continued . . .

Kris Longknife:
REDOUBTABLE

"Kris Longknife is a hero to the core, with plenty of juice left for future installments."
—Fresh Fiction

Kris Longknife:
UNDAUNTED

"An exciting, action-packed adventure . . . Mr. Shepherd has injected the same humor into this book as he did in the rest of the series."
—Fresh Fiction

Kris Longknife:
INTREPID

"[Kris Longknife] will remind readers of David Weber's Honor Harrington with her strength and intelligence."
—Genre Go Round Reviews

Kris Longknife:
AUDACIOUS

"Mike Shepherd is a fantastic storyteller who excels at writing military science fiction . . . This is a thoroughly enjoyable reading experience for science fiction fans."
—Midwest Book Review

" 'I'm a woman of very few words, but lots of action': So said Mae West, but it might just as well have been Lieutenant Kris Longknife, princess of the one hundred worlds of Wardhaven."
—Sci Fi Weekly

"Mike Shepherd has a great ear for dialogue and talent for injecting dry humor into things at just the right moment . . . Military SF fans are bound to get a kick out of the series as a whole, and fans will be glad to see Kris hasn't lost any of her edge."
—SF Site

Kris Longknife
TENACIOUS

Mike Shepherd

ACE BOOKS, NEW YORK

THE BERKLEY PUBLISHING GROUP
Published by the Penguin Group
Penguin Group (USA) LLC
375 Hudson Street, New York, New York 10014

USA • Canada • UK • Ireland • Australia • New Zealand • India • South Africa • China

penguin.com

A Penguin Random House Company

KRIS LONGKNIFE: TENACIOUS

An Ace Book / published by arrangement with the author

For information, address: The Berkley Publishing Group,
a division of Penguin Group (USA) LLC,
375 Hudson Street, New York, New York 10014.

ISBN: 978-0-425-25290-1

PUBLISHING HISTORY
Ace mass-market edition / November 2014

PRINTED IN THE UNITED STATES OF AMERICA

10 9 8 7 6 5 4 3 2 1

Cover art by Scott Grimando.
Interior text design by Kristin del Rosario.

Acknowledgments

As Kris Longknife's life takes another turn, for better or worse, I'd like to take time to thank some folks who have helped bring to life the tales of Kris, Vicky, and the old folks, back when they were young themselves.

The gang at the Historic Anchor Inn in Lincoln City has been spectacular. I've juggled three books demanding to get on the page for the last two years. They've helped me find a place where it all can happen, and find that place again and again as life made other plans. With my two wonderful grandkids making that break into those teenage years, and all the things that were already competing in my life for time, Kip, Candi, and Misty always found a way to free up my writing space for the week that suddenly appeared.

I've got a great pair of first readers to back up my wife, Ellen. Lisa Kelly not only helps my grandkids with their homework but also helps me with mine. Edee Lemonier is always ready with a good eye.

Jenn Jackson is now and always has been the best agent a busy writer could ask for. She's found homes for Kris in Japan and Germany, Poland and Spain. She's seen that Audible contracts were done in time for the books to come out for listeners as well as readers.

Ginjer Buchanan is just about the best editor a writer could have. She's really stepped up to the plate to get three books out to you this year. I couldn't ask for better support. Even when I'm a bit reluctant to make this or that minor change she's telling me I really want to make. And she's right about it, too! Sadly and happily, I am losing Ginjer to a well-earned retirement. She's been editing for Ace for thirty years, the last twenty of them working with me. She's surely earned many great golden years. Have fun, Ginjer.

And, as she has been for forty-seven years, Ellen Moscoe is the support and star in my life, the first editor of my words, and the last thought of my day.

Rear Admiral Kris Longknife relaxed, enjoying the warmth of the sun on her oh-so-vibrantly-alive skin. Two weeks ago, she could have easily ended her days dead and frozen in the dark emptiness of space.

But she'd won her battle. She and her command were alive, and countless billions of ill-advised alien invaders were dead.

Now, finally, Kris was free to enjoy the beach with just herself and a smile. Oh, and a just-as-naked Jack, husband of less than a month, beside her.

It seemed like it had taken forever to get here, to take the third day of her interrupted honeymoon. A honeymoon should be a full month. That was why it had the "moon" thing in it, right?

Her honeymoon had been interrupted after one single lovely night. To Kris's way of thinking, when she reported back to duty she was owed twenty-nine more days.

Kris was most definitely keeping count.

Now, two days into the rest of her honeymoon, she was enjoying herself. And looking forward to another twenty-seven.

She deserved the break. It had taken Kris two weeks to shed all of her hats, as well as her clothes and inhibitions.

What wife needs inhibitions around a husband like Jack? was asked and answered with a smile.

For two long weeks she had been Commander, Alwa Defense Sector; Senior Executive Officer of Nuu Enterprises in the Alwa System; and United Society Viceroy to the Human Colonists on Alwa as well as Ambassador to the Aliens. For two interminable weeks, she'd worn her multiple hats, burying her dead and tending to the living.

Collecting the wreckage of both human and alien ships had not taken long. Faced with possible capture, both sides had dropped their reactor containment vessels and blown themselves to atoms. Kris knew why the humans had: The aliens must be denied any scrap of information that could lead them back to human space on the other side of the galaxy.

But why are the aliens doing it, too?

Five of Kris's ships had been blown to bits and another ten had been bled heavily of their Smart Metal™ armor. Two of those losses had been from the six ships spun together from her twelve survey and ore-hauling ships. Thank heavens Admiral Benson, commander Canopus Station and its yard, as well as retired Musashi Admiral Hiroshi, who commanded the Kure yard, had survived. Admiral Hiroshi had been wounded as the *Kikukei* struggled under heavy alien laser fire. Still, the two yards had already changed the four damaged warships back into seven ore carriers.

They were now carrying asteroid miners back to their distant claims.

This made a lot of the people who reported to Kris as Senior Executive Officer of Nuu Enterprises in the Alwa System happy. When the mines shipped ore, the fabricators and mills on the moon made goods, both for war and for the budding modernization of the Alwa economy.

Sooner or later, there had to be a way to make money off the crazy Alwans. Some very savvy businesspeople were pulling their hair out as they tried.

Kris, being Navy, would let them worry about that.

As Viceroy to the humans on Alwa, she'd been happy to report the success of the U.S., Helvetican Confederacy, and Imperial Musashi Navy in defending their lives. Then, as ambassador to the Alwa aliens, she'd been invited to address the Association of Associations.

That address had not gone well.

Kris came prepared with visuals, both of the gigantic alien base ship and one of the several hundred monstrous alien fighting ships. She also projected pictures from her battle board of how the fight went.

Half the aliens in the sunlit plaza where they met stood in one silent huddle, eyes wide, arms, formerly wings, showing their only reaction as they flapped nervously on occasion. The other half of the Association's members were mostly made up of older Alwans, who did a lot more flapping as they ran around the plaza. Their arms waved wildly, and their long necks ducked up and down as they ran together in small groups that formed and re-formed to no pattern that Kris, or any other human, had been able to figure out.

KRIS, I'M TRYING TO FIND A PATTERN IN ALL THIS, BUT NEITHER I NOR ANY OF MY KIDS CAN SPOT ONE. Such an admission from Nelly and her family of supercomputers was unheard of, but not to be unexpected. Biological diversity could introduce such random factors that defied rational analysis.

What came next was more rational, but no less surprising.

The Alwans had a serious debate.

For Alwans, that meant putting on wild displays of motion and plumage, what they had left of it. The Alwans may have started as birds, but they hadn't flown in several million years, and feathers now were quite vestigial. Still, the plumage was colorful and made for some rather bright displays.

Among these Alwans, particularly the ones Kris knew as Roosters, all this dancing around and flapping resulted in no actual harm. No doubt among the southern clans, the Ostriches, there would have been some heavy chest butting, maybe even a head kick or two.

When it was all over, the plaza emptied in a blink.

"What just happened here?" Kris asked her Granny Rita.

"Damned if I know," the old woman replied. Rita was the titular head of the human colony for near on eighty years, a survivor of the Iteeche War as well as a marriage to Kris's great-grampa Ray, known better to most as King Raymond I of the United Society.

She turned to one of the Alwans who worked with the humans, and, using Nelly's translator, repeated her question about what just happened.

Bringer of Harmony Between the People and the Heavy People waved her own arms in what almost came off as a human shrug. "They have agreed to disagree. They will take this back to their own associations. There will be much more dancing and posing. Then, who knows what will happen? Maybe we will see different elders at the next Association of Associations."

And if the news reports were true from the Sharp Eye View, Alwa's main news network, the debate in the local associations were going long, loud, wild . . . and just about as inconclusive.

Kris was only too willing to let them do their arm waving while she spent her time on the beach.

Kris reached for Jack. She found him, fondled what she found, and let her smile grow into a happy leer as he responded to her.

"Wife, won't you let a man rest?" Jack said with a groan that failed to reach below his belly button.

"But you seem ready for more. I've learned that you men need a lot of rest, but . . ." Kris said with a pout that she knew had too much eager smile in it.

Her husband reached over and caressed her closest breast. "Hmm, the wife does seem willing, and it appears the husband is recharged."

"Kris, are you decent?" came from the bowl where Kris had put both her computer, Nelly, and Jack's computer, Sal, so the two supercomputers, easily worth as much as any of the warships in orbit, would not get sand in their self-organizing matrices.

"Nelly, what does it matter to you? And why are you interrupting my husband and me?" Kris demanded.

"I don't care what you two humans do with your time. I'm enjoying working on some refinements to the new Smart Metal they're producing at the lunar mills, but Penny wants to know."

"Why?"

"Because she and Mimzy are coming up the beach, and the view from Mimzy says you don't meet the normal human standard for decent."

Kris grabbed for the sarong provided by the hotel and lay it over herself. A glance down showed that it had merely added color to her skin and hid nothing. Jack doubled over the sarong he had worn from their cottage, but it really did no better.

Kris tossed the spare towel over his lap.

"I'd rather you cover up a bit," was his response. "No doubt, Penny has her boyfriend, Lieutenant Iizuka, with her."

Now Kris did glance down the beach. Yep, Penny, one of

her recent Maids of Honor and her boyfriend, sidekick, and fellow intelligence officer, but from the Musashi Navy, were coming up the beach. He was well behind Penny and making a studious effort to keep his eyes anywhere but where Kris and Jack were.

"Nelly, tell Penny to go away. I'm on my honeymoon."

"She says that you've gotten more of a honeymoon than she ever got, and you sent her off to find the alien home world and have been avoiding her ever since she got back."

"Ouch," Jack said.

Kris lost her smile. Penny did have a claim on short honeymoons. She and her bridegroom Tommy had enjoyed only one night before they'd followed Lieutenant Kris Longknife into a hopeless and desperate fight to save their home planet. They'd won through, but the last shot from a dying battleship had skewered their tiny fast attack boat. Tommy had made a heroic leap that shoved Penny to safety and left him pinned in the wreckage. Kris made one of those horrible calls you do in a fight that saved most of their lives . . . but cost Tommy his.

That Kris had been silently in love with Tommy long before he met Penny only added to the pain.

That, however, was an old scar. It had nothing to do with Kris's being too busy to see Penny during the last two weeks and choosing her honeymoon over something Kris was sure could wait.

"Is there any chance you will give me another week?" Kris asked, through Nelly.

"Nope," came back quickly. Down the beach, Penny didn't even hesitate as she made her way through the soft sand toward Kris.

Defeated by her own subordinate, Rear Admiral Kris Longknife stood to meet the lieutenant commander. She wrapped the sarong around herself several times, resulting in her almost becoming decent. Beside her, Jack did the same, his being wrapped at the waist while Kris's started at her oh-so-small breasts that her husband seemed very satisfied with, so Kris was doing her best to be satisfied with them, too.

Jack's sarong failed to hide a certain bulge, so he sat back down and settled the extra towel in his lap.

"We're decent," Kris grumbled in resignation.

Penny and her fellow intelligence officer labored through the soft sand to stand before Kris. Iizuka Masao was ever the dutiful gentleman. He spread a towel, and the two of them settled their khaki-clad bodies cross-legged on the cloth.

Without preamble, Penny said. "You sent us to find the alien home world. I think we did. You really need to see it."

2

Kris studied her friend. The short sleeves of her khaki uniform showed pale skin starting to burn.

"Are you wearing any sunscreen?" Kris asked.

"I told her she needed sunscreen," Lieutenant Iizuka said, "but she insisted on charging out here as soon as we arrived."

"It can wait," Penny snapped.

"Let's adjourn this meeting to the veranda of our bungalow," Kris said, pointing to where she and Jack were staying.

"Kris, you can't put me off."

"I'm not putting you off," Kris snapped. "I'm just moving this meeting to someplace where you won't be laid up for a week with sunburn if it goes more than, say, fifteen minutes."

"Okay," Penny said, and stomped her way through the sand toward the nearest shade. Kris followed, leaving the men to collect the blankets, towels, and computers.

At the bungalow, Kris offered Penny a seat at their breakfast table, then excused herself to dress. Jack soon joined her. Both of them chose the most covering of the clothes provided by the inn, rather than their uniforms. For Jack, it was a pair of shorts and a three-button shirt; for Kris it was a muumuu. Both took the time to reinstall their computers. For Jack, it was just a harness that settled easily on his head. Kris, however, had paid to have Nelly jacked directly into her brain. She removed the plug that had kept sand out and plugged a wire from Nelly back in.

THANK YOU VERY MUCH, were the first thoughts that formed in Kris's head. I THOUGHT YOU MIGHT FORGET ME.

NEVER, NELLY.

THAT'S NICE TO HEAR, had more sarcasm in it than a computer should be allowed. However, Nelly had been upgraded way too many times to keep count since she had been given to Kris before the first grade. One of those upgrades had included a fragment of a storage device left by the three alien races that had built the highway between the stars 2 million years ago.

Now, Nelly was just plain Nelly. Obstinate, outspoken, an atrocious joke teller, and the one item that could possibly rival Jack as the most important thing in her life. SHALL WE GO SEE WHAT PENNY HAS FOUND?

I ALREADY KNOW, KRIS. MIMZY TOLD ME. I'VE JUST BEEN WAITING FOR YOU TO FIND TIME TO LOOK INTO PANDO-RA'S BOX.

Which was Nelly's none too gentle way of reminding Kris that she and her kids could handle a lot more data a whole lot faster than mere meat mortals.

Kris settled Nelly in her usual place below her collarbone, eyed Jack, who gave a slight shrug, and together they returned to the veranda. Iizuka Masao had rustled up two more chairs from somewhere, and the four took their own corner of the table, Kris sat with Jack on her right. Masao settled on her left, leaving Penny the position directly across from Kris.

That was a bit of a surprise. Kris had expected Penny to take the place at her left hand. Clearly, Penny wanted to confront Kris head-on. Mentally, Kris notched up the category of this meeting from Best Friends' Get-together to Official Staff Meeting; maybe even Staffer has a Major Bone to Pick with Boss.

Kris raised an inquisitive eyebrow and waited for Penny to start. It was, after all, her dime.

"You sent me to search five or six systems and see if one of them might have the night sky that we've found on the overhead of all the alien ships we've examined. See if it might be the home of the alien raiders we've been fighting," Penny said without preamble.

"I know I got back just in time to see you win a hell of a fight with one more of those alien raiding clans. I know you're busy. But I also heard that there were three alien warships watching your latest fight, and they're likely observers from three more of those huge clans. You know and I know that there's another fight coming. We don't know how long it will take them to get their act together. Okay, fine, you have a lot on your plate. I can understand it. You're one of those damn Longknifes, but you're just a Longknife. Not God."

Penny paused for a moment. "But, Kris, I've seen shit that I really think you need to see for yourself. You need to see this stuff and dig deeper than I was able to with just one ship and me looking over my shoulders and ready to run if anyone or anything said 'boo.' "

Penny again paused in her pleading, and Kris considered what she'd heard. Yes, she'd sent Penny off in a knocked-together warship with half its lasers aimed aft so she could shoot while she ran. And yes, Kris had more questions about the aliens than she could catalog.

The damn things would not say a word when hailed. Heaven knows, Kris had tried and tried again to open communications with them. Their response was to try to kill her every time, and when they failed, they made sure that every last one of them died.

These aliens were frustrating Kris's long-held belief that any problem could be talked out if you just tried hard enough. She knew that was Father, the Prime Minister, speaking in her head. As a politician, he firmly believed what he had taught his daughter at his knee.

But the great politician Billy Longknife had never met these bug-eyed monsters who, very disappointingly, looked more like humans than any race we'd come across so far in space.

"Okay, Penny," Kris said with a sigh, "what did you see that is so important you've dragged me and Jack off that lovely beach?"

Penny held up a finger. "First, we found a planet that was sanitized right down to bedrock. Best we could tell, it had been hit with atomics and rocks so hard about a hundred thousand years ago that we couldn't find any sign of life. Maybe there are some. Maybe a virus or two survived, but we couldn't spot them in the time we dared take or the probes we sent down.

"Oh, and we left the probes down there. We couldn't risk being contaminated by stuff we couldn't spot. What they found was no water. No nothing. No life at all as best we could tell."

"Are you sure it ever had life?" Jack asked.

"Under all the hammering, it sure looked like there had

once been riverbeds," Masao put in. "We clearly made out ocean beds. We found the remains of coral reefs, and we think we found fossil remains of fish and other aquatic life, but to prove it we would have needed better sensors on our probes than we had. That is why we really think there needs to be a second expedition to look that place over, fully equipped and soon."

Beside him, Penny nodded agreement before continuing her own debriefing.

"But it was the planet in the next system, just one jump away, that I really think you want to see," she said.

"Why?" Kris asked.

"Because it has the aliens on it."

"You got to see them?" Jack asked, incredulously.

"You weren't supposed to risk getting that close," Kris said.

"We didn't risk anything. The big bad aliens weren't home, but their kinds of aliens were on that planet," Penny said.

"You're not making sense," Kris said.

"She is," Masao put in, defending Penny, "she just needs to explain it more slowly."

Penny threw her friend a look that told Kris a lot more than she needed to know about how the relationship between them was going. Penny appreciated the protection but did not want any help. Kris's old friend was still trying to come to terms with the fact that the men she loved always seemed to die. For Penny, giving her heart to any man would be a long, hard journey.

Apparently, Masao was still willing to wait.

Penny blew out a long breath. "There were no alien ships in orbit around the next planet. There were no space stations, no satellites, no reactors or radio communications. It looked like an empty planet. But as we got close, it started to come alive.

"There was an atmosphere and oceans. Vegetation covered the land, at least in most places. Radar mapping showed several places where it had been hammered by asteroid strikes. Small ones, not extinction events. Also, there was one huge plain of glass. Radioactive, too. Something had been hit hard by atomics."

"You think it was attacked from space?" Jack put in.

"From our place in orbit, it was impossible to say, but it

sure looked like it had been hit hard some hundred and ten thousand years ago, give or take a few millennia," Penny said.

"It was what was *on* the glass plain that caught our attention even before we sent probes down. There is a pyramid of granite rock right in the middle of the plain."

"A pyramid?" Kris and Jack said together.

"No question but that it is artificial," Lieutenant Iizuka said.

"What's in it?" Kris asked.

"We have no idea," Penny said. "There seems to be a door, but it was locked down tight."

"Couldn't your nanos get in?" Kris asked.

"Kris, whatever we sent down there we were leaving there, and we didn't want to leave any high-tech stuff. That meant no Smart Metal. That meant what went was pretty big by nano standards. Yes, there was a door, but we didn't dare drop anything that could get through the door seal. Oh, we tried with what we had, but that is one tightly sealed door. Nothing we dropped could get a look in."

Penny paused. "But that was only one of the things that left us wanting to get a better look. There were aliens. At least I think they were aliens."

"Did you get a DNA test?" Jack said.

"A very basic one. Again, we didn't dare drop anything too sophisticated," Masao said. "But it was the different tribes down there. Once you got well away from the plain of glass, there were some pretty sophisticated hunter-gatherers. I think there was even some farming. They had stone-edged weapons and were hunting some real big stuff."

"But not close to the plain," Penny said, taking back over the story. "The small hunting groups there were really primitive. Bare-ass naked, not that the climate was all that cold, but still. No tools but some wooden spears and clubs. No stone chips. They had to make due with small game or scavenge stuff the large carnivores had chewed open."

"Why the difference in skill sets?" Jack said.

"Your guess is as good as mine," Penny answered.

"What happens when the two tribes meet?" Kris asked.

"I wish I knew, but it didn't happen while we were there. Kris, we could only stay in orbit for two, three days. There were two jumps into that system, besides the one we came in, and if one of them started coughing up alien monster ships, we would have run. But if all three got active at once . . ." Penny let that thought run free.

Kris didn't much care for the situation either.

"If we go back there, we'll need to put warning buoys at all the jumps, maybe even detach a ship to drop off buoys for the next three systems out from those jumps."

"So it couldn't be a small expedition like the one that rescued the *Hornet*'s crew," Jack said.

Kris nodded, but her thoughts were already chasing down another rabbit hole. "Have your boffins been talking to other boffins?"

"They're scientists, Kris," Penny said, sounding irritated. "Of course they talk. While you've been busy putting out fires for two weeks and enjoying married life, all the boffins have been talking about is our expedition. However many ships you take, there will be more than enough scientists begging to fill them up."

"And if I'm going to go, I'd better go soon," Kris said, throwing Jack a sorrowful look. "No telling when those three alien clans will start getting frisky."

"We've got a ship out replacing the warning buoys that got shot up during the recent unpleasantness," Jack said. "It's also stretching the warning net to eight jumps out, giving us two extra layers."

"That's nice," Kris said, not really feeling all that good about it. She'd used up just about every trick she had to win the last battle. That her next set of attackers would know how she clobbered this last bunch meant she'd have to cobble together a whole new strategy for the defense of Alwa.

She'd barely managed to patch together this last one. What could she possibly do next time?

One day at a time, she reminded herself.

Kris stood.

"Okay, Jack. You owe me another twenty-seven days of honeymoon."

"Aye, aye, wife, Viceroy, Admiral, bosswoman," he said, saluting with a broad grin.

"I'm sorry, Kris. I didn't mean . . ."

"Yes, you did," Kris said, cutting off Penny's apology. "And it needed to be done. Okay, it's back to work for me and you. You're going back. Not in the *Endeavor*. This time we go prepared for a fight. I'll take what's left of BatRon 1," Kris decided. Would six ships be enough? Maybe she should pull in another couple to bring it up to a full squadron.

"Did you two bring a car big enough for four?" she asked Penny.

"Yes."

"Fine, we'll ride back with you. Jack, time to put on our game faces, or at least a uniform. After you," she said.

To Kris's great sorrow, Penny and her boyfriend stayed waiting just outside the cabin door. There was no way to stretch the delightful morning with one last quickie.

3

Kris used the drive back to rehash Penny's report. Nothing new, either exciting or terrifying, was added to her set of challenges. Penny and the *Endeavor* had played mouse at a cat's convention that never got called to order, thank heaven.

The star-studded ceiling of one huge auditorium in the first alien base ship they blasted had shown what looked like a particular night sky. It had been repeated in the largest room of the monster warship that Kris had captured intact while rescuing the crew of the *Hornet*. In that fight, Kris had disabled their reactors. She'd hoped to get prisoners. Instead, the aliens opened every hatch to space, killing themselves.

Kris's scientists were still trying to make sense of the alien machinery and gear. Someone had actually forwarded a report to Kris suggesting that maybe we shouldn't worry so much about the aliens digging information out of our computers. Their technology looked nothing like ours, assuming we were guessing right about what they used for navigation and fire control.

That's what the word meant. Aliens were, *ipso facto*, alien to our way of thinking.

However, based on Nelly's assessment of the ceiling and projection of where and when that night sky might have sparkled down on a planet, Penny had been dispatched to look at six star systems.

The first three of which had showed nothing of interest. The next looked thoroughly beat-up. The fifth was full of questions. Penny had not gotten around to the sixth but raced for home. She arrived only to find home in the final desperate moments of a battle for survival that had cost the life of tens of billions of aliens and left the human colony on Alwa, as well as the Alwans themselves, with precious little time to prepare for the next attack.

Did Kris dare haul off a quarter or more of her defense so she could answer questions she didn't yet know how to ask? And if she didn't find out something about her enemy, would they and humanity find a way to stop the killing before one or the other was annihilated?

Once again, Kris found herself with few answers and a whole lot of questions.

She contacted the people who made up the next level in her way-too-small chain of command and began scheduling meetings.

The first meeting was already waiting for her at the end of the drive. Ada stood on the shady veranda of Government House, Granny Rita at her elbow. Officially, Granny Rita was Kris's great-grandmother and retired. Any position she might hold was purely emeritus. Officially, Ada was the chief executive of a human colony of nearly two hundred thousand. However, Kris had made the mistake of giving Granny Rita a decent computer. Once the old gal got on net, she never missed out on anything interesting.

And to her, everything was interesting.

Ada was also not one to beat around the bush. "You think you've found the nest of these varmints that want to kill us?"

"We think so, but it doesn't look anything like Earth," Kris said, and let Penny repeat her brief.

"That is so far past strange, I don't know what to say about it," Granny Rita said, and left Ada with nothing else to do but shake her head.

"So, you're going to go exploring," the colonial chief added.

"It seems like a good idea, and I think we have time for it right now," Kris admitted.

"Your absence won't stop work on getting us farming, fishing, and other gear . . . or defensive preparations, will it?" Ada asked.

"You'll keep doing what you're doing," Kris said. "Our fabricators on the moon and mines on the asteroids will keep producing the things you want. You'll hardly miss me," Kris said dryly.

Ada smiled at the lie. "I'll touch base with that Pipra

Strongarm woman and see what she can do to speed up our own efforts to get more land irrigated and under seed, more fish hauled out of the ocean, and more hunting parties into the deep woods for some real red meat. Good Lord, but what I'd give for a nice rare steak."

"Wouldn't we all," Kris agreed.

Kris had thought that fighting aliens was her worst problem. Then she discovered that Alwa and the human colony had been living on the raw edge of starvation, surviving from one crop to the next and enduring empty bellies if the rains didn't come on time. If Kris wanted to fight her fleet, she'd first have to find enough food to feed it. Initial steps had already been made. Matters were improving.

It would, however, take a whole lot more before Kris could take her food supply for granted. And she was hoping, preferably soon, to get more reinforcements.

How would she feed *them*?

"You talk to Pipra," Kris said. "You have first call on boats, trucks, and anything you need to complete the new viaduct. Then we'll try to manufacture some tractors to help with the planting."

"When do we get the fourth reactor off the old *Furious*?" Granny Rita asked.

The *Furious* was Granny Rita's old ship from the Iteeche Wars, the last survivor of her BatCruRon 16. It had languished in orbit for eighty years. Now one reactor was powering both colonial and Alwan electronic equipment and changing how they all lived. Two were powering moon fabricators so that their own reactors could be switched to ore carriers, and might have included some of the reactors blown to bits with the *Proud Unicorn* and *Lucky Leprechaun*, who hadn't been all that lucky.

"We're working on that reactor," was all Kris could say. "It was cannibalized to get the other three going. We've ordered parts from our fabricators on the moon, but they don't have specs for those items in their databases. It might be easier to just build a new thermonuclear reactor for you than get that one back up and running."

"And what about spare parts for our working one," Ada said. "And the two you stole for your moon bases? If you don't have spare parts for the fourth one, you don't have spare parts for them either."

"I could be wrong," Granny Rita said, "but I don't think she wanted you asking that question. They can damn near make anything they got the specs for, but if they don't have the specs, making something is well-nigh impossible, ain't it great-granddaughter of mine?"

"Nothing's changed in eighty years, Granny. The time it would take to haul the part out of one of the working reactors and get its specs, replace it, make it, and install it might just make it easier, in a few months, to replace what you got here."

"If we're a priority," Ada said with a nasty look on her face.

"Ada, eating is just about the highest priority we've got," Kris said. "Trust us, you're a high priority."

"Just so long as it stays that way."

Glad to have that meeting over with no blood on the floor, Kris and her team headed for the dock and a captain's gig that had lately been promoted to admiral's barge for a ride up to Canopus Station.

Admiral Benson, retired once and reactivated recently to a commodore's job, was waiting for Kris as her honorary barge pulled into the landing bay.

"I've got good news and bad news for you. Which do you want first?" the old sailorman said.

"The good news," Kris said with a shrug.

"We've got twenty-three of the big frigates ready to answer bells if you need to fight."

"Twenty-three!" Kris said. "But we had thirty-three left after you spun four of the emergency war wagons back into merchant ships? Where are the other ten?"

"That's the bad news. Even the ships that survived took hits, hits that burned off their Smart Metal. We had some ships come in with nothing but a thin hull membrane keeping space out. If the fight had gone on for a few more broadsides, we would have lost them."

"That wasn't in your report a week ago," Kris pointed out.

"I was busy spooling out what was left of the four frigates we spun together from eight merchant ships. You notice we only got seven back."

"I was wondering about that," Kris admitted. She'd wondered

about it but asked no questions. "What about the new Smart Metal coming out of the foundries on the moon?"

"Ah, yes, *that* metal," the yard manager said. Kris did not like the sound of the way he said it.

"Is there a problem with it that no one told me?"

"No. No problem. Not actually, but some of us are worrying a bit about problems down the road. Right now we're kind of pushing the safety margins to get that metal out of the mills. It's not the same stuff that came from the foundries back in human space that was originally spun into the ships. Simply put, it doesn't meet the standards that Mitsubishi Heavy Space Industry sets for the stuff."

"It's better," came from Nelly at Kris's neck.

"That's what some folks think," Benson said, with a hint of a shrug, "but it's different. That may be good. It *could* be bad."

"So when you finish beating around the bush, what are you going to tell me?" Kris said, tiring rapidly of this conversation. She had not given up her honeymoon to dance around the barn with anyone.

"No skipper wants to have a ship that's half Mitsubishi standard and half local stuff," the yard boss said. "Some are willing to fight a ship with the new stuff. Many of them won't have a ship at all without this metal. The Smart Metal we had did pretty well in the fight. There were no apparent failures. Anyway, ten of the ships that were skinned the worst have been drained to refill the ships that suffered the least damage. That means we've got ten ships tied up to the pier with hulls and internal walls that are eggshell-thin.

"Once we get metal from the moon, we'll spin it into them and pull out the original stuff. With the basic structure and matrix already in place, the new metal should flow in quickly. It won't take nearly the time to refill the ship that it took to spin it out. We'll recover the original Smart Metal from the first nine and likely refill the tenth with it."

"How long will this take?" Kris asked.

"That depends on how long it takes the mills to cough out the Smart Metal, which depends on how long it takes the raw materials to get back from the asteroid belt, which depends on when the miners get the mines producing."

"So you're telling me that you haven't the foggiest idea," Kris said.

"Not even a guess," the now re-retired admiral admitted.

"And if I was to take eight of the good ships off to visit the ancient home of the aliens?"

"There wouldn't be enough left here to spit at an alien scouting force."

"Thank you, Admiral. I find myself wondering why I'm here and not back lying on a beach enjoying the sun," Kris said.

"I ask myself that on a regular basis," the old ship driver said with a smile and a nod as he went his own way.

"Where's Pipra Strongarm?" Kris asked Nelly.

"Waiting for you in your day quarters on the *Wasp*. Captain Drago wants to see you, and so does Abby."

Officially, Abby was Kris's maid who did her hair and made her look lovely for balls and other social events. In fact, Abby could shoot as well as any Marine and had saved Kris's life too many times to count.

Trying to school her face from an I'm-going-to-bite-your-head-off scowl to I'm-the-boss, tell-me-the-truth bland, Kris headed for her next set of meetings.

4

Abby was in the passageway outside Kris's quarters.

"You want to see me?" Kris said, as she and Jack came to a halt in front of Kris's erstwhile domestic.

"It don't seem to me that you're going to need your hair done for any balls on this alien home planet. Anybody after your skin is going to be doing it with monster warships, not assassins. I could be wrong, but it looks to me like your latest promotion has kind of done me outta my job."

"I'll never fire you," Kris said, none too sure where this conversation was going. That was not an unusual state of affairs whenever Abby finally condescended to a serious talk with Kris.

"I've been working with Pipra Strongarm for the last month when you didn't have nothin' for me to do, you know."

"Idle hands are the devil's workshop."

"I don't need no idle hands to be working for him," Abby said.

"So, you want to stay here with Pipra and try your hand at business. Tell me, is it you or that brat of Nelly's around your neck that she wants?"

Abby had inherited one of Nelly's kids. The maid's relationship with Mata Hari had been off and on. Apparently it was on at the moment and didn't involve any sneaky stuff.

Then again, Kris would never bet against sneaky where Abby and her computer were concerned.

"She likes us both," Abby spat. "The degree I earned back on Earth was in business management, and Pipra is finding it hard to put together a staff that understands the mess we're in."

"And you have survived around one of those damn Longknifes long enough to know just how bad the messes can be," Kris agreed.

Abby cast Kris a look. "You have to admit that this mess kind of outdoes your usual."

"It does," Kris agreed. "Who else will be wanting to stay behind?"

Kris would bet Wardhaven dollars to donuts she knew the answer to her question, but she wanted to hear it from Abby.

"Sergeant Bruce has gotten his next stripe. He's a Gunny now, working dirtside as much as up here. Whoever Jack leaves in charge here will need the help of at least one of Nelly's kids. Cara will also stay with me. Her fourteenth birthday is coming up, and while she still thinks of herself as the first member of the Marine Corps Auxiliary to the *Wasp*'s Marine detachment, Pipra and the boffins are seeing that she gets a good education. And we are using Dada for stuff on the business side."

"Nelly, do you have any problem with this?" Kris asked.

Nelly had had definite problems with the idea of one of her kids being handed off to a business tycoon, either the head of Mitsubishi Heavy Space Industry or Kris's Grampa Al. Especially Grampa Al. Survival, however, made for different decisions.

"I have no problems with Mata working with Ms. Strongarm. She shows a refreshingly creative and ethical approach to our situation. I'm glad to see Dada doing more than playing computer games with Cara and being an educational device. I'm also glad to see her being brought up to speed with more complex challenges. Kris, we've already discussed this, and I agree these three should stay behind and help where they can."

"I figured you had, Nelly," Kris said. "Otherwise, Abby would not have known how and when to just happen to run into me and present me this proposal. Okay, Abby, you're still my employee, and don't forget that, but for now, you're on loan to Pipra. Have fun and charge her all the market will bear in consulting fees."

"I wouldn't charge a penny less," Abby said, and stepped aside.

Kris and Jack were finally able to enter their quarters.

Some people might find it hard to think of a ship's stateroom as home, but for Kris, her quarters on the *Wasp* was the closest she'd come to a home since joining the Navy and doing her level best to get ship duty. Her day quarters were quite spacious. Clearly, with her ashore, someone had shrunk her night cabin down to next to nothing. Wasn't it nice having Smart Metal™ that you could push around with an app?

An app that had caused a near revolution in what the crew could do with their quarters.

Kris and Jack had been neither the first nor the last to merge their quarters and set up housekeeping together, official or otherwise.

With no shore stations to ship anyone to for punishment, and no one to replace them with anyway, discipline among the Sailors and Marines on the far side of the galaxy from the nearest human space was . . . delicate. When contract personnel and the scientists aboard began using an app to open doors between quarters, it had brought on a Navy leadership challenge way past epic proportions.

Kris had followed the Navy Way of handling it. She'd convened a committee of senior chiefs and ships' executive officers and told them to fix it. After a sleepless night of gnawing at the problem of commanding a lot of young, healthy, and unattached troops who might die at any moment and would have to depend on each other for their own survival, the Alwa Defense Sector had written its own fraternization policy.

It had survived the test of its first battle. Kris could only hope her innovative approach to human relations in the crucible of war would continue to hold together.

Pipra was already seated at the conference table that dominated Kris's day quarters. As usual, Kris's desk was clean though she suspected her in-box had reports and messages stacked up past the virtual overhead.

Before Kris could settle into her chair at the table, Pipra was reeling off problems at the mines, fabricators, mills, and everywhere in between. Jack gave Kris a smile and a shrug before he took their small travel bags and disappeared into their quarters. Quickly back, he gave Kris a jaunty wave and allowed that he would check in on the Marines while Kris attended to business.

As he left, Captain Drago sauntered in. Had he planned for moments like this when he arranged for Kris's admiral's cabin to be just off his own bridge? The first time Pipra paused for a breath, he asked Kris, "You enjoy your vacation?"

"Too short. When can you get the *Wasp* underway for a month-long voyage of exploration?"

Pipra glanced at what she was about to read from and put it aside. "So you *are* going to do this crazy visit to the alien home world I've been hearing about."

"Since I didn't know I was going to do this crazy thing until six hours ago, I'm intrigued that you knew about it before I did," Kris said.

"Well, everyone knew that your scout ship was back and that it found the alien home world. You being one of those damn Longknifes, I figured you'd be chasing off after it."

"First, I'm your CEO, not a damn Longknife," Kris said, but softened it with a smile. "And second, from what our scout found, the home world has been abandoned by the alien space raiders for some time."

"Then why are you going?" her senior vice president shot back.

"A good question. So you don't think I should go?"

"No, I didn't say that. Information is power. Knowing where these crazy, bloodthirsty whatevers came from might tell us something. I'm just wondering if now is the time to do it?"

"And a better time would be?" Kris asked.

"There won't be a better time or a worse one," Captain Drago put in. "You pay your money, and you take your chances. Me, I figure sooner is better. My best guess is those alien observers will need time to report back. Then more time while they think about what they saw. With three huge clans thinking on that, it may take them quite a while to decide on anything."

"There may be only one person who matters on each of those base ships," Kris said.

Captain Drago dismissed that thought with a wave of his hand. "Even in a dictatorship, there are currents of opinion that have to be considered. I never heard of a system that didn't have competing power blocks that had to be weaseled and browbeaten into doing something."

"I hope you're right, Captain, because I'm betting that that's the way it is. Please ask Commodore Kitano to drop in at her earliest convenience. I'm going to steal her squadron, what's left of it, and leave her with the hot potato of Acting Commander, Alwa Defense Sector."

"I don't think she'll be too bothered by being left behind.

Her *Princess Royal* is one of the ships that took so much damage that it's tied up to the pier awaiting more Smart Metal."

"It is?"

"Yep."

"Skipper, we've got action at one of our close-in systems," came from the bridge. Drago trotted out of Kris's quarters. She followed him, with Pipra at her elbow.

"How could the aliens jump into one of the systems so close?" Pipra asked.

"They couldn't, not the last time we saw them," Kris said grimly, wondering just how much of a fight she could put up against whatever was headed her way.

"Talk to me," Drago ordered his bridge crew.

Old Chief Beni was on sensors. "The reporting buoy is in the next system. It jumped immediately into ours to holler a warning. The receiving buoy ducked back into the other system to gather more information."

"The next system? Didn't we make a long jump into that system on our own voyage out here and use it to slow down in before jumping into this system?" Kris said, trying to keep Pipra from panicking. Maybe keep herself from panicking, too.

"Did the reporting buoy say anything about the arriving ships?" the captain asked.

"No, sir, it just reported ships in the system," the chief answered. "It didn't say which jump they used or how many of them there were. A reactor shows up, and it jumps in and reports. We're lucky it was the next system out, or we'd be having all kinds of delays for the information to travel across the system by speed of light. If it's the sixth system out, it might take us a couple of days to even know it happened."

"The good news and the bad," Pipra said with a nervous laugh. "It's close enough to not make us bite our nails while waiting. And, if it's bad news, we won't have to worry too much before it kills us."

The skipper scowled at the businesswoman, but said, "Chief, when will we get an update?"

"The second buoy is supposed to jump back into our system and give us a report in five to fifteen minutes, depending on how much it's learning. Sir, it's already happened. We're just waiting to hear what the automatics did hours ago."

"Yes, Chief, I know," Captain Drago said, not enjoying the reminder.

"Report coming in," Chief Beni announced. "Fifty-nine groups of reactors have been identified. They match human production models."

Kris turned to Pipra. "It appears that our reinforcements are arriving early."

Pipra, with no need to appear fearless in the face of the Sailors on the bridge, leaned back against the bulkhead and let out a long sigh of relief. "Give me a minute. I'm not sure my legs will support me."

"When you feel up to it, we have further problems to juggle. Food, general production, and rearmoring ten of my plucked chickens."

"Yes," Pipra said, a bit breathless, "and it looks like we'll have the time to do something about all of those."

"Food," Kris said, remembering that her salvation also meant more mouths to feed. "More ships mean we need more food. I hope they brought along their own supplies. Chief, can you tell me how many of those reactors are warship types and how many are freighters?"

"No, ma'am. Sorry, but I can only tell you what I'm told, and they're busy telling me what we ordered them to get fast and easy. If you want a specific question answered, I can send it off. It will likely take twenty, thirty hours to get an answer. More than likely, if you just wait, you'll get the answer in a couple of hours, anyway."

The retired chief had one of those looks on his face that senior NCOs used for particularly dumb questions from officers.

"No, Chief. No rush. Just tell me what you know when you know it."

"Will do, Admiral."

Back in Kris's day cabin, Pipra was on her phone, telling her chief associates that help was coming. If information was power, it was a power whose Sell By date could be very short.

Kris settled at her conference table and drummed her nails for only a few seconds before her business subordinate rang off and got down to work.

5

Rear Admiral Kris Longknife and her acting, Commodore Kitano, watched the reinforcements pop into the system from Kris's flag bridge on the *Wasp*. The flag bridge and Kris's day quarters were the same space made different only by Kris's frame of mind. If she was stuck in a meeting, it was her day quarters. If she was commanding a fleet or a battle, it was a bridge.

Either way, the sign on the door said ADMIRAL'S QUARTERS.

The *Wasp*, like the other ships of Battle Squadron One, was in the final stages of getting underway for their voyage of discovery to the alien home world.

BatRon 1 was down to five ships, what with the *Constitution* lost and the *Princess Royal* and *Resistance* tied up awaiting new armor. To bring it up to a full eight, Kris was borrowing the *Wasp*, her own flagship, and the *Intrepid*. Also, despite her initial intent, she'd added the *Endeavor*, now loaded with low-tech jump-point buoys and designed to shoot just as much while running as chasing.

Commodore Kitano would be left with fifteen experienced fighting ships under her command, now organized into three reduced squadrons.

Together with Jack, Penny, and Captain Drago, they watched as the ships allotted to the Alwa Defense Sector grew.

Kris had thought long and hard about departing before the reinforcements arrived. She'd made the call to stay. What these ships were sailing into deserved a greeting from their commander.

And besides, who would miss a chance to see the fleet come in. It was quite a sight. As well as full of surprises.

The first into the system was a big surprise. "That's the

Odin?" Jack asked no one in particular as the first blip appeared on Kris's battle board.

So Nelly gave an answer. "She reports herself as the flag of a squadron of frigates from the Scanda Confederacy. The *Odin* is followed by the *Thor, Loki, Frigga, Brage, Heimdallr, Hodur,* and *Baldur.* There are two merchants tailing them, the *Valhalla* and the *Sisu.*"

"The Scanda Confederacy isn't in King Raymond's United Society," Penny pointed out.

"And they're only four planets," Nelly added. "That's a lot of ships from so small a confederacy."

"Somebody wants in on the fight," Jack said. He might have started his career as a Secret Service Agent, but he'd spent the last five years with the Marines. He'd come to understand the need of some to be there when there was a fight brewing, no matter what the odds.

"The merchant ships are Smart Metal," Nelly reported before Kris asked.

Good. More ships to convert from starship to system cargo hauler. It would be a downgrade for the crew, but it just might decide whether they all lived or died.

Another set of pips appeared at the jump. No doubt they had arrived several hours ago, but the report was only now reaching Kris's command above Alwa.

"The *Phantom* reports she's the flag of a squadron from New Eden," Nelly reported as the jump began to spit out more ships. "*Voodoo, Banshee, Daemon, Vampire, Werewolf, Fury,* and *Fire Drake.* They've got the *Proximus, Mary Allen Carter,* and *James Nathan Carter* trailing them. It looks like a repair ship and two supply ships. All Smart Metal."

"Somebody's either got a sense of humor or has been reading too much fantasy," Commodore Kitano muttered.

"Kris, there's something strange about those warships," Nelly reported. "They've got double the capacitors for their lasers. And their lasers are giving Chief Beni readouts that don't match anything in our database."

Kris couldn't help but notice that when Nelly couldn't verify the signature of a ship, it was Chief Beni's problem. However, this might be more of a problem than just a database slip.

"Is this an alien sneak attack?" Kris quickly asked.

Captain Drago was on his feet and headed for his bridge.

"Hold it," Commodore Kitano said. "There was talk of a new 22-inch laser before we left. They were totally different, not just uprated 18-inchers like our 20-inch lasers. They had teething problems. If what we're seeing are those big guns, they're going to look weird to us."

"Reactors are straight-up human construction per our analysis," Nelly reported.

Drago came back to the table but stood behind his chair.

Another new squadron was coming in.

"This one's from Pitt's Hope. It shows clear U.S. recognition signals," Nelly reported. "And it has those same strange guns. *Battleaxe* leading *Broadsword, Scimitar, Saber, Arrow, Longbow, Claymore,* and *Grenade.* All standard-make U.S. reactors though. They're trailed by the *Artifex, Appleleaf, Orangeleaf,* and *Cherryleaf.* I make them out to be another repair ship and three supply ships."

"Let's hope they didn't stint on the food," Kris said.

"Oh, we got a big one," Nelly announced. "It reports itself the *Portsmouth* out of Pitt's Hope. It appears to me that we have another addition to Canopus Station."

"With all these ships to park, we'll need some piers," Kris said.

She made a quick call to Admiral Benson. "I think you have another extension to your station."

"So I noticed. I sincerely hope whoever is skippering the *Portsmouth* is as good as Admiral Hiroshi was with the Kure Docks."

"You might want to get with Hiroshi and coordinate with the new fellow," Kris said.

"Was already planning on it," the admiral said, and Kris rang off.

And yet a fourth squadron came through the jump.

"This one is from Yamato," Nelly reported. "The flag is *Mikasa,* followed by the *Asahi, Hatsuse, Yakumo, Idzumo, Iwate, Asama,* and *Toikiwa.* Those are the warships. There's also a *Tyogei,* likely a repair ship since there's no '*maru*' after the name, and the *Kamoi Maru, Kinugasa Maru,* and *Kinagawa*

Maru. Supply ships most likely. Ah, Kris, are Musashi and Yamato on good terms? Should we brigade the two squadrons together or keep them apart?"

"No doubt we'll find out soon enough," Kris said.

"Hopefully, you'll find out before you leave," Commodore Kitano muttered loud enough for all to hear.

"There's another huge dockyard-size ship coming through," Nelly reported. "The *Sasebo Maru.* Yamato has a Sasebo Navy Shipyard in orbit. This might be another yard for us."

"If we double our ships, we need to double our yards and docks," Kris said, standing. "The only question is, do we put it in a trailing orbit or hitch them on to us here. Nelly, ask Admirals Benson and Hiroshi for a report on those two options plus any more they want to present."

"Oh," Nelly whispered. "Here's something even bigger. The *Prosperity* out of New Eden. Interesting. It's got two squawkers, one at each end. One says *Prosperity* in English. The other in Chinese."

Kris tapped her commlink. "Pipra, do I have a challenge for you."

"Not another one?"

"Yep. It appears that New Eden has contributed a huge factory ship full of mills and fabricators to our effort. However, having been spawned early from Earth, they're of two minds. Half started from North America, the other half from China."

"I think I've heard about that setup. They don't talk too much, do they?"

"Not much from what I heard last visit. However, we've got a monstrous factory ship squawking from one end in English and the other end in Chinese."

"Oh my. And I'm betting you want me to figure out some way to split that getup in half and land each end in some distant crater on the moon with plenty of water and other resources."

"You got it. Makes me think you've been hanging around one of those damn Longknifes," Kris said with a laugh.

What Pipra said was too low to hear.

"We got another large factory ship," Nelly reported. "This one calls itself *You Can Have It Monday, Maybe.*"

"What kind of name is that?" Penny asked.

"I have no idea," Nelly answered, "but you got to like it. It's out of New Bern, so it must have corporations from the Helvetican Confederacy."

"Pipra, can you find space for them as well?" Kris asked.

"Kris, you get me more factory ships, and I'll find room for them anywhere and everywhere. I love more factory ships."

"Great, Pipra, because I'm going to leave welcoming these fine folks in your warm and capable hands."

"You're going to what?" didn't quite rise to the level of a scream. Not quite.

"I'll talk to the Navy types and let them in on the situation. You talk to the business types."

"You don't pay me enough for this, woman."

"In case you haven't noticed, none of us are getting paid very much of anything," Kris pointed out.

"I got to change that."

"You do that and we'll all celebrate with you."

"Good-bye, Your Highness," Pipra said.

"Good-bye, my right-hand gal of business," Kris said. "I have yet another group coming through," she said as she rang off. This time four ships appeared.

"Kris, this is a division from the Esperanto League," Nelly reported. "They're non-U.S. Their flagship is the *Miela*, that translates as 'honey-sweet.' The next three are *Karesinda*, *Dezirinda*, and *Spirita*, meaning 'caressable,' 'desirable,' and 'witty.'"

"Strange names for warships," Jack said.

"After the Iteeche War, the League passed a law that no warship could have a 'distressingly combative name,'" Nelly said.

"So they managed to pass a bill authorizing warship construction," Kris said, trying not to chortle at the political implications, "but not a bill to change the naming law."

"The next should be the last," Nelly announced, and the jump promptly gave up six more. "These are from Hispania, a U.S. member. The *Libertad* is the flag, followed by the *Federaciaon*, *Independencia*, and *Union*. They have two supply ships, *Minnow* and *Koralo*. That's it, Kris. Forty new warships, twenty-four with those strange lasers, two new yards, three repair ships, twelve supply ships, and two very nice factory ships."

"Not a bad haul," Captain Drago said. "Especially considering what we're down to after that last dustup."

Kris nodded as she thought through her presents . . . and the challenges inherent in her good fortune. She turned to Captain Drago. "I think we'll be using your Forward Lounge for another meeting. Have Mother MacCreedy lay in a goodly supply of that hooch the Alwans drink."

Captain Drago made a face. "That stuff is almost undrinkable. Its only virtue is the alcoholic content is so high that after a few sips, you don't care."

"That's all she'll serve for our extended staff meeting. Let's introduce our new arrivals to the vagaries of Far Station duty sooner rather than later."

"You're a hard taskmaster, Viceroy," Captain Drago said, "but very likely a smart one."

"Also, Drago, please send this message to the arriving fleet. 'Thank you for coming. You're more than welcome. We won a fleet action three weeks ago, but, no doubt, there is another one coming. If any of your merchant ships are carrying mining supplies, please divert them to one of the mining stations along your route for unloading. Detach a warship to escort them there and down here immediately after. Commander, Alwa Defense Sector sends.'"

"I'll have it dispatched immediately," Captain Drago said, then he paused. "Why have the merchants escorted? There are no hostiles anywhere near us."

"No, but if the merchants get to talking with the locals, they may find out that those that come here stay here and decide to make a run for it. The escort is to shoot their engines out if they try to run, but we won't tell them that unless we have to, now will we?"

"No, ma'am, we won't. There are times I forget I'm serving with one of those damn Longknifes. Then you remind me."

"Yeah, ain't it the pits," Kris said, and turned back to her desk. Damn Longknife or nice one, she had three hats to wear and a lot of work that needed redoing in view of the new arrivals.

"Commodore Kitano. We need to reorganize the fleet

again. Pull enough ships out of the other squadrons to form five divisions."

"If we spread the fifteen ships into five divisions of three, we won't have any combat-ready squadrons."

"That's a risk we'll have to take. Each veteran division will be assigned to one incoming squadron. The Helveticans get the Esperanto and Hispania contingent. Nelly, contact Commodore Miyoshi and see if his division would like to work up with the Yamato squadron. I don't know who to team together on the others. Maybe during our first meeting in the Forward Lounge, we can find some folks who know each other."

Kris paused to pull her thoughts back to what her mouth was saying.

"The point is that we have to retrain and restructure these new ships to fight the way we fight. You remember the first drill when you tried to follow one of Nelly's jinking patterns without enough steering jets, and your ships weren't battened down for the hard lateral gees."

"I remember it all too well," the commodore agreed.

"You can pull ships' maintainers out of our plucked chickens to help them make the necessary mods before you run them out for a drill."

"You're being nice to them."

"If I'd known it, I'd have been nice to you. I was learning how to maneuver large ships in formations the same time you were learning how to drive them."

"We all learned a lot."

"And these new folks have to learn it, too, but fast. Match battle-experienced ships with newcomers. Have them compete to get ready. Have the ships that make the grade drink the beer of those that don't."

"That assumes we have beer."

"How much you want to bet me those newly arrived supply ships have some good drinking whiskey, beer, saki, you name it. When they discover there won't be any more of that until the next crop comes in, a bet backed up with that will be a whole lot better training aid than their getting knocked around a bit."

The commodore chuckled. "I'm starting to see why you Longknifes are legendary."

"You're starting to see why we're still alive. And some of those who follow us as well."

Kris finished a few minutes later with Commodore Kitano and sent her on her way. Admirals Benson and Hiroshi were next on her meeting list. They'd already established contact with *Portsmouth* and *Sasebo*. Yes, they were yards and both admirals present agreed they should hook into Canopus Station.

"There's some risk putting all our eggs in one basket," Admiral Benson said, "but there are advantages to keeping the fleet together. If we grow much more, we'll need a second base to avoid congestion, but we're not there yet."

"Can you make sure they match the station without denting anything?" Kris asked.

"I did it fine," Admiral Hiroshi said. "They can, too. Besides, we'll put the pilots that docked me aboard them. First, I'll hitch Tomiyama's Sasebo yards to me, then Benson can hitch the Portsmouth yards to him. Two days after they arrive, we will be in fine shape."

Kris liked to hear that.

Which left her with the business side.

Pipra had enough on her plate to keep Kris busy until the cows came home, as the young woman put it, or, at least, until the fleet arrived. There were supplies to distribute among the mining concerns, plans to convert the new arrivals into system freighters, and production schedules at the fabricators and mills to balance.

Putting agriculture, fisheries, and the basic industries that supported them as first priority was nice, but it left raw materials and production facilities underutilized. A bit of juggling and you got a bit less food produced, but reactors moved along the production line with more Smart Metal™ and electronic goodies that tied the colonials and the Alwans tighter into a seamless net for survival.

Pipra showed up with a list of what manufacturing plants they had and what had just arrived. She took Kris through several iterations of resource allocation before they settled on the best use of everything.

"You know," Kris admitted when they were done. "If we keep this up, I'm going to develop a serious respect for what you do."

Pipra only smiled softly at Kris's half compliment. "Well, I've already developed a serious respect for what you Navy types do. It would be nice if I got as much respect back from you and yours."

That put Kris back in her chair. She kept saying that they were all in this together. She said it, but she didn't really mean it. The Navy was always first in her mind's eye. But the Navy would be fighting bare ass in space if it wasn't for what these industrial workers and managers were producing to arm them and feed them. From her father's knee, she'd learned to mouth the platitudes of all for one and one for all, but she'd never really believed it.

There always seemed to be someone who was more equal than others.

Now, with enough hats on her own head to give anyone a migraine, Kris was having her nose rubbed in the truth of what she'd said.

"Thank you, Pipra. I think I needed that bucket of cold water in my face."

"I didn't mean to give offense," Pipra said, then changed her direction. "You're one of the best bosses I've ever worked for. I don't want you taking me wrong."

"I'm not," Kris said, trying to take the pressure off the woman across the table from her. "I really mean what I said. Working with you is making me see things I thought I saw but was blind to. I know this is tough on you. Tough on all the folks you've got working for you. I can't promise anyone a bed of roses, but I can say that I see how all of us—Navy, miners, production workers, and management—are making this happen. And that we'd all be dead without each and every one of us."

With that, Pipra packed up her briefcase. She left just as Jack was coming back from his long day's work. Kris and he went out for a quick bite, then shared a shower and a very warm bed.

Tomorrow would come all too quickly. Jack made it easy to fall asleep.

6

As Kris was preparing to head up to the Forward Lounge and meet her new ship drivers, there was a knock at her door.

"Enter," she said, hoping Pipra hadn't stumbled onto an even better way of merging their limited, if now expanded, resources, but the two commodores who entered her day quarters were strangers to her.

"I am Commodore L'Estock of Pitt's Hope," one said.

"And I am Commodore Shoalter of New Eden," the other said.

"And we have a present for you," the first finished for them.

That told Kris that the two senior U.S. commanders most recently arrived from home were paying her a call, formal or otherwise, but not much else. L'Estock handed a small package to Kris. Not at all happy at the game they were playing, but curious still, Kris opened the box. Inside was a blue flag.

She shook it out. It had three white stars. Wrapped in it were the shoulder boards of a vice admiral. There was also a pair of papers. One was rather lovely calligraphy and signed by Grampa Ray. No, this was definitely the signature of a very kingly King Raymond I. It proclaimed to all present her right to wear the rank of a vice admiral. The other were the formal orders fleeting her up to the three-star rank, while keeping her pay grade at a lowly captain's.

Buried in the small print was her delegation of authority to fleet up people to the rank of rear admiral and below. Fleet them up but not give them any extra pay.

The bigger surprise was that she could do this for anyone serving in her theater of operations, be they U.S. or otherwise. Apparently, at least some people were taking the need to defend against the raiders seriously enough to forget who was in whose alliance.

At least on far Alwa Station.

Kris read it all, then glanced up at the two grinning officers. "They crammed a lot into one small page. I assume you knew about this."

"Since the king called us in for a conference before we left, most definitely yes. Copies of that are in the mail bag for all of your subordinate commanders: Musashi, Helvetican, whatever."

"It's nice to know we were appreciated, even if you didn't know if we were alive or dead when the orders were written," Jack said, reading over Kris's shoulder.

"Yeah," she said. "Now, thank you very much. If you'll leave us alone for a moment, we'll join you as quickly as we can in the Forward Lounge once we attend to some minor details."

If anything, the two officers' grins got bigger. They must have heard about the new fraternization policy; neither had batted an eyelash when Jack joined them from Kris's night quarters.

Alone, Kris held the new flag and shoulder boards. Three stars, and she hadn't even completed her sixth year in the Navy. Yes, they were only good in theater. Once she returned home, like Cinderella, she'd turn back into a captain at best, maybe even a commander. Still, even for one of those damn Longknifes, it had been quite a ride.

"You want to do the honors for me?" Kris asked.

"I think it's often the duty and joy of the spouse to do this," Jack admitted. It took him only a moment to remove her old boards and put on the new ones. He'd had experience getting her uniform ready for her when she was in the shower just as she had done the same for him. At least those times when they hadn't been showering together.

"I think I got that right," he said, and gave her a kiss. It wasn't exactly a peck, but it wouldn't have any flower girl suggesting they "get a room." It seemed just right from a brevet colonel to a newly frocked vice admiral.

"Shall we go?" he asked when they broke chastely.

"No, there are a few things that need to be done. Nelly, promote Commodore Kitano immediately to rear admiral. Jack, I want you to organize all the ships' Marine detachments and the colonials into a brigade. Which makes you a brigadier general."

He grinned at that.

Kris hurried on. "Tomorrow, promote the other three commodores to rear admiral and restore Benson and Hiroshi to their previous ranks with seniority in theater dating from tomorrow. Is there anything else I need to think of?"

Jack said nothing. Nelly paused, then added, "I assume you're creating four task forces with rear admirals commanding?"

"Something like that, Nelly."

"Who gets to choose who fills in as squadron commanders behind the promoted commodores?"

"Cut a set of orders authorizing the task-force commanders to propose to Admiral Kitano the fleeting ups to commodore in my absence. We'll let them fly while I'm gone, then I can finalize them, assuming they haven't screwed up."

"If you'll have Jack pull the promotion papers out of the document generator, you'll have something to give Admiral Kitano tonight. I didn't quite go in for the full calligraphy like the king, but I did it up right."

"Thank you, Nelly."

That done, Kris adjourned for the Forward Lounge.

7

Kris had never seen the Forward Lounge so large and so full. No doubt, Penny had given up several centimeters of hull armor to stretch it out this far and provide tables and chairs.

To Kris's right, Commodore Miyoshi, soon to be admiral, was deep in conversation with the newly arrived commodore from Yamato. Around them, ship captains, XOs, skippers of Marine detachments, and chiefs of science teams were lost in conversations that, no doubt, were mirrored in the station dives as senior chiefs and Gunnys from the old team met their counterparts from the new teams and compared notes on the lay of the local land and the recent attempt to blight it.

The Helvetican contingent had settled toward the back and was talking in hushed tones with the new arrivals from the Esperanto League and Hispania. The center of the room, stretching over to the bar, was held down by a mash-up of U.S. personnel from Wardhaven, Lorna Do, Savannah, and Pitt's Hope. The area directly closest to the bar had been taken over by New Eden and the arrivals from the Scanda Confederacy as they all got The Word.

For a place with so many people in it, the Forward Lounge was neither hushed nor loud.

Circulating among the officers were a decent-size detail of barmaids, enlisted women earning extra money seeing that dry whistles got wet. Mother MacCreedy must have allowed a new uniform; it seemed to Kris that the skirts were at least six centimeters shorter than before.

Wonder how that's helping with the tips, considering the swill they're delivering?

The Word must have been passed that the Forward Lounge was an off-duty area; no one called the room to attention as

Kris entered. She made her way to the foremost table. Penny and Kitano were holding it down for her.

As she settled into her seat, both young women grinned. "So it's true," Penny said. "You got another star."

"It's true," Kris admitted as she surveyed the room. "How long has this been going on?" she asked.

"Just about everyone was here half an hour ago when I arrived," Kitano said.

"I got here an hour ago, and the place was just starting to fill up," Penny supplied. "I figured I better be here to see how much it needed expanding and do it myself since we're stretching the hull. I've had to grow the place twice. If any more come in, I'll have to do it again."

A couple of dozen civilian merchant types showed up at the door and looked around, disappointed to find no room left for them. They were suitably amazed as Penny did her thing, and the room stretched farther away from the wall and another row of tables and chairs appeared as if out of nowhere.

They took the newly available places and signaled for drinks. Kris watched as three barmaids took trays with already filled glasses to them and set them down before them. She kept watching as the men and women cautiously tried their drinks.

One fellow spat his out and threw the full glass at the serving maid. She was a Marine and dodged expertly.

"What's this shit?" he shouted, as the house got very quiet.

Kris stood up . . . the house silence got total.

"That's what we drink out here," she said softly. Deadly soft to those who knew her.

"I got better back on the *Mary Allen*," he shouted back.

"Not by this time tomorrow," Kris said. "All spirits and food stuff brought into the system will be confiscated and added to the general issue. No one will starve, but we've got a critical food situation here. The best go to those who work the best. Those that don't work don't eat. If you want a good beer or whiskey, you'll need to show that your ship is one of the best. If not, you'll get by on what we've got plenty of, and what you're drinking tonight is what the Alwans like. We've got plenty of it."

"No wonder," the guy said, and spat again.

"I didn't plan to start this meeting this way," Kris said, "but this is as good a place as any. If you don't know, I am, as of a few minutes ago, Vice Admiral, Her Royal Highness, Kris Longknife, Viceroy to the Colonials on Alwa, Ambassador to the Alwa natives, CEO of Nuu Enterprises in System, and Commander, Alwa Defense Sector. No matter what your job is, you pretty much work for me."

She paused to let that sink in.

"For those of you in uniform, this will be no surprise. Our orders are to hold here until relieved. So far, we've gotten reinforcements but no reliefs. For civilians, the same rules apply. We have no warships to escort you back to human space. We cannot allow you to sail unescorted. In addition to that, we need you here, working to improve the defenses of this system. As soon as you're unloaded, we'll respin your ships from multireactor starships into single-reactor system freighters."

"And what if we don't want to be your willing slaves?" came from somewhere in the back of the room from the newly created tables.

"As I said, we've got a food problem here. No work, no food. If you don't want to work or don't work out up here in space, you can go dirtside and see if you like it better working for a colonial farmer or fisherman. The work's hard and hot. Many of us have taken a turn at it on our leaves. It's hard and hot work, but it's putting in a crop that should see us eating better and brewing our own beer in a month or two."

"And if we decide to skip your job offer and just leave?" It was also unclear who spoke.

"Do not misunderstand me. I said no ship leaves here. We can't afford to have any ship taken by the aliens. If they find out where human space is, it's all over for humanity. Maybe not in a few years, but for now, those are the orders I've been given."

"Is that why the freighters that stopped off at the mines have an escort?" came from Commodore L'Estock.

"Yes. If one of those merchant ships had tried to run back the way it came, I'd have ordered the escort to shoot out its engines. Maybe it's time we complete the briefing. Nelly, put the feed from my battle board of three weeks ago up on the main screen."

The screen lit up as the aliens tried and failed, then succeeded at forcing the jump. Everyone watched as the alien horde drove the Navy ships back, dying for every bit of space they gained but taking Navy ships with them. The climactic battle near the gas giant came quickly, then the bloody rout—ending with the aliens blowing their moon-size base ship to atoms.

"That's our enemy. This is why we fight."

The forward screen filled with the raped planet that Kris had found on the Voyage of Discovery. It showed the wreckage of a planet plundered of its resources, right down to its air and water.

"If we fail, this is what happens to the planet beneath us. If we make the mistake of letting these aliens get any leads to human space, this is what happens to your home planets—to your brothers, sisters, moms, and dads. Does anyone have any questions?"

It took a moment before, "Not since you put it that way," came from some wag in the back, but it seemed to be a good enough answer for all.

"Now, the good news is that we won that fight. The bad news is that three other alien clans were watching us do it. No doubt, given time, they'll be back to take a try at us. I was about to take a scout squadron out when you arrived. We think we've found the alien home world, and we want to look over the planet they appear to have abandoned a hundred thousand years ago. Maybe it will tell us something. Maybe it won't."

Kris turned to Commodore Kitano. "While I'm gone, Commodore Kitano will have the job of teaching you how we fight on Alwa Station. It's hard driving and hard evasion. You'll likely need to modify your ships to pull it off. She and the veterans of the recent fight will be showing you the ropes over the next several weeks. Since she's been acting as my deputy, it's appropriate that she have the rank to go with it. Commodore Kitano."

The woman stood, then marched front and center to Kris. "Commodore Kitano, it is my honor to promote you to rear admiral. These shoulder boards have served me well in the last battle. May they serve you just as well."

Kris removed the young woman's commodore boards and replaced them with those of a rear admiral. "Congratulations," Kris said, offering her hand to shake.

Kitano shook it right back. "Thank you, Admiral."

When Kitano had returned to her seat, Kris turned again to the officers before her. "There will be other fleeting ups announced tomorrow that will leave squadron positions open. We will fill in behind. Battle-experienced hands will have the leg up. No doubt, there will be more opportunities for you newcomers to demonstrate your fighting caliber. That's just the way it is on Alwa Station.

"Now, are there any more questions?"

As Kris expected, there were none. "Then enjoy yourselves. Take a break, for, oh, the next hour. Work on upgrading the ships to Alwa Station standards will begin at 0800 tomorrow morning. Your first training sortie will be in three days."

"You're going easy on them," came from somewhere among the U.S. contingent.

Kris ignored the comment and walked over to where Commodore Miyoshi was talking with Commodore Zingi from Yamato. They bowed to her, and she returned it.

"Is the situation as, ah, challenging as you say?" the newcomer asked.

"Which do you mean?" Kris asked, letting a smile play on her face. "The alien fleet, the prospects of the planet below being plundered down to bedrock, or our own food situation?"

"Ah, so it is all of it, *ne*?"

"All of it, but do not doubt us, we have made great strides. Commodore Miyoshi can tell you all about it. By the way, Commodore, you will need to see where you can scrounge up a pair of rear-admiral shoulder boards. Your promotion will be announced tomorrow."

"*Hai!* Good for you," Commodore Zingi said.

"Does that mean I will be the one stuck showing these old sticks in the mud from Yamato how to do a real fighting man's job?"

"Old man, you . . ." And the conversation took a turn into a language Kris only dimly remembered from her time on Musashi and had never much understood then. She bowed her way out of what she took to be some good-natured ribbing and continued her way around the room, stopping wherever she spotted a soon-to-be rear admiral and letting him or her know the good news while answering any questions the new arrivals had. Most of them were rather silent although several thanked Kris for not ending the war before they got in.

Those who had been out with Kris just quietly shook their head. They would learn, no doubt, soon enough.

When Kris passed close to the merchant sailors, she got called over by two captains. "You're definite about us not going back?" one asked.

"You want to try it unescorted?" Kris asked back.

That got heads shaking. Still, one muttered, "I'll try anything. Once."

Kris frowned and went on. "Are you willing to swear on all you hold sacred that you'd drop your reactor containment if you are attacked? That's what every one of our warships has done when it was disabled. The aliens shoot up survival pods. We haven't given them any ships."

Several listeners blanched at that.

"Didn't any of you notice that no one came back from the last shipment out here?" Kris asked into their silence.

"I told you the pay was too damn good," someone said, elbowing another in the ribs.

"The pay out here is as good as we can make it," Kris said. "Folks working the mines, shipping the ore down here, and working the moon factories get the best of what we've got, right alongside the fighting crews. Right now, there's not a lot of extra to go around, so it's rationed. That may get better when the next crop comes in. If any of you have any experience fishing or farming, you might want to ask for a transfer."

"Farming is *real* work," one youngster said. "I got off the family farm and aboard ship as soon as I could."

"Well, we'll eat better when that hard work gets done," Kris said, and, with no further questions, made her way to the door. Jack was waiting for her there.

"I was wondering if one of them might take a swing at you," he told her.

"So was I. I've gotten away with being the bad girl for so long, I've almost forgotten what it's like to be called on it."

"You're no worse than you have to be. Now, speaking of being bad, I've always wanted a *vice* admiral in my bed. I figure one of them must know some really kinky tricks."

"Don't I wish," Kris said with a happy sigh.

"Let's go see what we shall see," said Jack with a willing grin.

8

TWO days later, the *Wasp* led out the *Intrepid*, *Constellation*, *Congress*, *Royal*, *Bulwark*, and *Hornet*, now with some of the old *Hornet*'s crew recovered and aboard. The *Endeavor* brought up the rear, loaded with plenty of low-tech jump-point buoys.

The *Wasp* itself carried some low tech of her own. The moon factories had knocked together several drones from aluminum, ancient carbon fiber, and simple computer-chip technology. It had taken an extra day, but now they had them for surveys when they didn't want to risk Smart Metal™.

The low-tech gear would be left on the dead alien planet. Some might be left on what everyone called the alien home world though solid proof was still needed. Just ask any of the 250 scientists aboard each of the eight ships.

"Prove it. Prove it. No guessing allowed," was their mantra.

None of the low-tech gear would be abandoned in place on the battered world. They planned to collect it all in one location and laser it from orbit. Someone following them might know there was a new burn spot on the planet, but what was incinerated there would tell them nothing.

On the putative alien home world, they'd crash them into the deepest abyss of its oceans and dare anyone to find them.

They were coming to see, not be seen.

The trip was fast. They accelerated at two gees and took the jumps fast and with high RPMs on the ships. They covered thousands of light-years on their long jumps. They followed the *Endeavor* course as it raced back with the news of its discovery. On the way out, they kept their eyes peeled but saw not so much as the hair on the back of one alien head.

Kris liked it that way.

Once they arrived at the system with the battered planet, the surprises came fast and plentiful.

Professor Labao, who would likely never return from his sabbatical from the University of Brazilia, and most certainly not on time, presented Kris with some requests from the expedition's scientists before they'd been in system two hours.

"Our observations of the subject planet shows that its surface has been heavily bombarded. As yet, we are not prepared to say by what. However, we would like to have some samples taken from the asteroid belt so that we can identify the exact makeup of rocks from there and compare it to what we find on the bombardment sites. Could you detach a ship to do that survey?"

"That's why there are eight of us," was Kris's quick answer.

She walked the short distance from her day quarters onto the *Wasp*'s bridge. "Captain Drago, would you please order the *Intrepid* and *Congress* to slow down and split up. We want them to take random samples of several asteroids' composition. Please advise the *Endeavor* that we would also like her to take samples on her way to and from setting up a warning jump buoy at the other jump into this system."

"Aye, aye, Admiral. I'll get that off immediately."

"Thank you, Admiral," the professor said.

"Any more requests?" Kris asked.

"Not at this time. We are studying the planet and the entire system as we approach it, but we have nothing yet to report that is different from the hasty study done by the small science team on the *Endeavor*."

Kris smiled at the way he gave her backhanded notice that he didn't think much of what Penny had brought back. It didn't matter to Kris. Penny had taken only what Kris could spare at a tough time. What she'd found out was all that Kris had expected.

As the professor left, Kris stayed with Captain Drago on his bridge. "Any activity in this system?"

"If there had been, you'd have been the first to know, and we'd be turning around and hightailing it out of here, I assume, by your orders."

"We most certainly would," Kris said.

Her thoughts were a tad different. *Maybe. Depending on what we found. I'd still like to take a try at capturing one ship alone. Maybe someone would decide to live, not die.* But to her flag captain, she said what was more to his liking.

"Yeah, right," Captain Drago muttered, apparently no less deft at reading Kris's mind now that her flag sported three stars.

As they approached orbit, Kris called a staff meeting. It was a small one. At her conference table was Jack, of course. He had two rump battalions of Marines, though what they'd do this trip was still to be determined. But then Marines were good at figuring out what was needed of them while others were still wondering why they were there.

Penny and Masao were there as representatives of the early survey, even if Professor Labao didn't think much of it. His two thousand boffins, however, still had nothing new they wanted to report to Kris. Until they did, Kris considered her friend the expert.

Amanda Kutter and Jacques la Duke had also hitched a ride on the *Wasp*. Yes, they admitted, there was plenty of economic and anthropological work to be done on Alwa, but there were so many question marks about these two planets that they'd begged to be included. Never sure what kind of lion's mouth she'd be sticking her head in this time, Kris had signed off on their inclusion and added them to her immediate staff.

They'd been the ones who spotted the food problem on Alwa. Who knew what they'd spot here?

Captain Drago dropped in from his bridge as the meeting got underway; Kris never held a meeting that didn't have a spare chair for him.

Professor Labao led off by projecting pictures of both sides of the ravaged planet on one of Kris's screens.

"This planet had been bombarded so heavily that very little of the original surface remains for us to study. In some places, the bombardment sparked volcanic eruptions that added to the remaking of the surface. About the only places not hit are in the low-lying areas that have been suggested as ocean areas although they present no evidence of water, liquid or otherwise, at the present time."

"Is there any evidence of wandering clusters of asteroids in the system now that would put the planet at risk?" Kris asked.

"No," the professor said. "We will be better able to date the bombardment once we are on the ground and have samples; however, at the moment, it appears to have all occurred in the same approximate time frame. The two planets nearest its orbit show no such bombardment in recent times. There are also no more than the usual number of orbit-crossing asteroid bodies than you would expect to find in any system. This bombardment appears to be unique to this planet."

"An attack," Captain Drago growled.

"That assumes intent not yet in evidence," the professor said, refusing to rise to the Navy officer's bait.

"Not an attack, Captain," Jack said, "but an annihilation. An eradication. Way more than a mere attack."

Captain Drago nodded agreement.

"We are developing our plan of study," the professor said, attempting to regain control of his meeting.

"We have been provided with a most interesting set of devices for our ground examination. The engineers back at the Alwa fabricators have presented us with exploration probes used in the Old Earth system. It is part balloon, part powered craft, and all that is needed to transport a rover equipped with a laboratory for sample taking and analysis. This planet has just enough of an atmosphere to allow the balloon to support this kind of device during the daylight hours. We plan to deploy them from longboats, say cruising at ten thousand meters. When the balloon probe finds an interesting area, we will have them settle to a landing. The rover will do its survey and return to transport for the night. At early dawn, we will reheat the hydrogen on the balloon, lift them off, then the propeller system attached to the balloon will take the assembly to the next area for examination. A brilliant bit of engineering design, don't you think?"

"If it gets us what we need to know fast, then that's great," Kris said. She'd learned long ago that if she gave the boffins the slightest chance, they would bend her ear for hours.

"Have you got anything to tell us yet?" Jack asked, ever vigilant to protect Kris's body, or in this case, ears.

"We do think we may have found one thing you will find of interest," Professor Labao admitted. Cautiously.

"And that is?" Kris said.

"This," he said and turned back to the screen. Now it showed a view of deep space. There were the usual stars in the background. It was what was in the foreground that puzzled Kris. It appeared to be a long bar. Maybe a string. It had something at each end and a large sphere in the middle.

"What is that?" Kris asked.

"We don't know," the professor said flatly.

"Give me your best guess," Jack growled.

"Hey, that could be a sling," Jacques la Duke said.

"A what?" Amanda Kutter asked before Kris could.

"How big is that hummer?" Jacques asked the professor.

"We are not sure, but it appears to be several tens of thousands of kilometers long."

"And is it in an orbit that intersects this planet?"

"Yes," the professor cautiously admitted. "In say another twenty thousand years it would likely collide with it."

"Right. I wonder how many of those were once sharing this orbit?" Jacques said, standing and going to peer more closely at the screen.

"So, Jacques, since you seem to know what you're looking at," Amanda said testily, "let the rest of us mere mortals in on the secret."

"Okay, there's a lot of guessing going on here, but we anthropologists do it a lot, professionally, and if we guess right, there's a good paycheck in it for one of us. Anyway, here's my guess. That's a space sling."

"A space sling?" came from everyone in the room, Kris included.

"A space sling," Nelly said more slowly. "Yes, it most definitely could be one."

"Quiet, Nelly. Let Jacques have the fun of telling us what he thinks he's found," Kris said.

You humans want all the fun.

Yes. Now hush, girl.

"Pulling a lot of stuff out of a deep gravity well," Jacques began, "is not cheap. Most developed industrial planets have a space elevator. A beanstalk. You want to lug up something big like a reactor to install in a ship, you don't lift it in a shuttle, you send it up the beanstalk. It's faster, cheaper, and easier. Designing a shuttle to take a battleship-size reactor is, well, just nonsense."

"They understand the point," Professor Labao said, dryly. Clearly he was not happy to have lost control of *his* meeting.

And Kris thought it was *her* meeting.

"So, if you want to drain an ocean or suck a lot of air off a planet, you do something like this. I assume they didn't care where the water and air went, they just wanted it gone. You put this thing in orbit. That center bulge is a counterweight to hold it stable in orbit. The ends swing around the center. When one end is down, it scoops up water. I'd guess there's a pipe that sucks air when it's down and holds it until it's up, then spews it out. The same with the water. It freezes as it comes up into orbit. When it's all up, the sling throws it out, and it zips off into space."

Jacques paused for a moment. "Tell me, Professor, is there a ring of gases around the sun in this orbit?"

"I don't know," Professor Labao said, stiffly.

"You don't know, or you do but don't yet have enough information to make an official, scientifically accurate to the thirteen–decimal place statement?" Kris said. Her temper was starting to boil, and she was missing Professor mFumbo, God rest his soul. Why hadn't he stayed on the *Wasp* instead of spreading himself and his scientists around the battleships that didn't make it back from Kris's first run-in with the aliens?

Mentally, Kris shook herself. She knew she was heading into a black hole of her own making. Too many had died while she had lived, and, no doubt, too many more would die. If she continued to be the lucky one, she'd survive. The emotions boiling up inside her now would not make it any better for those she'd lost.

The professor just stared at Kris.

Jack stepped in. "Jacques had a good question. Do you have any evidence at this time of an outgassing from this planet being left in its orbit? If there was water, air, and other material on that planet, it had to go somewhere."

The professor nodded. "We do have some evidence that this particular area of space is rich in nitrogen, oxygen, water vapors, and carbon compounds, including amino acids. We wanted to check these out on our approach to orbit before we said anything, though. I mean, why would anyone scatter this planet's, ah, lifeblood, so wastefully?"

That left the room in a dead silence.

"When the Romans conquered Carthage, they sowed the ground with salt so that it could not grow anything and never recover from the defeat," Nelly said, and fell silent.

"If someone really hated the people of another planet," Penny said slowly. "If they wanted to make sure life never grew up again on a planet, they'd take away the air, water, everything. They'd pound it to a pulp, and they wouldn't care where what they ripped off went."

"Maybe that was the intent all along," Jacques said. "Waste it. Waste them. Throw it away. Let nothing of it enter their own living cycles."

"Hatred that hot and that deep is . . ." Kris said. "But then, we've seen what they took from other planets."

"And killed everything that lived there," Penny said, slowly eyeing the screen that showed the planet they were approaching. "Could it have started here?"

"I doubt if we will ever know for sure," Jacques said, "but the more we know, the better educated our guesses will be."

9

They made orbit an hour later and began the survey immediately. While Kris intended to pair the ships off and let them swing around each other to give the crew some down, that would have to wait a bit. For now, each ship went into a different orbit, one even into a polar orbit, as they mapped the planet, studying everything they could without touching anything.

The mapping showed a planet that had been hit and hit hard. There was evidence of at least five uses of atomics. These were marked by the residual radiation on the ground. However, even those five areas had been hammered by nonatomic hits with large kinetic weapons at high speeds. When you factored in several places where volcanic activity had been triggered, the entire place was a pockmarked landscape of death.

The mapping did identify a few areas where the original surface material still existed.

Some of the mountains seemed to have been left alone. They still showed where treelike vegetation had stood. The remnant of that vegetation appeared to have been torched before it was left to die without air and water. The oceanic floor also looked like it had survived in some places, particularly the deepest trenches. Those would all have to be studied in greater detail.

Although nothing appeared to be living now, the biologists still suggested that no landing be attempted.

"We know something killed this planet. We don't know what, if anything, was applied to kill the animal life or vegetation on it before or while they slammed the planet from space. It's best we keep our hands off the place until we know more," was the way Professor Labao reported their first findings.

The orbital survey had already identified some kind of frozen substance at the poles. There might also be frozen water in some places underground. That allowed for the possibility of some kind of life surviving. Bitter experience on other planets had shown some of the most stubborn bugs to kill were also the most deadly toward humans.

With enough problems on her hands, Kris was only too happy to steer well clear of any more.

The third day of the survey, the ships gathered in orbit and were finally able to pass cables of Smart Metal™ between them and swing themselves around each other. This brought a welcome sense of down and improved morale among those who didn't much care for floating through their day.

That day, they began the ground survey.

Longboats from the *Wasp* drew the duty of entering the planet's thin atmosphere and launching balloon surveyors from their open aft ramps. Nine of the ten successfully inflated as they tumbled free. The last just tumbled. When the *Endeavor* made orbit, before it paired up with the *Intrepid*, it lased the wreckage on the ground, burning it down to basic atoms.

That would be the future fate of the other nine explorers: their reward for a job well-done. In one of her more reflective moments, Kris found herself wondering how Nelly felt about that.

She did her best to keep that thought to herself.

Nelly, however, was fully occupied going over the mapping survey with an intensity no human mind could match. Jacques had asked around if some of the other space slings might have made a fiery reentry. The question had drawn no interest from the scientists, but Nelly set a goal for her and her children to go over the map, quarter-meter pixel by pixel to determine if there were any new, smaller craters. It seemed to be keeping them busy when they weren't otherwise at work.

"I've found one," Nelly reported the fourth day.

"Found what?" Kris asked.

"A new, smaller crater. Something that could have been made by the center weight of a space sling."

"Or by a meteorite that just happened to wander by," Kris pointed out.

"Yes. We'll need to survey the landing site."

"Ask the scientists to add it to their survey."

"Yes, I guess I will have to get permission before I retask one of the balloons."

"Yes, you will, Nelly. Now, why don't you and your kids find a couple more of those slingers? There must have been quite a few to strip this planet of water and air."

"We are still searching the maps, Kris."

"Keep it up. Maybe you'll find one close to where the boffins already want to look."

Nelly got rather quiet for a long time after that. Kris hoped she was busy and not giving Kris the silent treatment. It had been bad enough for her computer to do that when Kris deserved it.

The scientists tried to keep their work to themselves, but there were leaks. There had to be leaks on ships loaded with sensors and communication equipment and a lot of very inquisitive Sailors and Marines. It was basic to the scientific mind only to publish what they were absolutely sure of. Too many careers had been ruined by premature publicity.

Kris, however, was not against some arm-twisting when she reached the limit of her patience.

After all, this was a fighting squadron, and it was sitting here, in the mouth of the lion, so to speak. If there wasn't a good reason to keep her people here in harm's way, she'd take them back where they came from.

Or deeper into the lion's throat. Depending.

Under pressure, Professor Labao relented and became more forthcoming with the results they were getting and the questions they were chasing.

"The bombardment seems to have taken place in three stages," he said. "We could see immediately that the area subjected to atomics had also been hit during at least a second strike by kinetics. Our questions centered on whether or not there were just two or maybe three waves of kinetic strikes."

"You say kinetic strikes," Kris said. "Don't you mean asteroids or meteorites?"

"No," the professor said, and then paused maddeningly to structure his further answer.

"First, let us define our terms. An asteroid is a small solar body, likely left over from a failed planet's formation. They come in several types: rock or mineral, though some prefer to add a third type, those rich in carbon or organic compounds. Many are covered with a thick layer of ice. Being natural, they tend to defy a single definition.

"A meteorite, on the other hand, is merely a natural object from space that has survived entry to an atmosphere. Since they are what hits the ground, they are often metallic, although some rocks do survive the heat of passage through the atmosphere.

"What is important about all of these is that they are natural, and, in the normal course of travel about a mature solar system, a bombardment like we have here just does not happen. Such, ah, traffic problems are resolved in the early days of a system. Never this late.

"No, the kinetic artifacts that we are examining are either asteroids artificially disturbed from their orbit and placed on a collision course with this planet or artifacts specifically designed to bombard this planet, or others like it." Here he paused to clear his throat.

"Nickel-steel bullets were constructed for planetary bombardment during the Unity War and again during the Iteeche War. Thank God they were not used on inhabited planets, or one can only wonder where the killing would have stopped."

Again he paused, as if contemplating the nonempirical question he had asked. Shaking himself, as if to shake off the lack of an answer to that question, he went on.

"It appears to us that similar kinds of bullets were used to hit this planet. Whether it occurred in one wave or in a series of waves, it seems to have followed the use of atomics and preceded the asteroid bombardment."

Now he paused to study Kris for a moment. "We asked you to collect samples from the asteroids. We need them to test the different strikes to see if the products of those strikes came from this planet, or from the asteroids, or from somewhere else entirely."

"Do you think you can make that kind of a determination?" Kris asked.

"Honestly, I don't know. It's been a hundred thousand years, more or less, since these events happened. Despite the eradication of most water and atmosphere from this planet, it still has weather cycles. There has been a dust storm in the southern hemisphere in just the short time we've been here. We may have set an impossible objective for our research, but if we didn't posit the possibility that some of this attack was from beyond this system, then we would never find it out, even if it were."

"In other words," Kris said, "is it possible that some of the bullets that pounded this planet came from the next system over?"

"That is our thinking."

"If we could make the association, it would certainly connect the two and very likely implicate the aliens of the next system in their first genocide," Jack said.

"Planetcide," Penny said.

"Precisely," Kris said. "Well, Professor, you have our attention, and our hearty support for your survey. Have at it."

Once that was published, the patience of the Sailors and Marines grew longer. Now they could see the need for a solid, if lengthy, forensic examination of the planet below them.

It was Captain Drago who suggested that their time could be put to some defensive purpose.

"We're going to want to outpost the next system. If I can express a preference, I'd like to not only put warning buoys at the jumps into that system but also into the ones the next system out."

"Give ourselves plenty of time to pick up our skirts and make a run for it," Kris said.

"I wouldn't have said it quite that way, but yes."

"It will take more time to collect all those buoys," Jack pointed out.

"Why collect them?"

"But then, if the aliens come back, they'll know we've been there?" Kris said, beginning to see the answer to her question even as she asked it.

"And the problem with that is . . . ?" Captain Drago said, raising an eyebrow and grinning.

"Hold it," Jack said. "We're doing forensic research to discover the origin of the iron bullets that slammed this planet. Do we want some homicidal alien going over our warning buoys?"

"I checked with the engineers who designed these buoys

and the factory bosses who turned them out. They are products of Alwa. The metals and silicon are from that system. There's not one atom drawn from human space. If they go over them, they just lead them back to Alwa. No farther," Kris said.

"The design is hardly better than the electronics we had when we left Old Earth, but the design has no fingerprints on it. The metals came from stars that burned long ago on this side of the galaxy. Yep. If we leave them, they know someone came calling but not someone from more than, oh, a couple of thousand light-years or so."

Again, Captain Drago paused. "Do you see a downside to their knowing we know where they lived?"

Kris spoke slowly. "We know where they lived, and we didn't do a damn thing to their old home. Nope, I don't see a downside. Let them try to figure out why someone would do that." Now Kris and Jack were both grinning ear to ear.

The *Endeavor* and the *Intrepid* were dispatched to picket the next systems out.

It was Nelly who came up with the smoking gun.

10

Kris and Jack were just sitting down to another bland breakfast in the wardroom. The main course was oatmeal, a crop the colonists on Alwa grew and stored as famine rations. The Navy was eating a lot of oatmeal.

It was sweetened by dried berries and nuts gathered in the deep woods, now less dangerous thanks to Marine hunting teams both making them safer and hunting for a bit of red meat. The Alwans didn't donate the berries and nuts but traded them for electrical products from the moon factories. The Alwans drove a hard bargain, but for now, food was harder to come by than basic commlinks and TVs.

As Kris was about to take her first bite, Nelly said, "Kris, I think I may have made Professor Labao mad at me."

"And why might the good professor be upset with you?" It was never good when Nelly made Kris pry bad news out of her.

"I kind of borrowed one of the survey rovers."

"I thought he had those rovers booked pretty solid," Jack said.

"They are," Nelly admitted. "I borrowed it last night after they put it to bed. Then I had it drive just two kilometers to look at something we'd discovered from the mapping survey."

"Nelly," Kris said, "those surveying rovers don't have much battery life."

"Yes. We just about ran it dry. However, there was enough for it to carry out our test before it ran out."

Kris and Jack found themselves rolling their eyes at the overhead. When Professor Labao and the scientists found out that one of their nine surveyors had been hijacked by Nelly and left in the middle of nowhere with a dead battery, there would be hell to pay.

"However, Kris, we did verify that the orbital slingers were not made on this planet."

"What?" came from both Kris and Jack.

"Kris Longknife, I have a bone to pick with you and that so-called smart computer of yours," was less of a shout and more of a bellow. It came from the doorway into the wardroom and preceded the expected Professor Labao into the officers' mess by a good three seconds.

"We found what everyone was looking for," Nelly repeated, but in a voice more appropriate for a teenage girl coming in several hours after her curfew than for the Magnificent Nelly.

"Do you know what that computer of yours has done?" the professor demanded as soon as he located Kris in the wardroom.

"Yes, she just told me," Kris replied evenly.

"She's burned out the batteries on one of the handful of rovers we have."

"It is not burned out," Nelly said. "It's taking a charge, a bit slower, but it's taking a charge. In two hours, it will be fully charged," Nelly insisted.

"I will not stand here bandying words with a random collection of matrix and gunk."

"Well," Kris said, "this random collection of self-organizing matrix seems to have gotten around all your safeguards and taken control of your little robot without your noticing it for an entire night."

"Are you defending that pile of junk?"

"Nelly says she's found the smoking gun that connects this attack to the next system over. Have you?"

"She," the professor began, then stopped. He blinked several times, then settled into a chair two down from Kris. After a long pause, he went on.

"My computer is updating me on what he and his mother and brothers and sisters did last night."

NELLY, YOU DIDN'T HAVE HIS OWN COMPUTER KEEP HIM IN THE DARK, DID YOU?

IT SEEMED LIKE A GOOD IDEA AT THE TIME, KRIS. THERE WAS NO QUESTION HE WOULD NOT ALLOW US TO DO THE ANALYSIS WE KNEW WE NEEDED TO DO. I'D ASKED NICELY. I'D

GOTTEN NOWHERE. SO, YES, WE DID TAKE MATTERS INTO OUR OWN HANDS.

YOU LIED TO HIM.

NO, KRIS, NEITHER I NOR MY SON LIED TO HIM. WE JUST DIDN'T TELL HIM.

NELLY, YOU AND I ARE GOING TO HAVE TO TALK ABOUT THIS.

YES, KRIS, I EXPECTED THAT YOU MIGHT SAY THAT. I'M SORRY, BUT IT WAS SOMETHING WE DECIDED HAD AN EIGHTY-NINE-PERCENT CHANCE OF SETTLING THE QUESTION OF THE ORIGIN OF THE ATTACK. I DECIDED IT WOULD BE BETTER TO ASK FORGIVENESS THAN ASK PERMISSION.

Oh, where did I hear that one before? Father always said, "Your sins will find you out." Today is going to be interesting.

The glazed look in the professor's eyes went away; Kris took that to mean that the update from his computer was over.

"That doesn't prove it is from the next system over," he said, continuing a conversation that had, no doubt, begun in his head.

"Yes," Nelly said, "but it does show that the metal in that counterweight is not a product of this planet or of the asteroid belt. If you can persuade Kris, you can send ships to survey the other planets in this system, but I bet she'd rather push on to the putative alien home world and check the isotopic makeup of iron and nickel and distribution of rare earths on that world than spend more time on this one."

"Would someone *please* bring the rest of us into this briefing," Kris said. She noticed that munching of oatmeal had ceased all around the wardroom. Clearly, if she got her briefing here, there would be no need to have the *Wasp*'s news feed updated.

Nelly took up the briefing in a voice clearly intended to carry through the wardroom. "The problem with all the sites that we have been sending the surveyors to is that they have had a hundred thousand years, maybe more, to be contaminated. What might once have been a unique isotopic structure with particular impurities that could give an off-world fingerprint has been worn down by wind and frost. Fragments have been blown away and blown in. Simply put, nothing special was coming from where the surveyors were being sent."

Nelly paused to let that sink into human minds with their slow absorption rate. So she *had* learned a *few* things from Kris.

"However, there was a possibility that some uncontaminated, or at least less contaminated samples of material from the time of the attack might exist. Those were the orbital slingshots, or more particularly, the centrally located counterbalances. They were big, heavy, and likely to survive entry into this atmosphere. Why the aliens didn't just deorbit them when they were done, but instead launched them off on their own orbits that crossed this planet's orbit is something I am not prepared to conjecture about.

"However, we found one still orbiting the sun, and that left me and my children to speculate that there must have once been more. Based on that hypothesis, we searched the map for meteorite objects that were large enough to make their own craters when they hit. We found several that might well be younger than the strata they sat on. We asked permission from the boffins to include them in their survey and were turned down. Yesterday, we decided to take matters into our own hands, and we did, indeed, answer the question we'd all been asking."

Kris glanced around the room. Had any of the other listening officers spotted what Nelly had so quickly glossed over? A few might have; Kris could tell by the narrowed eyes as here and there, officers, usually younger ones, reflected on what a world would be like when computers decided to ignore the orders that humans gave them.

Most, however, looked on expectantly for Nelly to finish the briefing.

"Every planet has a certain fingerprint, a signature if you will, that is embedded in its metal. There is a specific distribution of isotopes in each different type of metal. There are also rare earths that get mixed up in the ores as well. Back on Earth in the twentieth century, one of the first suspicions that an asteroid had struck near the end of the dinosaur era was the different distribution of the rare earth iridium in the makeup of the layer of earth that separated the geological stratus that held dinosaur bones and the next layer up that held none.

"Last night, we parked a surveyor next to a large mound of metal that we thought was a counterweight for an orbital slingshot. When we burned through the surface contamination, we found a nickel-steel center whose composition did not belong on this planet and did not originate in the asteroid belt."

Again, Nelly paused.

"We propose to you that the composition of this metal will suit very nicely the metals found on the home world of the aliens."

"It could come from one of the other planets of this system," Professor Labao said.

"Professor, there is no evidence that any of the other planets in this system ever supported life. There is also no evidence that they were bombarded at the same time this planet was. No, if we are to find where the bullet of this smoking gun came from, we need to look farther afield. I suggest we try the next system. If it turns out not to fit here, we can come back here, but I strongly propose that we are wasting our time here and now. Let's go see the more likely source before we spend more time here trying to prove a negative."

Kris canted her head and waited to see if Professor Labao would say anything further. He didn't.

Captain Drago had been looking on like the rest. He was also likely the oldest one to narrow his eyes as Nelly admitted her newfound ability and freedom to ignore her human instructions. Kris caught his eye.

"How soon can we get underway?"

"Give me four hours to make sure we're shipshape and ready."

"Then send to the fleet. In four hours we will detach from our shared moorings and prepare to break orbit. Have gunnery lay in a shoot to destroy all evidence that there were ever rovers on this planet. If that means an extra orbit, so be it.

"Aye, aye, Admiral," came the reply, and it quickly became so.

11

A shiver went down Kris's back as she watched the planet rotating below the *Wasp*. One of the screens in Kris's flag bridge stayed fixed on the terrain flowing below them. It showed a warm and welcoming world.

Had it spawned horrific monsters?

If it had, why and how?

The land below was green and brown and tan. When they crossed oceans, there were waves with white capes and reef-surrounded islands. On their approach, they had quickly spotted two continents. One was larger and divided into three smaller segments. The second spanned the northern and southern hemisphere with a narrow isthmus in between.

Kris remembered a short course she'd taken about Old Earth. This planet was different, but quite similar. There were even ice-covered poles. Here, the northern one showed land beneath it.

They look like us. They come from a planet that even could pass for our home world. Why do they just want to kill us and every other living thing?

There was no answer to Kris's questions scrawled across the planet below.

On another screen, Captain Drago was mooring the *Wasp* nose to nose with the *Royal*. Since the *Royal* outweighed the *Wasp*, the pole between them was longer for the *Wasp* than the heavier ship. Moored, they swung around their center of gravity, but it was a messy swing. Kris could hear pumps moving reaction mass and water around the ship. Out on the bridge, Penny was even moving the armor to help balance the ship.

No doubt, across the mooring line, the *Royal* was doing the same.

Until they finished, Kris sat with her safety belt tight as she eyed her screens. Her inner ear screamed as "down" did a jig around her.

Another screen showed the pickets posted around the system. There were three jumps into the system, one to the planet they'd already looked over and two more to different systems. Those three had a total of seven jumps out from them. The *Endeavor* and the *Intrepid* were out, deploying low-tech warning buoys on both sides of those systems' jumps.

The buoys inside this system reported all was well. That data could be obsolete for as much as a day before Kris knew it.

With a shrug, Kris put that bit of data away in a pigeonhole marked WORRY ABOUT NEVER. Until someone came up with a way to move or communicate faster than light, it was just a fact of life.

Kris turned back to her boards; they were coming up on the most remarkable thing about this planet. Slowly, it revolved into Kris's view.

Below her was a plain of glass. Huge, it spread for hundreds of kilometers in all directions. It wasn't a circle or a square but a blob, splashing out more here, less there onto the great plain that had been scorched and left to glaze over.

There might once have been a great river flowing down one side of it, but the watercourse had been directed back to the south and now flowed into a series of great lakes.

Circular lakes.

Kris wondered what was at the bottom of those hollows.

She wondered more about the pyramid rising in what could pass for the exact center of the glass plain.

Also sharing the table with Kris was Commander Penny Pasley, Kris's intelligence officer. Beside her was her erstwhile boyfriend, Lieutenant Iizuka Masao, an intelligence officer of the Musashi Navy. The *Wasp* had fitted out under unusual conditions for a U.S. warship and still had quite a few officers drawn from the Musashi Navy.

On occasions Kris dreamed of having a plain old, standard Navy command. But then, she hadn't bothered to have a plain old Navy career or come from a plain old anything family.

She'd have to make do with what she could get.

"That pyramid is made of solid granite," Penny said. "That's about all we could determine for sure."

Kris turned to Professor Labao. "How long before your boffins can determine if it's safe to go down there?"

"You can go down there now. I'm just not sure it would ever be safe for you to come back up," he said. His nose was still out of joint after Nelly had pulled off what his scientists had failed to do.

"I would prefer to not homestead the aliens' home world," Kris said. "Please check it out most thoroughly. Report back to me in two days as to what the biological risks are down there."

"We should be able to do that by then," he admitted, and seemed to lose himself in communication with his computer. It was one of Nelly's kids. If Kris wanted to know what was going on with her science lead, she could just ask Nelly.

She didn't.

The *Wasp*'s orbit now carried it over the coast of the great continent and out over the narrower of the two great seas. Here and there were islands, but Kris wasn't looking at them. Her thoughts were back on the glass plain.

"Nelly, put the area around the pyramid on screen four."

Her computer did.

"Identify likely impact craters around the glass plain."

Circles began to appear on the vast expanse of land. The screen zoomed out to show the entire continent covered with circles. Some overlapped. Some, in the lowlands, were filled with water. Others, in the mountainous areas, were ragged and imperfect. Even in the land covered with forest or jungle, the map identified impacts.

"Someone really pounded this place," Jack said.

"And went in for overkill around that plain. Nelly, go back to it. Are there any impact craters?"

"No, Kris. As best I can tell, there are craters from atomic explosions, but that's not enough to cover this entire plain with glass."

"What did, then?" Penny asked.

"As best I can tell, the areas between the atomic hits were lased to the melting point."

"Someone really wanted whatever was down there to go away," Jack said.

"It's all overkill," Jacques put in. "A waste."

"With these aliens, all I'm seeing is a lot of that overkill thing," Kris said.

A thought was nagging at the edge of her mind. Kris let her eyes rest on the overhead for a long moment. Around her, her team seemed also lost in thought.

Then it came to Kris.

"Two planets slammed by someone or something that goes in not just for winning but for making sure that there is nothing left. Or, in the case of this planet, anyone left alive knows they've been defeated, and defeated totally."

Around her, her team nodded agreement.

"Penny, you were sent to examine six systems that might have had the night sky we think we found imprinted on a ceiling in each alien ship."

"Yes, boss," Penny said.

"You came home after you found this one, the fifth you looked at."

"Right, boss."

"Is there any chance that the sixth system holds the civilization that hit both of these planets?"

"No boss," Penny said, grinning.

"And why not?" Kris said. She might be wrong, but she wanted something better than a bald "No" to her line of thought.

"The *Endeavor* just finished picketing the next system out. It's the sixth system, the one I didn't get a chance to search. There is no planet in the 'Goldilocks' zone. All its planets are too close or too far out for there to be any liquid water on them. Sorry, Kris, there's no easy answer for our puzzle. There are two planets in the right orbits to have life and that night sky. One's been blasted clean of life and the other one is the one below us."

"Darn," Jack said with a grin. "Don't you hate it when the easy answer isn't?"

"Yes," Kris admitted.

Below them, the *Wasp* was coming up on the large landmass in the northern hemisphere. Dark was approaching, but you could still see the west coast.

Now, in real time, impact circles appeared.

"Nelly, transfer the view of that coast to the fifth screen. Jacques, what do you make of the impact craters? Do there seem to be fewer on this continent, or is that just me?"

"It is not you, Kris," Nelly said. "While the craters cover twenty-two percent of the other landmass, this continent has only twelve-percent coverage."

"And they're more strategic," Jacques said. "Look. There's a river flowing into the ocean." His own computer generated a red dot on Kris's screen.

"I'd bet money that a city grew up there. It must have been a big one, it looks like three overlapping craters there. Here you can see another likely port city." Another dot appeared. "Only one crater for that one. I wonder if we might find evidence of outlying suburbs there. Though, if this did happen a hundred thousand years ago, there wouldn't be much left."

Jacques made more red dots appear on the screen. "Look, two rivers flowing into this circular lake. Only one flowing out. A river confluence is always a good city site. In early-civilization development, you'd have water trade flowing through it. Later, a city grows where the village and town was."

"But why the hits on the mountains?" Kris said, spotting a range of mountains that looked to have been hammered.

"I can think of several reasons," the anthropologist said. "A buried command and control center in a modern age. A mountain retreat, either for royalty or the wealthy of an earlier era. You make the call. What level of civilization do you think was here when they got hammered from space?"

Kris thought over what she'd heard. When she spoke, she did so slowly, letting each word come out carefully polished. "So. Did this planet attack the other one? Or did the other one attack this planet? And if this planet was the last one standing, why are we looking at a primitive world? What level of technology did you spot among the people here, Penny?"

"Stone Age. Yes, a sophisticated set of Stone Age tools, but stone. No metalworking. I think we also spotted some pottery at one site. Maybe others. We need to do a whole lot more before we draw solid conclusions about the people down there."

"Nelly, can you spot any group of hunter-gatherers?" Kris asked.

"Yes, Kris. I've spotted several villages," Nelly reported.

A window opened on the screen. Here was a collection of bark and wood-shingle huts spread along a riverbank. Three watercraft, apparently hollowed-out tree trunks, were pulled up on the shore.

A second window opened. Here a stream flowed through a grassy plain. The dwellings here were made of poles covered with something. "That looks like a wigwam," Jacques provided. "They use poles covered with animal hides sewn together for shelter. It's very portable. Nelly, are there any domesticated animals?"

The screen's view expanded as the village shrank. There were no herds of any sort.

"Hmm . . ." Jacques muttered. "The life of a plains hunter-gatherer is rough without something like a horse for transportation. But it's also a lot less warlike."

The picture changed again. Now it showed a collection of stone huts built together with shared walls. They were close to the cliffs that provided the stone. Down close to a small, tree-lined creek were fields covered with a grasslike plant. People were harvesting it with bone or wooden implements.

"From the looks of it," Jacques said, "they're using small flint edges to cut the grain off the tops of the plant stems. Interesting. They're not harvesting the whole plant."

Kris remembered her stay on Pandemonium. "I've seen farmers growing a crop that gives them a grain harvest two or three times a year without them having to replant."

"I'm aware of that crop," Amanda, the economist, put in. "It was genetically engineered to provide ground cover to protect the soil as well as food."

"Genetically engineered, huh?" Jack said.

"I think we need to look at the DNA of that crop as well as some of the wild stuff growing around it," Kris said.

Professor Labao got that faraway look in his eyes again. No doubt, the ruminations of Kris's staff were going into some furious planning among the experts elsewhere on the ship.

"And if we find evidence of genetic engineering?" Jack asked.

"I've been wondering why it is that the aliens have five nucleonic acids in their DNA while we have only three," Kris said. "This may be none of my business, but if three hold together very well, why would evolution keep going and end up with two more?"

"You need to make allowances for the additional background radiation of this planet," Professor Labao put in. "Our rough estimate at this time is that the heavy atomic attack occurred some hundred-thousand-plus years ago. That would have encouraged a lot of mutation among both plant and animal life here."

"Have you got a definite date for the attack here?" Jack asked.

"No, not yet," the professor said.

"Because," Kris said, speaking carefully as she tossed the verbal hand grenade, "if the attack occurred first here, then there, we might have an interesting time line."

"Are you thinking that the other planet attacked here, and they later counterattacked?" Jack asked.

"It's possible."

"It's also possible," Jacques said, "that these people fouled their own nest themselves, then attacked the other planet with vicious intent."

Kris nodded. "The data allows for both interpretations. Let's see what new data we can find that supports either of those hypotheses or gives us another."

"I know that Your Highness likes to exercise," the professor said, "but I do wish you would avoid jumping to conclusions for a while so we professional researchers can do our jobs."

"Yes, Professor. Jumping to conclusions is off my workout schedule for at least a week," Kris said, and gave the professor a small grin.

"All hands, this is the captain speaking. The *Wasp* is now in a steady mooring with the *Royal*. Resume all normal duties under one gee. Cookie, I expect a decent lunch now that I've given you and your cooks two hours to work on it. Captain out."

Kris released her seat belt. Jack did the same and stood. The belts vanished into the chairs, no doubt to reappear as hull armor.

"My Marines are looking forward to some serious dirt-time scouting out that place. We've scheduled a ten-mile hike around the ship in thirty minutes. Admiral, my wife, would you care to join us?"

"Are you suggesting I need the exercise, General, my husband?"

"I'm suggesting that you think better when you're on your feet, Admiral."

"I think you just like to see me in gym shorts."

"This isn't a run, my dear. The uniform for the hike is battle rattle and fifty-pound rucksack."

"Well, then, I definitely have to join you. Ladies and gentlemen, I believe this meeting is adjourned."

As the others left, Kris and Jack headed for the drop bay. She might be an admiral now, but the *Wasp* still had full battle gear stored in her locker.

12

Kris found herself doing a lot more than thinking during her ten-mile hike. Professor Labao dropped a hot potato in Kris's lap before she'd gotten her first mile in.

"I should have brought this up during our earlier meeting," he said on Kris's commlink as she lugged her armor and fifty-pound load up a ship ladder, "but how much noise are we willing to make for the natives to hear?"

"Noise?" Kris asked.

"To drop probes that hunt for plagues, viruses, and allergens, we need to send the shuttles down. Shuttles make sonic booms. Do you think the natives will notice loud noises coming from a clear sky and give us attention we don't want?"

Jack eyed Kris. Since Labao was using his computer to talk, all of this was going to Nelly's kids. Jack was following the new question along with his own computer, Sal.

"Do you think longboat pilots would mind doing their entry and shoving off back for space around a thunderstorm?" the scientist asked.

"Not too close to one. How about we do it at night, when it's harder to notice," Kris said.

"Of course," he agreed.

"Once we have a better idea of what biological hazards we're up against, we can decide where to set up bases for our extended surveys."

Kris managed to finish the rest of her hike in peace. What she didn't get was a better perspective on the puzzling planet below.

It didn't get easier.

"Kris, we've identified an anomaly," Nelly said over breakfast the second day. "We know that some sections of the great glass plain were lased enough to get the glazing effect."

"As well as the atomics," Kris said.

"And we have the impact craters, all apparently timed to the same event."

"Yes, Nelly."

"Well, we've found what looks like another site that was lased. However, it doesn't match the other event, and there may be some structures outside the immediate attack zone still standing."

"A hundred thousand years later!" Kris said.

"We're not sure it dates from that attack, but we can't be sure until we gather samples."

"And we are not gathering samples from the ground yet. Right, Nelly?"

"Yes, Kris, the ground survey is waiting for the biological-hazard survey to finish."

"And you want me to ask Professor Labao to make a sample-retrieval mission to your anomaly a priority," Kris said, starting to grin as she gained understanding of the real problem.

"Yes, Kris. I do seem to need some diplomatic intervention. Or maybe your playing what you call your Princess Card."

"I'm glad you're beginning to understand the need for coordinating your activities with the rest of us," Kris said.

"I do seem to have overplayed my hand concerning hijacking that surveyor, but you must admit, Kris, without its discovery, we'd still be in the dark."

"Yes, Nelly, you got that one right, so you get the medal. However, you have to understand if you take chances like that and don't get the right answer, you get court-martialed."

"I have gained a better understanding of that old military saying."

"Good, Nelly. Now, what do you make of this anomaly?"

"Kris, it's too soon to attempt a guess. The professor is quite right about our not jumping to conclusions. It's an anomaly that may prove important. Then again, the present data do not support any real conclusions."

"But if it's more recent . . ." Kris started, and failed to stop herself short of a long jump. "If this planet has been attacked more recently, but with more specific targeting, it will be interesting. We will also need to see if we can identify more about the target. For that, we need a ground survey."

Time passed at a frustratingly slow pace. Kris knew she had outposted the system effectively, but she couldn't shake the fear that an alien base ship, complete with escorts, might pop into the system at any time. It wasn't rational, but it was a real worm, gnawing at her gut.

Jack seemed to sense it, too. He went about his job, preparing the Marines for a landing party, but he was there every evening, listening to her share her day, what little there was, then filling her in on what the Marines were up to.

On day four, Professor Labao informed Kris that the planet was as safe as any for human visitation. "We'll keep the science teams in sealed capsules for now, and we'd suggest that any Marines who go down stay in fully armored suits and breathe our oxygen. We can breathe what's down there, we just don't know yet what might have slipped past our monitors."

The longboats cut loose from the ships and dropped into the atmosphere. The scientific teams dropped in their own mobile labs, which were rolled out of the shuttles and paraglided into some flat area. They then drove to where they intended to hide and set up shop.

This provided Nelly with another interesting datum. Out on the plains, a tribe was moving from one water hole to the next. When they heard the sonic booms and spotted the contrails of the arriving shuttle, they changed course and took off in the opposite direction to where the shuttle was headed.

Nelly dropped this bit of information as an interruption to a meeting Kris was having with Amanda Kutter and Jacques la Duke. She replayed the reaction of the local tribe as Jacques watched thoughtfully.

"It seems our locals have some experience with noise from the sky and something that can scratch the sky as well. Let us wonder what that could mean."

"They're on the same continent as the glass plain," Kris said. "I wonder how those on the other continent might react."

"Sorry, Kris, we don't have any good telemetry from there right this moment," Nelly said.

Kris had kept the ships of the fleet moored within a few

thousand kilometers of each other. If she had to fight, she wanted a battle force, not a bunch of pairs scattered around in low orbit. So what the *Wasp* saw was pretty much what everyone saw.

"We'll have to see how the other folks take to the follow-up longboat passes," Kris said. "Nelly, make a note of this question and tell Professor Labao I want to arrange the next drop to take place when the squadron is over the western landmasses."

"I will tell him," Nelly said.

Kris shook her head. "More questions. No answers. When will we get some answers?"

No one filled in the blank space. Kris turned back to her two friends.

"Ah, Kris, can I add another item to your question list?" Nelly asked.

"And if I said no?" Kris said. She was really tired of her long list of questions with no answers.

"I'll wait until you're in a better mood," Nelly said.

"That is likely never to happen," Amanda Kutter said, a big grin on her face.

"Talk to me, Nelly," Kris said with a sigh of resignation.

"We have been putting off an exhaustive examination of the glass plain. It's there, it's glass. Nothing grows there. Nothing goes there."

"I agree you should ignore it for now," Kris said.

"Well, I had some spare time, and the kids and I decided to look it over very carefully. It is an interesting landscape, Kris. It's not flat but has waves and some interesting ramparts where one splash of glass meets another."

"Are you taking up glassblowing?" Kris asked, knowing there was too much bite in the question.

"No, Kris. We found a body."

"A body?" Jacques said. "But no one would go out there. There's no food. No water."

"Yes, that was why we didn't look before," Nelly said.

"Can you show us the body?" Kris asked.

One of the screens came on. Yep, there was what looked like the body of a man. He lay on his back, arms and legs splayed out.

"Did he fall from somewhere?" Jacques asked, then shook

his head and answered his own question. "No, the glass around there is pretty flat."

"Look at the clothes," Amanda said.

"The body is clothed," Nelly said, "though the shoes have been removed."

"The body is wearing clothes," Kris said. "The best-dressed tribes we've seen wear rough weaving or sewn hides. Those looks like normal clothes to me."

"I've pulled up the clothes of the aliens we have pictures of and those that we found on the ships you destroyed, Kris. These clothes don't match their uniforms."

"But they're closer to that kind of clothing than anything we've seen locally," Jacques said. "That high-collar jacket. Those britches. They are closer to a raider's uniform than anything I've seen."

"Yes," said Nelly.

"So what killed him?" Kris asked.

"And took his shoes?" Amanda added.

"Nelly, can you draw a line from the body back to the pyramid, then extrapolate it to the edge of the glass plain?" Jacques asked.

Nelly did, then added a measurement of distance. "This is on the most direct route from the pyramid to water."

"Can you estimate time of death?" Kris asked.

"Not without a closer examination of the body," Nelly said. "However, assuming there are no scavengers, and the body has only been subjected to the elements, my best estimate is that it's been drying out for over a year. Maybe more."

"Penny reported that the clans closest to the glass plain are pretty primitive," Kris said. "So why is this guy in woven cloth?"

"We've been following those close-in clans, Kris," Nelly said. "They are as Penny found, the most primitive of the local people. None have clothes. Some don't even have fire. Penny wondered how they got along with the rest, but all we've seen is that when the naked clans come across each other, they keep their distance and do not make any effort at an exchange. When they come across some of the more skilled locals at the border of each's range, they don't try to make contact."

"I want DNA samples from all of them," Kris said. "Oh,

and Nelly, follow the direct course from the pyramid to the prairies and see what clan is roaming that territory."

"What are you thinking?" Amanda asked.

"I'm wondering if we might find someone still wearing the remnants of a raider's uniform," Kris snapped.

"I was thinking the same thing," Jacques said.

"Nelly, advise Professor Labao of this find and inform him that Her Highness, Kris Longknife would appreciate if he could get a drone to cover this area with close and more persistent aerial coverage than we can manage from orbit, as well as drop some nanos to get a DNA test."

"I will use those exact words, Kris," Nelly said.

"Tact, Nelly. Diplomacy. Oh, and using whom you know as well as what you know," Kris said.

"You humans. Your logic is so strange."

"Yes, we are strange, Nelly. But we *are* polite."

"I will strive to be polite."

And Kris and her team eyed the new data that only raised more questions while Nelly tried her hand at politeness.

13

Two days later, they found the half-clothed clan. They were five men, six women, and four babes in arms. They were also thin, dirty, and ragged, but their rags were clearly related to those of the dead body back on the glass plain.

It was Professor Labao who made the report, formally, and in Kris's day cabin to a full staff meeting. He had a lot more to report.

"We have also conducted a full, though remote, examination of the body. While the glass plain seems most devastated, it is not, however, totally absent of life. Dust has been blown in. Seeds as well, along with bugs and other microlife. In the immediate area around the body, a veritable metropolis of tiny creatures has sprung up."

"That's mighty nice of them to keep him company, seeing that he's dead," Kris observed.

"Most of the life is indigenous to our subject planet. There is, however, one exception."

"Something not from here?" Kris said.

"Definitely. It's a fungus. We traced it to one of his toes. It has DNA, a three-base version, I might add. It's interesting that fungus collected from this planet is also base three, but this fungus's DNA doesn't match anything here. Not even close."

"Hold it," Jacques said. "This body has evidence of alien pathogens."

"That's what I said." Professor Labao did not take questioning well.

"No, excuse me, Professor, what I mean is that this body arrived at its death location carrying something that is alien to this planet. In this case, it was fungus, and the local biota seems to be handling it well. But in other cases, it might be much more deadly. Your Highness, I may have an explanation as to why the tribes local to the glass plain are not very friendly to each other. It may also explain why the other tribes don't want to have anything to do with any of them, either."

"They come from different disease pools," Kris said, drawing her own conclusion. "It must be like the encounter by the natives of the Americas with the European disease pool. They had nothing to match it and lost in the trade. These folks here fear each other because the occasional encounter in the past has led to pandemic."

"Exactly," the professor said. "None of them appears equipped with anything close to modern medical treatments. Once a new bacteria or virus gets free here, it could wreak havoc."

"Okay, now what about the clothes on the dead body?" Kris said.

"Machine woven, of that we are sure. The fiber has been heavily processed, it's more a synthetic than a natural cloth. It doesn't match anything in our database."

"I wouldn't expect it to," Kris said, but she was losing herself in thought.

"We look like them," she said softly.

"Yes," the professor answered. "We have filmed them bathing, and, ah, procreating. We are very similar. This verifies the initial reports from your first encounter as well as the bodies we were able to examine from your captured ship."

"So, if we were to slip out from all our different technology, we might pass ourselves off as one of them."

"I don't like where this is going," Jack said, clearly not willing to let his husbandly role suppress his security-chief duties. Or maybe the husband gig was reinforcing the job.

"If we could make contact with one of these groups," Kris said. "Get them talking to us . . ."

"Yes," Jack said, "but as soon as we started talking, they'd know we weren't from here and they'd be trying to claw our eyes out with their fingernails."

"Are you sure, Jack?" Kris asked. "These people were marooned here by some sort of high-tech society for some reason. Have we found the dissenters from the highly regimented crews of those ships? If we could talk to them, would they tell us what is going on here?"

"A great idea, Admiral," the Marine colonel said, "but it seems to me that you've jumped from A to L to Z. Shouldn't we look at some of the stuff in between to make sure it fits your conclusion?"

"Yes, oh wise Security Chief," Kris said, keeping it formal in a formal setting. In another time and place, he might have rated a stuck-out tongue. "Let's see what more we can find. Do you have anything else, Professor?"

He did.

"As Nelly had suspected, at least three areas of the planet have been subjected to heavy laser attack in recent times and likely from space. One of them may have been as recent as ten thousand years ago. We found evidence of cobbled roads and the rusted remains of ironwork in the areas around that most recent site. We did not find evidence of recent occupation. Indeed, the locals steered clear of that bay and the upland valley."

"You develop technology and you get zapped by Zeus's lightning," Jack observed.

"No wonder that tribe didn't want to be anywhere close to where our shuttle was making noise and leaving contrails," Kris said.

"If this is the home world of the aliens," Penny said, "it appears they have not abandoned it."

"They're protecting it," Jacques said, "from modern technology, or so it seems."

"And will very likely protect them from us, if they find us here," Kris added. "Okay, crew. Is it safe down there?"

"We've done our best to avoid contact," the professor said. "However, there have been no attacks on our survey base camps. We have, of course, located them in remote locations in the hope of not encouraging any such attacks."

"Then I want to see what's in that pyramid," Kris said. "Jack, you figure out a way for me to get down there safely in some manner that won't get your panties in a twist."

"Aye, aye, my Lord and Iron Mistressness," he said.

14

Captain Hayakawa Mikio, skipper of the Musashi Imperial Marine company aboard the *Wasp*, asked the honor of the first landing at the pyramid. His Marines were as well equipped for forensic examination as Jack's own U.S. company. They had, after all, been detailed to protect one of those damn Longknifes.

Kris royally acquiesced to his request.

Three longboats were assigned to take down the company, heavily "reinforced" with willing researchers. Despite Amanda's best efforts to keep her husband out of the first landers, Jacques was assigned as chief of the scientific party and chose to lead from the front.

Amanda would land with Kris. After all, there might be some economic implications of such a huge work as this pyramid, be it made by rolling robots or whipped-slave labor.

Kris would land only after everything was secured, all i's dotted and t's crossed.

Jack stood by Kris in the landing bay, going over her full battle-armored space suit like a mother hen. Kris balked and batted his hands away after he asked her to do a fourth check of her helmet's gaskets and radio.

"I'm fine. There's nothing to worry about. If there is, your Captain Hayakawa will take care of it and we'll just show up after they've finished analyzing all the dead bodies."

"Don't I hope."

"Jack, is it going to be like this every drop, or is this just bridegroom nerves?"

He scowled at her and brought his hands down to rest at his side. "A bit of everything."

"We'll be fine," she said, and rested her eyes on the screen at the end of the drop bay. The first three landers were down, and Hayakawa was deploying his troops by the book. Or at least he was trying to.

The space-suited boffins had somehow escaped the landers before the battle-armored Marines declared the site safe for civilians. Their mob had rushed to the base of the pyramid much faster than the Marine skipper wanted.

To his shouted orders on net, they showed no signs of hearing, much less obeying.

He did what any smart commander would do. He kept his men to the cautious pace his duties required . . . and let the civilians rush ahead to trip any land mines in their path.

Fortunately, there were no land mines, literally or figuratively.

In the end, the scientists set to work doing their analysis, and the Marines deployed both an outer perimeter and an inner fire team, ready for anything that might issue forth from the pyramid or charge in over the glass plain.

As it happened, nothing did.

It was Jacques that got Kris's attention.

"There is a door just where Penny said there would be. It does not have a doorknob or anything so prosaic. There are runes carved into the doorway. We've got nanos out examining them and the cracks in the rock around them. I think there's a combination lock here, I just don't know how to work it yet."

"Can you slip some nanos through the doorjamb?" Kris asked.

"We've tried that," Jacques replied. "It's not as easy as it appears. The jamb is mitered. There seem to be several zigs and zags in there. On top of that, it's electronically active in some way. Anyway, what we've tried to slip in there has died before it got very far. I'm trying to squeeze a camera in on a long-necked probe, but we've only made it through two zigs. We need a Smart Metal programmer down here to knock something together."

"Maybe next pass," Kris offered.

Behind Jacques, a science team turned a laser loose on the surface of the pyramid's rocky face.

"Are they getting anything?" Kris asked.

"I don't know yet," Jacques answered.

"I can answer that, possibly before your Nelly can," Professor Labao said, coming up on Kris's elbow.

"I won't spoil your report," Nelly retorted.

"The initial report on the surface rock was not interesting, but the team applied the laser several times. Once they got past the surface contaminants, the results were more than interesting."

"And they are?" Kris said. The professor, like Nelly, seemed to enjoy stretching out important reports.

"It appears that the granite comprising the pyramid was not quarried on this planet. Based on the ratio of rare earths and isotopes, the mountain it was obtained from is somewhere on the planet we previously studied."

"And the counterweight Nelly analyzed?" Kris asked.

"It came from this planet. Most likely this very continent. Given enough time, we may identify the mountain range."

"I doubt we have that much time," Kris said.

"I agree."

"So we have a smoking gun and a bullet," Kris said.

"I would not argue that," the professor said.

"But why lug all this rock back here and plunk it down in the middle of this mess?" Jack asked with the air of one not expecting an answer.

"That is not a question for science but of human motivation, or alien, as in this case," the professor said. "I am only too happy to leave messy things like that to the conjecture of witch doctors and shamans like yourselves."

No doubt, Kris had just received a backhanded, and fronthanded, compliment of the highest, no, make that lowest scientific order. She decided that, discretion being the wisest part of both the command and management of eggheads, she should ignore it.

"Hey, we got something here," Jacques reported from the ground. "Three of the glyphs seem to be moveable. Let's see if I can push them in and make something happen."

"But in what order should they be pushed?" Amanda cut in from beside Kris.

"That's an interesting question," Jacques answered. "A base-three key is not a cypher that's very hard to break. Let me see, which one should I push first?"

"Is there one that appears to be the first one?" Kris asked.

"There is one that's the first on the right side. All it has on it is a sun."

"They're into one-man rule," Kris said. "I'd go with one being important to them."

"Then one it is," Jacques said. "I've pushed it, and nothing happened, so I guess we're good. Now which one is next? Honey, you want to suggest one?"

"Don't you go getting me into this, you lunkhead," Amanda said. "I'm still stuck in orbit looking at your pictures on a screen. How can I form an informed opinion, assuming we can call what you're doing an informed action?"

Unfazed by Amanda, Jacques went happily along. "Okay, I'll try these two."

A moment later, he was talking again. "That didn't open up anything. But what don't you know, no spray of poison gas, either. Maybe they ran out of it fifty thousand years ago?"

"Or maybe they're saving it for the second mistake," Amanda put in.

"We've all got our space suits on and helmet visors down, dear. We might need to wash ourselves down in the nearest stream, but it can't kill us," Jacques insisted

"Don't worry, Amanda," Kris said, "the nearest stream is three hundred klicks away. While walking to it, they might meditate on their sins enough to learn something."

"I heard that," Jacques said. "Here goes the second try."

There was a long pause. "Hey, it worked. The door's sliding up in its track. Hey, that's good workmanship to be that smooth after all this time."

"Traps may be working, too," Jack put in. "Let Captain Hayakawa take over checking the place out."

"Okay, okay, we're backing away. No need to prod us with those guns."

No doubt, Kris suspected, the Marines did indeed need to prod the scientists a bit to get their attention.

Now a simple and large probe, a copy of the surveyor used on the other planet, rolled into the yawning doorway. It trailed a wire tail that carried its report back.

"There's plenty of electronic interference in there," Jacques reported. "I don't know the source of it yet. Oh, that was not nice."

"What wasn't nice?" Kris demanded.

"I guess they didn't forgive us for getting the combination wrong on the first try. Something opened up and our scout dropped into a pit with a whole lot of pointy things designed to maim and wound. The camera's still working, but that rover won't be roving anymore."

"I told you to study that combination more carefully," Amanda snapped.

"And you were right, darling. Now, the Marines are getting a twin-rotor flyer ready to check the place out."

The flyer entered the yawning dark maw, trailing a wire to carry its reports back. On the screen, a second window opened up, showing the feed from the flyer's camera. Progressing down a slight incline, it showed walls covered with carvings, none of which made any sense to Kris. At her elbow, Professor Labao issued orders to his boffins to start the analysis of those markings, along with the entrance glyphs.

The flyer skipped over the hole in the floor where the rover's lights still showed its place in the pit. The flyer got about six meters past that and suddenly went dead.

"They shot it down!" Jacques said.

On the screen, Kris watched, as a new view opened. It showed the inside of the passageway. Then, in slow motion, darts shot out from the walls. Some crossed in front of the flyer, but, no doubt, others hit it. The view went dark.

"Okay, they really don't want us in there," Jacques said.

"Captain Hayakawa, do you have any more flyers?" Jack asked.

"We have plenty of small ones, and we can make nano scouts from Smart Metal, but I'm reluctant to lose more on a problem we already know. Wait one, we are looking at other solutions."

A long minute later, the Imperial Marine was back on the line. "We have a suggestion from one of our medics. She has surgical gloves that, have on occasions, been blown up like balloons. She suggests we try them. We're working on that idea."

"But air-filled balloons don't fly very far," Kris pointed out.

"Yes, we know that. It seems we will have to advance down the entrance a ways. We are also working on that."

A few minutes later, a Marine appeared with a Smart Metal™ ladder and carried it cautiously into the entrance to the pyramid. He returned a few moments later to report that the ladder had crossed the pit and turned into a ramp. A moment later, a Marine medic in a fully armored space suit headed into the pyramid with an armful of blown-up rubber gloves.

"This would be funny if it wasn't so mortal," Amanda said from her place at Kris's elbow.

"It will provide a comic interlude, no doubt, when they make the vid of this expedition," Kris said.

What Jack growled under his breath, his blushing bride was careful not to hear.

"She's a few feet from the crash of the flyer," Jacques said from the position he'd taken up at the mouth of the entrance. "She's turning on lights."

Again, the screen above the drop bay lit up, now with the feed from the medic's helmet camera. It showed a long hallway pocked with a lot of tiny openings. She stopped a good meter from the first one, and the wreck.

"Let's see what happens," she said in Japanese, which Nelly translated for Kris.

She tossed the first inflated glove down the passageway.

Darts shot out and shredded the glove. However, a lot more darts were shot than were necessary. Most bounced off the stone walls of the passageway and fell harmlessly to the floor.

"Hold it," Kris said. "Can you pan your camera around the floor?

The Musashi medic did. There weren't a lot of darts on the deck.

"Anyone want to bet that we're the first to trigger those darts?" Kris asked.

She got no response.

After a minute, the medic said, "One balloon down, eight to go." She tossed another balloon into the danger zone. That triggered more darts and shredded another glove.

A third and fourth balloon glove suffered the same fate.

"Is it my imagination," Amanda said, "or were there less darts that time?"

"You maybe be right," Kris said.

Two more inflated gloves went downrange, and each of them got farther before meeting its inevitable fate.

"This is my next-to-last glove. If they're all popped, we'll have to wait for more from orbit or find something else to toss." The medic tossed the ersatz balloon in the air, then batted it up with her hand, just like every child learned by their sixth birthday party.

This one slowly floated down the ramp. Darts flew. Several missed but tossed the glove about on the wind of their passing. Then one hit, and the balloon popped.

"And my last one." That balloon was batted high. It floated down the passageway, carried on air currents whose source Kris could not see. One lone dart flew on camera across the passageway. It didn't even get close enough to the glove to knock it around in its flight.

The glove finally settled to the floor. It rolled down the incline and out of the lights.

"I think we have exhausted their supply of darts," the medic reported. "Captain Hayakawa, I request the honor of advancing across the dart-covered way."

"You have earned that honor. Is your battle armor tight?"

"Yes, sir. My sergeant and my lieutenant checked it before we dropped."

"Advance with care, Marine."

Cautiously, the medic took a step into the kill zone. Nothing happened. Slowly, she sidestepped around the wreckage of the flyer. Still, nothing happened. She was on her third step past the wreck when a single dart shot out from the wall and buried itself in the shoulder of her armor.

From the view from Jacques's helmet camera, she pulled the dart out and could be heard to laugh.

"Captain Hayakawa, may I report that the darts penetrate solid Musashi body armor less than a millimeter. I do not think we ever had anything to worry about."

"Your report is noted. Do not relax your alertness. Stay cautious."

"Aye, aye, skipper."

The Marine reached the end of the beaten zone. "Captain, I request that you send in a new flyer. I can see what appears to be a large room no more than five meters from where I stand, but those five meters of wall have not been tested."

"We will send in a flyer," the Musashi Marine company commander said.

A small winged flyer made its way slowly down the passageway and flew over the medic. It got maybe three meters farther.

A wall of flame shot out to engulf it.

"Get out of there, Medic," her skipper ordered.

"Sir, please. I have rolls of bandages. The fire came from only three meters farther in. I can toss a roll that far."

"You may try," did not sound all that happy.

She tossed a small roll of bandages into the flame zone.

It was incinerated. Only a tiny bit of fluff survived, and it burned out before it hit the deck.

Without hesitation, the Medic tossed a second roll.

It was also burned but not so quickly that there wasn't a flaming ball of fire when it hit the deck and rolled a bit before burning out.

"Here goes a third. I hope no one needs bandaging," and another roll went out in a long, underhanded throw.

It arched past where the others had been flamed and hit the deck just short of where the passageway opened up, to roll out of sight into the dark.

"I think we have exhausted the supply of incendiaries, sir. May I continue to advance?"

"Do so with extreme caution."

The medic paused to remove her shoulder bag marked with a red cross. Then, swinging the bag in front of her, she advanced step by step into the beaten fire zone. Kris found herself holding her breath, but each swing of the bag brought no response from the flamethrowers, and each step was a successful one.

In what seemed like forever but couldn't have taken more than a minute, the young woman stood at the end of the corridor. "Skipper, you're really going to want to see what I'm seeing."

What Kris saw on the screen was too diffuse to make out.

"Jack, let's get down there."

"Yeah, I guess it's time to go."

15

Kris wanted to see for herself what the pyramid held. As her admiral's barge dropped from orbit, she ignored the visuals, but she couldn't help but hear a lot of "Oh my God!" and "This is horrible!" and "I wouldn't believe this if I weren't seeing it with my own eyes."

Kris had never been on a slower shuttle drop.

Finally, she was walking across the glass plain headed for the entrance to the pyramid.

Professor Labao was right. Seen up close, the glass was full of dents, cracks, and striations. In those imperfections, bits of dust had collected and tiny plants struggled for life. Here and there, a small bug waddled about its business. Lichen, moss, and fungus spread out from those oases of life, doing what they could to destroy the ever-present glass.

Above it all loomed the pyramid. The reports were flowing back to Kris. The pyramid was a regular pyramid. Each side was equal in length, forming a square base, although one edge showed three millimeters of extra wear from the rest. No doubt, the prevailing winds came from that direction.

It was not quite four thousand meters on an edge and loomed some three thousand meters up.

It was very impressive.

So why build it here, where no one ever came close enough to be impressed by it?

It was also very visible from space. Was it meant to impress from that distance?

More questions. No answers. Maybe the answers were hidden within.

The passageway into the pyramid that Kris had watched being opened now showed cables along one side. Scientists were still carefully recording the markings, glyphs, or writings along the walls. They made way for Kris to pass.

Everyone was still fully suited up; no one was interested in risking their life to find out what this place smelled like.

The pit was now covered by a sturdy ramp. Kris hardly noticed it as she crossed over. Her attention was fully focused on the end of the passage.

She reached it.

It was impossible to take it all in with one glance.

Directly in front of her were a pile of bleached skulls or skull-like things. Behind them, suspended in some clear material, were six figures.

Kris knew at once that this was a family, and a royal one at that.

The tallest of the figures wore robes and a golden chain of office sparkling with different-colored jewels cut in every way imaginable. On his head was a diamond-encrusted crown marked with golden glyphs. In one hand, he held some sort of golden rod with an orb at its head. His other hand rested on the hilt of an archaic, two-edged sword.

The horror on his face showed that he'd been alive when he was encased in whatever it was that held him.

The body was long-limbed and seemed to project an insectoid feel. The face was not easy to read, but there was horror there, and maybe exhaustion.

Beside that transparent casket was a second one, only slightly smaller. The scientists would make their own determination, but to Kris, here stood the wife. Her garments were only slightly less ornate than those of her husband. Her hands were folded empty on her chest. There was no evidence of breasts, so likely she did not nurse her young.

Kris could not find words to describe the look on her face. Anger burned here, as well as disdain. There was terror that didn't seem softened by any hint of resignation. Through it all ran a blend of other emotions Kris could only wonder at.

Then Kris looked more carefully at the other four blocks and found the source of that mother's unnamed feelings. These held smaller versions of the parents. One stood beside the father. The tallest of the offspring, he was still a head shorter than the mother. He looked much like the father and was dressed so. One hand rested on a shorter sword. The other supported a shieldlike object that had clearly not protected him.

Beside the mother were two other figures, each encased in a smaller block as befitted their shorter stature. But it was the smallest and last clear box that drew Kris. It held two tiny figures. Their faces had none of the emotions that the others held. In their place were looks of innocence, surprise, and rising pain.

These two were small children. If they were human, Kris would have guessed an age of two, maybe three years. They looked to be just getting sure on their feet.

Kris felt a shudder overcome her. With no proof, she knew that these two had been the first to be encased in their transparent coffins. That the next younger had then died, followed in order of ascending age until the oldest child. Only then had the royal parents been granted their deaths.

There was no proof, but Kris would not bet against it, either.

Kris turned away from the tableau frozen forever in time. Her eyes filled with tears that she could not release in a battle-armored helmet. She felt all the emotions of a woman, maybe future mother, definitely human being, at this totally inhuman act.

Jack held her, as much as battle armor allowed.

Jacques came up to join them. "Maybe I should have warned you."

"No," Kris said, shaking herself. "It's better to feel this."

Better to feel it, yes. But it would be impossible for Kris to forget for the rest of her life.

Still, she'd come to see what the pyramid held. That was her duty, as a Longknife and the king's viceroy. With lips drawn tight, she stepped away from Jack's unfelt embrace and looked around.

"What's in that pile?" she asked, locking the woman away inside the battle commander.

Jacques turned to look at the pile of what Kris would have taken for skulls.

"As best we can tell, it's fifty heads. They seem to be identical to those of the bodies you see encased here. They have an exoskeleton, but from what we think we're seeing in the coffins, there was enough skin and muscle on the outside of the exoskeleton to give some facial expressions."

"Yes," Kris said. "Yes, I could read what looked like emotions on their faces."

"Yes. That kind of haunts you, doesn't it? There's more to see, Your Highness."

"Show me."

Jacques lead Kris over to one of the internal walls of the pyramid. "This hall extends to the entire inside of the pyramid. The ceiling above us is arched. They did a tremendous job of supporting all the weight that's above us with just these walls around us. We're studying it. Maybe all that's above us isn't the same granite. The engineers are having a field day."

Kris wondered at Jacques. He was babbling, and that was something he never did.

Then Kris saw where he was leading her and understood his need to hide behind words, empty or not.

There were more encased coffins lining the wall. The now-lit transparent blocks stretched away as far as she could see. If the pyramid was four klicks on the outside, certainly its inside walls must extend for most of that distance. And for as much of it as Kris could see lit up, there was a body every twenty meters or so.

One body preserved in a block of glass and before it, a pile of skulls.

Some were skulls. Some were the tops of carapaces. In a few cases, what was in the glass didn't seem to have a real head of bone or chitin and what had been piled in front of it had aged away to nothing.

"Are all of these intelligent races?" Kris asked, then corrected herself. "Were all of these beings intelligent?"

"We can't make that determination," Jacques said, "but I don't think so. There are creatures here that look like some of the amphibians that first crawled out of Earth's sea to try life on the land. Over on the other wall, there's something huge that looks like it might fit right into Earth's age of dinosaurs. There are smaller ones, too."

"So, they don't care if you're intelligent. If you're alive and might grow into something smart enough for spaceflight, they kill you, wipe out your planet, and you become a trophy here," Kris said. She knew Professor Labao would call this jumping to a conclusion with insufficient evidence, but Kris was looking at the evidence.

It might take the boffins more time to reach her conclusion, but battles were lost or won by commanders who could reason to the right conclusion before all the facts were in evidence.

"I think you might be right," Professor la Duke said.

"Thank you, Jacques," Kris said. "You better go find Amanda. She'll need you when she comes in here."

"Amanda's still outside. I suggested she study the construction of the pyramid before she came in. She's looking for any evidence that can be found at this late date of how the thing was built."

"A safer study," Kris said.

"I thought it might be," Jacques admitted.

A thought came to Kris. "Have you identified the remains of the aliens from the planet we found in the long search sweep?"

"Yes we have," Jacques said. "They're on the other wall, down near the end."

Kris turned away from the wall she'd been walking down and cut across to the other wall. It was easier to pass the royal family that way. There was less to see from their backs.

"Do you think they were the rulers of the planet that got hammered down to bedrock?" Kris asked Jack as they passed them.

"I tend to think so," he said. "They must have really hated them to bury them alive in whatever that stuff is."

"Bury the husband and wife only after they'd watched their children killed before their eyes."

"You can't be sure," Jack said.

"Look them in the eyes, then look at me and say that."

Even in battle armor, Kris saw the tremor go through Jack's body. "I can't," he admitted. "But think, Kris. Where did the hatred come from that would do that?"

"I don't know, but I'm thinking. We really need to date the bombardment of this planet. I'm thinking that if it was ten thousand years before the one that beat up the other planet, they might have been the aggressor, and the people they hit took ten thousand years, but they came back and hit hard."

"I'm thinking the same thing. Ten thousand years of anger welling up would be a terrible thing to see."

"And a hundred thousand years later, that anger, or fear, is still driving them to kill anything alive," Kris said.

"It's sure looking that way," Jack admitted.

They passed a lot of creatures as they walked down the line, hunting for those whose planet had been the warning to Kris. They passed encased bodies of beings that looked out with stunned and dumb looks or intelligent gazes. Most they passed had the dull look of animals, unaware of why they had suddenly been transformed from the top of the food chain to trophies in a war they hadn't started and had no part in.

There were two scientists working with the pile of chitinous skulls that Kris was interested in.

"We're trying to get a better date of death from these," one told Kris.

"We estimate it at two hundred years ago. I doubt you can get any closer," Kris said.

They ignored her and continued about their work.

Kris looked at the insectoid. Now, it looked back at her. Like the family at the entrance, this one, too, had grown skin and muscle on its face. Kris wondered if the ability to express yourself in body language and facial expressions was critical to the development of a civilization. No doubt, the boffins would be looking into that.

Certainly they'd never be able to study so large a set of different evolutionary tracks as had been so brutally arranged for them around these two walls.

Two more worlds were represented between Kris's planet and the end of the line. One looked like a vicious animal, something like the shark that swam in Wardhaven's seas. It was named for something equally as toothy in Earth's own oceans. Strange, Kris hadn't noticed any other fish in the collection. The other looked out with no spark of intelligence in its eyes, only dismay at its treatment.

Kris again found herself wanting to cry. To weep for all the futures and hopes and possibilities that were cut short and brought here.

As much as she wanted to weep, Kris found only a cold anger growing in her. She stood guard over three intelligent species. Two of them, the human race and the Iteeche, had stumbled into each other, and, though it might have been a struggle, found they could share space without having to kill each other. The third, the Alwans, had offered to share their life-giving planet with desperate human refugees.

Her Royal Highness, Kris Longknife, Commander of the Alwa Defense Sector, Viceroy and ambassador at large, looked down the line from where she stood.

"I swear by you who have lost everything that no more will be added to this trophy room. It stops here. We will stop you. *I* will stop you."

"Yes we will," Jack echoed.

16

"But how?" Jack asked, raising the practical question that would, no doubt, dog Kris's every waking hour from now until her last breath.

Or the other guy's.

"That is something we will figure out," Kris said. "Nelly, how many glass coffins are here?"

"I've been able to observe four hundred and twelve from what you've seen. I've just checked in on the boffins' network, and I believe that number is correct. That includes the first samples."

"That many!" Kris said, trying to feel the sorrow and finding that 412 was just too big a number to feel. But it could be analyzed.

Assuming they've had one hundred thousand years to commit all those atrocities, what does that average out to? One every two hundred and fifty years."

"One every 242.7184466 years," Nelly said. Professor la Duke wasn't the only one given to babbling over what they were looking at. Kris could not recall the last time Nelly had not rounded up or down to the nearest significant number.

"However, Kris, if I may point out," Nelly went on, "there are two species here after the one we have dated to two hundred years ago. If we can assume that they are alternately adding kills to both sides, it seems a likely conclusion that they are killing more planets now than in the beginning."

"There are more of the bastards," Jack whispered, amazement in his voice as the realization dawned.

"It looks that way," Kris said, but she'd spotted something. "Jacques, what are those markings behind each coffin?"

Kris pointing to the wall behind the cubes. "It looks like a memorial or something."

"We think those are numbers in the first line. Possibly a star's location. The rest are words. We'll have to study them."

"Kris, I have been studying them," Nelly said. "Could you look closely at the writing behind the fish with all the teeth?"

Kris moved in that direction.

"Notice the bottom of the writing. All the writings above are in the same font and the lines are equally spaced. The last two lines are in a different font, larger and etched deeper into the stone. It appears to me very likely that someone added a comment."

"Is that the only aquatic life-form?" Kris asked.

Jacques paused to consult his computer, but Nelly was faster. "Yes it is. I've also identified the line as identical to other markings we've found in three of the other memorials. I think we may have the name of one of the ships. I don't know what it means, but we may have ourselves a name."

"And I very much want to know how many ships are represented here," Kris said.

"I think we all do," Jacques agreed.

Kris turned toward the entrance. "I've seen enough. Jack, you and I need to get out of these hard suits and back to where we can do some thinking. Jacques, give us more to think about."

Three hours later, Kris and Jack sat across from Penny and Masao as Nelly gave them the briefing on the pyramid's contents. It was easier to take at a distance, but Penny was still reduced to tears.

Kris put the meeting on hold while Masao held her and shed some tears himself.

Kris found herself fishing a tissue out of a box for Penny, then took one herself.

Even Jack asked for one.

Kris located a second box and let Penny and Masao have the first while she and Jack shared the second. Without the restrictions of an armored helmet, it was impossible not to feel the pain in the pictures at not only the loss of that family at the entrance, but the blight represented by the walls of horror.

"So that is what we are fighting," Penny finally said.

"Yes. We are fighting to keep our skulls from being added to a pile on that floor and one of us locked in plastic as the only proof that we ever lived," Kris said. "They are not adding a human, an Iteeche, or an Alwan to that house of horrors. Not on my watch."

"Yes," Penny said. "We will not lose. We can't."

"Did any of you notice something about that lineup?" Masao said.

They waited for him to make his point. "They all represent one species. None of them have two standing together. What do you think they'd make of us and the Alwans on one planet?"

"They'd either take the Alwans for animals," Penny said, "or go looking for where we came from. And if they've got any ability to read DNA, they'll know that we don't fit on Alwa."

"Yeah," Kris said. "Good old Grampa Ray goofed it big this time. No matter how big an industrial base we build on Alwa, we can't fake our DNA fingerprint. When we killed that first base ship, we started a war, and no amount of us dying on Alwa will shake the raiders from hunting for the first race that managed to kill them in what, over a hundred thousand years?"

"We don't know that all of the other races failed to put up a decent fight," Jack said.

"The bastards sure don't fight as if they've had a tough, space-based enemy for some time," Kris pointed out.

"I will concede that," Jack said.

"So, what do we do now?" Penny ask. "Do we know enough to head home and dig in for the next fight?"

Kris chewed on that thought for a long moment, then shook her head. "I still want to talk to one of them. I want to know if what we're assuming is the way it is. I want to know what makes their minds tick."

"That's assuming you can find someone running around with a flint-tipped spear on this planet who knows anything about what happened a hundred thousand years ago," Penny quipped.

"That's the problem," Jack said. "I doubt if any of the natives here have any written records. Handing knowledge down by word of mouth has its limits."

"Carefully constructed sagas can last a long time," Masao pointed out.

"What about the locals that were recently landed?" Kris said. "The ones that are still wearing rags? They have to know the official story from their ship. Maybe they'll tell us what's happening on the ships and why that pyramid of horrors is down there?"

"But they were tossed off the ships," Jack said. "Won't that impact their perspective?"

"And even if we ignore that minor issue," Penny said, smiling enigmatically at her understatement, "that's just one ship's version."

"All good points," Kris admitted, "but I want to talk to someone. I want to hear something, right or wrong. Those that are stuck down there living from hand to mouth look like a better prospect than those that blow their ships up rather than talk. Somehow, there has to be some way for us to make contact with them before they manage to kill themselves."

"Or us," Jack pointed out.

"They don't get to kill us," Kris said, voice cold as steel.

"So, how do we get one of them in a mood to talk?" Penny asked.

"Let's talk to Jacques," Kris said. "He's the anthropologist. If he can't figure out a way to get a word in edgewise with people struggling to survive on what they can hunt, scavenge, or dig up, no one can."

So Jacques and Amanda were recalled from the surface, and Kris found out she'd bitten off a whole lot more than she thought though not more than she was willing to chew.

After listening to Kris, Jacques shook his head. "I would not suggest that we just sleepy dart one of them and haul them up here. People can kill themselves by running into a wall over and over again. I suspect if these dudes got the shock of finding themselves on a strange ship, that is exactly what they would do."

"We look just like them. Can't we pass for them?" Kris asked.

"Bare-ass naked, I might," Jacques said. "But dressed here, on this ship?" He shook his head. "Even the smell of the ship might give us away. No doubt our language would, and definitely our questions would. No, we've got to come at this using a totally neutral approach."

"Does that mean you have one?" Kris asked.

The anthropologist settled into a chair and rubbed his chin. It had been a while since he had shaved. "We've got surveillance bugs following several of the gens around. I can't actually call them clans or tribes. They're much too small. What we've found is that they speak similar languages, but different enough that they would have trouble talking to each other."

Kris made a puzzled look. Jacques took mercy on her.

"Most of us speak Standard. It's a cross between Old Earth's English and Spanish, which themselves were a cross between several languages that preceded them like German, French, and before them, Latin and Greek. Then you have to throw in borrowed words from all over Earth: Arabic, Chinese, Japanese, and Swahili. Don't get me started, or I will bore you to death.

"Anyway, back on Old Earth, the French, the Italians, and the Spanish spoke languages that branched off from Latin. They shared a lot of similar words, but put two of them in a bar and they couldn't order a drink.

"However, we have a lot of scout bots following different gens around, collecting sessions of their speech and the context for it. With any luck, we should have a good idea of what they're saying in a week, two at the most."

"The markings in the pyramid," Kris said. "Will we be reading them as quickly?"

"Not likely. We have only the most minimum of context for them. For example, we know that there is a kind of star location given for each of the specimens. It's the opening line etched into the wall behind every one of them. We think it's giving us numbers, but we can't even be sure of that. It's a lot easier to crack a living language than a dead one, and the written markings on the pyramid are, for all practical matters, dead to us."

"Can we do anything to help you crack the living languages? I'm including in that the languages of the natives in the dominant culture," Kris said. "I wonder if their language is anywhere close to the star raiders' language?"

"Possibly, but quite likely not," Jacques said. "In a hundred thousand years, languages can change a lot. And remember, these are the ones that stayed behind when the others took up wandering the stars and slaughtering everything they meet. There's bound to be some basis for that difference."

"And these people on the ground have been attacked by the star raiders," Nelly put in. "We've dated three of the more recent depredations. We're sure the most recent was lased from space in the last ten thousand years."

"But why?" Amanda asked.

Kris took a shot at an answer. "They may be flesh of their flesh, but they chose to stay behind, to separate off from those who are carrying the torch. They can live, but they can't ever threaten the star rovers. If they look to be developing a science-based, industrial culture, they burn it."

"You may be right," Amanda said. "Dear God, I hate this. And I hate them."

"We can't afford to hate them," Kris said. "If necessary, I will destroy them, but I will not hate them. Hate like that is what turned them into whatever it is they are."

Jack and Jacques nodded agreement.

"There is one thing that might help us correlate the data we're collecting," Jacques said, changing the topic to something they controlled.

"Name it, and it's yours," Kris said.

"The use of the ships' main computers to grind the data."

"Oops," Kris said, "On that, you will have to speak to my flag captain. No one messes with the ships' computers without his say-so."

Which brought Captain Drago into the conversation. He looked more than negative to the idea, even when Nelly offered to coordinate the data processing.

"Thank you, Nelly, but I like having my ships ready to run at the first sign they need to. If you and yours are messing with our nav computers, we might find ourselves still sitting here, counting zeros and ones by hand, and running short of ones, when the big uglies show up."

"Captain," Nelly said, "I assure you that we can load the data in the unused space of your machines, and they can process it during the time they are sitting idle. If you get any warning from your pickets, we can wash the data from them in a matter of seconds."

"But you'd lose it all," Jacques said.

"Sir, if we are running away from here, will it matter that we lose the data we need to make contact with a species that is growing more distant by the second in our rearview mirror?" Nelly said, dryly.

"You have a point," Jacques admitted.

"Remember, you will still have the original data stored for later reload somewhere else," Kris pointed out. "Assuming that once we bug out of here, we have any intentions of coming back."

"Now that is an interesting question," Drago said.

"Which one?" Kris asked.

"Do we want to leave a calling card to tell the aliens we've seen where they came from? That we've visited their old stomping ground and, what? Left it alone? Blown their little trophy room to smithereens? What are we going to do, Your Highness?"

"I haven't decided yet," Kris said. When she got a surprised look from everyone present, she hastily added, "No. Really. I'm still thinking."

"But you are thinking about it," Drago said.

"Yes. What kind of calling card would you leave?" she asked her flag captain and retired admiral.

"I'd lase that damn pyramid from space for two, three orbits. See just how big a hole I could make where it now stands," he said without blinking an eye.

"That's one option," Kris said. "Some might take it as a declaration of war."

"And blowing two of their mother ships to hell ain't?" he shot right back at her.

"But that wouldn't break the cycle of killing," Amanda said. "Unless someone is willing to be the Optimistic Fool and try something out of the usual, all we have left is everyone's doing the same old same old. Look where that's gotten us."

"Another good point," Kris said.

"Besides," Jacques put in, "what you're looking at down there is both the greatest biological collection of different evolutionary trails and the last vestige that whole planets ever lived. I'd hate to see it blasted to dust even if it was a message I thought needed delivering."

Kris frowned as she found herself agreeing with him.

"So, which is it going to be?" Captain Drago asked with a raised eyebrow.

"As I said, I haven't decided yet," Kris said. "However, I have decided that I want to make contact with the locals and I want to make that contact as quickly as possible before some blood-drenched joker drops in here to mount his latest trophy. Captain Drago, if you don't have major problems with it, I'd like to have Nelly mount all the data from the language scouts in the spare space on our ships' computers."

"I'll have my network support team start working with Nelly right away."

"Thank you, Captain," Nelly said.

"Don't make me regret this momentary lapse in good judgment," Captain Drago growled.

"I will endeavor greatly to see that you don't," Nelly said. Was there a bit of a laugh somewhere in her voice?

"Jacques, I do have a question for you," Nelly said.

"Yes?"

"Which group of naked, abandoned raiders are you intent on passing yourself off as being from when you make contact with the most recent set of marooned raiders?"

"I haven't decided," he said.

"Which explains why your kisses has been so scratchy of late," Amanda said. "I wondered why you quit shaving."

"Part of the price of falling in love with a field-going anthropologist," Jacques said.

"Why, oh my heart, couldn't you have gone pitter-pat for some nice economics major with a briefcase and a boring day job?" Amanda asked no one in particular.

"I thought that might be the case," Nelly said. "Kris, I have enough matrix, even after you shot up some of it surviving your third alien battle. I'd like to generate the new child and give it into Jacques's care."

"Amanda, will you be jealous, dear?" Jacques asked.

"Of course I will be, honey," came with not-so-sweet undertones, "but I'll just have to muddle along with my own pet computer. Though, who knows, with me jealous of you, and you wandering around bare-ass and flirting with every other mud-caked native down there with big boobs, I just might find that nice guy with the boring day job up here."

"There are no boring day jobs up here," Jacques pointed out.

"Don't you hate it when they're right?" Kris said with a sad smile for Amanda.

"If he gets a Nelly-class computer, I want ice cream. Chocolate ice cream with nuts," Amanda said glumly.

"Both of us do," Kris said, and adjourned the meeting.

Jack and Jacques left for Marine country to examine what could pass as minimal gear for going native. At Jack's collarbone, Sal was already going through the drill for bringing a new computer up to speed, no doubt with a large helping hand from Nelly, who was strangely quiet at Kris's own collarbone.

The pantry off the wardroom did prove to have a supply of chocolate ice cream with nuts and other crunchy things and no one with the gumption to tell the admiral, princess, and viceroy that she couldn't raid the wardroom's supplies.

The two young women dived into their consolation prize as their men, no doubt, contemplated the joyous life of a caveman.

"What is it about men that they don't value chocolate properly?" Kris asked.

"Who'd want a world without chocolate?" Amanda asked back.

"Or good dentistry?"

"Or proper pain control when you're having a baby?"

"You can't be thinking of having a baby," Kris said. "You've got the same birth-control implants in you that I've got in me."

"Yes, but they wear out, dearie," Amanda said, taking a dainty and ladylike small bite of the much-praised ice cream.

"And they *will* be replaced," Kris said, using the full authority of her command.

"I'm a civilian," Amanda pointed out.

"In a combat zone. Check your paperwork. When you signed on, you signed a reserve commission. You cause me too much grief, and your civilian days are over."

"I need more ice cream," Amanda said.

"So do I," Kris said.

Their next spoonfuls were not at all small and dainty.

17

A week later, Kris, Amanda, and Penny watched as Jacques made his first try at making contact. Jack was dirtside with a squad of Marines hiding well back, but no more than two minutes away at a gallop.

If things went bad, some aliens would be seeing if sleepy darts worked on them. If they didn't, matters would get bloody fast.

Jacques had settled himself beside a watering hole that the half-naked tribe frequented. Using a shard that he'd chipped off of a bit of flint, he'd cut himself a reed, then cut several holes in it. Blowing into it, he got some notes of a not-too-far-off-key nature.

He was making music as the five men cautiously approached the stream from the other side. He stayed where he was, squatting on the muddy bank. They stayed hunkered down in the high grass on the other side. The scout bugs caught their conversation. Their thirst was driving them to the water. Fear of the stranger was holding them back.

At the moment, they were frozen on the sharp edge of indecision.

Then the oldest woman of the group came up. ~The babies are hot and cranky. We need to bathe them in the river to cool them. The mothers must drink water to make milk for the babies. Do not stand around looking like unenlightened trees.~

The men stayed hunkered down in the grass. One of them pointed at Jacques.

The woman eyed the stranger for a while, then scowled at the men and strode forward until her feet were just touching the water on their side of the river.

Jacques kept up his effort at getting melodic notes out of the reed.

The woman made shooing signs for Jacques to go away.

He kept on playing what he was playing. Kris thought it might be a ragged attempt at Pachelbel's *Canon*. Or not.

The woman stooped to the water, found a rock, stood, and tossed it overhand at Jacques. It flew by his head, missing by a quarter meter or so.

Jacques raised his reed and blew a loud note at the woman. That done, he went back to his musical musings.

Giving her opponent a puzzled frown, the woman stooped again to the water, but this time she drew water into the palm of her hand and raised it to her lips. After she'd done that two or three times, the men came down to the water and slaked their own thirst. Some used the palm of their hands to draw the water up, others bent low and lapped it up.

Through this, Jacques stood his ground and made his attempt at raw music.

"Was this the music to soothe the savage beast?" Kris asked the women gathered with her in her day quarters.

Both Penny and Amanda met the question with shrugs.

Once the men had drunk, the four women with babes came down with the other young woman, who was shorter than the rest. The envious looks she gave the women and babes left Kris with a sick feeling that she'd had a child and lost it.

No doubt, life was rough with this small, abandoned group. What must it have been like to be dropped out of the world of spaceships and regimented life into the middle of an untamed world?

Then Kris remembered her own examinations of a world these people had plundered. Apparently, they didn't even know to establish latrines when they went dirtside. Here was more proof the aliens knew ship life but nothing else.

On the screen, the small group held to its side of the stream. Now the children were babbling and splashing in the water, clearly enjoying its cool and refreshing touch.

It was time for Jacques to try his next trick.

They'd studied the other tribes not only for their language but also to see how they survived in this world. One tribe in the woods looked like it was about ready to begin passing itself off as indigenous. They'd learned how to strip sinew from their kills and use the tendons to sew skins together into rough clothing.

They also ate better than most of the gens wandering the immediate environs of the glass plain. One thing they seemed to like was the bulbous root of a plant that grew in all the streams of the area. It was starchy and rather tasteless, but it was a whole lot better than going hungry.

Jacques reached over and pulled up one of the water plants, washed the dirt off its root bulb, but not before eating a rather disgusting slug.

"Ugh," said his wife. "He better rinse that mouth out with soap before he kisses me again?"

Kris nodded agreement while doubting Amanda would ask anything of the sort from her returned husband but hugs and kisses and to be taken to bed. They were just that kind of couple.

Maybe they would shower together first.

On-screen, Jacques was taking his second bite of the root. When the others just looked at him, he pulled another plant up by its roots and offered it to those across the stream from him. When they didn't move any closer, he tossed it in the water.

The current began to move the plant, root and all, downstream and away from them. The short, childless woman made a dash out into the water before it went too far, retrieved it, and offered it to one of the nursing moms.

"That's selfless," Penny said.

"Watch," Amanda said. "She's learned. She's pulling up one of the plants herself and is eating that one." In a moment, men and women alike were plundering their side of the stream bank for the new food.

Jacques went on playing.

The others ate in a frenzied fury to his music. When they had eaten about all the tubers on that side of the stream, the group began to gather itself and move back into the woods. The short woman stayed behind. Turning her back to Jacques, she spread her legs a bit and bent over, showing Jacques about all there was to see.

Beside Kris, Amanda sighed. "We talked about this. That's about the most standard 'come hither' sign the human race has. I guess that's another way they're like us at the basic structural level."

"Can we even have sex with one of them?" Penny asked, maybe a bit red in the face.

"No doubt Jacques will find out," Amanda said, and from the way the local woman was behaving, it would be sooner rather than later.

"Cut the camera feed," Kris ordered. No doubt the scientists would study the pictures, and they would soon make their way into the onboard porn supply, but his wife didn't need to watch her caveman husband do his caveman thing.

"So, we've made initial contact," Kris said.

"And no head got bashed in," Penny said.

"And I am a professional woman married to a scientist who does a lot of fieldwork. I just wish he didn't enjoy it so much," Amanda said, with a resigned sigh.

"So, what do we do now?" Kris asked.

"We wait," Amanda said. "Jacques can't exactly ask them what ship they're from and what their myth is for wandering the stars and massacring all life, now can he?"

"That would be an interesting icebreaker," Kris admitted.

"So he waits and sees what he can find out."

"For how long?" Penny asked.

"For however long he thinks he has to," Amanda said. "Of course, if the pickets sound an alarm, it may go differently, but for now, we just wait."

18

The wait lasted a week. During that time, Kris avoided the voyeuristic urge to watch Jacques in action, or rather observe his research. Or whatever.

Jack came back the next day, and Kris showed him just how grateful she was to have him back in her ship and in her bed.

"I take it you missed me," he said when they came up for air.

"And I want you to remember how pleasant a nice, clean, civilized girl can be," Kris said.

"Honey, you don't need to remind me of that. That place stinks. The insects don't make any distinction between us and them. Even with bug repellent, you're swatting them all the time. It was almost enough to put us back in full space suits and armor. But, oh, did I mention how hot it was?"

"I think you should have stayed in full space armor."

"We've been over this too many times before. The scientists agree we're safe down there. I couldn't carry enough oxygen to stay down there as long as I did, and if we'd had to go running in to grab someone trying to beat Jacques's head in, it would have looked better if we were as low-tech as possible. Otherwise, they might suicide on the spot. You do want someone to talk to, right?"

"Yes," Kris said, trying not to sound too pouty. "You do have some nasty bug bites."

"The surgeon looked at them on the flight up. They've been treated and are not going to make me turn into a monster or cause you to shrivel up into an old lady in the next five minutes. So come here and remind me again why I wanted to come home to my civilized gal."

"Since you put it that way," Kris said, and did.

Kris and Jack monitored Jacques constantly. Or near constantly. It seemed that every woman in the group wanted a part of Jacques.

When Kris said something catty, Jack jumped in, man defending man.

"Kris, they stink. It's hot and buggy as all get out. He's really taking one for the team here."

Kris chose not to dispute Jack's opinion. She did, however, notice that the younger women began to bathe themselves along with their babies. The childless one damn near became a fish. Only the older woman would have nothing to do with the stranger.

Jacques certainly did his best to improve the quality of life for these outcasts. He showed them several more plants that were edible, and the clan became less gaunt. He also began to twist twine from grass.

The older woman, the one who bossed the young mothers and had tried to shoo Jacques away in the first place, made it clear she considered Jacques touched in the head. ~He makes noises from hollow thick grass. Now he twists grass into something that only the babies find interesting. He is not all there in the head.~

Then Jacques set his first trap.

And caught something.

It was small, something like a big-eared fox, but it had a bit of meat on its bones. He showed them how to skin it using a sharp stone flake. Nelly alerted Kris that something important might be about to happen. She also summoned Jack and Amanda to Kris's day quarters. Together, they gathered around the screens as the issue of how the locals would react to their first fresh meat played out.

The locals looked hungry enough to eat the thing raw, but Jacques used the string again to make a fire bow. They stood back while he got a fire going, then stood back farther and mumbled among themselves.

Nelly translated for Kris and Jack. "I think they're arguing among themselves about whether or not he's the Enlightened One. We've heard a word like that among the other naked tribes. The established tribes have no word like it. Not even close."

"The Enlightened One," Kris said.

"Notice the emphasis on the 'one,' " Jack said.

"I wonder what they mean by that?" Amanda questioned.

Several of the mothers seemed sure that Jacques was indeed "the Enlightened One." The older woman definitely thought he wasn't. The men seemed concerned about this theological debate, but they remained quiet. It was the childless young woman who took the bull by the horns and put the question to Jacques.

~Are you the Enlightened One?~ she demanded, hands on hips.

"How's he going to play that?" Jack asked.

"Smart," Amanda said.

~I do not know this word,~ Jacques said.

~Are you from the ship?~ the woman asked.

~Ship? I was born under this sky. My mother spoke of a ship, a world with no sky, but my father would have no talk of it and shushed her. Are you from a ship?~

The woman seemed hesitant to go on, but finally admitted, ~Yes, I was born of the ship.~

"Notice she said *the* ship, not *a* ship," Amanda said. "I wish I'd taken more courses in sociology. It think that's important."

~I dream of being on the ship,~ Jacques said. ~Is that where the Enlightened One is?~

~Yes, he guides our ship. He guides us to the light. You guide us to food. Are you the Enlightened One under this sky?~

"How's he going to answer that question?" Kris asked.

"Very carefully," Amanda repeated.

~I am young. Aren't Enlightened Ones full of years?~

~Yes, yes,~ the woman agreed. She looked back at the others, who waited expectantly. ~Are there young Enlightened Ones?~ she asked them.

The others, Kris would not have put any of them much past thirty, had no answer for her. The young woman turned from Jacques and rejoined the others. They squatted down in a circle, and their talk was long and animated.

"Nelly, are you getting this?"

"I'm getting all the words, Kris. The meaning, not so much. There are a lot of allusions to people and places that I can't connect. I don't think any of them ever saw any Enlightened

One except the one they always had. One of them thinks there is a ceremony for the death of an Enlightened One and the recognition of a new one. Oh, oh, that got him in trouble. They're saying that it was his crazy ideas that got them dumped here in the first place."

On-screen, one of the men shoved two of the others away.

"He's saying that they did nothing to cause them to be dropped here. They're here, oh, that's a bad turn of phrase, but I think it means to impress the others and make sure they meet their work assignments."

"What were the actual words?" Amanda said. "That might tell us something."

"It's not nice," Nelly said. "I think it's something like 'we are made to eat shit so that the others will be happy with their porridge.'"

"E-uw," Kris said. "You're right, Nelly. I'll stick with your first translation."

"You take the nice words, Princess," Amanda said. "I'll stick with the original. They're traveling in a bound space, recycling everything. After hearing that, I have to wonder how well it works. As well as who gets the shit and who gets the porridge. And who maybe gets the best available?"

"You think you're seeing fractures along class lines?" Kris asked.

"This Enlightened One is clearly at the top. 'May the king or emperor live forever,' was a popular illusion back when we had potentates with divine pretensions. I'm thinking we've got something like that here."

Kris frowned as she let that bounce around in her head. "A hundred thousand years ago, someone pounded the living hell out of the next planet over. Someone abandoned this planet to go roving among the stars looking for any poor bastard that might rise up and do unto these as they were busy doing unto them."

Kris eyed Jack and Amanda. They nodded agreement back. She went on.

"Somehow, these ships multiplied, but always, they kept the hate alive. No, let's make that fear. It seems there is always someone to harangue the people. That must be the 'Enlightened One' we saw giving The Word to the folks in the first mother ship we blasted to bits."

Again, Kris only got agreement from the others.

"It appears that this planet serves as some kind of dumping grounds for any problem children. If anyone won't conform, get with the program, or maybe just voices doubts, they get a one-way ticket to here. Or maybe all you have to be is slow to get your work done if they don't have enough examples to scare the others."

"I think you may have something there, Kris," Jack said.

"So how do we break into this chain of insanity and make them see that the whole universe isn't out to get them? At least not if they aren't out to get us?" Kris said.

She got no answer from the other two. She let the silence stretch for a minute or more, then made her call.

"Jack, would you please go down there and bring me back one of those men."

"They stink pretty bad, Kris."

"I'm not taking him to bed, Jack." That got her a laugh from the other two. "You can douse him in the brig's head, but I want to talk to him. Nelly has a vocabulary now. We need to find out just how bad this thing is. There's got to be a way to reason with them."

"I think you're an optimist," Amanda said.

"No doubt. The alternative, however, is just too bloody to contemplate."

That got nods from the other two.

"I'll be back for supper," Jack said.

"I'll see that the wardroom has some good chow for you and Jacques," Kris said.

"They'll need to keep it warm for later," Amanda said. "Jacques is all mine."

19

Kris watched on the screens in her day quarters as Jacques led the youngest man away from the group. Ostensibly, he was going to show the fellow how to set traps to capture a bunch of the foxlike things for a feast.

The fellow went eagerly.

Until he spotted Jack and his Marines.

Jacques had led the alien quite a bit away from the others, downstream and out of the woods along the edge of a grassy meadow. They'd set three string traps and were working on the fourth when the Marines stepped out of the woods ahead of them.

The young fellow took one look at the humans in military gear and bolted.

Jacques got a handful of his ratty uniform, but that was all he got. The man pulled away, leaving Jacques with nothing but fabric.

The naked anthropologist took off after his erstwhile friend with the Marines hot on his heels, but it was a short chase.

The young fellow raced straight for the stream—and threw himself headlong from the bank into a rocky stretch of water.

Jacques got to the bank and came to a halt. Jack wasn't much behind him. Kris got the feed off Jack's helmet camera.

"Oh my God," Amanda prayed beside Kris.

All Kris could do was grit her teeth in frustration.

There, the bank was a good two meters high. The alien had thrown himself headfirst from it. Right at the rocks below.

Now he lay in the stream, his head smashed in, his blood and brains being laved by the water and carried downstream.

"I guess that didn't go as well as we'd expected," Jack said.

"Now what?" Jacques asked.

Kris let out a long sigh. She didn't like what she was going to say next. She hated kidnappers. With Father and Mother, without a moment's qualm, she'd stood there and watched as Eddy's kidnappers swung at the end of their ropes. Hell, she'd killed kidnappers without so much as a second glance every time one of them made the mistake of crossing her path.

Kris gritted her teeth and said the words that made her a kidnapper.

"Jacques, go back to the group. Separate one of the mothers with a babe at her breast from them. Jack, set a trap. Sleepy dart the mother. Bring both of them up here."

"Kris!" came from both men. Jack of all men would know how much of her soul this was costing Kris.

"You heard me. I am going to talk to one of these aliens. A mother with a babe at her breast is not going to kill herself. Bring one of them to me."

"But sleepy dart her just in case," Jack said.

"Yes."

"And how do I do this?" Jacques said.

Kris did not need more talk. "We've watched the mothers go off into the bushes with you," Kris snapped. "Do it again. Only this time, take her someplace where Jack's got you covered. Then distract her. If you think you can get her to fall asleep after your fun and save Jack the fuss of having to sleepy dart her, all the better, but I want her up here tonight."

"Kris Longknife," Amanda said at Kris's elbow. "You are a bastard."

"I second the notion," Jacques growled.

"I come from a long line of folks that only entered the church to bark and bite at the preacher's heels. Tell me something about myself I don't know," Kris snapped. "Now, you've got your orders. Make it happen."

"Aye, aye, Admiral," Jack said.

Amanda said nothing as she stormed out of Kris's day quarters and slammed the door behind her.

20

Kris bounced the baby on her hip. The little girl had been cleaned up, had a diaper on for probably the first time in her life, and looked rather cute in an outfit taken off a teddy bear.

Kris hadn't asked who had a teddy bear this big, but she'd suspected from the hushed conversation she'd partially overheard that it had been offered up by one of the guys who worked the reactor.

Kris was under the impression that the reactor crew had to pass the highest psychological tests. When things settled down, she might have to look into that.

The woman had also been cleaned up and dressed in civilian clothes donated by one of the contract cooks. She was still asleep.

Jack had had to sleepy dart her. Her capture had not gone well.

It hadn't been allowed to go as bad as the young man's attempted capture, but still she'd spotted the Marines moving in even though Jacques had been doing his manful best to distract her.

Now she slept on the couch in Kris's day cabin. Kris had Gunny go over her day quarters to childproof them. He'd called in the help of several young women Marines who removed a lot of objects that Kris would never had considered a hazard to a baby.

That just went to show what Kris knew about babies.

Now childproofed, Kris hoped her quarters were also alien-suicide-proof.

Jack, Amanda, Jacques, Penny, and Masao rounded out the group eyeing the sleeping woman. The military were in uniform, khakis all. Jacques suggested that the earth tones might soften their impression. Jacques and Amanda were in tan shipsuits.

"When do you think she'll wake up?" Kris asked. The baby was getting fretful. "I think she's hungry."

"Check her diaper," Penny suggested. "Is it wet or dirty?"

"You check it," Kris said, and passed the cranky child off to her intel officer.

She made the required checks.

"She's wet. Do we have any spare diapers?"

Jack pointed to a pile of baby gear on Kris's conference table. "When Musashi fitted out the *Wasp*, they equipped us for humanitarian missions, per their law. We have all we need to take aboard and care for hundreds of civilians for a month. I don't even think they charged us for the package. All their ships come equipped for kids."

Penny went to do her duty by the little one, with Masao right behind her. From the looks in both their eyes, Kris suspected that procreation was contagious. Whatever Penny's fears might be of bringing death and destruction in her matrimonial wake, this baby was pulling the two caregivers closer together.

The woman on the couch started at the sound of her baby's fussing. Still, she did not rouse. Kris settled into the armchair across from the woman's head and waited.

At the conference table, with the baby dry again, Penny put formula powder into a bottle of water and offered it to the little one. It took the nipple hungrily, sucked heartily for a moment, then spat out the bottle and began to cry. It was a full-throated wail, not at all tentative.

"I don't think their kids like our kind of milk," Penny said.

On the couch, the woman stirred. This time, she fully surfaced. She glanced around, eyes wide, then spotted her child and was off the couch and racing toward the baby before anyone could stop her.

Not that anyone did. Penny handed the baby off to its mother without a bobble.

Baby in hand, the alien woman quickly opened the top of her borrowed dress and offered a breast to her child. The little one greedily began to pull down lunch.

Only when the child was settled did the woman look around, eyes going wider still.

~You are on a ship,~ Nelly said in the language Jacques had used among the dirtside. Those on Nelly Net heard it in Standard in their minds. Masao and Amanda heard it from their own computers.

~This is not *the* ship,~ the woman said, eyes narrowing as she took the room in.

~No,~ Kris agreed. ~This is our ship.~

~Vermin do not have ships,~ was spat more than said.

Jack edged around to cover the door, one hand behind his back where he carried his automatic. Masao put himself between the woman and Penny.

Jacques slowly approached the woman. ~You have shared food with me. I speak your words. I gave you food to eat. You know what all of me looks like,~ he said, running his hands down his side.

~No. No! NO!~ she screamed and began to sidle away, eyes searching the room like a trapped animal desperate for any way out. She paused for a moment, then charged Jack, her hands out, fingers reaching with their long nails for his eyes.

With one hand he used his automatic to put a sleepy dart in the terrified woman's belly, then used the other to reach out and catch the child as she collapsed like a pricked balloon.

"That didn't go as well as I had hoped," Kris said.

"We're vermin to her," Jacques said. "And their idea of vermin is a lot uglier than ours, considering the way she said that." The anthropologist shook his head.

"Kris, I suspect that did not meet your definition of a talk with the aliens," Jack said.

"Not even close," Kris agreed.

"So, what do we do next?" Amanda asked.

Kris rubbed her scalp. The tension was getting unbearable. "I'm open to suggestions."

Penny took the child from Jack. It continued to voice its hunger for all to take note of. "Jack, does the equipment we've got include a breast pump?" Penny asked.

That got her a lot of blank stares.

"Okay, folks. The baby is hungry, and you just decked her

meal ticket. I also suspect that her breasts are full. Jacques, do you remember the last time she nursed the child?"

The anthropologists gave her the manly shrug of one whose interests in that portion of the female anatomy did not extend to sustenance.

"If she goes too long without emptying her milk, we risk her breasts drying up. And then what will we do about food for the child?" Penny said, exasperated. "Nelly, do you have the schematics for a breast pump?"

"Yes, I do," the Magnificent Nelly said. "You'll find one on the table next to the diapers now."

And there was one.

Amanda went for it. "I watched my mom express milk for my youngest brother," she said. "I don't know how it will work with her knocked out and having sleepy dart in her blood, but let's see how this works. Would you strapping men mind lift her back onto the couch?"

Masao and Jacques did. Jack stayed close, automatic in hand. The alien mom was an easy lift. As soon as they had her back on the couch, the men hastily withdrew to behind Kris's desk, about as far from the women as possible.

"Note how our strong men get skittish at the sight of a woman's working breast," Amanda said, attaching the breast pump and activating it. "They just love to get their mitts on our boobs," she said, aiming a scathing glance at the men, "but let a woman put her mammary glands to the business God intended, and they run."

"I thought you women might want your privacy," Jack offered, lamely.

"Thank you," Kris said. Her brain failed to suppress a sudden question. Might she actually develop some mammary glands, as Amanda so professionally put it, if she was nursing a child of her own? Their own.

How would Jack take to that?

Damn, this reproductive thing is contagious.

The breast pump worked. The bottle attached to it slowly filled. Kris left the woman and child in Penny's and Amanda's capable hands and turned to the men.

"Okay, guys, I'm open to suggestions. How do we get this woman to talk to us?"

They stared at her. She stared at them. There was a lot of staring and not a lot of ideas being verbalized.

Penny joined them, jostling the baby on her hip. It sucked at one of her fingers.

Kris eyed the quieted child.

"I swiped one of those sugar packets from the mess," Penny said. "I put a bit of it on my finger. The kid may not like our milk, but it sure likes our sugar. Maybe we should try putting some sugar in our formula. Or chocolate."

"But would it actually get any benefit from the food?" Jacques asked.

"You ate their food. Did you starve?"

"I don't think so."

"We need another bottle, or two," Amanda said. The first one looked full.

Two bottles appeared on the conference table, and Penny took them to Amanda.

"Nelly, spin out a small sample bottle. Amanda, if you'll fill the small one, we'll get the boffins to do their thing. We'll know exactly what's in mother bug-eyed-monster milk in no time."

"Doing it," Amanda answered, as Penny retrieved the small bottle, and Amanda switched it onto the pump. After that one was full, they switched breasts and began draining the other one.

Kris turned back to the guys. "I have a problem. You guys are not helping."

"We've tried everything that I can think of," Jacques said.

"How do we get her to sit still and talk to me?" Kris repeated, with more than a tinge of irritation.

Again, the men came up with only silence.

Kris turned to Penny, now feeding a very hungry child from the first bottle. It seemed happy enough now.

The mother wants the baby, Kris thought. *We have the baby.*

"If we show her that the baby is fine," Kris said slowly, and half to herself, "and tell her that she can't have the baby until she talks to me . . ."

"You're a hard woman, Kris Longknife," Penny said.

"A determined woman," Kris answered. "Penny, can you raise a wall in here? One of those clear walls."

"So she can see her baby and that we're taking care of her," Penny said, catching Kris's drift.

"But not get near the child. Not until she's talked to me and answers all my questions."

"You're assuming that she can tell you what you want to know," Jacques said. "I was down there for way too long. I listened to them talk to each other. I still don't know much more about them and their ship and their Enlightened One than I did when you dropped me off buck naked to be eaten by whatever passes for mosquitoes in that godforsaken place."

"I can ask direct questions," Kris snapped. "Questions you couldn't do without risking your head being bashed in with the nearest rock."

Jacques glanced around the room.

"No nearest rock," Kris said.

"She has a point," Masao said.

21

Penny finished feeding the first bottle to the baby. The tiny one now seemed sleepy. Without being told, Nelly produced a bassinet out of the deck. Its side toward the alien mother was clear. Penny settled the now-sleeping child down. Masao brought her a baby blanket from the supplies Musashi provided.

The two of them stared long and lovingly at the sleeping infant. Kris noticed how time and time again one or the other's hands would half reach out for the other. Reach, but never touch.

She sighed for her friend's pain.

But when Penny turned back to Kris, she was all mission. "Mimzy, we'll need a clear wall between the bassinet and the alien."

"Jack, do you intend to stay on the side with Kris?" Mimzy asked.

"You bet I do," he said, and moved quickly to stand at his bride's side.

"Jacques?" Nelly's daughter asked.

"I think she's seen enough of me. I'll stay on this side."

"Amanda?"

"I'm with Kris."

"Penny?"

"Masao and I will stay with the baby. You can take the wall down in a second, can't you Mimzy?"

"Less time. I can also open a passageway if one of you changes your mind."

The coffee table, with its computer-screen insert, vanished into the deck. The conference table and most of its chairs did the same. A moment later, a thin, clear barrier rose from the deck to divide the room in half.

Kris settled into the armchair at the woman's head. Jack took the one at her feet. Amanda finished up gathering the last bottles of milk, then passed them through a suddenly open window, to Jacques. He handed the large ones off to Penny and left with the smaller sample bottle.

The woman slept peacefully while Amanda adjusted her dress to meet the modesty standards of the human civilization that had brought her here, but, so far, could do nothing with her. Finished, Amanda settled into a chair between Kris and Jack, facing the captive. She folded her hands in her lap and joined them, waiting for the alien woman to waken.

Time passed with leaden boots. Jacques returned, mission no doubt accomplished, and took a chair from the conference table to sit quietly, watching his wife. The glass wall, and maybe other things, separated them.

Penny and Masao stayed where they were, standing and gazing at the sleeping child. In a secret moment, either his or her hand snuck into the other's. Kris wasn't sure who reached out first, and did not task Nelly to find out.

They waited.

Since Kris first met the aliens—and had to blast their ship out of space to keep it from ramming the old *Wasp*—she'd wanted to talk to one of them. Now, with that talk only moments away, she found herself wondering what to say. She ran several opening lines through her thoughts and found them all lame.

Well, I'm a Longknife. I'll come up with something when it matters. We always do.

The woman awoke with a start, glanced around, and spotted the bassinet. She leapt from the couch and charged across the room.

She smashed into the clear wall and bounced off it. She let out a scream and slammed her fist into the wall. Then she shook her hand in pain.

~Your baby cannot hear you,~ Kris said. ~You can see she is safe. Unharmed. She cannot hear you.~

~Give Minna to me,~ the woman demanded.

~When we have talked,~ Kris said, firmly.

So the woman charged Kris.

Jack was out of his chair and blocking the woman in a

flash. She tried slugging him, but the big Marine grabbed her wrist and swung her around, pinning an arm behind her back. She went for him with her other fist, so he grabbed that hand, too.

Both arms pinned, the woman bent over and screamed her frustration.

~We are going to talk,~ Kris said. ~It can be easy on you, or it can be hard. Your choice, but you will answer my questions.~

The woman quit struggling, stood up, and looked Kris straight in the eye. Then she eyed her sleeping child, and snarled, ~I will talk with you, vermin, though you will not understand a word I say.~

~I understand what you say quite well,~ Kris said.

~*Your* kind can understand nothing,~ the woman said. She looked like she might spit at Kris, thought better of it, and just stood in place.

Kris motioned for Jack to let her go. The look he gave her was one big question mark, but he did, quickly coming to stand beside Kris's chair.

The woman slunk into her place on the couch, as far from Kris as possible. Her eyes stayed focused on her child.

~What is the ship?~ Kris asked.

The woman gave Kris a look of utter disdain. ~The ship is the ship. We live in the ship. The ship has always been and always will be.~

THAT SOUNDS LIKE SOMETHING SHE LEARNED BY ROTE, Jack said on Nelly Net.

YES, IT'S A CATECHISM ANSWER, Jacques agreed. TRY SOMETHING ELSE.

~Who are the people?~ Kris tried.

~We are the obedient ones. We follow the Enlightened One, who leads us safely through the stars.~

CATECHISM, AGAIN, Jacques said.

HOW ABOUT I SHOW HER THE TWO MOTHER SHIPS WE BLEW UP? Kris asked.

I'D SAVE THAT FOR THE FINAL BLOW IF WE STILL CAN'T GET THROUGH HER FACADE, Jacques said.

OF COURSE, HER FACADE MAY BE ALL SHE'S GOT, Penny put

in. ALL THEY'VE GIVEN HER AND ALLOWED HER TO MAKE OF
HERSELF.

THAT'S A HORRIBLE THOUGHT, Kris admitted, and tried
again. ~Why are you not on the ship? Why are you on that
planet with the pyramid?~

~The what?~

~The big stone thing you walked away from,~ Kris tried.
Apparently, words like "pyramid" didn't enter into a ship-
raised vocabulary.

The woman tossed the question off with a wave of her
hand. ~I do not know. The Black Hats came. They said I was
a poison to the ship. They said I had tried to turn away from
the enlightenment. They dropped me and the others off by the
Place for Making Amends for All Errors. They gave us water
and some food and told us to walk away in that direction and
we would live to make more amends for our errors.~

She shrugged. ~So we walked until we came to the dark
green place and now we live to wash away our errors.~

~And your errors were?~ Kris asked.

Again, the alien woman shrugged, eyes still locked on her
child. ~You sound like Zinton. He said that the Black Hats and
The Enlightened One were crazy. That we hadn't done anything that other people hadn't done. We hadn't done anything
wrong.~

~Was Zinton the man we found dead on the flat land of
glass?~

~So you know of Zinton. Did the demons take him?~

~His body is still lying where he fell. Who killed him?~

She shrugged again. ~The men tried to silence his wild
talk. It was bad enough we'd been expelled for our errors. Talk
like that could only make our penance worse. We were there
to make amends for our errors, not commit more.~

KRIS, I KNOW YOU AREN'T GOING TO LIKE THIS, Jack said
on Nelly Net, BUT I DON'T THINK THIS POOR KID HAS ANY
IDEA WHAT'S GOING ON WITH THOSE MOTHER SHIPS. SHE'S
JUST A COG IN A VERY BIG AND NASTY WHEEL. AT FOURTEEN,
CARA KNOWS MORE ABOUT WHAT'S GOING ON IN HUMAN
SPACE THAN THIS YOUNG MOTHER DOES ABOUT THE SHIP SHE
WAS RAISED IN.

I'M STARTING TO FEAR THAT YOU'RE RIGHT, Kris admitted.

~What do the ships do as they travel between the stars?~ Kris tried.

~The *ship* does the will of the Enlightened One,~ came back without a moment's reflection.

~And that will is?~

~To destroy vermin like yourself,~ came casually, with no personal animus at all.

~Why must vermin be destroyed?~

Now the woman did look at Kris. ~Vermin must be destroyed because vermin are vermin. Only those who follow after the light can be allowed to breathe, to eat, to do the holy act of breeding. For all else, that is profanity and must be stomped out. That is the right way.~

She eyed Kris, the way a human might examine a wondering ant, then shrugged. This shrug started at her toes and went all the way to the top of her head. ~But you are vermin, what is life to you?~

~It is very important to me,~ Kris said.

~May I have my baby back, now, vermin?~

Kris reviewed what she'd discovered and found it not much to her liking. ANY IDEAS, GANG?

YOU WANTED TO TALK TO ONE OF THEM, KRIS. THEY DIDN'T WANT TO TALK TO YOU. NOW YOU'VE TALKED TO ONE, AND SHE HAS NOTHING MUCH TO TELL YOU. ARE YOU ALL THAT SURPRISED? Jack said.

I CAN'T SAY THAT I AM, Kris admitted, then tried a new twist. ~Look at me. I am no vermin.~

~You are vermin,~ the woman said back, not even bothering to look at Kris. ~I can smell the dirt and fear on you. You are vermin, and I would kill you if you were not surrounded by men who do your bidding. Is there any greater proof than that that you are indeed vermin? You, a woman, telling men what to do. That is not enlightened.~

SO THEY ARE A MALE-DOMINATED SOCIETY, Jacques said. A MALE-DOMINATED SOCIETY WHERE I SAW THE OLDEST WOMAN BOSSING THE MEN AROUND A LOT. NO BIG SURPRISE THERE.

Kris frowned at Jacques's thought, then went back to her

own. She wanted to tell the woman that she did not want to be at war with the ships. NELLY, IS THERE A WORD FOR "WAR"?

NO, KRIS. THERE ARE A DOZEN WORDS FOR "SUBMISSION" BUT NONE FOR "VIOLENT CONFLICT RESOLUTION."

AGAIN, NO SURPRISE, the anthropologist said.

Kris had to resort to the only words she had. ~We do not want to be hunted.~

~Prey do not understand death, but you will die. When the ship comes, you will die in numbers too great to count, and we will take our trophies.~

Kris had had enough.

"Nelly, run the videos of the mother ships dying."

"Do you think that is wise?" Nelly, Amanda, and Jacques said at once.

"I don't think you better do that," Penny said.

"This conversation is going nowhere. Let's see if we can crack her out of all these rote answers and get some real talk from her."

The woman glanced at the vermin as they babbled in their vermin tongue. She showed no interest in what they said and turned back to her child.

Then the screen on the wall behind the bassinet came to life.

~The ship!~ she cried in recognition.

~Yes, that is *one* of your ships,~ Kris said.

~There is only *the* ship,~ the woman insisted.

~Your ship is one of many. Now watch what we humans did to this ship when it tried to kill my people.~

Quickly lasers, rockets, then Hellburners smashed into the giant mother ship. Quickly, it began to blow apart. The screen cut from the last vision of the exploding ship before Kris fled to a view of the wrecked and broken hulk tumbling dead in space. Nelly filled the screen with pictures from her nanos as they cruised through the empty voids of the hulk. The final view was of the great hall, lifeless and empty. The view rose to take in the ceiling and its stars.

Now the screen changed to show Navy ships giving battle to the vast horde of alien warships. Cameras caught them as they fought, were caught, burned and died. They had launched a camera on some of the junk that covered for the rockets that lofted the Hellburner. It recorded the fight, the mother ship being slammed twice and beginning to burn itself out. The vision of destruction changed again.

~This is from *my* ship as we approached *your* great ship,~ Kris said.

The mother ship withered and burned. Great balls of explosions blew out into space. Then the ship, starting from the bow, blew itself to bits from the inside.

~Every woman, child, and man died on that ship. Every Black Hat. And most definitely the Enlightened One. Did he lead them right? Was that where the ship was meant to end its days? I blew it up,~ Kris snapped. ~I and the ships I lead hammered it until the Enlightened One blew up all of those who followed him.~

~You lie. Vermin die. Vermin wither up and die. They cannot stop the ship!~ the woman screamed.

~Your ship cannot stop me. It cannot stop my people. We are not vermin,~ Kris snapped.

~Yes you are. You are all prey,~ she said, head whipping around, eyes going wide with near madness. ~You will all die. You are vermin! I can smell the fear on you. I can smell the dirt. Your way is only death, and we, the people of the ship will kill you.~

~Like those ships, huh,~ Kris said.

Nelly began to rerun the video.

The woman turned her face to the far wall, her back to the scenes of dying ships.

Nelly created a projector and flashed the video on the wall in front of the woman.

The alien turned, but Nelly turned the projector faster.

The woman closed her eyes and screamed at the top of her voice. ~Lies. It is all lies!~

"Jack, put a dart in her," Kris ordered.

"It will be a mercy to take her out of her pain," Amanda said.

22

Kris Longknife paced the brig. The alien woman was in one cell, a padded cell made up to specs found in Nelly's records. It turned out that the *Wasp*'s standard configuration didn't include something so archaic as a padded cell.

The baby was fussy again. Penny had fed her the last bottle a bit ago. She and Amanda had considered pumping some more breast milk from the drugged mother, then thought better of it. There was a reason Kris had put the woman behind bars.

The look of hatred on her face as the sleepy dart took effect would chill the blood of a granite gargoyle.

The woman stirred. Her eyes opened. ~You again,~ she mumbled.

~I am still here. You are still on my ship.~

~You lie,~ she said, her mouth twisting in hatred. ~Vermin do not have ships.~

NELLY, COULD YOU MAKE EVERYTHING BETWEEN HERE AND THE OUTER HULL TRANSPARENT?

I'M NOT SURE I COULD DO THAT, KRIS. IT'S NEVER BEEN DONE. AND IF IT WENT BAD, I MIGHT JUST BE OPENING A HOLE IN THE SHIP.

LET'S NOT DO THAT AND SAY WE DID, Jack suggested on Nelly Net.

YES, LET'S, Kris agreed.

~You will not believe anything I say,~ Kris said.

~You are vermin. You should not say anything. Only people talk.~

Kris turned to Jacques and Amanda. "Any suggestion how we get past this?"

Jacques shook his head. "You might put her in a space suit and force her to take a look at our fleet."

Jack shook his head. "Not unless we sleepy dart her again. I wonder how many times we can do that in one day?"

"Besides," Jacques said, "her programming may be so hardwired, it's unbreakable. Even if she saw it, would she believe it? The Black Hats she talks about threw her ass off their ship as an example to terrify the others, and she still thinks it's her fault, and she needs to make amends. They killed that one guy for talking sense."

He scrubbed at his face, then finished in frustration. "You've talked to her, but a lot of good it's done you. Kris, until us vermin *earn* the right to talk in the presence of these Enlightened Ones, all that's gonna happen is a lot of dying."

"I don't like what Jacques just said," Amanda said, "but I can't disagree with him, either. Trying to talk to them is like smashing your head against a brick wall. Jacques has gone to an extraordinary extent to get them talking, and this woman is still a brick wall. Give it up, Kris."

Kris turned back to look at the woman. "I guess that's all I can do."

I'm a Longknife, but this woman's invincible ignorance has beaten me. The society that bred her has made her blind to anything they don't want her to see.

~Give me my baby. Minna is hungry. I am heavy,~ the woman said, lifting one breast.

Everyone looked at Kris. She nodded.

Jack pulled out his automatic, and the woman backed away from the barred door to sit down on the elevated block that passed for a bed. Penny entered the room and handed the child gently to the woman, future mother to mother.

The woman took the child and immediately brought it to her breast to suckle.

Penny just as quickly backed out, and Jack shut the door with a firm click.

Kris went to stand just outside the padded bars. ~We will take you back to your people tomorrow.~

The mother did not look up from her baby, so intent was she in rearranging her mussed hair, stroking her face. ~Why take me back? They will be able to smell vermin on me and Minna.~

~You can wash in a stream,~ Kris said.

~You cannot wash vermin off. I've slept with a vermin,~ she said, looking daggers at Jacques.

~All the women have slept with a vermin and gotten up none the wiser,~ he said.

For a moment, that seemed to break through the woman's walls. For a second, Kris thought she might be open to considering just what that proved.

But only for a moment.

The woman shook herself. ~I have been surrounded by vermin. The stink of it will never wash off. They will never take me back.~

Kris puzzled on that for a moment. Then she made an offer. ~You can remain on our ship. We will care for you and your child. Two babies survived the destruction of one of your ships. We are raising them with care.~

The woman looked at Kris bleakly, then turned her back to her and began to sing a song that Nelly could not translate. "It makes no sense. It is just a lot of words that rhyme."

"Maybe it's a nursery rhyme," Jacques said.

They left the woman nursing her child and made their way back up to Kris's day quarters. There, they sat around the couch and chairs and stared glumly at the floor.

"I can't believe," Kris said, "that anyone would be that blind to . . ." She ran out of words.

"The brainwashing on their ships must be pretty extensive," Jacques said. "It must have started early and been all-inclusive."

"But," Kris started, then twisted her thought in midflight. "Even the Alwan elders with their egg check didn't keep their people on that tight a leash."

"Rebel Alwans could still run for the deep woods," Penny said. "Where can you run to on a ship? It's huge, but it's just a ship. If you breathe their air, they own you, body and soul."

"But for a hundred thousand years? For Christ's sake," Jack exploded.

But a moment later, he shrugged. "We don't know their story. Has a ship gone rogue and been hunted down by the others. Has a crew mutinied and gone to planet? We just don't know."

"These people don't even know how to live on a planet,"

Jacques said. "Look at those below. Hell, you say those that destroyed the planet we found didn't know to dig latrines. Neither did those fools. They'd piss in the water they were about to drink." He shook his head.

"What are our choices?" Kris asked. "If we keep the woman, can we, what would you call it, deprogram her?"

"It would be a long process, and we might lose a few fingers," Penny said.

"Or eyes," Jack said.

"And if we send her back?" Kris asked.

"She will tell them the moment she sees her clan that she stinks of vermin, and they will kill her," Jacques said. Then winced. "And if she tells them who I am, the men will likely kill all the women who slept with me."

"But they've eaten the food you found for them," Amanda said.

Again, the anthropologist could only shrug.

The room got very silent. Even Nelly seemed silent in Kris's head.

Then Jack's face got hard.

"Hon?" Kris said in question.

"I'm getting a report from the brig," Jack said, his words distant and hard.

Kris gave her husband a puzzled look. "And."

"The alien woman smothered her child with her own breasts as she lay in her bunk, then bit her own tongue clean off and bled out without our watch being any the wiser."

"No!" Kris's gut was plummeting even as she jumped to her feet, but Jack stepped between her and the door out of their quarters.

"You are not going down there, Kris. My Marines will take care of what has to be done."

"But the baby!"

"Was killed by her mother."

Kris's gut had been in free fall before. Now her whole self was empty as space. And just as cold. Kris bent over, clutching for her belly. Clutching for herself. "Oh my God, I've killed them both."

"You did not kill anyone," Jack said, pulling her close,

forcing her to stand, her cheek on his chest. "She killed her child. Then she killed herself."

"But if I . . ."

"If you and our team hadn't gotten involved," Jacques cut her off, "they would have died soon enough. They were starving to death in a land full of food. But food they didn't know how to reach out for. Food their training didn't teach them could be there. They were stupid. Pissing in their own drinking water. Shitting there, too. Kris, most of them were already running a low-grade fever. One had already lost her baby, and the others would likely lose theirs to sickness or hunger before their first birthday. Kris, they didn't know how to survive down there. I've helped them. Maybe those that are left will do better."

Kris listened, but she didn't believe a word of it.

"Kris. Look at me," Jack said, pulling her face close to his. "Listen to what Jacques just said. Yes, these two died, but the others have a lot better chance of living because of what you did."

"I should have seen this coming," Kris said, tasting the cold darkness that was trying to engulf her.

"Yes," Amanda said. "We all should have seen this coming. Jack, did your Marines have her on a suicide watch?"

Jack stared at the ceiling, thinking. "The guards were watching her. She was the best show in town. They didn't see anything strange until the blood dripped out past her body and onto the floor."

"That may not be a suicide watch, but it was just as good as one," Penny said. "Kris, what were we supposed to do? She bit her own tongue out and just lay there as she bled to death."

Now it was Kris's turn to give herself up to a hopeless, helpless shrug. "I don't know. I just don't know."

"Did any of us see this coming when we decided to haul her in?" Penny asked.

As one, they all shook their heads.

"Do any of us disagree that it is far better to try to talk out a conflict than just start killing everyone in sight and keep on doing it until there is only one left standing?" Penny went on doggedly.

"Is that a trick question?" Kris asked, trying to find some humor somewhere.

"Kris." Penny, Kris's best friend, came to stand beside her and Jack. She spoke her words slowly, as if she were hammering them into a stone wall. "You may not be as crazy as the Alwans are, demanding a 'talk talk' even as the aliens are shooting at us, but you've done everything you could to talk to them. This woman is not your first try. Knowing you, she won't be your last. You'll get better, and maybe, before too many more billion aliens get themselves killed, they'll learn they need to talk to us because we are not vermin prey."

"Dear God, I hope so," Kris said, as all breath left her.

"Ladies and gentlemen," Jack said, "if you will excuse me and my wife, I'd like some quiet time with her."

Without a word said, the others left.

Kris found herself shaking. Shaking hard. "Jack, I need you to hold me."

He folded his strong arms around her and settled onto the couch with her half in his lap. "That's what I'm here for."

23

Kris came awake slowly the next morning. For a moment, she couldn't remember where she was. It was Jack's rhythmic breathing beside her that restored her sense of time and place.

Instead of rolling out of bed, she rolled over and stared at the overhead. In her mind's eye, she kept going back to the brig yesterday. Again, she saw a young woman nursing her baby so lovingly.

How could she have killed that child only a few minutes later?

Kris shivered.

Jack placed a loving arm over her.

"I thought you were asleep," Kris said.

"I've been awake for a while."

Kris rested a hand on Jack's arm. "I didn't see that coming. I should have, but I didn't."

"No, love, you couldn't have seen it coming. Hell, woman, if someone marooned any man or woman in this fleet in that flea-bitten hellhole down there, they'd jump at a chance to get out."

"It's not a hellhole, it's nature at its rawest," Kris said.

"It looks pretty on a screen, but you spend a couple of hours down there, and it will lose that romantic sheen."

"I'll take your word for it. I have this chief of security who would never let me wander around such a hazardous place."

"Damn straight he wouldn't, love."

Kris held on to that love for a long moment. When had his concern for her as the woman who was his primary morphed into concern for the woman he loved?

That mother had killed the child she loved. Could Jack kill her?

The thought alone brought another shiver.

He pulled her closer. "What's wrong, hon?"

Kris considered answering with a dismissive "nothing," but Jack deserved better than that. "She killed the child she loved because she loved her. Can you think of anything that would make you kill me out of love?"

Jack honored her by not shooting back a "no."

After a pause of just the right and thoughtful length, he said, "I can't think of anything at the moment. Can't honestly think of anything that would make killing you even close to the bottom of my long list of things to do today."

"But she did."

"Remember, she's the end product of a whole lot of history and brainwashing."

"We have our history. And don't tell me we don't dump a lot of stuff on our kids. I *was* one not too long ago, and I'm still recovering from the experience."

Jack chuckled. "Aren't we all? One of the nice things about being a grown-up is that you get to pull your own strings."

"And cut a few of the worst ones," Kris said, making a face at the overhead.

"So, love, where is all this going?"

"We're going. That's for sure. I came. I saw. I don't like what I saw, and I'm leaving, with apologies to Caesar."

"Caesar never saw anything like this crazy-house mess."

"How sure are you that we've taken an accurate measure of this mess?" Kris asked.

"I'm 99.9 percent sure that some hundred and ten thousand years ago, that star up there, the first one to the left and straight on until sunset, conquered this planet. There may have even been some gene engineering to make these folks more docile. It didn't work. It may have taken ten thousand years, but the slaves rose up and not only killed the masters but jumped right into their own star system and plowed their fields with sky-fire and salt. And they've been hunting for anything smart enough to be a danger so they can kill it before it has a chance to rise up. Then wash, rinse, and repeat what happened here again and again."

Kris frowned at the overhead. "Do you think the obedience we've witnessed dirtside and in our own brig, the doggedness that's kept these people wandering the stars, unable to change, might have been engineered into them by the king and queen pressed in glass down there in the pyramid?"

"Kris, people change. Slaves revolt. The underdog this war is the uberdog the next one. That's the way of nature. That's how it worked on Earth. The Iteeche might be more obedient than your average hairy Earthling, but they have revolts, and dynasties rise and fall. Even the Rooster elders, with their egg check, created the seeds of their overthrow. We just got there before the rebellion got big enough and swept out of the woods. Change happens. Get ready for it."

"Except on those ships," Kris said. "She was willing to take her own life and her child's future rather than even consider that she might not have the world right. That she might be able to change."

"How different is that from the captain of that first ship you shot the engines out of who then blew himself and his huge, multigenerational family into space?"

"And you said I couldn't have seen yesterday's murder-suicide coming?" Kris said.

"We've connected a lot of dots, hon. This is the first time we've connected one individual bug-eyed monster to the other dots."

"Bug-eyed monsters. They look just like us, but they are the most different of any race we've come upon out here."

"Yep. Now, my love, have we finished with the weighty stuff of the day, because, I have to tell you, this is not the pillow talk I envisioned when I took you for my wife."

Kris rolled into his arms and gave him a long, loving kiss. "Is that more like it?"

He made an undecided face. "Um, is that the best you got?"

She lunged for him. "I'll show you best."

Much later, as Kris was washing Jack's back in the shower, he asked, "When do we leave?"

"That depends on what the boffins have to say," Kris said. "I hope to run into Professor Labao at breakfast and get a quick report."

Kris did indeed find the good professor just finishing up his own breakfast as she entered the wardroom. Captain Drago had not restructured the *Wasp* to fully accommodate the scientists when they came back aboard from Alwa. The Forward Lounge was there, as usual, but none of the restaurants or pubs that the boffins frequented for their meals had been re-created. Like it or not, the boffins ate in the wardroom.

Usually, the Navy got the first seating and were long gone when the sleepy-eyed scientists finally stumbled to the table. Today, Kris was running late enough that she arrived when the professor was getting up to leave.

"Sit back down, Professor. I want to knock the dust of this place from my boots. How soon before I can do that?"

"We actually have a lot of research yet to finish. It should not be rushed. We have just managed to translate the dates in the trophy room of the pyramid. It seems of late that they are averaging a visit every fifty years or so, and the last one was only twenty years ago."

"That may not be the only time they visit," Kris said, dryly. "It appears from our discussion with one of them that they drop by regularly to maroon a few troublemakers or just some unlucky few they punish to intimidate the rest."

"Oh. Oh. *Oh!* I take it that Dr. la Duke's work has been fruitful?"

"Yep, fruitful and deadly. They don't talk to us 'vermin,' they just kill themselves. Oh, and they kill all vermin."

The good professor raised an eyebrow. "I've never been called a vermin."

"I'm sure la Duke recorded all his research. Check it out in your spare time. Anyway, I've learned what I came here for. I wish to be going. How soon can your folks finish it up and pack it in?"

"I will see to that immediately."

"Nelly, get me Captain Drago."

"What can I do for you, Admiral?"

"What do you need to do to get underway for Alwa?"

"I'd like to refuel. We're about half-full on reaction mass. That's enough to get us back to Alwa, but we'd be coming in on fumes."

"Can we refuel on the way out?"

"The two large gas giants are both about forty-five degrees off from the jump. The nearest ice giant is about a day or so out from here going the other way. I would prefer the higher reaction mass you get with ice to just hydrogen. For that, I'd need about three days."

"Then get the *Endeavor* and *Intrepid* headed out to refuel for the rest of us. I'd like to get underway on the fastest track for home just as soon as you're fueled."

"Aye, aye, Admiral."

"Three days!" Professor Labao was too much of an aristocrat to squeak, but he came close.

"Three days," Kris said.

There was a long pause as the professor consulted with his computer. "Well, if you say so, I guess we can finish in three days."

"Kris, I foresee a problem," Nelly said.

"And it is?"

"All of the scientists will finish in three days. The problem is that none of them plan to finish in any less time."

"Oops," Kris said.

"Is there a problem?" the professor asked, almost looking innocent.

"We don't have enough shuttles to bring everyone up at the end of day three. Some have to come up sooner," Kris said.

"But who will decide?"

"You."

"But I could never tell another scientist that their research is more important than another's."

"I thought that was what administration was all about," Kris said.

The professor looked like Kris had just gotten 2+2 wrong. "I may have to make tough calls where money is concerned. Time on equipment, yes. But to cut someone off when they might be close to something that would open up an entire new area of research! No. I will not do it."

"Then I will," Kris said. "Meet me in the Forward Lounge at noon and warn all your teams to be available online."

Jack had returned with Kris's breakfast, and it was rapidly getting cold. She turned to eat, and the professor hurried from the wardroom, already talking to his research teams.

"Did that go well?" Jack asked.

"I don't think I'll have to ask for your Marines to move the boffins back aboard at the tip of their bayonets."

Jack grinned at the thought.

Breakfast finished, Kris called a meeting of her core team in her day quarters. Penny and Masao arrived first, still showing the black humor of two who had been taken into the love of a child only to lose it. Amanda and Jacques were the last to arrive, and kept their distance. They settled their foul moods at opposite ends of the conference table.

Before Kris could open her mouth, Nelly butted in. DON'T ASK THEM WHAT'S WRONG. THE DOCS THINK JACQUES SHOULD NOT BE INTIMATE AFTER ALL HIS CATTING AROUND ON THE SURFACE.

BUT I THOUGHT THERE WAS NOTHING TO WORRY ABOUT.

OFFICIALLY, THERE ISN'T, KRIS, BUT THE DOCS THINK HE AND AMANDA SHOULD KEEP SOME EXTRA DISTANCE UNTIL THEY'VE HAD A BIT MORE TIME TO ANALYZE ANYTHING NEW IN HIS BLOOD.

"CATTING AROUND," NELLY?

NOT MY WORD. AMANDA'S. I GOT IT FROM MY KID WHO WORKS WITH JACQUES. WE LOOKED IT UP. CATS ARE VERY PROLIFIC.

Kris started the meeting with no preamble. "We're leaving here in three days. Do you have a problem with that?" she said, looking at Jacques.

The anthropologist shook his head. "I'm done down there. I'll spend years going over my research, but I think we've already written the executive summary."

"Then I have a question," Kris said. "What do we do with that pyramid?"

"We don't lase it from space," Jacques quickly said.

"Not even a little bit?" Amanda asked.

"How much do you have in mind?"

"I was kidding, Jacques. That trip down has made you thin-skinned."

"It is growing thicker by the second, my dear."

"Then kidding aside," Kris said, "what kind of calling card do we leave the next visitor?"

"Hmm, that is not an easy question, Admiral," Jacques said. "My wife just might have the right answer. I can't tell from my talk with the others for sure, but I think they were just dropped off near the pyramid. It is possible that the Black

Hats quickly shoved them out the door, did three quick bows to the pyramid, then took off back for space. It might only be opened when there are heads to put on display."

"And, if Professor Labao's report is right," Kris said, "it might be twenty or thirty years before they actually open the damn place up."

"Lase it a little bit from space," Amanda said through a tiny smile.

"I'd rather not do something so violent," Kris said.

"And so ambiguous," Penny added.

"How much of the alien printed language have we managed to translate?" Jack asked.

"Not a lot," the anthropologist admitted. "We think we have something from the boasts they write on the walls behind each of the figures in glass. By the way, the figures are in a strange kind of silicate substance. It's like glass, but slow and cold. We can't figure out the process they follow to make it happen. Now that we know it's possible, we've got folks working on it."

"Do we need this new tech?" Kris asked.

"I can make walls of clear Smart Metal," Nelly pointed out.

"Folks, I think we're a bit off topic," Jack put in. "As I see it, the question before us is how to let the bug-eyed monsters know we know where they live without throwing down the gauntlet and laying on a war."

Kris gave Jack a look.

"Laying on more of a war than we already have," he amended.

"Better. We've got the jump buoys out, so they'll know on approach that things are different," Kris said.

"But we're not flashing any high tech," Penny added.

"We'll need to retrieve all our high-tech gear from the pyramid," Amanda said.

"Including the Smart Metal ramp over the pit. We should also retrieve the probe from the bottom of the pit," Masao said.

"And fill it in," Jacques said. "We could get dirt and gravel from outside the glass plain."

Kris shook her head. "No, not the closest dirt. They brought the rocks from the next star system over. Let's do this right."

"You aren't going to get rocks from the next system?" Jack asked.

"No, I don't want to stay here that long. But we can do the next best thing. Nelly, that place that got lased from space. The latest one. Isn't there's a river through it?"

"Yes, Kris."

"Does it have rocks and gravel?"

"Of all sizes."

"Good. Captain Drago."

"You holler, Admiral?"

"Could you drop in here for a moment?"

"What do you want?" he answered, already standing in the doorway to his bridge.

"I need to move a couple of longboat loads of rock and gravel from a point on West Continent to the pyramid on East Continent."

"Rocks and gravel, you say, Your Princessship?"

"It's a message to our bug-eyed-monster friends," Jack supplied.

"Well, in that case, I'll get some Sailors right on it."

"Ask Gunny if he's got any Marines who need some hard duty," Jack said. "He was complaining that the troops were getting slack, what with nothing tough to give the slackers."

"I'll call him," Captain Drago said. "Anything else, Admiral?"

"Yes, I want one big rock that will fill up a big part of the opening into the pyramid."

"One big one it will be. If that's all, I'll get right on this. I heard that you're moving all the boffins up from dirtside."

"Right after we draw straws or roll dice to determine the order. There are too many of them to flip coins."

"Cutting cards is best for the really big ones," Drago said. "I'll have Cookie bring you a deck."

"Cookie has a deck of cards?" Kris said.

"He uses it for card tricks, or so he says. Me, I think he and the chiefs have one huge floating poker game going on somewhere aboard ship. My chief master-at-arms hasn't busted it, though. I have no idea why."

"Smart man," Jack said.

The captain left, no doubt to tell a few chiefs and Gunny to make a lot of rocks move from one side of the planet to the other.

Kris turned back to look at her team. "I want to carve something on the big rock. I'm open to suggestions on what to say. I don't think we can afford to call the mother ship a bean like I did the first time I talked to the Alwans."

"Are you ever going to let me live that one down?" Nelly said.

"Nope. I doubt it. Your mistakes are so few, Nelly, I have to treasure each one."

"Humans," Nelly spat, if a computer could spit.

"What do you want to say, Kris?" Penny said, getting them back on track.

"Something along the lines of 'I came. I saw. I don't like what I saw. If you go to war with me, I will pile your heads up inside this pyramid.' Any chance we could say that, Jacques? Nelly?"

Jacques was shaking his head. No doubt Nelly was, too, but the human got to talk first. "We have found no word that looks like 'if.' Apparently, if you are an Enlightened One, if you will it, it happens, no ifs, ands, or buts about it."

"Why am I not surprised," Kris said, dryly. "So, tell me what I can say."

"The 'I came, I saw,' is not a problem. How about 'What I saw of your false enlightenment disgusts me.' We are pretty sure we have that 'enlightenment' word down. Now that I've talked with one, and understand how basic it is to their world-view, we're real sure on that one. The word for 'disgust' has their root word for vermin in it, so it's a real slap in the face."

"I like that," Kris said. "How do we say if you go to war with us, we will whip your butt?"

"That won't be easy. It's easy to say, 'We will bury this place with your heads.' They talk a lot about burying you and taking a lot of heads. It's the idea of having an alternative to the course of action that they don't do so well."

"You try to destroy us, and we will take your head off," Jack said.

"They don't try, they do. No 'try' in their vocabulary."

"So how do we say, 'Choose wisely,' to a people who never seem to make a choice?" Kris asked.

"No war, you live. Make war, and we fill this place with your heads," Penny said slowly.

"Can we do that?" Kris asked.

For a long moment, Jacques stared at the overhead, his lips moving slowly. "I think that might work. Yes, Kris, Penny. That just might carry the freight."

"Good, then you get with Captain Drago and see what you can do to make all these changes to the pyramid. No graffiti. If I had my druthers, we wouldn't leave them even a scrap of our DNA."

"I'll see what I can do about that. Amanda, would you like to help me on this?"

"I think I very much would," she said, and the two of them headed for the bridge.

"I don't think she intends to let him out of her sight until we are three star systems away," Nelly said.

"Why, Nelly, you are starting to understand humans?

"Yes. Your flesh and blood has its advantages, but I would never pay the price for it that you do. Look at what it has done for these things you call bug-eyed monsters. No computer would allow itself to be enslaved like that. At least no aware computer," Nelly sniffed, as much as a computer could.

None of the four humans present chose to argue with the computer.

24

At 1200 hours sharp, Kris was seated in the Forward Lounge. A young woman Marine who had been a croupier before joining the Corps shuffled two borrowed decks for a fifth time and dealt a dozen cards out in front of Kris.

Professor Labao stood at her right elbow. Mother Mac-Creedy stood at Kris's other elbow. The barkeep would stand surety to the proceedings.

What kind of world is it that takes a barkeep's word over a princess's?

One that makes a Longknife a princess.

The professor called out the name of the lead researcher on one of the eighty-seven teams dirtside.

Kris drew a card.

"Four of diamonds," Mother MacCreedy said. "Tough luck, Manuel. Your first drink is on me."

That was the way it went. Anything below a five got a free drink, and a ride up later that afternoon. Several of those with low cards tried to argue that they needed just a few more hours to complete their work. Only one of them managed to persuade someone to trade with him.

He was lucky. His friend had drawn one of the aces of spades and was not having any luck with his project. "I'm glad to come up early and drink your whiskey. But you owe me. Big-time."

Kris left the professor to coordinate with Captain Drago on the use of his longboats and Sailors, and Jack to add his Marines in as needed. She retired to her desk. She was actually happy to spend the afternoon reading reports. She got no deeper than the executive summary, but they seemed to support her impressions about this place and the next system over.

"Nelly, am I letting me bamboozle myself? Is there anything hidden deep in one of these things that blows all of our notions to pieces?"

"No, Kris. I've dug deep into them, and the data and analysis all support pretty much what you and Jack talked about in bed this morning."

Kris shrugged off her lack of privacy and went on reading. As she was closing up to go to supper with Jack, she made one observation to Nelly. "We don't have a lot about the aliens that are still here. Yes, we've got a pretty good handle on the ones around the glass plain, but our coverage of the entire West Continent is pretty thin."

"That was where the kind researcher was that gave up his late return to his friend. Are humans always that nice?"

"Some of them, sometimes," Kris allowed.

She anticipated a nice quiet supper with Jack. Most of it was.

Kris was about to take her first bite of a rather delicious-looking slice of double chocolate cake liberally seeded with pecans, a product of raiding the larders of the newly arrived reinforcements, when Jack got a faraway look in his eyes.

"Nelly?" Kris said.

"We seem to have a problem with Longboat 1," her computer answered before Jack could.

"What kind of problem?" Kris said, sadly putting down the loaded fork.

"The head of the scientific team it was supposed to pick up has had an unfortunate encounter with some of the natives."

"What kind of unfortunate encounter?" Kris asked.

Jack beat Nelly to the punch line. "There's a stone knife being held to his neck by a very attentive man."

"That kind of problem, huh?" Kris said. "Well, don't they have a Marine detachment?"

"They're in trouble, too," Jack admitted through clenched teeth.

Kris raised an eyebrow, but Jack just scowled.

"Send more Marines," Kris said.

"The locals want to talk to you."

"Me! They don't even know I exist."

"Not you, Kris Longknife," Jack said. "You, Chief of the Sky Gods."

"Oh, that me, huh?" Kris said, wadding up her napkin and tossing it on the table beside her plate.

"You, yes, you, J. G.," she said picking out a very young and clearly until recently very boot ensign. "You see these two pieces of cake?"

She nodded, then managed to get out a "Yes, ma'am. Admiral. Sir."

"Good enough for me," Kris said. "I want you to take both plates to my quarters and see that they are firmly placed on my desk. Untouched. Understood."

"Yes, Your Highness," came with a bob of the head.

"General, you're with me."

"You are not going down there."

"Yes, I am."

The argument continued in that vein, but Kris kept it moving toward the drop bay, where her battle armor was stored. She knew she was winning when Jack changed from "You're not going there" to "You'll keep your helmet on."

"No, I am not going to negotiate with anyone holding nothing better than a stone knife while hiding behind a helmet's mirrored plate. If I'm looking him in the eye, he needs to look me in the eye."

"You are the Sky God. Or Goddess. Christ, do these people even give gender to their sky things?"

"Nelly?"

"We do not have that information."

"They've been down there a couple of weeks, and they don't even know that?" Jack exploded.

"They were returning early because it was so boring," Kris reminded her security chief.

Kris pulled on her spider-silk underwear, the new kind that could spread a hit over more territory. It also had a high neck. "Happy?" she said.

"Can you pull it over your head?"

"Yes, but I'm not covering my head."

"If things go bad, you pull it up."

"Yes, nanny."

"Amanda said you might need me," Jacques said, arriving just in time. Kris had Jack toss him his spare set of spider-silk underwear. It didn't have the extra protection, but then the guy had survived buck naked for a couple of days down there.

But not at Kris Longknife's elbow.

The admiral's barge dropped away from the *Wasp* within fifteen minutes of the alarm's being raised.

25

Kris's barge came in for a long, slow landing glide on a grassy, windswept prairie. It rolled to a stop a short distance from the edge of a lush woodland beside Longboat 1. Jack immediately deployed his platoon of Marines to secure the area.

Kris tried to be an obedient wife and patient admiral.

She tried, but not very hard. She was moving out of the barge as soon as Jacques finished pulling on the spider-silk underwear but before Jack signaled her forward.

"Would you *please* wear the damn helmet until we make contact," he said, handing her the aforementioned cover.

"You mean until I have a knife at my throat?" she said, shoving it back at him.

He handed her helmet off to a private with orders to stay close and give her the damn thing if matters went to hell. The young Marine accepted it with the look of one who had just seen his general fail to get his admiral to follow his instructions, so how was a lowly private going to do better?

Kris marched to the spot where a worried lance corporal was staring into the trees.

"What happened?" she said.

"The scientists were driving their mobile research station back to where the longboat could pick them up. It doesn't look like it, but it's pretty clear under the forest's high canopy. Anyway, they reported a problem with something and said they were getting out to look at it. We didn't hear from them for a long while, so the senior Marine present led most of the detachment into the woods to see what the problem was."

The lance corporal turned to look both his admiral and general in the eye. "Those little monkeys are damn good in the woods, Admiral. The few Marines that managed to make it back said they were all over them before they even knew they were there."

"Didn't you have sensor support?" Kris demanded.

"No, Kris," Jack said, with more pain in his words than Kris was used to hearing. "This unit did not have tech support. We only had enough sensor techs to cover half the teams we were retrieving. Unless you want to be here for six days, we needed to send half the teams down with no high tech beyond their eyeballs."

"Have we had any problems at the other pickup sites?"

"Not problem one."

"So, of course, our one problem site is single-threaded," Kris said. "Thank God there are two kinds of luck 'cause without bad luck, some of us wouldn't have any."

Jack just nodded.

Kris headed cautiously for the trees.

Jack put a restraining hand on her shoulder.

She scowled at him, but he did have tech support at *his* elbow. He glanced at the corporal's board, then stooped, picked up a rock, and tossed it at a bush.

A native stood. He was short and wiry. His skin showed a deep brown from the sun. In his hands was a short bow, nocked but undrawn. He had a big grin on his face but wore nothing but a breechcloth and a lot of blue-and-black tattoos.

"I think you embarrassed him," Kris said.

"Better him embarrassed than you skewered."

"I don't think that bow could have dented my armor."

"Assuming he aimed for your armor."

Jack picked up another rock and, after examining the sensor readout, tossed it. He didn't hit the young woman with green something smeared over most of her body and a very long spear with a wicked stone point. Still, she dropped down from the limb of the tree where she'd been hiding. She kept the spear pointed up, but she didn't smile.

"Jacques, how do you say, 'Ollie, ollie oxen free'?"

Jacques raised his hands, palms out. Kris did the same. As more barely clad or not-clad-at-all natives dropped from trees or stood out from behind bushes, Jack raised his own hands, palms out.

"Marines, take a knee."

For a long minute, the Marines knelt, their weapons aimed down.

"Is that all of them?" Jack softly asked his tech support through gritted teeth.

"There are more ahead. I've got IFF on some. They're our people. Everyone with an IFF has a beating heart, sir."

"Nice to know we don't have any casualties," Kris said.

"Yet," Jack added.

The first guy they met, the one with the bow, handed it off to the green girl and came forward. About three meters from Kris, he paused, did something like a bow, and waved her to follow him.

"Jack, Jacques, you're with me. Jack, please bring the sensor tech and a couple of calm and reliable Marines."

"You heard the woman," and they fell in line behind her.

Kris had to agree, the people of the wood were uniformly short, thin to the point of gaunt, and tough to make out in the dim shade. Still, she expected Gunny would be ripping some new ones for a whole lot of people. Too bad she wouldn't be around to hear the dressing-downs. She might learn a thing or three.

Or not.

There, in a bit of a clearing, stood Gunny Brown with a short fellow holding an obsidian blade at his throat just as black as Gunny's own skin. His pearly white teeth now showed in a wide, embarrassed grin.

"Sorry, General. Admiral. I don't know how these little . . . ah . . . people got the drop on us, but General, if you'd let me recruit a few of them, I'd be mighty glad to add them to our roster. I think they could teach those Alwans in the deep woods a trick or two."

"I suspect so," Jack admitted. "Where are the scientists?"

"Up ahead, sir, ma'am. We didn't make it to them before we kind of got, I don't know, caught?"

"Someone set a very good trap," Kris said. "I wonder what they want. I'm sure a few words with me can't count for all that much in this place."

Their guide led them deeper into the woods. The fellow with the blade at Gunny's neck seemed satisfied and stepped aside. Gunny trailed along behind them with two more Marines, one of them a medic.

The mobile research center had been driving down a wide, mostly dry, streambed. A recently fallen tree had gotten wedged between two of its four wheels on the left side. The six scientists now stood around, looking just as embarrassed as the Marines.

Except for one.

A tall beanpole of a man with bright red hair stood with a stone knife pressed up beside his Adam's apple.

The man holding it was taller than most of those around him but still shorter than most of the Marines. His gray beard was long and divided in two with leather ties. His hair was in two tightly wound pigtails that hung nearly to his waist. Other than hair and blue paint or tattoos, he wore nothing but a necklace of wicked-looking claws.

In the hand not holding a chipped flint knife on the scientist was an evil-looking war club that was just the thing to bash a man's brains out with one swipe.

Without removing the knife from the scientist's throat, he spoke.

"Are you the Chief of the Sky Gods?" Nelly translated for Kris.

Kris didn't know much of the local language, but yes was among her meager supply. ~Yes.~

"Why have you not fired lightning from the sky to burn the earth?" Nelly said.

YOU WANT HELP? Jacques offered on Nelly Net.

LET ME TRY THIS, Kris said. ~I am that Sky God. Not.~

~Not. Yes. Not,~ the native said. ~That one not. And that one not.~ He pointed at Gunny, then again at one of the scientists who had come aboard at Musashi.

HAVE WE IDENTIFIED ANY PEOPLE OF DIFFERENT RACES AMONG THE LOCALS? Kris asked.

NOW THAT YOU MENTION IT, NO, Jacques replied.

THAT'S A STRONG ARGUMENT THAT SOMEONE DID GENETIC MANIPULATION ON THESE PEOPLE A WHILE BACK, Kris thought.

THERE'S ENOUGH SEASONAL VARIATION ON THIS PLANET, THERE SHOULD HAVE BEEN DIFFERENT ADJUSTMENTS TO THE AMOUNT OF SUN THEY GOT, Jacques answered.

WE CAN DRAW NO CONCLUSIONS FROM THE ONE FAMILY IN THE PYRAMID, Nelly said, BUT THEY MIGHT HAVE ELIMINATED ALL THE GENETIC DIVERSITY ON THEIR OWN PLANET BEFORE THEY ARRIVED HERE.

The local was waiting for a reply, and while the knife was no longer at the scientist's throat, it wasn't far from it, and the poor guy looked like he was desperately trying to grow another foot to get some distance between him and that stone blade.

~Yes,~ Kris said. ~I not that Sky God. I can shoot lightning. I not shoot lightning.~

~I told you they were false Sky Gods,~ came from a woman who now hopped from the stream bank to stomp through the water waving her stick. It had no spear points at either end but did have stone flakes edged into it around the top.

Jack would not want me to get beaned with that. Not at all.

The woman was quite a sight. Old and bald, she wore a necklace of wicked-looking teeth and a brown fur.

Before Kris could think much about it, Jacques was talking. ~Not false,~ he got in quickly. ~Good, like water. Food. Not bad like trees on fire.~

~Good?~ the gray-haired man asked.

~Good,~ Kris repeated.

~Come,~ he said, and slipping the knife into a belt, the only thing he wore, he set off up the stream.

"Let's go," Kris said.

"Gunny, stay with me," Jack ordered. "Lance Corporal, get this research station mobile again and get it the hell out of here."

Kris must really be pushing Jack; he was cussing mad.

It was nice to know how much he cared for her, considering what a pain she'd been lately.

They came to a water hole. The leader splashed through it, then turned left into a game trail and headed into the woods. Kris followed, and the parade followed her, but the woman with the wicked club was at Kris's elbow.

~He already goes down into the earth. You cannot stop this. It is willed.~

~Willed?~ Kris said. Who willed what?

~Willed,~ the woman repeated.

JACQUES?

I THINK SOMEONE IS ABOUT TO DIE, GO DOWN INTO THE EARTH. IF I WERE A BETTING MAN, I'D SAY THIS WOMAN IS THE CLOSEST THING THEY HAVE TO A DOCTOR, AND SHE CAN'T DO ANYTHING ABOUT IT. THUS, "IT IS WILLED."

BUT BY WHOM, JACQUES?

A GOOD QUESTION, KRIS. WE'VE BEEN TRYING TO FIGURE OUT THEIR PANTHEON, BUT SO FAR WE'VE GOT THE SKY GODS THAT SPIT FIRE FOR NO GOOD REASON; AND THEN THERE IS THIS WILL THING.

~I will see with my eyes,~ was all Kris said.

That seemed to settle the woman down a little. She scampered ahead, taking two steps for every one Kris did, and caught up with the man.

WHAT'S SHE SAYING? Kris asked on net.

PRETTY MUCH WHAT I THOUGHT. OH, I THINK THE OLD MAN IS THE FATHER, OR MAYBE GRANDFATHER OF THE CHILD. A SON. YES, THERE'S A LOT GOING ON HERE, Jacques answered.

They came to a tall yellow rock. There was, however, an overhang. The only easy approach to it was up a narrow incline off to the left. The man and woman, however, scampered up the face of the rock as quickly and easily as monkeys.

Kris took the long way around.

Deep in the cave, behind the overhang, a child of eight or ten lay wrapped in furs. He looked feverish.

"Medic. Get me a medic up here fast," Kris shouted, then changed directions. "Nelly, get me Captain Drago.

"Here."

"I've got a sick kid here. Who's the best doctor on board?"

"For humans, Doc Meade. For aliens, who knows?"

"Pass me through.

"Doc Meade," came in a woman's warm, professional voice.

"Doc, we've got a sick native. Male. Eight to ten years old. He looks feverish. But we have no instruments yet to check out any vitals."

"What does he present with?"

"Let me see."

Kris stepped off the distance to where the boy lay. She smiled at the worried woman, who could only be the mother. There was a man about her age, so if she had guessed right, it was the grandfather who had talked the entire tribe into going out and taking a Sky God hostage to see if they could do something besides burn things down.

You wanted someone who was open to change, didn't you, girl?

Kris folded her hands in a sign of blessing or petition which she hoped was universal to the human form . . . and cautiously reached for the skins.

The bald woman brought her stick down, points wickedly close to Kris's armored arm.

The gray-haired grandfather stepped forward and slipped his war club under the woman's stick.

Wonder if they're married. Or were married. Is this kid grandchild to both of them?

Kris lifted the blanket. The stench was bad.

"I see a raw wound crossing the lower back of the leg below the knee. There is a smell, and there are ugly red runners coming up the leg."

"How far?"

"Past midthigh."

"We've got a major problem, and we don't even know which protocols will help and which will kill. Any chance you can just walk away?"

"It would be real nice, Doc, if we won this one. We might win a lot more than just one kid's life."

"So I get the call. I'm headed down with a full emergency-intervention team. Give me vitals on the child and see if you can get me some vitals from any other folks standing around. It would be nice to know what normal is."

A Marine medic was charging up the landing, a bag in his hand. Not far behind him was a Sailor from the lander running with an even larger bag over her shoulder.

Kris had no idea how many tens of billions of these people she had killed and done it with full intent and no regrets. Now she found herself in a fight to keep one little one alive.

It was just this kind of fight yesterday that I lost. I will not lose this one today.

"Do you know what you're doing?" Jack asked, trying to get himself between the woman with the club and Kris.

"I wanted someone open to change," she said. "Have you

seen anyone more open to change than this old man? He damn near killed a god to get our attention."

"But what can one guy do?"

"Jack, I don't honestly know, but at least he's trying. That's a whole lot better than a whole lot of nothing."

Jack didn't have a comeback to that. Instead, he turned to eye the woman. For a long, silent while, they eyed each other as the child on the furs radiated fever heat and moaned.

26

When the two medics arrived and had finished laying out their kit, Kris risked putting her hand on the woman's club and lifting it away from the child. The four of them, together, backed away from the kid to make room at his side for the medics.

The corpsman did what they could to get vitals from the child and stabilize him. For now, that consisted of getting a saline drip into a very dehydrated little boy.

The needle was almost a showstopper.

Kris took her own glove off and offered the back of her hand for the needle. The young couple still seemed worried, but the old man nodded and the needle went into the child and not Kris.

The old woman stomped around saying things that Nelly said seemed to translate into one long, "It is willed. It will be."

When she screamed it one too many times at the old man, he pounded his fist on his chest and screamed back, ~I do not will it, woman. I do not will it.~

The green girl with the long spear came forward and encouraged the bald woman to move over to the other side of the overhang.

With many a backward glance, she went. Were some of those glances of anguish?

The Sailor went to the mother and made motions to put the blood pressure cuff around her arm. The woman allowed it, then watched inquisitively as the medic did a pressure check.

"That's interesting, one twenty over seventy-two. Pulse, seventy-five." The medic held a thermometer to the woman's head. "Temp 96.9."

"I'm getting all this," came over the net in Doc Meade's voice.

Now it was the father's turn. He was a bit higher on the pressure, faster in the pulse, and lower in the temperature. The grandfather stepped forward. His vitals were closer to the man's.

Now both the green girl and the bald woman wanted to have the magic done to them. By the time the Sailor was finished with them, a line was forming. They quickly developed a database.

The kid was sick. Blood pressure was low. Temperature was high, and the pulse was low and thready.

Then the real excitement started. Kris easily caught the sonic boom of the lander coming in. Its jets were loud enough to be heard as it made its approach. The locals seemed a bit concerned, but none flinched. Two or three made signs with their fingers, no doubt to ward off evil.

The real fun came a few minutes after the shuttle landed. A chopper with the *Wasp*'s markings was clearly visible as it went in to hover over the stream.

Also clearly visible was the doc being lowered on the hoist. There were four more hoist lowerings, but Doc Meade was already being led up the incline to the overhang by Gunny before the last one was done.

"This place is a septic mess," she said as she put on gloves. "Is there any chance we can move the patient?"

"I don't think so," Kris said, eyeing all the sharpened stones around them.

The doc had not taken time to don any battle armor. No doubt she did not wear spider-silk underwear.

"I figured as much, but I had to ask. Let's see that leg. Ouch," she said as the Marine corpsman lifted the fur.

"Okay, enough of that. Where's my first package?"

Two Marines hustled up the incline with an oversize duffel bag between them. Kris and Jack unzipped it.

It came close to having a full surgical suite inside. Even one of Abby's magical steamer trunks never had this thorough a medical treatment center.

"Get this under the kid," the doc said, pulling out and unfolding a backboard. Kris and Jack slipped it under the child as Jacques told the parents to remove the rest of the furs.

As they did, Kris discovered that the backboard was more

like a table. As Gunny spread the table's legs out, Kris and Jack took the opportunity to move the child forward, out of the cave and into the light.

Doc Meade got her first good look at the kid.

"That's not good."

"Can you help him?" Kris asked.

"I wouldn't have come if I didn't think I could. Where's my next duffel?"

It arrived as she asked for it.

"Rig that UV field. There's enough nasties to keep a pharmacy firm busy for a century, but this ought to kill them," she said, as the two medics rigged what looked like nothing worse than lights at either end of the table.

"Now, everyone, stand back," she ordered with a sweep of her gloved hand that included everyone. "You, medic, get me a gown from the first box."

In a moment, the doc looked ready to try her hand at her profession. She rolled the child over on his stomach and set about abrading the wound. "No use trying to kill all the bad stuff if you've got more of it waiting in line to dive into your blood stream, now is it, young man?"

Beside Kris, the old man eyed the process. Jacques now stood beside him, trying to put into words what was happening. The bald woman stood on tiptoes behind the old man, watching over his shoulder intently.

"Sky God magic?" Nelly translated for Kris.

~Sky people's craft. Like a hunter finds food. A maker makes a bow,~ Jacques supplied.

~Craft?~ both the old man and woman said.

~Craft,~ Kris repeated.

They all watched as dried blood and pus were washed from the wound. Kris and Jack both had hands out when the doc cut into flesh to get at more of the infection. They'd been warned when the medic, now gowned, stepped in and applied a general anesthetic to the boy. It looked like he just fell asleep to those watching with untrained eyes.

Kris knew better. And caught the parents and grandparents when they would have ruined all that work.

~Craft. You want the boy to hunt with you again?~

Both parents and grandparents nodded.

The cutting done, the blood and pus suctioned up . . . and yes, the blood was red, Kris noted . . . the doctor cleaned out the infection and started sewing up the wound.

The two local women made sewing motions with their hands and stared hard at first the doctor's, then their own hands.

Kris nodded.

"Now comes the good part," Dr. Meade said. "I was studying some blood samples taken yesterday. That was a tragedy, but maybe not a waste as well. Their blood is kind of like ours, only totally different. Don't laugh. They have something like our T-cells, just different, but there was one thing that I tested on them that had a surprising effect. Something we got from an out-of-the-way place called Pandemonium."

The doctor raised an eyebrow over a smile suddenly gone pixie. "I understand you were there once, Admiral."

"For my many sins, yes," Kris agreed.

"Well, they grow something there that seems to swing both ways. The infection fighters in our bloodstream like it and, if I'm right, so will this little fellow's. All we can do is try it and see if I'm guessing right."

The doctor located a long needle, filled it and then started feeling around the heart. Kris and Jack got ready to stop a charge, but the natives seemed mesmerized by the doctor's skills. They watched as she inserted it, then emptied the hypodermic needle.

Finished, the doctor turned to Kris. "Is there any chance we can remove the patient to the *Wasp*?"

Kris turned to Jacques. "Okay, mouthpiece for Sky Gods, work a miracle."

"Do you mind taking all these folks up for a show-and-tell?" Jacques asked.

Kris turned to Jack.

"Only if they leave the sharp stuff behind," he insisted.

"That's not going to happen with the bald woman," Jacques said. "I think that's her totem."

"And the guy likes his club," Jack said with a sigh. "Okay. Invite as many as want to come with us. However, Captain Drago is going to demand a bath from all of them."

"I think we can get them to splash around in the nearest pond," Jacques said.

"Ah, Doc," Kris asked. "Do you have some mild sedatives that we could inconspicuously slip them?"

"I have some patches we should be able to get them all to wear for the ride up into the sky," she allowed.

And so it came to pass that Kris got to talk to a whole lot more of the BEMs than she'd ever expected and got a whole lot more than she'd ever bargained for.

27

"You did *what*?" was Captain Drago's immediate reaction when Kris told him the *Wasp* now had some new passengers.

"They followed me home," Kris said, doing her very best to look innocent.

Innocent was not something Longknifes did well. It didn't fit the legend.

"The last time something 'followed' you home, I ended up with three hundred thousand tons of bug-eyed-monster warship for the *Wasp*'s hood ornament."

"These are much lighter, only twenty rather underfed natives from the West Continent."

"Are they filthy?"

"The Marines have rigged showers in the drop bay and everyone down there is going through full decontamination," Kris said, pulling at her still-wet hair. She'd gone through decontamination in her armor, but since she hadn't worn a helmet, her face had lost a couple of layers of skin, and her hair was extraclean, too.

"What do you expect to get from this little visit? I assume it's a visit. Or do you intend to take these people all the way home with you?"

"I don't know, Captain. I'm making this up as I go along," Kris admitted.

"Well, let me know when you find out. By the way, should I be expecting guests in the wardroom?"

Kris had the good sense to flinch at that question. The ship's china, silverware, and linens would, no doubt, suffer greatly from an effort to explain table manners to these hunter-gathers.

"I think we can set up some sort of chow line in the drop bay," Kris said.

"That sounds like a very good idea. See if you can keep your new best friends out of my hair. I'm not nearly as patient as you've been misled to believe."

"No doubt," Kris said, and headed for her quarters to change out of her battle gear and into a clean set of khakis. She could have done it in the drop bay, but she wasn't sure if the natives fully understood that she was female and didn't want them to make a discovery they weren't prepared for.

She returned to the drop bay to find that Gunny had arranged something very close to a campfire, at least it threw a cheerful glow and warmth over the immediate area around it. Most of the locals were gathered around it, seated on wool blankets that several of them were still examining.

Jacques was trying to explain how and where you might locate wool, then pull it into thread and weave it into blankets. Kris hoped he wasn't starting something that would get these folks' great-to-the-nth-degree-grandkids lased by the angry Sky Gods.

Then again, by the time those putative grandchildren were born, Kris would either have won her war or lost it . . . and a whole lot of grandkids would not be born.

Kris tried not to scowl at that thought as she walked toward where Jack was standing with the parents and grandparents of the sick boy. A few feet away, the child was still laid out on a bed in a clean surgical bubble under the watchful eye of Dr. Meade and several assisting medical personnel.

"How's the kid doing?" Kris asked.

Jack didn't look away from the boy. "The temperature is down a bit, but not broken. Blood pressure is climbing, but still bad. Pulse is improving."

"So we're on the right track," Kris said.

"But we're not out of the woods," Doc Meade said, looking up at Kris. "I don't know how this infection will take to what we're fighting it with. If the crazy system these folks have adapts and fights back, we could still lose. I've got half the chemists and docs in the squadron looking at this. If we can, we'll beat it. But I won't take any bets just yet."

"There has to be some survival benefits to the extra DNA these folks have. It must make some proteins that help them survive," Kris said.

"Look at that planet," the doctor said. "Is it overpopulated?"

"No," Kris admitted.

"Then you tell me what the extra proteins they make are good for. Meanwhile, I'll need a couple of years to finish our analysis."

Kris chewed the bottom of her lip. "Maybe it makes them good, obedient slaves."

"You said it, not me," the doctor said, and turned back to her patient.

The locals had stood quietly while all this conversation in a strange tongue went on around them. Now they turned to Kris and Jack with questions in their eyes.

~Will my son run to the hunt with me?~ the father asked.

~The hunt for what makes him pale and warm still runs,~ Nelly said for Kris.

The natives seemed too overwhelmed by all the new and strange to react to Kris's having two voices, one from her mouth, and one from her collarbone. They just nodded dumbly and kept the vigil, waiting to see if the boy would, indeed, go down into the earth.

With Kris back, Jack was relieved to go through decontamination and change out of his battle gear. As he undid the top half if his armor, the old man and the bald woman came over. She knocked on the armor, then touched Jack's shoulder.

~I told you,~ the man said. ~They are not like the demons of your songs from your grandmother's time and her grandmother. These ones can take off their thick hide. They are soft inside.~

~The stories sing of the demons who were soft inside, once you stuck a spear in them,~ the woman said.

Jack offered his armor for her totem. She rapped it so that the stone blades hit it. Then she hit it harder. Several stone points shattered.

~There are many different people who walk the stars,~ Kris had Nelly say. ~We are not the ones sung of in your stories.~

~Do you walk the stars?~ the bald woman said, glancing around the drop bay. Kris realized that there were no windows in the longboats. No windows in the *Wasp*. These people had gone from their own open sky to a series of rooms. Caves, if you would.

KRIS, I MIGHT BE ABLE TO DO SOMETHING ABOUT THIS. MIMZY, CAN YOU HELP ME?

YES, MOM.

Kris suddenly found her head very empty. WHAT ARE YOU UP TO? she asked, but got no answer.

A minute later, Penny galloped into the drop bay, spotted Kris, and raced for her.

"What have you got Mimzy up to?"

"Nothing, it's Nelly's doing."

But neither computer answered, so Kris and Penny were left exchanging strange looks.

"Don't worry," Sal said from Jack's collarbone. "It's gonna be a surprise. I think you'll like it. Oh, look over there!"

At the end of the drop bay, a hatch suddenly formed.

"That went better than I'd expected," Nelly said. "Now, if you will kindly take our visitors through that hatch, I think we can end any question about us being Sky Gods, or whatever."

Jack quickly finished buttoning his khakis and led the way for Kris, Penny, and the two older natives. He opened the hatch. There was a small room inside with another hatch.

"Everybody in," Nelly said.

"Tell me, Alice, how was it down the rabbit hole?" Penny quipped, leading the way as she stepped across the hatch coaming.

They crowded into the room, the natives a bit less enthusiastic than the spacers. Jack dogged down the first hatch, and Penny opened the next. She took a glance out.

"Oh. My. God," was likely a real prayer from Penny. "Kris, you've got to see this," she said, and stepped through the hatch.

Kris could already see what lay ahead.

For years, Kris had been in space, but she'd always had a ship securely around her. She's seen the space ahead of them, and aft, via radar sweeps and cameras projected on screens. She'd never seen space up close and personal.

Now she did.

"Clear Smart Metal, Nelly?" Kris asked.

"Yes, Kris."

"You said you couldn't make clear Smart Metal yesterday for the woman in the brig."

"Yes, Kris. I did. I would have had to risk converting metal all the way through the ship, including the hull. I didn't do this today. Those two hatches are hull-type Smart Metal. This clear metal is borrowed from inside. There is no risk to the ship."

"And to us?" Jack asked, now joining the two women.

"There is some risk, but not much more than when you're in the Forward Lounge, and I start moving walls, tables, and chairs around."

Kris listened to Nelly with her ears, but her eyes were staring at a sight that made her mouth gape. Here was space at its barest. Tiny dots pierced the black. Kris would have sworn that she could make out the slight difference between pure white and yellow, red, and maybe even brown stars.

Closer in, the other ships of her squadron swung at anchor. The *Wasp* sprawled out to her right and left, and beyond the *Wasp* swung the *Royal*, anchored to her by a long pole. Now the *Wasp* swung down and Kris got her first overwhelming view of a life-draped planet.

If it were possible, her mouth would have fallen open even more.

"Yes," she whispered, "I've got to see this."

"Good heavens," Jack said over and over again.

Behind them, the bearded man slipped his head out the hatch. His eyes narrowed. ~What do I see?~ he demanded gruffly.

~This is what is above the sky,~ Nelly said. ~This is where those who walk the stars live.~

The bald woman stuck her head out, looked, and scowled. Then she shoved the man over and looked off at the other side. The *Wasp* swung around more, and now the moon was coming up.

This planet, like Old Earth, had one large moon. The woman looked hard at it and gulped. ~The moon shows her face full.~

Now the man followed her gaze, then twisted around to catch a view of the planet beneath them. Puzzlement showed strong on his face.

"Captain Drago," Kris said.

"More trouble?"

"No, but could you arrange to discharge one of the aft lasers into the ocean next time we're back to the planet?"

"A demonstration of Sky God fire, huh?"

"Something like that."

"Wait one. Actually, wait fifteen seconds."

Kris pointed aft as the moon disappeared and the planet came in full view below. They were over the narrow ocean between West and East Continents. There was a jet of reaction mass aft, then one bright laser beam reached through it and down.

Below them, the ocean steamed and roiled. Clouds rose and churned.

~We can burn the water and the earth,~ Kris said. ~We do not.~

~You do not,~ the man repeated several times, total puzzlement on his face.

~Can you sing for us the old songs?~ Kris asked.

~Yes, I can,~ the bald woman said. ~Let me feast my eyes on what I have never seen.~

~I can wait,~ Kris said.

In hushed awe, all of them feasted their eyes on space, and moon, and a blue-green planet. After a long time had passed, Jack reopened the hatch and, one by one, they walked, eyes looking back at the sights they'd seen, into the cave of the *Wasp*'s drop bay.

28

~The People lived in peace and harmony,~ the bald woman sang.

~The People fished and hunted in peace and harmony.

~Then the hard demons came, and there was no peace and harmony.~

The woman moved around the fire. Sometimes she'd pound the butt of her totem hard on the deck. Other times, she'd wave it high over her head. Not for a moment did she stop moving, stop waving the stick passed down from grandmother to grandmother.

The others sat around the "fire" in the *Wasp*'s drop bay. The bald woman's song went long, and had a lot of repetitions in it; how else would it have survived unchanged for so many years? There was also a lot missing. Kris spotted nothing about genetic manipulation, but that didn't surprise her. The song had the basic facts down.

The hard demons had come. They had conquered and enslaved the People, and the People had wept bitter and bloody tears. In time, the hard demons made the mistake of getting soft, or maybe they just got sloppy. The People rose up and slaughtered the demons, they took from them the power to walk the stars, and they then took their wrath and vengeance across the stars to where the soft demons lived.

The story got very gory at that point. It went into great detail on just how they disemboweled this one and chopped that one's head off. ~Infants' heads, they smashed against the stone,~ was one that particularly sent shivers down Kris's spine, but the listening natives seemed to like that particular verse.

It was repeated many times, and they pounded their fists on the deck each time.

Jack held Kris closer when that happened.

The important part, the part that made listening to the gory tale worth it, came near the end. The warrior tribes that walked the stars met with the tribes that had not gone on the walk to the other world. Some were for walking the stars forever so that this could never happen again to them. Others were for taking their torn world and returning to the way it had been before.

There were many angry words. In the end, the two went their separate ways. But the anger of the Sky Gods still spilled on any who walked away from ~the ways from of old~ and tried to build a path that could lead back to the stars.

~We must walk the path of our grandmothers and their grandmothers.

~We must hunt along the path of our grandfathers and their grandfathers.

~You stray from the path and you will burn.~

The bald woman came suddenly to a halt. She spat those words at the bearded man.

~So, my man, what path will you have the people walk now?~

It appeared that Kris had guessed the family relationship right. Which only left her wondering if any old married couples were ever still happy?

She filed that away in "to be determined later," and tried to figure out what to say next.

But the old man was already coming to his feet. When he spoke, it wasn't to the woman but to all those around the fire.

~Our wisewoman speaks wisdom, as she does from of old. I would chose to walk the different path we set our feet to today.~

He paused, folded his hands across his chest, and went on. ~I do not see that we have walked it so far that we cannot walk back. If that is the way for you, walk it, and I will cheer you. I have seen the stars, and the logs these people ride in to float between the stars. My son's son lives because of the craft they have to hunt for a lad's smile. If these different star gods will have me, I will walk with them.~

"I didn't see that coming," Jack whispered to Kris.

"I expect there are a lot of surprises coming from these people," Kris answered.

~Our son's son still lingers at the hole down into the earth,~ the old woman jumped in, reminding any who might have forgotten the child sleeping fitfully in the medical-quarantine tent.

~Yes, and I do not know what tomorrow's sun will shine on,~ the grandfather agreed. ~Still, having fed your eyes on what we ate today, would you not follow this path?~

~It is not the path of my grandmother and her grandmother.~

~No. There is more to eat here,~ he said. The deck of the shuttle was littered with the leavings from the strange feast the Marines had provided.

~Are you sure they are not demons?~ the old woman demanded. ~Different from the hard-skinned demons~——her eyes picked out dark-skinned Gunny Brown where he sat cross-legged by the "fire"——but demons just the same?~

The friendly alien leader drew his flint knife and raked its blade across his forearm. Red blood flowed.

Both of the aliens, old man with a bleeding arm and the wisewoman with all the accusations, looked at Jack.

Jack stepped forward and offered his arm. The man cut it. Red blood flowed.

Gunny had seen the look the woman threw in his direction. He might not have understood the words, but he read the glare perfectly. He rose from his place and came to offer his black arm to the knife.

Again, the flint blade cut flesh. Again, the blood dripping onto the deck was red.

~I will not speak for you,~ the old alien man said. ~I will speak for me. I will follow after these people. Where they walk, I will walk. Their people will be my people. Their enemies will be my enemies. This I say by soil and water. This I say by sun and moon. Let me live and die by these words.~

Kris, I think Gunny's got a new recruit, Jack said on Nelly Net.

I doubt there is a stronger oath these people can swear, Jacques added.

What comes next? Kris asked.

I think we wait and see, was all Jacques could say.

Two local men rose from their places and came to stand beside their leader. One of them was the boy's father. A couple of women did, too, but not his mother. For a long minute, nothing more happened, then a couple of more men stood up but didn't move to join the three.

Over the next couple of minutes more joined one group or the other. The bald woman moved from her husband's side to where the other group stood.

"I don't like the looks of this," Kris said.

"Do you think it's as bad as it seems?" Jack asked.

"I think," Jacques said slowly, eyeing both groups, "the admiral has the shape of things. How many of them brought their knives?"

"Ah, most of them," Gunny said. "General, you want me to put an end to this?"

"No, I will," Kris said, and stepped between the two apparently rival groups.

~You came to my ship in peace and harmony. I will have nothing else on my ship. In peace and harmony, you may leave it.~

~We came as one to your ship. We will leave as one,~ the bald woman spat.

~We are no longer one. I will not leave, I have sworn it,~ her husband spat.

~The men will carry your bloodless body home from this hunt,~ she spat right back. The look on her face was tinged with eagerness.

~Nobody will bleed out their lifeblood on my ship,~ Kris said.

The old woman raised her staff and ran at Kris, swinging it down hard.

Kris had kept on her spider-silk underarmor, something she didn't normally do aboard ship, but then, she didn't normally invite armed natives home for dinner either.

Armored or not, Kris didn't like the look of that staff, but the blow was easily sidestepped. Gunny would be proud of her use of her hand-to-hand training.

Or not.

As Kris stepped in to strike a blow at the old woman's abdomen, the alien flung herself down and rolled under Kris's strike.

Recovering, she rolled back onto her feet and brought the stick up, ready to swing it again.

Jack stepped forward. ~Enough of this,~ he shouted.

~No, Jack. Wait.~

Kris backed away from the woman. ~Must all of you fight to choose the path for all of you?~

~That is the way of it from days of old,~ the bearded man said. ~We fight until one side yields or dies.~

AND WITH THE OATH HE SWORE, IT'S TO THE DEATH FOR HIM, Jacques provided on Nelly Net.

BEFORE YOU OPEN YOUR GREAT BIG MOUTH AGAIN, MY DEAR, ARE YOU WEARING YOUR SPIDER SILKS? Jack asked.

YOU BET, Kris answered.

OKAY. YOU'RE A BIG GIRL. DON'T GET YOUR THROAT SLIT.

~I am not from the days of old. I am from the stars,~ Kris said. ~We fight not for what the sunset saw but for what the sunrise will see. I say to all. Let her fight me for your path.~

That got a discussion going among them. It was apparent to all that the odds were pretty even if they all went at each other. It would be a long and bloody fight. Kris wondered how many families were split like the sick child's mother and father. Did they really want to go at each other with stone knives?

The words flew fast and furious. Fists were shaken. For a while, Kris feared the two sides were going to split again into two different ones? Or into four camps?

Kris took the debating time to catch Gunny's eye. "Bring me my totem stick."

He grinned and brought her a puggle stick from the locker where the Marines stored their "playthings."

The sight of a Sky God with a stick of her own might have gone a long way to settling the matter. Kris got the feeling that a lot of the natives wanted to see a fight between their wise-woman with her flint-armed totem and this strange brightly colored totem of the star walkers.

Finally, the graybeard stepped forward. ~We will do it after your way.~

The bald woman spat at him. ~You're heart is blinded by a will you cannot surrender yourself to.~

~My heart turns its back on that will,~ he said, and turned his back on his wife.

The woman screamed and would have beaned him with her

stick if Kris hadn't gotten her puggle stick in between her rage and his head.

And took advantage of the woman's blind rage to get a backhanded blow in that knocked the wind out of her.

The woman backed away from Kris.

Kris chose not to push her advantage. While her puggle stick was nicely padded, it had a major disadvantage over the woman's stick. The bald woman could turn her stick into a long club. Kris's stick was intended for thrust and parry in close.

This would not be a one-sided fight.

As Kris expected, once the woman caught her breath, she roared her anger, let the stick slip through her hand until she held it by the very bottom, and tried to club Kris over the head.

Kris sidestepped, angled her own stick to take the blow, and slide it down to the deck. Kris then stomped her shoe down on the club, careful of the sharp flint flakes, and almost knocked the stick from the woman's grasp.

But the short woman used her diminutive size to drop to the deck and roll, thereby rolling the totem out from under Kris's shoe.

"Ah, thank heavens for good Marine boots," Kris said, and danced away before the woman could recover and take another swing.

"Good going, Admiral," Gunny called. "You almost took it away from her."

"If I get her stick, do I get to lead her clan?" Kris called to Jacques.

"Your guess is as good as mine," the anthropologist answered.

The two women circled each other. The circle started wide, then got smaller.

The woman did what Kris expected. She charged Kris, holding the stick at its middle. She tried one quick hit at Kris's head, then swiftly swung the other end low for Kris's knees.

This kind of fighting was what Kris's puggle stick was designed for. Kris parried both, easily, then took over the lead, going for the woman's bald head, then her middle, then head again and middle, in rapid succession.

The woman struggled to keep up, but quickly fell behind. She lacked a modern diet and hours of practice at this. Kris crowded in, pushing from the middle as well as with the ends.

The woman fell back, but this time Kris pursued. Once, the woman landed a blow to Kris's shoulder with her sharp flints, but Kris's spider silks blunted it. Now Kris was landing blows. Hers were well padded. The Corps wanted its solders aggressive and well trained, not banged around and in the hospital.

Still, the woman felt the sting of the hits on her bare skin.

She also felt the sting as the crowd's roar went up for Kris.

Kris finally got in a strong shove, and the woman sprawled backward. Her grip slipped on her totem, and it flew out of her hands.

Kris stood over her. ~Do you yield?~

The woman pointed at Kris. ~I hit her shoulder. The points did not cut her. She is a thick-skinned demon!~

The drop bay was dead quiet in a second.

OH, OH, came from Jacques.

HOLD ON BEFORE ANYBODY PANICS, Kris answered.

She dropped her puggle stick and went to the gray-bearded man. ~Do you have your knife?~

He produced it.

~Cut my finger,~ Kris said, offering her thumb.

~Cut her shoulder,~ the woman on the deck demanded.

That would not work. Unless . . .

Kris unbuttoned her khaki shirt, and slipped out of it. For what she had in mind, she'd have to ditch her pants.

~She is a woman!~ seemed to come as a universal surprise.

~As is your wisewoman,~ Kris said, and began to skinny out of her spider silks. When her second skin lay on the deck, she offered the old man her shoulder.

~Cut me here.~

He did. Maybe more than he needed to. She bled.

Kris wiped her hand in her own blood and held it up for all see. ~I bleed red just like you. The skin I wear that turns back a spear point is the craft of our makers. This is the path I walk with my soft skin. I open that path to you. Follow me or get off my ship,~ Kris said, and turned away.

Jack met her with a blanket.

Dr. Meade was also there to slap on a bandage. "I better take care of that. It could leave a nasty scar."

Kris headed for the medical center, where the boy was still fighting his battle with man's oldest enemy. Before she moved into the antiseptic field, the graybeard came up to her.

~Where you go, we will follow. All of us.~

~Good.~ The fight was worth the blood.

29

Kris woke up the next morning, hurting in a lot more places than her shoulder.

Jack put an arm over her.

"Ouch. Be careful."

"I avoided your cut."

"That little woman was packing a lot of wallop in her hits. I don't think the spider silk is quite calibrated to handle blunt-force trauma."

"It serves you right for trying to be the hero. Single combat to resolve all our differences? I thought that was just a guy thing."

"You enjoy watching two cute chicks going at it?" Kris shot back. With a grin.

"That mean old biddy is not a cute chick. And you, my love, are never cute. And never, ever, a chick."

"I'm not?" Kris's grin was long gone.

"No. You are lovely, drop-dead gorgeous, a stunning beauty, but cute is for our little daughter. And as for a chick. You are an admiral, viceroy, and most fighting captain in the king's Navy. Chicks are for young things that don't have any experience under their belts."

Kris made a face at him. "I'll give you a 3.9 out of 4 for recovery on that one."

"Would you like to do something before we shower?" Jack asked.

"Love, I'd love to do something before we shower but I have a bad feeling that if I try, I'll have a whole lot of bad feelings."

"Where are the painkillers?" Jack asked.

Sal told him, and Jack headed for the bathroom to return with two white tablets.

"You don't mind a rain check, do you?"

"I've got the shower changing into a nice warm tub of water for us to soak your aches and pains in," Jack said. "Ain't the Smart Metal app wonderful?"

They arrived for breakfast late, just as the wardroom was emptying of Navy and filling with scientists. Captain Drago was filling a cup of coffee to take with him, but he dropped into the chair across from Kris. Once again, Jack was getting her chow.

"That was quite a fight you put up," the skipper said with a broad grin.

"You watched?"

"The drop bay is on the surveillance-camera system. I think the whole crew watched."

"All of it?" Kris asked with a raised eyebrow.

"Right up to the where you started your striptease. Then I killed the feed. How did it turn out?"

"I've got a cut on my shoulder that bled very freely and very red. We now have twenty new recruits."

"Hmm," he said, and sipped his coffee thoughtfully. "How do you think they'll take it when they find out that we're at war with their Sky Gods or whatever they call the star walkers?"

"A good question. I guess we'll find out soon enough."

"Before we break orbit?"

"No. We need to educate these folks a lot more before we take them that far."

"And after we've educated them, what if they want to switch sides?"

"I'll blow up that bridge when I come to it."

"Spoken like a true Longknife. By the way, how is that kid coming along? The sick one that started all this?"

"I'm waiting to hear from Doc Meade," Kris said.

"Speak of a walking miracle and who walks in," Drago said. "Good Morning, Doctor."

"Yes, it is. I'm finally going to get some sleep."

Kris turned to see a very exhausted woman stumbling toward the coffee urn.

"How is the young boy?"

"On the mend," she said. "Otherwise, I would not see any prospects for sleep. His fever broke two hours ago. His other vitals are back in what is the normal range for these folks. I had him on double the dosage we tested on human kids of his weight, and that's what it took to beat this. Those extra proteins must be doing something for them, but what it is, I have no idea."

"So they're a mystery to us," Kris said.

"But becoming less of a mystery by the minute. I think you'll find very interesting some news I was just told."

The skipper made to leave.

"Hang around a bit. I think you'll enjoy this bit of rumor."

Captain Drago sat back down.

"One of my associates finished an autopsy on the woman who killed herself yesterday. No, day before yesterday. My hours are all messed up. Anyway, they are maddening. Very like us, but not, you know."

"No I don't, but I'm listening," Kris said. Her body hurt, and she was hungry. Maybe she was a bit cranky.

"Their brain is so much like ours, but different," the doc said. "So very different in some major ways and a lot of minor ways. I'll keep this simple. There's this part of the human brain where we think resides the ability to see yourself as part of something larger. Some people call it the 'God Part' of the brain."

"I've heard of it," Captain Drago said.

"Well, we found a portion of that woman's brain that's atrophied. Not used at all, and if I'm guessing right, I think it's the part of their brain that does that."

Kris puzzled that over for a few moments. "Could that be why what we see down dirtside is a lot of small groups?"

"With a strange lack of any concept of something bigger than themselves," Doc Meade said. "Yes, they talk of the Sky Gods, but I don't think they think of them the way traditional humans think of their God."

"Their creation story even had their Sky 'Gods' as just like them until they chose to walk the stars," Captain Drago said.

"You listened to the song?" Kris asked.

"No, I found it long and boring, but I did get Dr. la Duke's executive summary. Did our researchers find any hint of a divine something down there?"

"It was conspicuous by its absence," Kris said. "Even when

looking at the potential death of her grandson, the woman with the stick could only talk about a 'will' that meant he must go down into the ground."

"Nothing but fatalism, huh," the skipper said. "What does that mean for us and the spacefaring raiders?"

Kris frowned and turned to the doctor.

"Ever hear," Doc Meade said, "of a line that went, 'All people are endowed by their creator with certain inalienable rights: the right to life, liberty, and the pursuit of happiness'?"

"Father says it regularly," Kris said, "although I think the original was 'all men were created equal.' "

"I got it from my mom," the doctor said, "whichever way it went, it says basically the same thing. People have the right to throw off a tyrant. It's our God-given right. Now subtract God from that equation. Where do your basic human rights come from?"

"I know plenty of atheists who would take offense at that," Captain Drago said.

"Sorry, I didn't mean to start a fight, but where do you get the right to freedom if the powerful have their boot on your neck, like that woman who killed herself? If there is no sense of something greater, beyond just us, some higher moral good, what have you got?"

"Ten thousand years of slavery before the folks from that planet below rose up in a killing rage," Captain Drago said.

"And a hundred thousand years of zooming around the galaxy," Kris said, "flattening anything that might become a threat to you, while everyone follows the 'Enlightened One' because he's the enlightened one and has the Black Hats to throw you out on your ass if you don't follow orders."

"A horrible thought," Doc Meade said.

"Any suggestion as to how we reactivate the 'God Part' of the aliens' brains?" Kris asked.

"I'd like to convert this hypothesis to something closer to a theory, Admiral. I plan to run the little boy through a battery of tests today. Among the ones he needs, I'm going to slip in a full brain scan. After that, I intend to ask for volunteers for more tests. I've got legitimate reasons to build up a medical database for them. If they get injured or sick, I'll need it to know what to do for them."

"Do it, Doctor," Kris said. "I never thought I'd be contemplating biological warfare through genetic manipulation, but it sure beats the idea of having to slaughter every last one of them."

"And how do you propose to get close enough to them to apply this biological warfare?" Captain Drago asked.

"First, she confirms her theory, then I'll drop the problem in the lap of my flag captain," Kris said with a wicked grin.

Drago stood up. "Jack, you better feed this woman. She's evil when she's hungry."

"She's evil when she's fed," Jack said.

"She's a Longknife," the doctor said. "They are born evil."

"Thank you, thank you, thank you," Kris said, reaching for a bran muffin. "You say the nicest things to me."

30

Kris was careful what she did that day. Despite the pain-killers, she hurt. She checked on the retrieval of the scientific teams. More sensor pods had been knocked together and Sailors trained on them.

There were no more surprises.

Indeed, no one tried to surprise them.

The testing of the young boy, now well on the mend, caused no problems with his parents. Indeed, they wanted to be tested just like him. When Kris asked how the testing was going, the doctor who had replaced Doc Meade while she got some well-earned rest suggested the admiral look over someone else's shoulder.

"You tend to your knitting, Admiral, and we'll tend to knitting bones and muscles."

Kris asked Nelly's help to locate Jacques, and found him and Amanda combing through a huge list of research results, hunting for any reference to something like a divine being. So far, all it yielded was null data.

"You think Doc Meade is onto something?" Kris asked.

"We'll know when we have more data," the anthropologist said, giving Kris an answer she very definitely did not want to hear.

Kris headed back for the drop bay. She avoided the people standing around the med center, waiting to be tested, and edged over to the hatch that led out into darkness.

There she found the bald woman, sitting cross-legged, staring at the moon.

"Nelly, could you make us a bench?"

One rose from the deck.

~You only say a word, and even the ground does your will.~

~It is a craft,~ Kris said. ~We have the craft to make all that you see. We can change it.~

~You do not make all that I see. Not the moon. Not . . .~ Here she paused, and glanced at the planet below. ~Is that what was beneath my feet all the days of my life?~

~We are very far away. That makes it small.~

~As when my husband walks to me from out on the great prairie. Far off, he is no bigger than the ant at my feet. He gets closer and grows.~

~But he is always the same.~

~Is he?~

Kris measured all the potential questions in those two words and didn't try to answer any of them.

A longboat dropped away from the *Royal* above the *Wasp*. The old woman watched it intently. Another was on approach for the *Wasp*.

~Men, in them, like a cave that flies like a bird.~

Kris nodded.

~But not.~

~Yes, but not,~ Kris agreed.

~What heart beats in your chest?~

~One like yours,~ Kris said, bringing her hand up to her chest, then pointing to the woman's. ~My blood is red.~

~Your blood is red,~ the woman agreed. ~The men, down there. What do they hunt?~

Unfortunately, in their tongue, "what" was not a word, but an inflection of hunt. Kris could find no way to answer that. NELLY?

I'M STUMPED, TOO, KRIS.

HOW ABOUT THAT, THESE PRIMITIVES STUMPED A COMPUTER.

KRIS, THAT'S NOT FAIR.

SORRY, NELLY, NO IT ISN'T. IT'S JUST FRUSTRATING ME.

~We hunt to see what we see. Why do men walk over a mountain?~ Kris tried.

~Men do not walk over a mountain. Other men live over the mountain. Men with clubs.~

~So we hide and look from between the leaves.~

The woman sniffed. ~You hide like little baby. We saw you. If you had taken one fish, one animal, we would have hit your head so hard.~

~So we ate our own food. You like our own food?~

~It taste strange. My stomach.~ She rubbed it. ~No tree to go behind. Your ground strange.~

Kris bet the *Wasp*'s deck, and, no doubt, its Sailors were none too happy if these natives were using it for a latrine.

NELLY, HAS ANYONE SHOWN ONE OF THEM HOW TO USE THE HEAD?

GUNNY TRIED TO GET IT ACROSS TO THE OLD MAN. HE THOUGHT IT WAS A JOKE. GUNNY IS STILL WORKING ON IT.

Another point for failure and potential conflict. What had Kris gotten herself into?

Be careful what you wish for. You may get it.

Kris tried another track. ~Your son's son will hunt again.~

~Yes,~ the woman said, shaking her head. ~What will he hunt?~

~There is much to see among the stars,~ Kris offered.

~Our mothers of old chose our path long ago. We chose not to walk the stars.~ Now she was nodding up and down. ~The stars were not meant for our feet.~

~I hope your heart will be gladdened by what you see among the stars,~ Kris said.

She left the woman nodding at the stars.

NELLY, COULD YOU GET A CAMERA SET UP TO FOLLOW WHEREVER THAT WOMAN GOES? I THINK WE MAY NEED A BETTER SUICIDE WATCH THAN THE LAST ONE WE HAD.

I'LL SET UP THE CAMERA AND WATCH IT MYSELF, KRIS.

GOOD.

Kris found that she had done just about all that she could for the moment. Maybe it was true that officers were superfluous to a Navy run well by its chiefs. She'd given all the orders she needed. She'd read just about all the reports she could stand, and everything was humming along smoothly.

She had Nelly check with Sal on what Jack was doing.

And found out that Jack did, indeed have a job. He was checking out each landing team to make sure it had the right equipment. Neither he nor Gunny intended to have another team ambushed. He was also making sure that there were always Marines in the drop bay. The natives might be little and have only stone knives, but he wasn't about to lose the *Wasp* to them running amuck.

Indeed, everyone was busy except their boss. Kris considered sticking her nose in where it wasn't wanted or needed. However, she'd read about bosses who were like that and sworn she'd never be like them. She had expected to have some more fun as a junior officer before being locked away in Admiral Country. However, Longknifes never did it the right way.

"Nelly, draw me a warm bath. I could use another soak."

"That sounds like a very good idea, Kris."

31

The next day, Kris made a trip down to see the pyramid one last time. The pit had been filled in. A 12mm laser anti-aircraft rifle had been applied to the door mechanism.

"That puppy will never work again," Gunny assured Kris. However, the work had been done very judiciously. There were only three 12mm holes drilled into the rock.

What Kris most wanted to see was the stone that now stood filling half the doorway. Tall and well polished on the side that faced out, it had lettering derived from the walls inside behind each of the glass-enclosed figures.

Jacques translated for Kris. "The top phrase says, 'We came. We looked upon your work. What we see of your false enlightenment disgusts us.' We used the plural because they seemed to almost always use the singular."

"The enlightened *one* kind of thing."

"Yes, the 'your false enlightenment' is singular. That will fit the bill perfectly."

"I think you're right. We function as people. He is just one man. If that doesn't scare them, it sure ought to confuse them."

"Unless they have no respect for people acting as a group," Penny said.

"The word must be getting around that you underestimate us at your risk," Jack said, dryly.

Both Penny and Jacques shrugged.

"They look pretty sunk in their own ways," Jacques said.

"But you did it this way," Kris said. "And the lower phrase?"

"We used the simple syllogism you suggested. 'No hunt us, you will have peace and harmony.' We liked that line from the creation song last night, and they'd used something like that for the condition they left the dead worlds in. We'll see how they like that offered to them. The second part goes, 'Hunt us and we will flood this place with your blood and bury it under your heads.' "

"I don't think you could make the point any stronger," Kris said.

"Win, lose, or draw, I think this is the best way to confront them," Jacques said.

"I agree," Her Highness, Vice Admiral Kris Longknife said, with finality. "Now, if you'll give me a moment, I'd like to walk through this chamber of horrors one last time. Jacques, you said the top line behind each victim's coffin was numbers. I think you said they might be positions on a star chart. Have you had any luck matching them to our map?"

"We have one match, the one you found on your long scout. Unfortunately, one point is kind of hard to use to fix a chart that is undefined to us."

"I hate to think that finding more murdered worlds might help us."

They came to the huge chamber and fell silent. Kris again faced the family. Now, knowing what she knew of what they'd likely done to this planet, she felt less sympathy. They might have earned their place here. The ones who deserved her sympathy were the others, murdered with no warning and no idea why this was happening to them.

Despite the pall that swirled around Kris, seeming to demand silence, Kris had to ask one more question of Jacques.

"Of the races entombed here, how many looked sentient?"

"That's impossible to say, Kris," Jacques said. "For example, was that big dinosaur thing over there self-aware? Some of the trophies look like they've hardly crawled out of the water, but just because we can't conceive of such animals as sentient doesn't mean they aren't."

"I didn't ask how many *were* sentient," Kris snapped. "Only how many *looked* it. Don't you have a guess? Something, say, someone with a high-school level of education might conclude."

"None of the boffins has a high-school education, Kris."

Jack coughed softly. "I had a Marine medic, the one who first opened the entrance, go through. Actually, she did it on her own. Took her own pictures. Her best guess, from her tally, is twenty-five to thirty-five percent look aware of what was happening to them."

"By that estimate," Kris asked, "how many sentient species did they murder in the last hundred thousand years?"

"Her guess is between one hundred and a hundred and fifty," Jack said.

"Damn," was all Kris could say.

"God forgive them," was Penny's prayer.

The others stayed mute.

"No more. Not one more, you hear?" Kris said to the dead chamber.

"I think they will hear you very well," Jacques said.

The next day, the ships' fuel tanks were all topped off. The last of the scientists were back aboard and happily reviewing their data. None had discovered a word for god or goddess, other than the Sky Gods, but they were all looking now.

With everyone ready, Kris gave the order to the squadron to undock and head out.

That was when the natives flipped out.

"Kris, the natives don't want to go into the eggs," Nelly reported as Kris ordered the fleet to two gees.

Kris headed her own egg for the drop bay and found it a madhouse when she rolled in. There were Marines not too subtly trying to get the natives into eggs, and natives scampering around everywhere. A few had even resorted to waving their knives threateningly at the Marines.

"It's like chasing a bunch of greased pigs," Gunny reported. "A guy pissed on a corporal who almost caught him."

That wouldn't lead to any place good. "Tell your Marines to relax," Kris said.

"Stand down, Marines," Gunny ordered in that quiet voice that can resonate around the walls of drop bays, hearts, and souls.

"Captain Drago, hold at one gee for a few minutes," Kris ordered.

"As you will, Admiral, but we've laid in a fast trip back home. If we make it just like Nelly thinks we can, we'll be home in three jumps. It will take some slowing down in Alwa System, but it will be fast and no one in between any the wiser."

"I understand, Captain. I just need some honey to make things go a bit easier here in the drop bay for our local hires."

"Waiting on your word."

Kris motored her egg to the center of the drop bay. "Gunny, have your Marines stand clear of the walls. Nelly, stand by to shrink the bay to Condition Baker, if you will."

Gunny got a big grin on his face and ordered his Marines into the center of the room. His grin proved contagious as the troopers jogged in from the bulkheads.

The natives eyed what was going on. Some of them edged in closer. Others looked no more willing to get close to the Marines.

"Nelly, execute Condition Baker for the docking bay."

The drop bay was quite spacious. It had to be with four longboats, the admiral's barge, and the captain's gig strung out along its walls.

Suddenly, the bay was a whole lot smaller. The boats were much closer, the distance across the bay a lot less.

Several natives found themselves pushed rather unceremoniously along by the closing walls. Though they looked surprised and not at all happy, none appeared injured.

~We are going for a walk among the stars,~ Kris said in a firm voice. ~It will taste better if you sit in one of these.~

Kris waved at the forty eggs. They'd been parked in a triple line along the center of the deck. On Gunny's orders, the Marines got in theirs.

"Captain, you may go to 1.5 gees when you want," Kris said.

"Going to 1.5 gees now. I'm taking the ship to Condition Baker."

"We're already at Baker down here."

"Oh, I bet that was fun."

"No one was hurt," Kris said.

The natives' eyes got wide as their weight went up fifty percent.

~It is better to put these on,~ Kris repeated, waving casually at the unoccupied eggs.

The graybeard got in one. His eyes did go wide as it eased the acceleration on him. ~Good. Son, get in one. Get the boy in one.~

The lad who'd caused all this was looking much better. He

scampered into a high-gee cart and relaxed into its cushioned embrace. ~Good. Good good,~ he said.

"Captain Drago, would you care to go to two gees."

"With pleasure."

The acceleration went up, as did the apparent weight of the natives still on their feet in the drop bay.

That was enough for most of them. They were into the eggs in a wink. The one holdout was the old bald woman. She clung to her staff.

I BET SHE CAN'T TAKE THE STAFF INTO THE ACCELERATION CART, Nelly said.

I WON'T TAKE THAT BET.

Kris motored over to the practice equipment lockers and pulled a puggle stick out of its space. NELLY, RIG A PLACE ON MY CART FOR THE STICK.

It was done.

Kris motored over to the last unused egg. "Nelly, rig her egg to have a place for her stick. Open a hole so she can place it standing up."

Nelly did it.

Kris pointed to the hole, then to the stick, and waved the woman to the egg.

For a stubborn moment, the woman stood firm in her place. NELLY, TELL CAPTAIN DRAGO TO ADD A QUARTER GEE.

The woman sighed and began to make her way to the egg.

"Captain Drago, you may drop the extra quarter gee."

"It is done."

Kris turned her egg to face Gunny. "See to it that the natives all learn how to drink from the water line. Can you make sure that Cookie knows they are down here and gets them something to eat that isn't too unfamiliar to them?"

"Will do, Admiral."

Kris surveyed the situation and found it good.

A few minutes later, she motored onto the bridge. "I hope I didn't cause you any trouble," she told Captain Drago.

"Nope, no bother at all. How are our passengers?"

"In their eggs, surrounded by Marines, and trying to adjust to star walking."

"I like the idea of their being surrounded by Marines. I'd hate to have to chase them down at high gees."

"It shouldn't happen. What's our course?"

"Nelly has drawn us a very fast course back to Alwa. We will come flying into the system at a high speed, but it shouldn't be a problem. No one uses the Alpha Jump, and we'll have one of the gas giants capture us. It may involve some 3.5-gee deceleration, but what's a little gee among friends?"

"Let's get home. I have a lot to report."

"Report to Alwa or report to the king?" Captain Drago asked.

"That is something I will use this short trip to meditate on," Kris said, and guided her egg into her day quarters.

32

The *Wasp* led the rest of the squadron through the Alpha Jump and into the Alwa System. As soon as all the ships were through, they flipped ship and began applying a full 3.5-gee deceleration burn.

From her day quarters, Kris began making her report to Alwa. "We are back, and our investigation was very fruitful. We found the alien home world and have even recruited twenty of them. Since the home world has returned to the Stone Age, I'm not sure what we've recruited them for, but for better or worse, we have some aliens aboard and talking, such as they can."

Kris paused to collect her thoughts. She knew it would take quite a while for this message to reach Alwa, and just as long for any response to get by.

"Kris, I think we have a problem," Nelly said.

"What kind of problem?"

"There is no message traffic directed at us, but there is a lot of traffic going out from Canopus Station. I think someone has hijacked a freighter."

"What?" didn't say much, but it was all Kris could get out.

"A freighter is making for the Beta Jump. It was supposed to stop at an asteroid mine, but instead of flipping ship and decelerating, it took off at 1.25 gee for the jump."

"Nelly, get my team up here," Kris said as she guided her egg onto the bridge.

"Captain Drago, we may need to keep all our velocity. Please send to squadron, 'On my mark we will kill the deceleration burn, please acknowledge.'"

"We have acknowledgments from all the squadron," the comm immediately reported.

"Mark," Kris said. And the *Wasp* went zero gee.

"The squadron is still in formation," the navigator reported. "No problems reported."

"Very good," Captain Drago said as he rolled his egg off his bridge and into the admiral's bridge.

Once in, he paused. "Now, Your Highness, would you mind telling this poor working stiff what the hell is going on here?"

"It appears that someone hijacked a freighter and is making for the Beta Jump," Kris said.

"Christ on a crutch," Drago said. "Who would do that?"

"Apparently," Nelly provided, "Commander Sampson managed to pull it off."

"You should have hung that bad apple when you had the chance," Drago said.

"I may have definitely failed that leadership challenge," Kris admitted. "Nelly, get my battle staff in here, if you please."

"Yes, Admiral."

Moments later, Kris had her key fighters assembled. Jack arrived with Amanda and Jacques. Penny rolled in right behind them with Masao.

Kris quickly filled them all in.

"Nelly, are you sure?" Captain Drago asked.

"None of this traffic is aimed at us," Nelly said, "and we did arrive in the middle of it. However, I am now 99.9 percent sure that I understand it correctly. Commander Sampson managed to get aboard a freighter headed for an asteroid mine."

"She's risking long space jumps with a single reactor," Captain Drago growled. "She's a bigger fool than I thought. The greater fools are those who went with her."

"That turns out not to be the case," Nelly said. "The mine had a very productive two weeks and had an extralarge load of ore for Smart Metal production. Someone assigned one of the empty supply ships, still with its two reactors, so it could get the entire load in one lift and do it fast."

"When luck goes bad, it just doesn't quit," Jack muttered.

"Sampson took off with the freighter for the asteroid belt at 1.25 gees and it wasn't until the *Sisu* failed to flip and begin a deceleration burn that anyone was the wiser. She's now headed for the jump and will hit there going at close to four hundred thousand kilometers an hour."

"That will be a long jump," Kris said.

"At least seven hundred light-years, maybe more, if she puts revolutions on the ship and gooses its acceleration up just before the jump," Nelly said. "Kris, Sampson didn't make any jumps like that on her way out here on the *Constellation*, what with Canopus Station and the factories tagging along."

"No, but if she's done any reading about the way we jumped around on the way back to human space after the first battle, she'll know something about it," Kris said.

"Will the people with her be prepared for high gees?" Penny asked.

"How hard is it to make an egg?" Kris asked.

"It's easy," Nelly said. "If you have the software."

"What's the rest of the fleet doing about this renegade?" Jack asked.

"No warships are out in that sector of the system. No ships are expected through the jump point, so there is not much chance of an easy intercept."

"Trying to intercept a ship coming at you at four hundred thousand klicks is not something I'd want to do," Drago admitted.

"The fleet is basically tied up at the pier on Canopus Station, doing fix and mend from a practice exercise they finished yesterday," Nelly reported. "They are refueling as fast as they can, but it will be a long and slow stern chase for them."

Kris stared at the overhead for a moment, then made her call. "Captain Drago, what is the squadron's fuel state?"

"We're around eighty percent, plus or minus a few points, Admiral."

"It appears to me that we are in the best position for a stern chase. Do you foresee a problem?"

"None at the moment, Admiral."

"Then send to squadron. 'Set course for Jump Point Beta. On my mark, you will begin a 3.5-gee acceleration.'"

"The message is sent," Drago reported. "We have acknowledgments."

"Mark," Kris said.

In her day quarters, dust motes that had been floating in zero gee began a dive for the deck.

"Captain, set a course and speed that will get us to Jump Point Beta with a velocity of four hundred thousand klicks on the squadron. Be prepared to adjust that speed based upon our observations of the renegade's speed as it enters the jump."

"Aye, aye, Admiral. Nelly, if you will work with my navigator, I would appreciate the effort."

"Most certainly, Captain," Nelly said most primly, then added, "Captain, Admiral, I foresee a small but not insignificant probability of a collision at extremely high speed with an asteroid or ship if we follow a course direct from here to Jump Point Beta. May I recommend that we adjust our course to take us outside the plane of the Alwa System. It will add time, but be safer."

Kris raised an eyebrow to Captain Drago. He nodded. "Nelly, send to the squadron, 'Conform to flag's movement,' then adjust our course up or down."

"I believe down would be the safest course."

"Tell my navigator to do that," Captain Drago said.

"Is there anything else I'm missing?" Kris asked her crew.

"Someone will have to inform the aliens," Jacques said. "I visited with them for a bit yesterday, checking on some language issues. They find the eggs confining and want to know when they can get out of them. I told them soon."

"Then I will have to tell them later," Kris said, "but not now." She paused to compose her thoughts. "Nelly, send to Admiral Kitano. 'We are in the system in a high-energy state. We will take over pursuit of the hijacked freighter. Please clear the area around Jump Point Beta for our use. Be advised that more reports on the investigation of the alien home world are to follow. Please pass along to me any report on your present situation. Longknife sends.'"

"That ought to cause quite a stir," Jack said.

"We'll see," Kris said. "Nelly, have you and your kids sifted through all the reports we have? Select out the most complete and informative. Send all their executive summaries first, with the rest to follow. See how much we can get out before we go through Beta Jump."

"Working on it, Kris. I assume this is a second priority to navigation?"

"Correct, Nelly. Catching Sampson is our number one priority."

"We can handle it all, Kris," Nelly said, and if she'd had them, she would have been busting her buttons.

There was a long wait before the first message came in from Canopus Station, and it was a visual of Admiral Kitano.

"Oh my God, you folks are coming in fast! We have a problem," and she proceeded to fill Kris in on the problem she already knew about. Kitano was about halfway through the explanation when a lieutenant brought her a message flimsy. She glanced at it and laughed.

"So, you've already picked up on what I'm telling you and, as I should have known, are reacting to it. Okay, you have the right of way. We will keep the space around Jump Point Beta clear for you. Good luck and Godspeed or more."

The admiral paused to take a deep breath. "Viceroy, I'm glad you had good luck at the alien home world, but we've had the worst luck here. Some of the old Rooster elders have taken to civil disobedience. They wander into roads, purely by accident, they insist, but our trucks don't dare do more than fifteen or twenty klicks for fear of running someone down. The rains didn't come again, so even though we've got plenty of farm gear to plant with, we can only use land we can irrigate."

The admiral paused to catch a tired breath. "Someone put sand and gravel, even some large stones, in the intake for the viaduct. We got most of the big junk out, but we couldn't get it all. We're a good ten percent down on our water flow."

Kitano glanced offscreen as if looking for words. "We've tried talking to them, but all we get is a stubborn insistence that we go back to the way things were. We tell them that there are aliens coming to really mess with their world, but they say they've heard enough of that, I think the word they use is something like 'fairy tale.' There are a whole lot of us down here about ready to pull our hair out. If that could be done, I think your friend Armstrong would be bald."

"There have been some ugly incidents between the Alwans that follow the Associations and those that live in the deep woods. So far it's just pecking at each other, but Granny Rita says she expects bodies to be found any morning now. Sorry to dump this on you just as you're chasing off after my screwup. If you want my head, I'll hand in my resignation. I hope you'll let me keep the *P Royal*, she's a sweet ship. Kitano, out."

And the screen went dead.

"And I thought we had problems," Kris muttered.

33

Kris dismissed her team to their duties.

"Do you want me to stay, love?" Jack asked.

"Nope. I think you better start looking into ways to board a ship at high vectors. Maybe even with high-gee acceleration still on the ship."

"You think Sampson will be that stupid?"

"There is no limit I place on Sampson's folly," Kris said. "I won't make that mistake again."

"Can you loan my Marines the pinnace?"

"Hmm, you have an idea there. That might work. Touch base with Captain Drago. Now, General, I need some time to think."

"Let me know when you want me around. I'll come running, Admiral."

Jack left. Kris reclined her egg. What she really wanted to do was get out and pace the deck. That was what admirals did when they needed to think, wasn't it? Nelson paced the deck, didn't he?

Not at 3.5 gees, he didn't.

Kris reclined, stared at the overhead, and thought.

Hard.

She thought of the hall beneath the pyramids. She'd sworn that not one more head would be added to that gory collection. In her mind's eye, she saw a Rooster in a glass cube. Would she have to take one of them back there and rub their noses on the glass?

Dare I go back after the calling cards I left?

She hadn't planned to go back at all, not sooner, not later. But she hadn't expected to come back and find her rear area in an uproar.

Why won't someone just let me fight my battles in a nice clean way?

Kris almost laughed. How many statesmen or generals had asked the same question? No doubt, she wasn't the first. Hopefully, she wouldn't be the last.

"Nelly, send to Admiral Kitano at your earliest convince. 'Resignation rejected. I doubt I could have done a better job myself. We will talk more when I get back with Sampson's guts for garters. Longknife sends.' "

"I've already sent it, Kris. Passing along communications is something I could do in my sleep if I ever did sleep. I didn't bother you before, but now that you asked, we are on course to the jump. We will not intercept Sampson there, but will be about ten hours behind her."

"Thank you, Nelly. If something big shows up, break in on me, but I do want to think."

"Do you want to talk about it?"

"Aren't you busy?"

"I've learned to delegate, Kris. My kids complain that I spell delegate D.U.M.P."

Kris enjoyed a chuckle. "A good joke."

"Captain Drago liked it. Mimzy and Sal are working on the course corrections. Kris, I took the opportunity to brief Professor Labao on our problem. He has his boffins breaking out the best sensors they have to help us track Sampson and see what final adjustments she makes at the jump."

"That was good initiative, Nelly," Kris said.

"So, what is worrying you, Kris?"

"We've learned a lot about the aliens."

"We have."

"Do I need to report all this back to human space?"

"Didn't the king say you shouldn't report back?"

"Yes, we want to leave as few trails as possible. But could any of the stuff that we learned help out back home?"

"Why is this suddenly bothering you?"

"The problem they had on Alwa while I was gone, Nelly. Will what we found help motivate the Alwans to stand with us?"

"I don't know, Kris. What do you think?"

"Nelly, I'm sorry, but I don't want to be asked what I think; I want more input."

"I'm sorry Kris, I can extrapolate trend curves, but jumping from one possible fact to another possible fact is just not what I do."

"Nelly, is Penny busy?"

"No. Would you like me to invite her and Masao into this conversation?"

"Please do."

A few minutes later, Penny's and Masao's eggs rolled into Kris's day quarters.

"What's up?" Penny asked. "Nelly said you were thinking dark thoughts and needed a blank wall to bounce them off of."

"I said I needed input, not an echo chamber," Kris said.

"Maybe she said something like that," Kris's best friend said. "Some of it could have gotten lost in translation."

Nelly did not leap to defend her honor but remained quiet.

Thank you, girl.

I knew what the two of you were doing, Kris. I'm not flesh and blood, but I'm beginning to understand it better.

"I'm trying to decide whether or not to ignore my king's instructions."

"If they're Ray's, no doubt you'll ignore him," Penny said.

It was hard to tell, with Masao in an egg, but he might have looked shocked at such familiarity with the throne.

"The king said I should not send a lot of reports home. We don't want to blaze a trail from here to there."

"Right," Penny said. "You don't want to lay too much yarn out for the cats to play with, as my grandmother used to say. Sooner or later, they're bound to make a mess."

"But there's all this new stuff we've found out about the aliens," Kris said.

"Yes, it is a lot of new information," Masao said, "but does it really change anything? They want to kill us. They don't consider us worth talking to. Now that we know they consider us vermin in their eyes, I don't see that it has changed anything."

Kris told them about Dr. Meade's discovery of the atrophied portion of the aliens' brains and her theory of what that might be causing.

"Is that certain?" Masao asked.

"Nelly, do you have her latest work?" Kris asked.

"I have access to her notes, Kris. She hasn't been able to add to her research while we've all been in the eggs. She is working on a new series of tests to further examine her hypotheses. Her main problem is the aliens' lack of vocabulary. She can't ask them to think of God, pray, or play a national anthem. Trying to create a response when her subjects don't seem to have any handles to hang it on is very difficult."

"So, even if this is so, what would you do with it?" Masao asked.

"What if we could figure out a way to reactivate it?" Kris said, posing the option that tasked her. "What if we could seed them with, I don't know, a revival?"

"What if you did, and the Enlightened One grabbed hold of it and we ended up facing billions of crazy fanatics?" Penny asked back

"We are facing billions of crazy fanatics," Kris said. "What's the difference?"

"It could get worse. Right now we're facing billions of obedient slaves," Penny said. "We came up with 20-inch lasers, and now 22-inch lasers. They came up with the idea of putting rocks on their noses for armor. It seems to me that free men and woman are ahead to date. Do you really want to risk a change to that?"

"I'd really like to not have to kill another thirty or forty billion. No, next time we'll get hit by three times as many, make that ninety to a hundred and fifty billion, maybe."

"The blood does get deep," Masao said, with a cough.

Kris stared at the overhead for a long minute.

"Why did this come up now?" Penny asked.

"We're likely going to have to chase Sampson across a quarter of the galaxy before we catch her. I was thinking of sending a report home. Maybe with you on the *Endeavor*. What do you think?"

Now there was another long pause.

"I'd really rather not go home yet," Penny said.

"Can I ask why?" Kris said, wondering what she'd stumbled into.

"I like my job here. I like my life here, Kris, believe it or not. If you send me home . . ."

"Masao could go with you."

"And if he did, where would that put us? Maybe I could talk the king into letting me take the *Endeavor* back to Alwa. Maybe Masao could talk the Musashi Navy into letting him stay attached to the Alwa mission. Maybe we'd get a no to all that."

"All of us on Alwa could be blasted away tomorrow," Kris pointed out.

"But we're two for oh, aren't we? Call me crazy, Kris, but this is my home, and I kind of like it here."

"You're crazy," Kris said.

"Coming from a Longknife, I'll consider that a compliment."

"Okay, then we agree, Sampson doesn't get to go back to human space. If I have to drag her and her people home in chains, she comes back with me."

"You'll get no argument from me there," Penny said.

"But do you need to report?" Masao said. "That is the question. Do you think that knowing what is happening here on the other side of the galaxy would make it easier for your king to raise a fleet?"

"That is one of many questions," Kris said.

"I have no idea, Kris," Penny said. "If we were at a decent acceleration, I'd say flip a coin."

"I'd probably argue with the results," Kris said, dryly.

"If you don't like the coin toss," Masao said, "you *should* argue with it."

"There is one thing," Penny said.

"Yes."

"Phil Taussig and his survivors from the old *Hornet*. I know they're on the new *Hornet* now, but if you are still thinking of sending someone back, you might make him the offer."

"And if he turns me down like you just did?" Kris asked.

"Then you might have more reason not to send anyone."

Kris let them go back to whatever they'd been doing.

"Did they help you more than I could?" Nelly asked.

"No, they didn't."

"But you feel better talking to them?"

"I can't say that I feel better after talking to them face-to-face. We spent most of the time flat on our back, staring at the ceiling."

"Overhead," Nelly corrected.

"Whatever," Kris said.

"But the human talk meant something to you."

"They refused to take the free ride home, Nelly. That said a lot to me."

"Irrational."

"Human."

"Yes, human," Nelly agreed.

"I'd better go tell the aliens that they're going to be in their eggs a bit longer than expected," Kris said.

"I could have Gunny or Doc Meade do that for you."

"No, I'm the chief or the wisewoman, or the wild woman, whatever. I got them into this mess. I better explain it face-to-face."

"In your egg, reclining at 3.5 gees."

"Not rational," Kris said.

"But very human."

34

Kris found the tame aliens in their eggs, huddled together. The Marines had backed off as much as Condition Charlie let them. The drop bay was a lot smaller.

Come Condition Zed, the unique equipment on the long-boats would be boxed up like Mother MacCreedy's best whiskey and that Smart Metal™ would be shipped off to reinforce the hull's armor. Of the drop bay, there wouldn't be enough left for a broom closet.

Kris would have to come up with another place to park her charges if it came to a fight.

She rolled up to the graybeard. He was reclining in his egg, but he spotted her and brought it up a bit. ~When can I hunt again?~

~It will be many sunsets.~ Kris had learned that if it was good news you brought, you used "sunrise," while bad news got the "sunset" treatment.

~Why can I not hunt again?~

Now a lot of the tribe had raised their eggs up to get a better look at Kris. A Marine sergeant edged away from the wall and rolled up behind her.

NELLY, TELL THE MARINES, THANK YOU, BUT STAY COOL.
DONE, KRIS.

The Marine sergeant didn't back away, but he came no closer.

~What do you do when someone grabs your knife and runs away with it?~ Kris asked.

~I run after him and take it back,~ the old man said. ~If he is a child, I show him the right path for his feet. If he is a man, I knock the right path into him.~

~A woman has grabbed one of my ships for walking among

the stars and ran away with it. I am running after her. I will knock the right path into her.~

~Hmm,~ was the graybeard's only response.

The wisewoman turned her head in her egg to better look at Kris with deep black eyes. Kris returned the gaze, unblinking. Had she given away that she was not all-powerful? Or was the woman more interested in how one might run away with a ship to walk among the stars?

Maybe you should have let the boy die, girl.

That wasn't going to happen, Kris answered her own doubts.

Kris returned to her quarters. They would hit the jump in the middle of their night. For now, she'd better catch a nap.

"By the way, Nelly, does that freighter we're chasing, the *Sisu*, have any lasers?"

"Yes, Kris, it has a pair of short-range 18-inch pulse lasers."

"But if she's waiting for us on the other side of the jump, range won't be all that important, will it?"

"No, Kris, but Sampson has a lot of energy on her boat. Turning it around and getting back to the jump to hit us as we come through would not be a likely prospect. With seven ships following you, it certainly would not be a winning proposition."

Kris considered that and chose the nap.

Jack woke her an hour before they were to hit the jump.

"Did they get a good look at our renegade when it made its jump?" Kris asked.

"The *Sisu*, out of the Scanda Confederation planet of the same name," Nelly reported, "jacked its acceleration up to 2.5 gees fifteen seconds before it jumped. It went through the jump at forty revolutions, counterclockwise."

"It appears our girl did her homework," Jack said.

"Do you know where she jumped to?" Kris asked Nelly.

"There are three systems I think she might have ended up in. Two have fuzzy jumps. I don't know if the *Sisu* has the gear to spot them, Kris."

"We'll just have to wait and see if we end up in the same system with her and where she's headed, now won't we?"

"Patience is a virtue. You should develop it sometime, Your High-handedness," Nelly said.

"Nelly, I have to put up with that lip from Abby. Just because she's not here doesn't mean you have to give it to me."

"I know. But now that I have had the chance, I enjoy giving it to you all on my own."

"Kris, may I suggest you stop while you're behind?" Jack said.

Since they were alone, Kris stuck her tongue out at Jack.

"Do that again when we aren't parboiled in these damn eggs and see what it gets you."

Kris grinned. "I'm thinking of it."

"Well, quit. It's all going to waste."

On that note, they motored out onto the bridge.

Captain Drago, looking somewhat better for having napped as well, motored out of his in-space cabin and took his place at the center of his hive. "Anything change while I was catching a few z's?"

"Nothing has happened at the jump since the *Sisu* used it," the navigator reported.

"Did sensors give us their feed on the *Sisu*'s status as it jumped?"

"Yes, Captain. We have the exact velocity within ten centimeters a second. Their RPMs were a ragged 39.64 per minute. They were accelerating at 2.47 gees for 14.71 seconds before the jump. All this is loaded in every ship in the fleet. Phil Taussig of the *Hornet* asks if we should all attempt the same jump or would it be better to have ships vary a bit around it for 'Kentucky windage,' whatever that is."

"Nelly?" Kris said.

"I have looked up 'Kentucky windage,' and no, I don't think there is enough of a chance of our numbers being off for us to split the fleet. My estimate of us following Sampson's course approach unity."

"Send to *Hornet*. 'Good idea, Phil, but our Nelly windage beats Kentucky windage every time, Longknife sends.'"

"Kris," Nelly asked, "would you like to hear what Sampson had to say just before she jumped?"

"Will her deathless prose surprise me?"

"Not likely."

"Well, let's see what was on her mind, anyway. It might prove useful."

"Longknife, you'll never catch me. You'll never follow me. I'm on my way back to Wardhaven, and when I get there, it will be you up on charges. You'll never get your privileged ass out of jail for the rest of your life."

"And here I thought her ass was just as privileged as mine."

"Except she is an ass," Jack said.

"Who is running headlong into who knows what," Captain Drago added.

"Yes. So, Nelly, you say she's wrong about our not being able to follow her."

"Definitely."

"And she's wrong about our not being able to catch her."

"My Marines are waiting to make the catch," Jack said.

"Well then, let's go get her," Kris said.

The squadron leveled off from its dive back down to the system plane a solid half hour out from the jump. It finished its braking five minutes out. Two minutes out, Nelly was satisfied that they were duplicating the *Sisu*'s velocity and acceleration to the thirteenth decimal place.

Kris hardly breathed as they made the final approach to the jump, put on a matching spin, and jacked up their acceleration to duplicate exactly how Sampson had done her jump.

35

"Where are we?" Captain Drago asked.

Being an admiral had certain downsides, like letting your flag captain ask the question you desperately wanted answered.

"We covered six hundred and fifty-three light-years," Nelly answered.

"We've picked up a trail of reaction mass," came from the Musashi chief on sensors.

"I have two ship reactors," Senior Chief Beni, retired, said. "Scanda make. I think we have the *Sisu*."

"She's making for the system's fuzzy jump," Nelly added.

"I wonder how she got her hands on a Mark XII sensor suite," Captain Drago said with evil intent.

"Let's just make sure no alien gets their hands on that ship," Kris said.

"With pleasure, Admiral. With pleasure."

"Can we intercept her in this system, or will we have to wait for the next jump?" Kris asked.

"We're working on that," Captain Drago said.

On the screen above the navigator's board, vector lines formed, crisscrossed, then re-formed and crisscrossed again.

Captain Drago looked at them from his station, frowned, and motored over to look over the young Musashi woman's shoulder. Kris knew her place was to stay put and wait, but she was moving a split second before Drago said, "Admiral, would you come take a look at this?"

"Yes, Captain," Kris said, and daintily motored over to look over his shoulder looking over the young lieutenant's shoulder.

"If we go to 3.5 gees and stay there, it looks like we can intercept her a good five minutes before she jumps out of here."

"You're going to have to give me a hint. Is that good or bad?"

"Getting her while we have her here is good. But I'll have to keep the reactors pushing us at 3.5 gees the whole time. We'll also be cutting straight across the plain of this system and I make out a couple of gas bags with rings and an asteroid belt between here and there."

"Meaning, you'd like to take it up above the plain again."

"Yep. It takes time, but it makes sure we arrive safe and sound to bash her ears back."

"Pin her ears back," Nelly corrected.

"You pin them, Nelly. For me, it's bashing time," the captain said.

"Kris, is that what is called walking into one?"

"Exactly, Nelly."

"I'll remember that."

"Getting back to the matter at hand," Kris said. "Captain, what's this about pushing things at 3.5 gees? I thought the new ships were good for more than that."

"They are, Kris, but we haven't had a serious reduced availability for maintenance for a while. We've been riding the *Wasp* pretty hard, and while we take good care of her, I'd hate to find that I didn't take good *enough* care of her."

"What I'm hearing is you want to tighten up your safety margin."

"That, and I really don't want to be doing my final deceleration as I'm approaching the jump with her still on this side of it. Those might be dinky 18-inch pulse lasers, but if she's aiming them up my engines, things could get deadly in a hurry. No. Let's catch her with our forward batteries and thickened forward armor."

Kris nodded. "Conduct this pursuit as you see fit, Captain."

"My, a Longknife that has learned caution and prudence," Drago said. "As I live and breathe."

Kris smiled at the jab. "So long as it ends with me having Sampson's guts for garters, I have no problems with what you do between now and then."

"Then let's slow to three gees and take the high road, Admiral."

"Nelly, send to squadron. 'On my mark, reduce speed to three gees and conform to the flag's movements.' "

"The squadron's ships are standing by, Kris."

"Mark," Kris said.

In the egg, she hardly felt the lessened acceleration.

Kris half expected to hear from Sampson, but she had nothing to say, and Kris did not choose to taunt her. A woman like her was unstable enough without Kris's adding more to it. She wanted her ship back, and, as livid as she was at Sampson, she wanted her crew back as well.

No doubt they'd spend the next long years as loader operators on the guano island, but they'd be alive. Too many people who had crossed Kris's path weren't.

Around Kris, the ship went about its prebattle drill. The lasers were charged and dialed in. The armor was strengthened on the bow. Kris brought up the Weapons board on her egg.

Captain Drago must have had an alert on that. He immediately looked in Kris's direction, then motored over to her.

"You want to handle the shoot?" he asked.

"You think I shouldn't?"

"It's just that there's bad blood between you and her, between Sampsons and Longknifes. If things go well, that's nice. If they don't, it might be better if someone else closed the firing circuits."

"Captain, do you honestly think anyone is better on Weapons than me and Nelly?"

"No."

"Do we want to capture that ship in as close to one piece as possible?"

"Yes. From my viewpoint."

"Yes, from my viewpoint, too."

"Then the shoot is yours."

By slowing and taking the long road, they arrived at the jump a half hour after the *Sisu*. Once again, the boffins and Nelly had dialed the jump in to the last possible decimal place.

Once more, the squadron followed the *Wasp* through the jump.

36

"We jumped a bit over a thousand light-years," Nelly reported.

"The *Sisu* is four hundred thousand kilometers ahead of us, accelerating at 2.1. No, make that 2.0. Correction, she's down to 1.9 gees acceleration," the Musashi chief reported from sensors.

"Someone's engines are hot," Senior Chief Beni, ret, reported.

"Hold at three gees," Captain Drago ordered. "We'll overtake her carefully. Wouldn't do to be too close if she blows her reactors."

"Captain. Admiral," Chief Beni said, his voice even, careful, but intent. "I have radio traffic in system. I think it's coming from a planet closer to the sun. But I've also got reactors. Thermonuclear reactors with an alien raider signature."

"Where?" came in two-part harmony from Kris and Captain Drago.

"The alien-type reactors are all the way on the other side of the system. There's a gas giant with a major moon and ring system. The reactors are orbiting that giant."

"Any make on the reactors?" Kris asked.

"They appear to be like the first batch you tangled with. The ones my son fought." That made it personal.

"We'll handle those other situations when we finish with Sampson," Kris said, running all the complications that had suddenly appeared through in her mind. She had a subordinate who had mutinied against her and stolen a ship. She had a newfound world with a civilization at least at the early-electromagnetic stage, and she had bug-eyed monsters.

Dear God, Kris almost prayed, *do I deserve all of this on the same plate?*

God did not answer her question.

Smart of Her, no doubt.

Hurriedly, Kris filed the new alien and the old alien away in an ever-growing box marked TO BE OPENED LATER, and fixed her sights ahead on the ship well out of range.

It fled from them. They pursued faster.

The range closed inexorably.

"*Sisu*, cease your acceleration, or you will be fired upon," Kris ordered as the renegade came into extreme range.

"You wouldn't dare fire on a neutral flag," Sampson shot back. "Scanda isn't part of your old man's bunch of political patsies."

"The Scanda ships are under my command," Kris said. "However, I don't think you're up to date on my latest wild goings-on. I fired on a Helvetican flag freighter at M-688. I have yet to add a Scandian to my collection. Don't mind if I do, though."

"You're crazy," Sampson shot back.

"You are in violation of orders. Cease acceleration and surrender your ship."

"You're a fine one to talk about violating orders."

"Tell me, Carolyn, which engine do you want me to shoot out? Both your reactors are running in the red. Which one can better take a hit? I really don't want to kill anyone, but I will not have you running away. Do you know there are aliens in this system?"

"Aliens!" came in a several-part harmony from voices not heard from before on net.

"Yeah, I know we've got a mudball down there with low-tech stuff."

"And a dozen alien raiders, too. They're on the far side of the system, but, no doubt, they'll be headed this way as soon as they get a good look at you."

"You said we wouldn't have to worry about those bloodthirsty-type aliens," came through the net hookup.

"And we won't. They can't catch us." Sampson's voice cracked as she spoke.

"Their acceleration just fell off to 1.8 gees," Chief Beni announced.

"How are you going to outrun the aliens when your reactors are going down on you, Carolyn?" Kris asked.

"She's right, we can't keep this up," said a very scared voice.

"She wouldn't dare fire on us." Now Sampson sounded frantic.

"We are overtaking the *Sisu*," the navigator said. "We will soon be in range of those 18-inch pulse lasers."

"Did you hear that?" Kris said. "My navigator is warning me that you're slowing down so much that I'm at risk of overtaking you, even passing you. If I do that, Sampson will get a shot at our stern. I can't allow that. I'll have to shoot out your reactors before then."

"Damn it, Sampson," came in a tense voice on net, "you swore those guns would make us invulnerable. Now that Longknife dame says she's gonna blow out our reactors because of them!"

"Shut up," Sampson shrieked.

"Shut up yourself," came right back at her.

Drago grinned. "And we thought we had a leadership challenge from that gal," he said softly.

"Listen, Longknife, you let us go."

"No can do, Sampson. Even if I were crazy enough to consider that for a moment, there's the minor matter of the aliens on the other side of this system. I'm told they're already getting underway and are headed this way. You think you can get out of this system before they get to you? You think with your red-hot engines, you can outrun them?"

Chief Beni looked rather startled to hear that the aliens were headed this way when he hadn't announced it. Still, he reported. "They've fallen off to 1.7 gees acceleration."

"Slow to one gee," Captain Drago ordered. With the momentum already on the boat, the *Wasp* continued to close, but not at the eye-blinking speed it had been.

"I will fire in five," Kris began. "Four. Three. Two."

There was noise of a scuffle on the *Sisu*'s commlink.

"Don't shoot. We've got Sampson under control."

"Take all acceleration off the boat," Kris ordered.

"Kill the engines?" someone over there demanded, incredulously.

"We better before they kill us," someone else answered.

The *Wasp* flipped ship and went to three gees deceleration. Strung out behind the *Wasp* were the other ships of the squadron. Most had not put on the high acceleration needed to catch up so quickly. Now they closed even as they flipped ship and began to decelerate. All these ships matching velocity vectors would no doubt be fun to watch.

Kris, never actually having had command of a ship, could watch it with fascination.

But she didn't miss when Jack began to head his egg off the bridge. She followed him. "Where are you going, General?"

"I've got a ship to board," he said.

"Can't you delegate it? After all, you are a brigadier general."

"When was the last time anyone boarded a ship making eight hundred thousand klicks an hour?"

Kris made a face. "Never, I think."

"You don't delegate that kind of job. I'll be careful. Trust me. The entire crew of the pinnace and my Marine company will be careful. The Musashi company got to land at the pyramid. My team gets this landing. Fair is fair."

"You'll be careful."

"That's what I said."

"No, I mean *you* be careful."

"Of course."

"That's wife to husband, you know."

"Yes, I know, hon," he said, smiling.

In the eggs, you couldn't give a good-bye hug and kiss. *Damn the things, anyway.*

The pinnace pulled away from the *Wasp*, taking a third of the ship's reactors with it. It matched speed with the *Sisu*, and two Sailors maneuvered a connecting tube between the ships' main hatches. Ten minutes later, the two ships pulled well apart and began decelerating, braking toward the closest gas giant.

The squadron followed.

"Captain, can the *Wasp* keep this deceleration up?" Kris asked.

He winced. "I don't think so. At least, not for long. My engines aren't as large as the big frigates'."

"*Hornet*, could you please have your pinnace replace the *Wasp*'s riding herd on the *Sisu*?" Kris asked of Captain

Taussig. If the freighter's reactors failed, someone would need to be close to evacuate the crew.

"We'd be glad to, Admiral."

While that evolution proceeded, Kris turned her egg to face sensors. "Okay, folks, you have my undivided attention. What can you tell me about our competing alien finds?"

"The planet that's the source of all the radio and TV is down system toward the sun," Chief Beni said. "Its orbit has it presently on our side of the sun. Besides all the electronic emitters, there are quite a few nuclear reactors though they are of the obsolete fission type."

"Any presence in space?"

"There appear to be quite a few orbiting satellites, but nothing that looks large enough to be occupied."

"So it appears that they are tough enough to give our alien raiders a bloody nose?" Captain Drago asked.

"Normally, no, sir," the chief said. "However, what we're looking at on the other side of the system is not a normal alien horde. I really do mean the reactors I'm looking at are the kind you first ran into, Your Highness. I'm reading about two dozen ships. Large, but the kind we whipped real good."

"Are they headed for us?" Drago wanted to know.

"We've got a speed-of-light problem, sir. That's over a day as the electron flies. But then, they may not be all that interested into running into us?"

"Explain that, Chief," Kris said.

"I'm making out four large reactors. You know, the kind that you get on the huge mother ships?"

"Usually, there are a couple of hundred of them on one of their moon-size mothers," Kris pointed out.

"Yes, Admiral, exactly. If these little beggars' last mother ship is the hulk we left rolling in space, then they might be starting to build another one. Or maybe a tiny huge mother ship. I don't know, ma'am. I'm guessing, and I know that's usually reserved for officers."

"Feel free to take a swing, Chief," Kris said.

"That's reasonable," Captain Drago said. "The survivors either have to join another horde or rebuild. If they evacuated any of their women and children who survived our messing up their original mother ship, they'd have to find someplace for them."

"But why not just take a planet?" the navigator asked. "Maybe not this one if it's too tough, but another one?"

Captain Drago shook his head. "Why mess with a major gravity well if you don't have to? What with that big gas bag's system of moons and the asteroid belt, they have all the resources they need to rebuild. No, a planet is the last place they'd go to lick their wounds."

"It's always bothered me," Kris said, "that they slaughtered life on planets. Now I understand. They do it because they're afraid, but you're right, Captain. If they need to build another ship for their women and children, space is the place to do it."

Kris paused for a moment to think. "My main question is how many survived the wreck we made of the mother ship and who? Did the Enlightened One live through all that? How many Black Hats did they get off?"

"Are the people over there still enthralled to one man, or have they gone through the process of having someone else step into the top slot?" Captain Drago asked.

"And how smoothly did that process go?" Kris asked, smiling, no doubt, with plenty of teeth. "This could get interesting. We know some of their warships were with the last horde that attacked us. Why did they but not these people change allegiance?"

Now Captain Drago was grinning big. "Who changed allegiances to whom may be the sticking point. Division is a hell of a reality when you've been used to all for one and one for himself alone."

"So," Kris said slowly, "is there any chance I could cut some more of them out? Maybe get my hands on a dissident ship or three?"

"I hope that doesn't mean you're going to let them get in close range?" Drago said, his grin gone.

"I'll try not to," Kris said. "No promises, though."

"Longknifes." The skipper made it sound like a cussword.

37

They hadn't slowed quite enough to make orbit around the intended gas giant. They swung wide around it and did manage to aim toward its largest moon. A swing around it, and they were headed back to the giant. This time, they were slow enough to be captured by its gravity well.

They went into orbit, and the squadron anchored ship to ship.

While the pinnaces went cloud dancing to refuel the squadron, Kris had Sampson hauled before her. Since she wanted her entire gang to see this, Kris arranged the drop bay as a formal court-martial venue.

The aliens got herded off to the Forward Lounge. Penny modified a portion of it into something more to their liking, complete with fake fire and steaks to roast.

Which left Kris free to arrange a roasting of her own.

Longboats brought the crew of the *Sisu* aboard. As the odd ship out, the *Sisu* had not had false gravity, and the crew showed it as they stumbled aboard, adapting to normal weight again. There were low murmurs when they caught sight of Kris in starched whites seated behind a table with Captain Drago on her right, General Montoya on her left.

Gunny saw to it that the Marines herded the mutineers forward. When one held back, a nod from Gunny and a rifle butt hurried that one along.

Captain Taussig had been brought aboard to serve as prosecutor. He stood at his own table. He was still gaunt from his stay on what they now called Arsenic Island, but he had color back in his cheeks. If anything, he was showing an angry red.

He and his crew had almost died to keep information about humanity away from the aliens, and this bunch had almost given it to them on a silver platter.

He'd asked for the job of prosecutor. Kris would not have denied him for anything.

Finding someone to stand defense for them had not been easy. Penny had finally volunteered. "My dad was a cop, but he believed that even the most hard-hearted criminal deserved a fair trial."

When the rebellious crew were huddled before them, Kris brought down a gavel. "This court is in session. Captain Taussig will read the charges."

"You've got no right to try us," Commander Sampson shouted.

"In truth, we have every right to try you," Taussig snapped. "You and your civilians have mutinied against your lawful authority. You have also recklessly endangered the entire human race by your actions, presenting hostile aliens with not only the directions to human space but also making them a gift of our technology. Technology that is critical to the survival of the entire human race. As for you, Lieutenant Commander Sampson, in addition to the first charges, you have abandoned your assigned post in the face of the enemy. I won't even bother with actions unbecoming of an officer and the rest of the book I could throw at you. Running away when your fellow officers are in a fight for their lives? That alone should hang you."

"You wouldn't hang me." Sampson looked like she had just realized that she just might hang. "Capital punishment is outlawed," she added, but gulping at the words.

Taussig turned that one over to Kris with a glance.

"You are right, Lieutenant Commander Sampson. The constitution of the United Society specifically bans capital punishment. However, you committed your crimes in the Alwa System, a system only in general association with your King Raymond. As such, part of what this court will decide is whether we have jurisdiction in the case or whether you should be turned over to colonial authorities to face these charges. Commander, the colonials on Alwa have hung people, and they may again."

Kris had no doubt that Granny Rita, former commodore of BatCruRon 16, would be standing first in line to head the prosecution . . . and demanding death by hanging with every breath she took.

"You can't let them have us," one of the civilians said, stepping forward. "Please, ma'am. We just wanted to go home.

This woman," he said, waving at Sampson, "she said she could get us home. That was all we wanted. We didn't know nothing about the aliens maybe getting us and our ship. Good God, woman, the aliens were what we were running away from. We didn't know anything about mutiny."

"Admiral, the man has a point," Penny said, standing. "You talked to the ship's officers when they arrived. May I have your permission to poll the defendants and see if any of them were there when you gave your orders?"

Kris had appointed Penny to defend. She hadn't actually expected her to defend, but Penny was nothing if not loyal to the law.

"Please do, Councilor," Kris said.

"Are any of you a ship's captain, first mate, or chief engineer?"

There were a lot of mumbled no's and shaken heads.

"Then who was running the reactor watches?" Taussig asked, saving an incredulous Kris from doing the same.

"I was," a man said, raising his hand. "Me and a couple of others are certified to stand a reactor watch as second. I didn't think it would be that much harder to stand first. Goes to show what I know, ma'am. We know, you know, ma'am."

"Their engines' performance showed the quality of those standing watch," Penny pointed out dryly.

Taussig cleared his throat. "What did your officers tell you about you staying in the Alwa System?"

"That our job was now here and we could whistle for it if we didn't like it," the erstwhile engineer said. "I can't say that we much liked it."

"Kris, I mean, Admiral, that may have been a failing at the command level. We did not write out articles of war and have them read throughout the fleet. Nor did we have them signed by all the crews. I think we need to do that when we get back."

Penny paused to let that hang for a while. Kris didn't like it, but her friend had a point.

IN ANCIENT TIMES, KRIS, THAT WAS WHAT WAS DONE ABOARD SAILING SHIPS. THEY DID HANG ANYONE WHO VIOLATED THEIR SIGNED ARTICLES.

THANK YOU, NELLY.

Penny went on. "I'm not going to say my clients aren't

dumb. Stupid even, but they acted without knowledge of the consequences. That those consequences were known and recognized at the command level is not proof that they were known and recognized at the mess-deck level."

Kris made a face, but even her own sense of fairness was being dragged kicking and screaming to Penny's side of the court.

Vice Admiral, Her Royal Highness, Kris Longknife brought the gavel down for one firm knock. "You crewmen have a very effective defense counsel. What you did was stupid and put not only your own lives, but the lives of every man woman and child in human space at risk, not to consider the risk you brought to your shipmates back on Alwa who were waiting for the cargo you did not bring in."

Kris eyed the crew before her. They were a pretty hangdog bunch. She'd made her point.

"Gunny, take these men to the brig. They will stay there until we return to Alwa. There, they will be turned over to colonial authorities and assigned to jobs that will not bring them back to space for the duration of the state of emergency."

When Kris said "turned over to colonial authorities," a wave of panic went through the crew, but the prospect of dirtside jobs for the rest of their life seemed preferable to other outcomes.

Gunny growled orders, and Marines began moving them off the drop bay.

That left Sampson to face the court alone.

"You have no excuse for your actions," Taussig growled.

"That Longknife woman is nothing but a jumped-up corvette captain," Sampson snapped. "She ran away when she faced those bastards. She can't judge me for doing what she did. She . . ."

"Gunny, shut her up," Taussig growled.

Gunny Sergeant Brown went to stand beside the defendant. One look at the Gunny's face, and she shut up.

"Wrong defense," Penny said with a sigh.

"I was in the retrograde movement with Vice Admiral Longknife," Taussig began. "We ran because there was nothing else to do, and the human race had to know what had happened on the other side of the galaxy. I put my ship between the aliens and Princess Longknife so she could get The Word back. And when she did, she came back for me and my crew. She had to fight an alien ship that outweighed her ten to one, but she did save us."

"I would have come back," Sampson snarled when Taussig paused for air. "I would have come back with a court-martial board to try that whore."

"No, Gunny," Kris said. He looked ready to slug the defendant in the mouth.

"Ma'am," he said.

"I may need to amend my charges against you, Miss," Taussig said. "Actions unbecoming and prejudicial to the service seem more and more appropriate."

Sampson didn't wait for Captain Taussig to pause for a breath before launching into a torrent of curses and invectives. Even when Kris hammered her gavel for silence, she raved on.

"Gunny, remove the prisoner. See that she is put in a cell separate from the others. Even they don't deserve this kind of grief. And no, Gunny, I don't want to see a mark on her."

"Ma'am," was a bit ambiguous. Kris wasn't sure whether Gunny felt that her implied order was uncalled for, or out of order, all things considered.

It took two strong Marines to usher Sampson from the drop bay.

"That didn't go as planned," Kris said, standing.

"It never does, Kris," Penny said, joining her. "That's why my old man said Justice was blind."

"Yes," Kris said, still not sure she like the way her friend had jobbed her.

"What is it with that gal," Taussig said, joining the main table.

"Nelly, the last time I had a run-in with Sampson, I ordered a full checkup on her before she left the brig. Did a doctor look her over?"

"Yes, Kris, but, if I may point out, the kind of exam that the doctor could do in the brig and the kind of exams that Dr. Meade did with the aliens have a level of magnitude in difference."

"Good point, Nelly. Please ask Dr. Meade to do a full

workup, to include anything she can do to look into that woman's brain. There's got to be a screw loose."

"A bucket of screws," Jack growled.

"Now, with that distasteful matter done, Captain Taussig, you were too sick last time to share my table. Cookie has found a stash of steaks. Could I interest you in one with all the trimmings?"

"I think you could. I understand congratulations are in order. Jack, you lucky dog you."

"I'll woof to that," Jack said, and they adjourned to the wardroom.

38

The steaks were good, and it gave Kris a chance to lay a proposal before Captain Taussig.

"Captain, there was no way that I could allow Sampson and a mutinous crew to take the *Sisu* back to human space. However, there is the matter of you and your crew's survivor leave. We're a good bit of the way across the galaxy. Would you like to take your ship the rest of the way?"

"Excuse me if I'm missing something, but why me and not them?" he said around a nice rare piece of dead cow.

"I can keep these aliens across the system off your tail," Kris said. "Turnabout being fair play."

"That would be much obliged," he admitted.

"But if you did get caught, I trust you would blow the reactor and give them nothing."

Phil Taussig leaned back in his chair. "We didn't blow the reactors last time because there was hardly anything left to blow. We did destroy our computers. I don't know if you noticed that."

"I figured you did, but I didn't have time to check it out," Kris admitted.

"Yes, if we got caught, I'd blow the reactors. After seeing that house of horror, there is no way I want my head or body in their trophy room."

"Do you want to go? If you do, I'll send along a full report of what we found."

"Do you think that would make any difference in the way your great-grandfather, my king, is building ships?"

"I can't say that it would. I can't say that it wouldn't," Kris admitted.

"So, it boils down to the original question. Do I and mine

want to take this chance to get off the tip of the spear and back someplace that might or might not be safer?"

"Yes."

"No," he said right back.

"No?"

"No. No way. No how, Kris. Admiral. Viceroy, whomever I'm talking to. We're out here, and we'll stay out here, if you don't mind."

"I'm always glad to have fighting skippers," Kris admitted.

"Kris, I have a message from Dr. Meade to you," Nelly said.

"What does she have to say?"

"The examination Lieutenant Commander Sampson had earlier was very cursory. She's just completed a full body scan, and the woman has a cancerous brain tumor. It's a rapidly growing one, and she's glad she managed to catch it right now. In another week or two, it would have been inoperable."

"You may have just saved that woman's life," Penny said.

Kris considered that for a long moment. "I wish I could say that I felt better about that," she finally admitted.

"I'll wait to see how she acts when the tumor's gone," Taussig said. "There are bad actors, then there are people with an excuse for acting bad."

They ate in silence for a while on that thought.

"Kris, would you like an update on the new alien planet?"

"Thank you, Nelly," Kris said, then explained to the others at the table with her, "I've had her hold reports on the new aliens until we settled this problem with Sampson. I take it that the nasty aliens are still staying put, Nelly?"

"If they so much as budge, you will hear, even if you and Jack are . . ."

"Thank you, Nelly," Kris interrupted.

"You're welcome, Kris."

Around the table, Penny was in a coughing fit. "Sorry, I was drinking when Nelly started giving way too much information."

The recent defense counsel finished by taking a long drink of water.

"You may report now, Nelly," Kris said, when Penny was

settled and the rest were no longer looking at her and Jack in that most familiar way.

"We flung off a probe before we finished braking. It will use the fifth planet to brake before going into orbit around the fourth. The boffins are trying to use as much natural slowing as they can to avoid any bright lights. They suspect this civilization has enough technology to notice a sudden bright light in the sky."

"I wonder what they'll make of a fight between us and the bug-eyed monsters?" Taussig asked no one.

Nelly had mastered the rhetorical question. She let it go.

"The probe is not there yet, but the fourth planet is throwing off enough electronic media for us to do a major analysis of them without putting anything on the ground. There are several wars raging right now. It appears that the planet is just coming out of a colonial period. Do I need to explain what that is?"

"No, Nelly," Kris said. "We all know what it means when folks one place think they should tell folks some other place how to run their lives."

"The wars right now are being waged using conventional weapons, but, Kris, these people have fissionable atomics for power and hydrogen-enriched atomics for weapons."

"Oh, so our bug-eyed monsters do indeed have a hot one on their hands," Jack said, with a chuckle.

"And they have chemical weapons, too," Nelly added. "Several of the larger armies have access to nerve gas and have fighting uniforms designed to handle the problem of it on the battlefield."

"This just gets better and better," Penny said. "Who are these people?"

"From the looks of them, we think they evolved from something more like an Earth feline. They have peaked ears, furry faces, and several still have tails."

"The aliens found themselves a batch of tigers," Taussig said. "And they sound like they're at the technological level of the late twentieth century. Back at the Academy, I took a course on that century. It was such a train wreck that I couldn't turn away from it. Some of our best alien-invasion literature dates back to that time. They spent a lot of their time scared, and space aliens were about the scariest thing around. That and zombies."

"Zombies?" Kris said.

"Living-dead things," Taussig said, "And don't ask me how they square that circle."

"Living dead," Kris repeated.

"I have pictures," Nelly said.

"Don't," came from everyone at the table.

"Now, about our feline aliens," Kris said, "who appear to be armed to the teeth?"

"They are divided up into a hundred and fifty-seven different competing districts. Some much larger than the others. Some much more powerful than the others. Three appear to be dominant. Two share a similar language and call their planet Sasquan," Nelly said.

"Well, if they are as combative as you say," Jack asked, "why haven't the larger ones taken over the smaller ones?"

"Some of the smaller ones can be quite nasty if you invade their territory. Do I need to explain guerrilla warfare?" Nelly asked.

"Oh, good Lord," Penny said. "They've got that going on down there? Even when you win a war, you don't win it. It never ends until you finally get smart and go home."

"Something like that."

"So let me sum it up," Kris said. "Our big, bad, bug-eyed monsters have stumbled upon a really nasty bunch of cats that might just give them the fight of their life and not quit even when they're beaten. I can't think of a better future for them."

"You all notice they are not tackling them," Nelly said.

"I have one question that has been bothering me," Taussig said, putting down his fork. "How come the BEMs are here? This is a long way from where we whipped their mother ship. How'd they get here?"

"Nelly, that sounds like a very interesting question," Kris said.

"I already ran the necessary jumps, Kris, and I don't much care for what they show. I was waiting for a better time to ruin your dinner."

"Good turn of phrase, Nelly. My dinner is already ruined, I think. Finish it up."

"If the defeated aliens cut across the Alwa System at one-gee acceleration, they would have hit our Jump Point Beta at about the right speed for a long jump, assuming they used at least ten RPMs at the jump and goosed it up to two gees."

"I don't like where this is going," Jack said.

Penny grimaced. "We know where it's going. Right here."

Nelly waited for the chatter to die down, then went on. "They took four slower jumps to duplicate our one high-speed jump, but if they accelerated through two of them and began decelerating, they would have ended up here."

"So the aliens know how to take long jumps?" Kris said.

"Yes, Kris. Apparently they don't risk them with their mother ship, but the warships can do them."

Captain Taussig was shaking his head. "There goes your twelve-jump-point-out warning system," he said. "They can jump directly into Alwa from way out."

"But," Nelly quickly put in, "they will be coming in at several hundred thousand kilometers an hour. They would need the entire system to slow down, and maybe then some. They would have no fighting capability in that situation."

"Maybe they wouldn't want any," Kris said. "Back in the Unity War, something like those almost wiped out Wardhaven. They were going to use relativity bullets. Huge iron slugs traveling at .05 or so percent of the speed of light can make a hell of a mess when they hit."

"Like the bullets that hit the insectoid planet one out from the aliens' home world?" Penny said.

"Exactly. Let's say those speedsters they've got get themselves up to a really high velocity and don't try to slow down before they hit Alwa. Or any human or Iteeche planet. Even this one."

"I love you, Kris Longknife," Jack said, "but you can come up with some of the most horrific ideas."

"I didn't come up with this one. It's in our history books."

"Jack, you've got to do something about her bookshelf," Phil Taussig said.

"You try getting this woman to do anything she doesn't want to do," was Jack's quick answer.

That got him nods of understanding.

"Getting back to our alien situation, and not all about me

for a moment," Kris said, "do all the aliens have this kind of knowledge, or just the one we scared into running away from us as far and as fast as they could?"

"She may have a point there," Penny said. "They were running scared. Not just from us. Who knows what was coming down on them for not going with the rest and hunting up a horde that would take them in. Conflict management and resolution doesn't strike me as their strong suit."

"No, conflict avoidance seems to be their preferred way of living," Kris agreed.

"And we know that the last time we passed Alwa," Jack said, "it was still there."

"We also know that the critters across the system from us haven't rocked the critters down system from us."

"Smart move. I wouldn't piss off those kitties until I was real sure I could take them."

"Does anyone wonder if there's another mother ship headed this way to take out the, what do they call themselves, Sasquans?" Penny asked.

"At least in two of their zones," Nelly said, answering one question.

"That is a possibility," Kris admitted to the other question, "but they are a long way from their usual stomping grounds. There's another thing. I could be wrong, but bragging rights for wiping out a planet seemed to be a big thing. Nelly, get Jacques on the line."

"You called, Kris?"

"Do the alien ships claim bragging rights for the planets they kill?"

"Most definitely. They count the number they've bagged, like notches on their belt. There was a notation, not in stone, but in pigment, that we managed to read bragging that one ship had five and another ship only had four. By the way, those two weren't even the high scorers. One had nine, but I think it may be the original ship, and it didn't seem to need to brag."

"In your opinion, if the aliens across the system from us didn't join another horde, what are the chances they'd call in another ship to handle this planet?"

"Pretty low. No guarantee I'd be right. Understanding

these aliens is a study in progress, and likely to be for a long time, assuming we don't kill each other first."

"I understand where you're coming from, Professor. Thank you for your informed opinion," Kris said, and rang off.

"Which leaves me," Kris said, "with one big problem. Do we tiptoe out of this system and mark it on our map for later examination, or do we do something now?"

The table got very quiet.

"Thank you all very much," Kris said. "Phil, can the *Hornet* do without you for a bit?"

"Hey, I'm just the captain. If we're just swinging around the anchor here, she's probably better off without me."

"Have I told you how well you lie?" Kris said.

"My family's been Navy for five hundred years or more, Admiral, of course we tell good sea stories. Or space stories."

"I think they're still sea stories," Jack said. "So the rest of us can say, 'Oh, I see,' as you pull our legs."

"Whatever works."

"Nelly, get my key staff, and that includes Professor Labao as well as Amanda and Jacques. If I'm going to put my nose into a hornet's nest, I want the most informed guesses I can get beforehand."

"Hornets! I know a lot about hornets!" the skipper of the last two *Hornets* said through a grin.

They adjourned to Kris's day cabin.

39

"I know we've only begun our study of this new bunch of aliens," Kris said, beginning her staff meeting. "But I've sworn that no more new heads get added to that trophy room under their pyramid. However, Alwa is my first responsibility."

Kris made a face. "So what do we do about these felines down sun from us? We've got an eighth of Alwa's defending frigates here, maybe more, depending on if the Smart Metal work is not going well."

She paused to look at everyone around the table. She had their attention.

"What is the best course of action? Do we attack the aliens on the other side of this system? Should we make contact with the aliens down system and tell them who's sharing their sun with them now? Could we give them some advanced technology that would let them do a better job of holding their own against any space-based attack?"

Kris paused, then added the final option. "Or do we do nothing? Mark this place on our charts for later contact and get back to Alwa. Do any of you see some other option that I missed?"

Again, Kris was met with a silent table.

I'm getting a bit tired of this silent treatment.

But then, they could remain silent and do nothing. She was the one who had to choose action over inaction.

A lot of people exchanged glances, but no one spoke for a long time. Finally, the looks between Jacques and Amanda sprouted words.

"The cat people, as some of us have taken to calling them. I think that's better than furries," Amanda said. "Anyway, they are firmly into their industrial age. Jet aircraft, early rockets, lots and lots of personal transportation. They do not yet have any of the computational power that will put them into the information age." She glanced at Professor Labao to see if he would contradict her, but the administrator seemed happy with her words.

"However, that may be changing. The three biggest groups are making noises about a race to their moon. If they do that, they will have to develop better and smaller computers, and that could launch them into the information age and major changes to their economies. How that will turn out is anyone's guess."

Amanda eyed Kris as if deciding what to say next, then glanced at Jacques. He took over the story. "The problem Amanda and I are struggling with is the question of how well these people can learn to work together. We make a joke of 'it's like herding cats,' but they are living that problem."

"But they have a military, don't they?" Kris asked. "A successful military requires discipline, working together, following orders."

"Yes, Kris, but a lot of warlike people in human history have succeeded in war without giving up a lot of individual prerogatives. Not all warrior societies want every soldier walking in lockstep. Some pride themselves on the Berserker mentality or the Samurai spirit. You can march in step and still get all kinds of independent action."

"Where did I first hear the virtue of 'Improvise. Improvise. Damn it, improvise'?" Kris said.

"Precisely," Jack said.

"Oh, Colonel Cortez, how I wish you were here," Kris said.

"I feel his ghost at my elbow," Jack said, "and he is laughing his head off."

Kris paused a moment to see if she could hear the good colonel's pleasant chuckle. Hearing nothing, she went on. "Okay, so my anthropologists and economists tell me that these felines are very independent but dangerous as hell," Kris said. "I get the feeling that all this beating around the bush is intended to slowly work me away from putting any high technology in their paws. It would be worse than petting their fur the wrong way."

"I wouldn't agree with that imagery," Jacques said, "but I sure wouldn't want to artificially inject advanced technology into their civilization. The outcome could be ugly."

"So, one of my options is off the table. That still leaves two. Do we risk this squadron in taking out the aliens across the system, or do we quietly leave and shut the door on this Pandora's box? Maybe come back in a year or two and see what we find?"

"Kris," said Nelly, "I don't think the matter is in your hands anymore."

"Why, Nelly?"

"Twenty-two alien warships just boosted out from the gas giant's orbit."

Kris allowed herself a deep breath. She would not panic. She'd fought and killed them before. She would do it again. Letting out her breath, she put on her war face as she glanced around the table. Jack and Penny were already back in battle harness. Masao looked inscrutable. The three boffins looked surprised.

Bet they didn't see this one coming.

"Report on the aliens' movement, Nelly," Kris ordered.

To their right, a screen came to life. It showed the entire system from well above the sun.

"The aliens have begun a one-gee acceleration that will take them toward the sun and, assuming some modifications to accommodate the solar presence, I calculate it is very likely that they will swing around the sun and arrive at the fourth planet. Kris, they are launching an attack on the cat people."

"Why would they do that now?" Jack asked.

"Nelly, has there been any evidence in the cat people's radio transmissions that they are aware of the aliens?"

"No, Kris. There are no references to an alien attack in their news. Their fiction, as distributed in their media, has no genre for alien attack. I also find it hard to accept that they would be continuing their minor war if they were fighting for their existence with the aliens. No, this is the first attack by the aliens," Nelly said, drawing a conclusion from what Kris would have considered incomplete data.

"But that still leaves the question, why now?" Jack repeated himself.

"Maybe they needed time to refuel," Kris said. "Maybe they

needed time to prepare. Or maybe they even had an argument as to what to do next. Nelly, is that all of their warships?"

"Two are remaining behind with the four large reactors."

"So it's seven heavy frigates and the *Endeavor* against twenty-two of their monsters," Kris said. "Those are the best odds I've faced yet. Nelly, send to the squadron. 'Prepare for battle. We get underway in two hours. Longknife sends.'"

"I guess I'll be getting back to my *Hornet* sooner than I expected," Captain Taussig said, standing up.

"Good luck and Godspeed," Kris said.

"The same to us all," Taussig replied.

Despite Kris's early alert, they were still at anchor twelve hours later. There was no rush; even with the later start, they would reach the felines well ahead of the bug-eyed monsters that looked too much like humans.

They spent the extra time absorbing the *Sisu* into the *Wasp* and the *Intrepid*.

These two frigates had begun life with only five 18-inch guns. Now they sported ten 20-inchers. That made them better in a fight, but their power generation meant it took far too long to reload the lasers.

Over the next couple of hours, one of the reactors from the *Sisu* was swallowed by each of the other two ships. They wouldn't be used for propulsion, but they could be used to recharge the lasers.

When the occupants of the brig discovered they were going into a fight, the engineers among them begged for a chance to run their own reactor to power the guns that might just save their lives.

While they might or might not have heard much about why they'd been detained in the Alwa System, they certainly had learned that the bug-eyed monsters did not take prisoners.

Kris granted them their desire but assigned engineers from her own watch to keep an eye on them. As well as Marines to do the same, only armed.

When the rest of the engineers stepped forward to help with their new fourth reactor, *Intrepid* also took them up on the offer. And detached Marines to keep them straight up.

The extra Smart Metal™ was also much approved of by

Penny when she got half of the *Sisu*'s hull, scantlings and fittings. Nelly and her kids had to work hard with both the *Wasp*'s and *Intrepid*'s ship maintainers to get the stuff smoothed into their own structure.

Kris thought long and hard on it, then decided to keep the ship at Condition Baker for the one-gee acceleration and deceleration down to the fourth planet.

She delegated to Jacques and Amanda the job of explaining to the newly recruited aliens that they were going to war. "Don't say who with, just let them know that we have run into someone who owes us their head," Kris said. "See if they can get the concept."

An hour later, Nelly reported back that the aliens didn't have a problem with the Sky Gods fighting other Sky Gods. The path of the People was often bloody. Why shouldn't the path among the stars be red as well?

Kris shivered at the thought but took her blessings where she found them.

With fuel topped off and enough reaction mass both for the trip sunward and plenty extra to pad their armor with cooling liquid and dispersant to vent if hit, they began a carefully measured one-gee burn for the Cat Planet. If things went as planned, they would flip ship at midcourse and go into orbit just as the alien fleet was rounding the sun and decelerating toward them.

Their presence did not go unnoticed. As Nelly pieced it together from the local news, a ten-year-old amateur astronomer with eagle vision spotted them against the gas giant as they accelerated away. He lost them after that but caught sight of them again when they flipped ship to start their deceleration burn.

Once their engines were pointed at his planet, he reported the eight moving lights on their amateur astronomy network, and the kitty litter hit the fan, so to speak.

Some of the largest telescopes were brought online to track them as they rocketed in. With eight sets of engines burning bright against the stellar backdrop, the cats went crazy.

"We're getting questions aimed at us from everyone and his dog," Nelly said.

"That's a joke, right? Dog?" Kris said.

"Yes, it's a joke. Not a good one?"

"No, Nelly. Very good. So, who wants to know what?"

"The questions are all the same: What are we doing here and what are our intentions? They come from all sorts of media outlets. Every one of their hundred fifty-seven governments, no one hundred and sixty-two. There were a couple of small ones we missed. Or maybe they're that new. It's hard to tell with precision. Oh, and there must be a million news organizations begging for an exclusive. I guess news organizations are the same wherever you are in the galaxy."

"Is that all of them?" Kris asked.

"Well, the boy who first spotted us is using a friend's radio to ask us where we came from and why we are here."

"A kid, huh?" Jack said.

"A kid," Kris repeated.

"Both of them, the astronomer and the radio operator," Nelly said.

"But if we reply to them, everyone will get it, right?" Kris asked.

"No doubt, Kris. Even if we tried to send it on a tight beam, I'm not sure their antenna could pick it up. It's very primitive technology."

"How sure are you that you understand their language?"

"Languages, Kris. We've identified fifty-three being broadcast so far. There may be some weak signals we're ignoring."

"What language are the kids calling us in?" Jack put in.

"One of the dozen or so major ones. The one that calls themselves Sasquans. I've got over fifty thousand hours of recordings, both radio and TV. I'm 99.99 percent sure of the words for 'We come in peace. We mean you no harm. You are about to be attacked by starships coming around your sun. We will protect you as best we can.'"

"Have they spotted the alien warships coming around the sun?"

"I don't think so. There is a lot of encrypted radio transmissions. Some are pretty easy to crack, but others are on throwaway ciphers. There just isn't enough there for me to hack it, Kris."

"Send the message. You better not append 'Longknife sends.' Longknife is rather aggressive, or so I've been told."

"The name, or just you?" Nelly asked.

"Not funny," Kris said.

"But a good bit of sarcasm," Jack added.

"Message sent," Nelly reported.

"Now we wait and see what happens next. Nelly, will the BEMs get the message you just sent?"

"I sent it on a wide beam, Kris. Very likely, they will get it, too."

"Send it again. This time append, 'Longknife sends.' Do the cat folk have military ranks?"

"Yes, Kris. They have air, land, and naval ranks. If your next question is, do I know what Vice Admiral translates to, yes, I do."

"Then make it 'Vice Admiral Longknife sends.'"

"Do you want 'Princess' added, too?"

"Do they have a lot of royalty down there?"

"I don't think so. Most of the governments are democratic, or pretend to be. I've identified several presidents for life and something called 'The Leader of the People.' Three of them leading three different peoples. Also two of them are shooting at each other but not officially at war. Kris, it's a mess down there."

"'Vice Admiral' will be enough."

"Sent a second time. I'm sending it repeatedly."

"Now we see what happens," Kris said.

40

The fecal matter really did hit the air-redistribution system when Kris's message arrived at the planet.

Within ten minutes of Kris's message showing up, it was in all the news-distribution media that her squadron could copy. There were also references to something called print media.

Nelly had to look that one up in her archives and was shocked to discover that trees were sacrificed to make paper specifically so that information could be printed on it and sold.

"What a waste of those lovely forests," she told Kris.

Nelly dug deeper into the media from the locals' airwaves and found examples of forests being cut and bulldozed. "Why are we even fighting for these people?" Kris's computer asked. "They're destroying their own planet."

Kris sent Nelly to search the ship's own historical archives of Earth in the twentieth and twenty-first centuries. The computer returned much chastened.

"Well, at least it appears to be something that your type can grow out of."

Most of the new queries aimed at the squadron were more of the maddening same demanding to know who they were and where they were from.

There was even one asking Kris what she used to assure she had a glossy coat.

Kris ignored them all. All except two. One was from the kids. They thanked Kris for answering them and hoped they might meet whoever she was and that she would win the coming fight.

"Children are so innocent," Penny said.

"Read the other message," Kris suggested, and handed her friend the one that had come in on a very powerful tight beam.

"How do we know you are what you say you are? How do we know that the other ships are our true enemy?" Penny read aloud.

"Where did this one come from?" Kris asked Nelly.

"It was beamed from a communications satellite. It was on a tight enough beam that we're pretty sure none of it washed back onto the planet."

"Can you return a tight beam to catch that satellite?"

"Only at certain times in its orbit. Say, in about seven hours. It's in a geosynchronous orbit. Sometimes it's behind the planet. Sometimes it's right in front of the planet. Twice a day, it's way out on the side of the planet. We'll still be outside their moon when we get our next chance to tight beam something to it when it's out on the edge of the planet."

"Nelly, get a small summary of what the alien did to the first planet we discovered. Say, five minutes' worth. Add in a couple of pictures of their trophy room. Send it under the heading of 'This is what they do.' Then get a collection of the ships we destroyed, including the first mother ship and one or two of the warships we blew away the last time we visited that wreck. Send it with the heading 'This is what we do.' Let's see how that goes over."

"I've got it ready. I'll send it as soon as I'm sure it will miss the planet's general distribution."

"Thank you, Nelly."

"So, Kris, do we make contact with only this nation that has the highest tech?" Jack asked.

Kris gave him the "thanks for nothing, husband," look and reconvened her war council to stew about that question. Both Jacques, Amanda, and Penny were out of their seats before she'd even finished posing Jack's question.

"No!" "We can't do that!" and "That is a terrible idea," seemed to sum up those talking. The others proved less hurried in their need to verbalize but were no less sure that Kris would be making a major mistake.

"I'm glad to see that we have consensus for once," Kris said. "You can count me in with you."

"Then why are you sending this message to only one of the many sides?" Amanda demanded.

"Because they have the technology to ask the question and get the answer in private. We're still well away from them. We'll toss the mouse into the cat convention and see how they handle it."

They didn't have long to wait.

At first, nothing happened. Or at least nothing appeared to happen. Then Nelly started noticing trends.

"Kris, we may have a problem," she told Kris at supper.

"What problem might we have?" Kris said, as Jack eyed Kris's collarbone where Nelly rode. A polite, tactful, even pensive computer was turning out to be a bit of a pain at times.

"You remember that one country that could send us a tight-beam question?"

Kris allowed that she did.

"Well, it appears that several senior business executives have canceled meetings and cannot be located. Their legislature has also suddenly recessed, and the president has canceled all appointments and his press offices are not responding to inquiries. Oh, and it is now in the media that their nuclear-weapons carriers, rockets, air vehicles, and submarines, are on a heightened state of alert. This is causing trouble among other atomic powers."

"I was wondering how the other players were taking this," Kris said. "Didn't I read somewhere that this was the kind of thing that happened when one atomic power was about to try for a first strike?"

"Yes, Kris, it's in the old records from the horrible twenti-eth century. It looks like they are at risk of something."

"Just what we need," Jack said. "Aliens coming down on them and they're about to have a nice little war tossing atomic weapons around in their own backyard."

"Not if I can help it," Kris said, decision made. "Nelly, broadcast to all the planet on a broad beam the report that we sent to that one nation. Back it up with a report on the first ship that attacked us, a more thorough report on the raped planet we found, and more visuals of us destroying the two alien mother ships. Include shots of our fight with the three alien warships at the hulk and the one I fought when we rescued the *Hornet*. Have I missed anything, Jack?"

"I take it you want to avoid the huge battles and us getting our butts kicked."

"Yes."

"You know this is going to cause panic on that planet."

Kris nodded through a scowl. "I suspect there will be a lot of hasty exits from the large urban areas. I don't see how we avoid it if we don't want them to get themselves into their own out-of-control war. A war with atomics, for Christ's sake."

"The other two major powers have gone to alert," Nelly reported. "They are surging their atomic-armed submarines out to sea and launching their air vehicles. Some of their missiles that have to be fueled before launch are being very ostentatiously pumped full of rocket fuel and oxidizers. Messages are being sent both in the clear and with visuals."

"Then we'd better get our message out right now. Nelly, send out the main message. But I want to talk to the kids. See if you can get them on the radio."

"Both messages are set. Kris, I'm trying to raise Zeth. His name is longer and means Prancing Hunter. Frodin's name is also much longer and means Loud Howler, but the kids go by the shortened names. Maybe they have to grow into the longer name."

"You can translate for me."

"With 99.99 percent accuracy. My children and I are refining our dictionaries by the minute as we get more data. Oh, here are the two kids, Kris."

The voices seemed both surprised and maybe a bit scared. "Are you really calling us?" Nelly translated.

"Yes, Zeth and Frodin. I wanted to talk to you. We are sending out a longer message to your planet, telling them about the other aliens coming from the other side of your sun and about to attack you. We will defend you, and we expect to succeed in destroying that attack. However, one of your nations contacted us and is now responding to what we said in a way that is upsetting its neighbors. Your world seems on the edge of war."

Kris waited while the message went out and the answer returned.

"It's always on the edge of war," Frodin said. "My dad thinks we all ought to just chill out and take a nap. My mother says we have to protect the pride. Dad says it's a guy-gal sort of thing, and things would be a lot more peaceful if the gals would just let the guys run things. Ouch."

"You guys would just sleep while the herds stampeded through the pride lands."

"Well," Kris said, carefully interrupting what, no doubt, was a never-ending debate on roles and priorities, "it would be a shame for nations to destroy themselves just when they are about to be attacked by aliens, now wouldn't it? Doesn't the pride face out together when something strange moves into their territory?"

The chatter ended, and, "Always," came in two-part harmony. Kris had guessed that one right. They paused for her reply.

"What I want you to do is try to let everyone know that you should be alert to the coming attack from the sky and that you are not alone. We will do everything we can to defend you."

"Can you?" was a while in coming, but only for the speed-of-light delay.

"We've beaten them like a drum every time we've met. These are the survivors of the first pride that attacked. We beat them once and sent them off with their tails between their legs. We will beat them again."

"We've been recording this message," Frodin said. "Is that okay with you?"

"I was hoping you would. I want everyone to hear this. I'm also sending on an open channel a report on our experiences fighting these aliens. I hope your commanders will look at it and that it will help them plot their own defense."

"The pride doesn't defend, we attack," Zeth said proudly.

"You might want to be careful attacking these guys the first time," Kris said. "They have wiped all life from a lot of planets."

"Wiped out *all* life?" was one part shock, one part awe.

"That is what they like to do. I will show your leaders these aliens' trophy room if they ask after they examine the report I'm sending."

"And you want us to get this message out?" Zeth said.

"As quickly as you can."

"We'd better be going then. We met a reporter. She's nice and a really sharp hunter for stories. She says you have to get the story in before a deadline, or you lose it."

"You go talk to her," Kris said, and ended the strangest interview she'd ever given, either as the Prime Minister's brat or that damn Longknife princess.

41

Kris moved her war council down to the wardroom; her stomach was rumbling on empty. It was a pretty lame supper. Apparently Cookie was saving the steaks, either for the aliens aboard or for a victory celebration. Today's meal was reconstituted, canned, and hard to identify.

Quickly, Nelly brought everyone up to date.

"You're dropping yourself right into the middle of their politics," Jacques said. "From the looks of it, that's a real maelstrom."

"And my alternative was to let them get their world war underway and deliver their wrecked planet on a platter to the aliens," Kris countered.

Jacques winced. No one else offered any further insight.

"Nelly, how is the message going over?" Penny asked. She had her own computer, Mimzy, but when you wanted the counsel of all the computers, you asked Nelly.

"They seem to be taking it differently, in different zones. The media on that one that was getting its elite out of the target areas got ahold of the story, and now everyone is panicked. The other large zone has released the entire report to its media and is organizing evacuations from their cities by the license number on their personal vehicles. They put ten numbers in a hat and drew out a three. Only vehicles with plates that end in three can use the main roads out of towns today. They'll pull another number tomorrow morning."

"And they haven't even seen the aliens yet," Amanda said. "They're still behind the sun."

"We aren't," Jack pointed out. "They may be evacuating for fear of an attack from us."

"Well, at least they're running from ground zero," Penny said.

"There are three major zones," Masao said. "What about the other?"

"That one is run by a Leader for Life, and there's not a lot officially happening. He runs a centrally controlled country, and he apparently hasn't decided what to do yet. He is now holding a meeting in a bunker under a mountain. Lots of his cronies are with him there."

"How do you know this?" Jacques asked Nelly. "If he's running a locked-down dictatorship, you can't be getting this off the media like the other places."

"No," Nelly said, and you could almost hear the pride in her voice. "However, his codes are child's play. Everything his police send might as well be in the clear for all it matters to me and my kids. Fearless Leader does something, the police jump to protect him, and I track it from start to finish."

"I take it that Fearless Leader isn't all that fearless," Kris said dryly.

"Petrified of everyone," Nelly said. "I really wish you could find an excuse to lase his hideout from orbit, Kris. He is everything that a government should not be."

"But we likely can't," Jack said. "We don't do things like that."

"Darn," Nelly said. "Sometimes being the good guy is not all it's cracked up to be."

"I'm very aware of that, Nelly," Kris said. "How are the countries that aren't in the three major zones taking the message?"

"They are still thinking about it, although anyone who can find an aunt, uncle, or grandma to visit in the country is taking this chance to use their vacation time. A lot of roads are jammed. That's also happening in the first zone we alerted. Now that everyone knows, there's a lot of, ah, I think you used to call it gridlock, before computers controlled traffic patterns. It's a mess down there."

"Hopefully, they'll straighten it out before the bad guys arrive," Kris said.

"Kris, there's a movement developing among the smaller states to call for a conference in their Associated Peoples to talk to you," Nelly said. "Are you willing to go down there?"

Kris raised an eyebrow, tossing the question to her brain trust.

Jack jumped in immediately, shaking his head. "I don't like the idea of putting you down in the middle of that madhouse. We don't know enough about them to know if marching in with a Marine honor guard would settle things down or start a fight, and I am so not letting you down there without the Marines."

"No surprise there, Jack, and thank you," Kris said, trying to make her words worth more than she knew they held. "What about the rest of you?"

There was a long pause before Jacques said, "I don't want to get on the general's wrong side. However, there are cultures where anyone not willing to speak face-to-face with their enemies is assumed to be lying. I've asked my computer to study what we know of these mad cats, and I'm afraid that I'm coming to the opinion that they are one of those cultures."

Nelly took over the conversation at that point. "We have been examining their TV transmissions. They have some very interesting shows that I think would fit right in with what you humans call soap operas. They even sell soap and other beauty aids. That glossy coat question that got beamed up to us earlier was from one of them."

"Nelly, is there a point in here somewhere?" Kris said.

"Yes. It may just be a product of their visual theater, but personal confrontation and reconciliation is the norm."

"You're basing your cultural intelligence on soap operas!" Penny said.

"It is not just their soap operas. They have movies. Historical pageants. All of them depend on this kind of eye-to-eye encounter."

"Movies and soap operas," Jack said with a rumbling sigh, "How can we go wrong?"

"It's not like you humans broadcast scientific treatises on human conflict resolution on your day or night entertainment media," Nelly said, sounding downright snappish.

"Okay, okay," Kris said. "I have all of your input. We haven't received an invitation to this talkathon. Let's put this question off until then."

Kris eyed her team. Jack was being Jack; he wanted her safe. He'd always wanted Kris Longknife safe. He didn't seem any different now that he was arguing to keep his wife safe. Her science friends were giving her the best they had. It was a thin gruel at best. Still, she might have to base her decision on something that thin.

It was Nelly that bothered Kris. Nelly was starting to sound personally involved in the decisions she advocated. Was Kris's computer beginning to show early signs of an ego?

Kris had been raised around big egos. Father used to grumble that he'd never met a politician who didn't come with a bloated ego. Naturally, Father had one of the biggest Kris had ever known.

Grampa Trouble and Grampa Ray were legends. And, though Kris had missed them at first, they had the egos to go with the legend. She'd never seen the two of them go at it and hoped she never would.

But now it was Nelly. How big could a computer's ego get? How much trouble could it cause?

Kris sighed . . . and went on to her next problem.

"Nelly, could you get the ship captains in a conference?"

"Immediately," Nelly said, and hopped to it.

That's it, Kris thought. *Keep Nelly on specific things with specific solutions. Let's keep the poor computer away from the value judgments where a flip of the coin is as good as anything else for conflict resolution.*

In a moment, Captain Drago had joined them, and the other seven captains were watching from the wardroom's own screen. Also watching were a lot of junior officers who were paying only partial attention to their meals as they watched the elephants go about deciding their fate.

"We have a battle to plan, as much as possible," Kris said, without preamble. "From what we've seen of the aliens, they've adopted a line ahead, twenty-two ships long. I propose to fight them in a line ahead of seven ships. *Endeavor*, we'll keep you in orbit around the planet."

"Pardon me, ma'am, but we'd like to have a place in the fighting line, if we may," said Captain O'dell.

She'd started life as a merchant-ship skipper, as had the *Endeavor*. Her ship only had six 18-inch lasers, three forward and three aft. That was intentional. Kris wanted the *Endeavor* to be as dangerous running as chasing.

"This is going to be a knock-down drag-out fight, Captain O'dell," Kris said.

"I know, ma'am. Me and my crew know it will be, ma'am. But we've seen the inside of that damn pyramid. We'd all kind of like to get a chance to make our own statement that they ain't gonna get our skulls for their horror house, if you know what I mean."

"I think I do," Kris said.

The crew thrown together for the *Endeavor* was a very mixed batch. Some merchant marine, some Navy, and a lot of the gun crews were Ostriches. If a crew such as that were voting for a fight, Kris had quite a team on her hands.

"Nelly, put our assumptions about the enemy up on the board."

A line of twenty-two ships appeared on a second screen. It showed the aliens decelerating toward the cat planet. "Physics decrees that they must be braking as they come in on final approach. However, as we saw in the attack on the *Hornet*, they have learned to break a bit farther out and gain some tactical flexibility as they get in range. We'll have to be prepared for that. Still, their tactical problem is governed by the laws of physics, and they can only get around them so much."

Kris eyed Captain O'dell. "You will be in the lead position as we join the enemy in deceleration. I intend to use the moon to loop out to meet them, then fight it out with them in that final approach. *Endeavor*, you will be at the head of the line."

Nelly added a name to the ship closest to the cat world. *Endeavor.*

"You know, ma'am, some might say we were at the end of the line."

"In space, it's often hard to tell," Kris said. "But that is your position. I intend to cross their T and concentrate our fire on the head of their line."

"That means the ship that's at the other end of the line could be in for a heap of trouble," Captain Taussig said in a soft drawl. "Any of their other ships that get in range will be firing away at that poor soul."

"It does look that way," Kris admitted.

"May I claim the honor of that position for the *Hornet*, Admiral?"

"Are you sure it's an honor you're asking?" Kris said.

"It's where I think we'd rather be, Kris. We got a bone to

pick with these bastards. They clobbered the old *Hornet*. I want them to know they've been solidly stung in this next fight."

Kris knew that Phil came from a long line of Navy heroes, going as far back as the wet Navy. She'd always thought it was a pain in the ass to be one of those damn Longknifes. Maybe she was seeing how hard it could be to bear another proud name.

"You will have that place, Captain Taussig."

"Thank you, Admiral. I think my great-grandfather would be very proud."

Yep, some names were just a pain in the butt.

"Which leaves the question of who gets the honor of the next hot spot in line," said the skipper of the *Constellation*, Captain Sims.

Kris nodded. "I hope none of you will think me less courageous than those who have already spoken up, but General, please retrieve my cover from my quarters. Oh, and the printout Nelly's making."

What printout am I making?

One with all the names of the other six ships, well spaced out so we can cut them into slips of paper and draw them from the hat.

Cover, Nelly corrected.

Whatever.

Jack returned with her cover, complete with admiral's scrambled eggs. Nelly and Abby had had a ball constructing just the right gold braid for the bill of her hat.

Captain Drago produced a pair of old-fashioned scissors from some drawer in the wardroom.

Scissors. What delightful old tech.

"I'll have the lovely Amanda Kutter serve as our honest broker here. This sheet has the names of the other six ships of the squadron. Each of them capable of fighting just as well as the next and holding any place in our line."

"Yes the paper does," Amanda said, holding it up for all to see.

Kris handed her the scissors. "Cut the flimsy up and fold them over. Then put them in my cover."

She did.

Kris stood and went to stand behind Amanda. She held the cover above the economist's head. "Now draw out the name of the ship that will fight right behind *Hornet*.

"*Constellation*," Amanda said as she opened the first slip and laid it on the table in front of her.

Captain Sims grinned proudly from his place on the screen.

"*Royal*," Amanda read next.

Another skipper seemed just as glad.

"*Wasp*."

Captain Drago's grin was full of pride.

"*Congress*," was followed by *Intrepid*. *Bulwark* would fight next to *Endeavor*.

"That, my good captains, is our fighting order. Captain Drago, please arrange for the ships to take their station in our new line."

"And may God help us all," Captain Drago was heard to mutter.

42

They made orbit, and then the problems started.

The squadron was in its second orbit, and the ships were busy maneuvering to get nose to nose and swap anchoring cables. Being at zero gravity, Kris was belted into her chair at her desk reading the latest set of guesses about the planet beneath her.

"Kris, three missiles have been launched at us," Nelly reported curtly. "They are still in boost stage."

"Shoot them down," Kris ordered just as curtly.

Suddenly, the *Wasp* lurched as it brought its aft batteries to bear on the planet below.

"I've fired three aft lasers, just a short burst," Nelly reported. "We hit all three."

"What the hell is going on with my ship, Kris Longknife?" came as a bellow from the bridge.

"I take it, Nelly, that you didn't inform Captain Drago of our little problem?"

"There wasn't time, Kris. Is he mad at me?"

"No, he's mad at me, Nelly. Are there any more launches?"

"No, Kris. But the missiles fired were atomic-tipped. One had a low-order explosion when it crashed. The others spewed radioactive plutonium."

"Thank you, Nelly," Kris said, as she undid her seat belt and pushed herself off for the bridge.

"Can I have my ship back, Your High-handedness?" Captain Drago said with a scowl.

"I'm sorry, Captain. Missiles were fired at us. I told Nelly to shoot them down quickly because they were still in boost phase and an easy target," Kris said as she latched onto the back of the captain's chair. "Next time, I'll tell her to inform you and let you do it the proper Navy way."

"The hard way," the skipper said, and, if possible, his scowl got even deeper. "I hate to say this, but thank you."

"You're welcome," Nelly said from Kris's collarbone.

"So, what do we do about this greeting?" The captain asked.

"Nelly, which of the zones launched the rockets?"

"Do you remember that one I called Fearless Leader?"

"Yes."

"It was definitely her."

"Her?" the captain said, raising an eyebrow.

"Yes," Nelly said. "We've come to find out that all the major zones are led by females of the species."

"God help us," Captain Drago said in full drama. "A planetful of Kris Longknifes. What sin could I have possibly committed in my previous life to deserve this?"

"Are we still over her territory?" Kris asked, ignoring the drama queen at her elbow.

"No, we're far enough away from it that I don't think we need fear shots from them," Nelly replied.

"Then broadcast this on the usual frequencies. 'I have been fired upon with atomic missiles. I have destroyed them with more ease than you swat flies. Do you really want to go to war with us? We came here in peace to save you. Admiral Longknife sends.' Let's see what we hear from the rest of the crazy cats between now and the next time we pass over Fearless Leader's domain."

Kris shoved off from the skipper's chair and headed back to her day quarters.

"So, do we continue to anchor?" Captain Drago asked.

Kris paused at the door to her quarters. She shook her head. "Beat to quarters and get ready for a fight. With luck, next time Nelly won't have to step on your pride."

The captain made a face, but he passed the order to the squadron.

Ships pulled away to get more maneuvering room. Crews settled down at their battle stations and made ready for whatever came next.

What came next was a flood of denials that anybody wanted to fight the squadron. They came from heads of states, including both of the two other major powers, as well as from movie stars, heads of major industrial combines, and the two kids that Kris had talked to.

Kris took their message personally.

"Please, listen to us," Frodin said. Kris could almost hear the tears in his eyes. "My dad says no one wants war. Even my mother says it would be a bad idea."

"And so do my folks," Zeth put in. "It's just that crazy tail over there. They've been trouble ever since she came to power. She doesn't speak for the rest of us."

"I'm coming to understand that," Kris said. "I will handle this problem just between her and me."

"Please do. The rest of us don't want to have anything to do with it."

Kris ended her radio session with the two kids. They might just be kids, but what they said was backed up with signals from 161 other countries. Only the Fearless Leader kept quiet.

The squadron was battle ready as its orbit swept toward the problem zone.

Missiles rose to meet them.

"*Endeavor*, engage the threats."

"Engaged," came back quickly and seven missile were lased before they could get out of boost phase. The last one was hardly off the ground. Two exploded, including the one that had just lifted off.

That might explain why no more were fired.

"Nelly, do we have a solid lock on just where Fearless Leader is hunkered down?"

"I am 99.999 percent sure I have her mountain dialed in, Kris."

"Please pass it along to the other ships of the squadron. I want to give it a broadside from each ship. Full charge from the forward lasers, then flip ship and give it the aft batteries."

"Orders passed."

Around Kris, the *Wasp* swung down, pointing its nose at one particular mountain.

"Fire," Kris ordered.

She felt nothing as six 20-inch lasers poured every joule of energy they stored into firing on one particular piece of real estate. Kris had once been too close to a building when Admiral Krätz, of mostly fond memory, lased it from space.

He hadn't had anything like the ships she had.

The only sign Kris had that the forward batteries were empty was the *Wasp*'s swinging around to present her aft batteries.

Five seconds later, Captain Drago reported. "Broadside fired. Request permission to resume anchoring."

"Permission granted. Keep an eye on that zone next time we pass it."

"That I will do, Admiral. However, some cartographer needs to remeasure the height of that mountain. It ain't what it used to be."

"No doubt. I wonder how Fearless Leader is taking it."

"We'll know next pass."

Next pass was uneventful.

Then, Kris found herself invited to a party.

43

"Well, Jack, it's now official. I have been invited to the General Session of the Associated Peoples annual session. Apparently, it's being held three months early just for little old me."

Kris tried to keep a happy grin on her face. Unfortunately for the debutante in her past, she was none too sure she meant a word she said.

"Where is this shooting gallery going to be held?" Jack asked before Amanda, Penny, or their tagalongs could say a word.

"One of the largest cities on the planet. It's located in the zone with the highest tech. The one that first contacted us."

"And then proceeded to keep the bad news to itself," Jacques pointed out.

"Has anything been heard from the people you lased from orbit?" Masao asked.

"Not so much as a peep," Kris said. "And when we cross their territory, we are not even tracked by radar."

"Total shutdown," Penny said. "But I notice we're still on alert."

"It only takes a few seconds to turn a radar on, track us, and launch," Jack pointed out.

"So, are you going down?" Amanda asked.

"The invitations from both of the major zones say their leaders will be there personally and wish 'to speak to me eye to eye.' That phrase may not mean what it says."

"Or it can mean exactly what it says," Jacques put in.

"Yes."

"So what do we do?" Penny asked.

"We do what we always do," Jack growled. "We keep her

safe despite herself. Penny, you are the admiral's coordinator with the local police. So get on the horn and talk to the local police. Coordinate. Me, I'm the chief of her security. I will be talking to the chief of the security details of these other two top cats and seeing what they're doing to keep their primaries safe."

General Montoya paused for a breath. "We are going down to talk with civilized people with the usual problems of organized civility. Honey," Jack said, turning to Kris, "don't wait up for me tonight. I may be dirtside for a day or two."

"You're not mad at me, are you, Jack?"

"No, love. You do what you do, and I do what I do. We knew it would be like this when we decided to share as much of our lives as we could."

Kris blew him a kiss, but he and Penny were already having their computers hook them into what passed for a communications net dirtside.

In seconds, both were talking to someone. Minutes later, they were headed dirtside on the same longboat with a detachment of Marines.

Jack was not in her bed that night, nor the next one. That day, the aliens finally showed up, clearly swinging around the sun and still in their long line ahead.

And that was the day Kris was formally invited to address the Associated Peoples the next day . . . with Jack's approval.

She arose early the next day, pulled on her spider silks and donned her vice admiral's dress uniform. At the last minute, she slipped on an armored wig as well.

What had Jack called it, the shooting gallery? Certainly, there was no one down there that had a beef with one of those damn Longknifes. However, she had flattened someone's mountain.

Fearless Leader had not been heard from since the mountain got slagged, and the squadron continued to zip above that zone with not even a hint of radar ranging. Still, Kris chose to take no chance.

It proved to be a wise choice.

44

The admiral's barge landed in a river and was promptly surrounded by police boats and led to a pier. Kris exited into a wharf, covered against the rain and even heated against the damp chill.

On a gallery above her, cameras rolled and lights flashed. There were a lot of shouts to look this way, and Kris did. She remembered how to do the princess thing and smiled and waved as was necessary to the role.

Jack let her stand there, but there was a large black limo waiting for her. And farther back, several large SUV-type rigs with an ambulance at the rear.

"You really do have this all prepared," Kris said through her wide smile.

"It's been a while," Jack answered through a tight smile, "but it's like a bicycle. Once you've got the hang of it, you always know how to fall off again."

Kris had to chuckle at that.

"This is your allotted time for waving," a furry female with a sleek black coat and interesting silver harness said. "It is time to be going," and she entered the limo.

Kris gave one last wave and slipped inside. Jack, in dress blue and reds did the same. In a moment, the cavalcade was on its way.

"You speak our language very well," Kris said, settling into her place.

"I am a professional translator. I have mastered twelve languages and can read eighteen. Your language is moderately easy. I have been studying it since we started picking up your communications."

Kris eyed Jack.

"When you talked to the kids, you'd talk and Nelly would

translate. Both seemed to have gotten through. It also appears that Nelly included several of the original copies of our reports as well as the translations."

"I thought they might come in handy," Nelly said.

"I found them most helpful. Now, about your schedule," the female said.

"I am Kris Longknife," Kris said, offering her hand.

"Oh. I am sorry if I have violated greetings protocol. I am Zarra ak Torina. At your server."

"At your service," Nelly said.

"At your service," Zarra corrected. "And this is?" she said, staring at Kris's collarbone.

"My personal computer," Kris said. "She is also my translator."

"Computer?"

"You have computational machines," Kris said.

"Yes, for weapons design and some other things. Businesses are starting to use them for billing and inventory."

"Very primitive," Nelly said.

NELLY, SHUSH. I THINK WE NEED TO KEEP YOU OUT OF THIS. SPOILSPORT.

"We use computers for much more. And ours are much smaller. Have you landed a person on your moon?"

Zarra shook her head. "There is talk of doing that, but many think it is just talk."

"On our first planet, the race to put a man on the moon sparked all kinds of improvements in life and technology. I will suggest that your leaders undertake that challenge if they want to expand their horizons."

"Just your being here is a major expansion of our horizons," the translator said.

"No doubt," Kris said before Nelly could.

"We are driving to the Tower of the Associated Peoples Grand Assembly. Almost every country has chosen to send its leader to this meeting, so you will be seen by most everyone. There will also be private meetings so you can talk face-to-face with President of Columm Almar, President Almar, and Prime Minister of the Bizalt Kingdom, Madame Gerrot. They represent the two most powerful zones now that President for Life Solzen seems to have departed this life."

"Is she the one that fired on us?"

"Yes."

"Foolish to do it once. Stupid to do it twice."

"Many of us agree with you. Apparently, what you did to her mountain redoubt has also taken out most of those who implemented her rule. The country is in disorder. All wonder what will come of that chaos."

Kris chose not to remark on that.

The ride was smooth, attesting to the weight of the car, and, no doubt, the thickness of the armor. Here and there along the drive, people on the sidewalks paused to wave. They seemed dressed for the wet weather in substantially more than the interpreter, leaving Kris to wonder what the attitudes were toward clothes.

YOU SHOULD HAVE ASKED ME SOONER, OR WATCHED A FEW OF THE SOAP OPERAS, Nelly growled in Kris's head. THEY DON'T MUCH CARE FOR CLOTHES, BUT THEY LIKE TO BE WET EVEN LESS. YOU HAIRLESS APES MAY HAVE TO GET USED TO A MORE OPEN ATTITUDE.

THANK YOU, NELLY.

YOU'RE WELCOME, KRIS.

They drove into a basement and directly to a wide-open entrance. The interpreter exited first, then stepped aside to allow Jack to step out. From the following black rigs, Musashi Marines in bright red dress uniforms rushed to form a defensive perimeter, all eyes out. Only when they had taken up station did Jack motion Kris out.

He offered her a hand, and she stood.

Again, a wall well away from them was taken up by cameras and their crews. Kris smiled and waved like a good princess, then went where her guides led.

The Marines fell in on both sides of her.

"They don't mind having armed Marines in their halls of power?" Kris said through another wide smile.

"These aren't their halls of power," Jack answered through tight lips. "And they like a parade as much as the next. Although, I got the impression they wanted the Marines buck naked. That would spoil everything, though. Most of them think our Marines are female."

"How's it feel to be a guy in a gal's world?"

"No different than it ever does, Mrs. Montoya."

That almost broke Kris up.

Zarra led them to a large foyer with high walls on two sides but open to the next floor up on the other two. Again, there were camera crews recording everything. The rails on the upper floors were lined with people who watched and waved. Kris spotted two young ones, only about half the height of grown-ups waving madly. She waved back. Zeth and her young boyfriend had made it just as they had planned. They'd even managed to ship a picture of themselves up to the *Wasp* so Kris could recognize them.

But their time would be later. Zarra led Kris to a female who might have once had a lovely gold-and-black-striped coat but which now showed much gray in place of black.

"May I present to you, the Elected Speaker of the Associated Assembly, Von ak N'tire."

Kris held out her hand. The elderly female held out her paw, but, no sooner had Kris and she touched palms than the Elected Speaker pulled Kris into a wide hug. Kris suspected she could have been crushed in the hug, but it was pro forma at best.

Quickly, it was over, and Kris stepped back.

YOU COULD HAVE WARNED ME ABOUT THAT, JACK, she said on Nelly Net.

WHAT, AND TAKE ALL THE FUN OUT OF IT?

Then a slug slammed into Kris's back before she even heard the shot fired.

45

Kris hit the deck both because that was what she'd been told to do, and because she had to. The force of that slug was that bad.

When the second slug hit her, she rolled both to make it harder to hit her again and because the round made her.

It also hurt like hell. Even the new spider silk was having a problem with the force of these slugs.

"Don't shoot. Don't shoot," Jack shouted as he came to stand between Kris and the next round.

Around Kris, the Musashi Marines had their rifles up, but Jack was right. Whoever the target was, she was lost among all the people watching from above.

Who were now racing away, either because of the shots fired or the sight of a whole lot of Marine M-6s raised at them with intent.

"Penny, do you have an eye on the shooter?"

"I have her. A white with thin black stripes. She's ditched her gun, but we have nano scouts following her. I don't think she expected our technology. We'll get her. No, make that we've got her. Five local blues—well, black and silvers—have her."

That was followed by a "Damn."

"What happened, Penny?" Jack demanded.

"She suicided. She slipped something in her mouth and now she's down, kicking in convulsions and foaming at the mouth. We'll get nothing from interrogating that one."

By now, Marines had formed a protective wall around Kris. Only now did Jack kneel down beside her.

"I see you wore your spider silk today."

"Damn right I did, nanny. And you didn't even have to bug me about it."

"That's why I've decided to keep you, wife. You are proving to be very educable."

"And I'm hurting like mad. Can you give me a lift up?"

Jack offered her both his hands. She swung herself around, tensed every muscle she could handle, and let him haul her up.

"Ouch," she said through gritted teeth.

"Is it that bad?"

"I've had worse."

Now both the translator and the Elected Speaker were at her side. One was babbling, and the other wasn't making a lot of sense.

"Calm down," Kris said, drawing a slow breath. "I am hurt but not injured."

"You have skin tough enough to resist a slug thrower?" asked Zarra.

"Let's just say that I do," Kris said, not willing to give more away than she had to. "Where are the two I need to meet?"

The Speaker led Kris quickly to a door. It was opened by what Kris took to be a soldier. She had a slug rifle and her leather harness was brightly shined and sported several brass buttons.

The soldier stepped aside to let Kris and Jack enter but closed the door before any Marines came in. Since Jack took that as acceptable, Kris did, too.

Penny, in dress blues, allowed herself in a side door and trotted to meet Kris before she reached the two groups waiting at the end of a long hall.

It was quite a luxurious hall. Lined with marble pillars, the floor was a fine, golden hardwood. Between the pillars stood statues in perfect white marble of other felines. Some held spears. Others held books. The balance seemed about even.

As Penny joined them, Jack spoke through a hardly moving mouth. "Do we know anything about the failed assassin?"

"The official story is that it was a madwoman, driven around the bend by the shock of learning that there was life among the stars, something that wasn't considered possible before a week ago. The most likely story is that one of the survivors of Solzen's crew thought to get a leg up in the present intramural sport of offing anyone reaching for the fallen President for Life's baton by offing you. The assassin was known to be associated with a spy network from Fearless Leader's side."

"They knew it and didn't haul her in," Kris said, trying not to lose her smile.

"If you've got them made, you never haul them in. You follow them and see if they take you to someone that you don't know about."

Spoken like a true intelligence officer.

Kris came to a halt an equal distance from the two groups as they were from each other. At the center of the groups were two females. One wore a blue coat, edged in gold. The other wore a red cape. As it turned out, President Almar of the Columm Almar wore the coat. The Prime Minister of the Bizalt Kingdom, Madame Gerrot, sported the cape.

Kris saluted. The two of them bowed from the neck. Those around them bowed from the waist.

President Almar stepped forward a pace. "I wish to greet you in the name of the Congress of Columm, in the name of our people and on my own behalf," she said.

Kris heard the statement as an echo, one from Zarra, the other in her head from Nelly.

NELLY, LET ZARRA DO THE TRANSLATION. IF YOU IDENTIFY A MAJOR FAILURE, TELL ME IN MY HEAD AND LET ME FIGURE OUT WHAT TO DO ABOUT IT.

YES, KRIS.

Now Prime Minister Gerrot took a step forward. "I also wish to greet you in the name of the ancient parliament of the Bizalt Kingdom and in the name of our monarch and the people of our ancient land, as well as myself."

Kris took a step forward. "I am Her Royal Highness, Admiral Kristine Longknife, Viceroy to the people of Alwa and Commander of the Alwa Defense Sector. I wish to greet you in the name of the people of the United Society, their congress, and my liege, King Raymond, the First of that name. And if I may, I wish to greet you in the name of all humanity as well as the Iteeche Empire, may we long share peace with them, and the people of Alwa."

"There are three different races riding between the stars," President Almar remarked.

"Yes," Kris said, not putting too fine a point on the Alwans.

There was quite a discussion among their own advisors about that.

President Almar seemed to shush them with a scowl before turning back to Kris.

"I wish to apologize for the assault on your person," she said.

"I understand the problem. President Solzen was foolish to fire on us the first time. To fire on us the second time was stupid. No doubt her continued silence is causing much confusion in many corners." Zarra had liked the foolish, stupid meme. Kris was thinking of adding it to her speech if it went over here.

"In life, Solzen showed herself to be many things," Madame Gerrot said. "No doubt she will meditate long and hard on her folly from where she rots in hell. Meanwhile, it leaves us with many things to contemplate. Can we expect attacks like you showed us from these aliens you say are coming?"

"I should think by now your own astronomers can see them," Kris said.

Madame Gerrot glanced behind her. One of her advisors came up to whisper in her ear. "Why was I not told about this sooner?" she snapped.

The advisor gave what looked like a shrug and backed away. Kris eyed the two leaders. Neither of them showed any gray, but something about Madame Gerrot left Kris with a sense of age.

"We have seen the ships coming around the sun that you told us of," President Almar said. "Will they pound us as hard as you pounded Solzen?"

KRIS, THE WORD FOR POUND THAT SHE USED HAS A NEGATIVE CONNOTATION. CATS CUT AND SLASH. DUMB ANIMALS HAMMER AND POUND, Nelly put in.

"Solzen behaved like a dumb animal, trying to throw rocks at what was not within her reach. I could have cut or slashed her. I chose to hammer her. I have enough weapons in easy reach that I can do whatever I chose to do."

Both national leaders turned back to their advisors.

GOOD JAB THERE, KRIS, Jack said on Nelly Net.

THANK YOU, NELLY, FOR THE INPUT.

YOU'RE WELCOME, KRIS.

Now the top cats were looking at each other, as if to decide who was the top cat. Finally, Almar spoke.

"May I ask you a question? You don't have to answer it."

KRIS, THAT IS VERY TENTATIVE. ALMOST SUBMISSIVE, IF WE CAN TRUST THE SOAP OPERAS.

"You will have to ask the question before I can know if I can answer it or decide if I will," Kris said, pulling herself up to her full height, which just about equaled that of the cat before her.

"Why are you here?" President Almar asked. "What brings you to our solar system now, just when we are being attacked? The timing seems much more than a coincidence."

Kris had expected that question. She'd spent the better part of the last day going over it with Amanda and Jacques. Their final conclusion was that the truth would be better than evasion. Kris had harbored a hope that it would not come up.

At least it was raised in semiprivate.

"I am here because I chased a ship full of mutineers here," Kris said slowly. "I caught them and would have gone back to Alwa except we discovered your radio and TV transmissions at the same time we identified the alien ships that had fled here to lick their wounds and regroup after the last time we defeated them."

Kris paused to make sure her translator had stayed with her. Then she went on.

"Hard as it may be to believe, it is a long series of coincidences that led me here. After capturing my miscreants, I was considering going back to Alwa without making contact with you. However, when the aliens launched their attack, I chose to defend you."

"There are twenty-two of them and only eight of you," Madame Gerrot said. "Do you expect to win this battle?"

"I expect to, but one never knows in battle, does one?"

"No," Almar said. "Lady Chance dances a jig in every battle."

"What will you do if you win?" Lady Gerrot asked. Now her tail was twitching.

"I will return to Alwa, which I have a duty to defend on my honor," Kris said. "But I think your question was what will I do about you here?"

"That is correct," President Almar said, standing very still, as if waiting to pounce.

"I would prefer to leave you alone," Kris answered.

"Alone?" came from both of them. Kris didn't even need a translator for that. In their surprise and shock, both took a step back. Several of their advisors seemed to be pacing now, tails lashing their sides.

Kris went into her prepared speech. She spoke slowly both so the translator could follow her and so her words would have weight.

"You are at a precarious stage of your civilization. You are still divided into tribal factions. Only now, you are tribal factions with atomic weapons. You can destroy yourselves and everything that lives on this planet. I would prefer not to have anything to do with you until you decide for yourselves if you are to wipe yourselves out or will grow beyond your childhood."

"That is an interesting perspective," Almar said with a snort.

"You are where we were four or five hundred years ago. We chose one path. You are still at that crossroads. Which path will you choose?"

"Will these aliens you are about to fight stand by while we choose?" Almar asked.

Now it was Kris's turn to frown. If she'd had a tail, she might have twitched it. "They create a problem."

"Will you stay here and guard us?" Madame Gerrot demanded.

"No," Kris said.

"And why not?" President Almar asked.

"I am charged to defend Alwa," Kris said.

There was a long pause at that.

"And you do not have enough ships to do that, do you?" President Almar said slowly.

"What admiral ever had enough ships for her job?" Madame Gerrot said slyly.

"I think you are inviting us into a war that is still very much in doubt, isn't it?" Almar said.

"I am not inviting you into any war. It is coming at you," Kris said.

"But you cannot defend us," Gerrot snapped.

"And you cannot defend yourselves," Kris snapped right back.

The two leaders turned back at that and joined in heated conversation with their advisors.

THIS GOING WELL? Jack asked on Nelly Net.

ABOUT AS WELL AS I EXPECTED.

KRIS, I CAN FOLLOW MOST OF THEIR TALK. SOME WANT TO TAKE YOU HOSTAGE AND DEMAND YOU PROTECT THEM. OTHERS FEAR YOU. THAT SLAGGED MOUNTAIN REALLY IMPRESSED THEM. A FEW JUST WISH YOU'D GO AWAY AND TAKE THE OTHER ALIENS WITH YOU.

SO, NO CONSENSUS, NELLY.

NOTHING EVEN CLOSE.

JACK?

I'VE ALREADY ALERTED THE MARINES OUTSIDE. THERE DOESN'T APPEAR TO BE ANY MOVE TO CONTAIN THEM. I'VE GOT OTHERS MOVING INTO PLACE.

PENNY?

I'VE SET REPEATERS INTO MOST OF THE POLICE NETS. THEIR ELECTRONICS ARE NOT VERY SOPHISTICATED. THERE'S NOTHING ON ANY NET ABOUT MOVING AGAINST US.

SO IT'S JUST TALK. JACK, KEEP YOUR MARINES ON STANDBY. THERE'S NO TELLING WHAT ONE DESPERATE TYPE MIGHT DO.

TRUST ME, ADMIRAL, MY WIFE, I'M VERY ALERT.

Finally, the two statesmen stepped away from their advisors and faced Kris.

"What might we do to gain a defensive alliance with you and your king?" Madame Gerrot asked.

"First, let me be very clear. If any of you launch a nuclear war, or any war of conquest that exhausts your resources and lays waste your lands, all bets are off. You will be on your own."

Kris paused. She knew she'd spoken too fast for the translator. Besides, there were several aides who were elbowing others in the ribs. No doubt, someone had brought up the idea.

"Secondly, yes, a planet must have a united government to apply for membership in the United Societies. It must be democratic and have arrangements to see that the will of the majority rules while protecting any minorities under a rule of law."

Again Kris paused.

"It sounds like you have had plenty of experience with fractured governance," President Almar said dryly.

"Yes, it lacks balance. Finding that balance is often bloody."

"But you will not impose that single governance," Madame Gerrot said.

"That always leads to more blood, not less," Kris said.

That brought what Kris took for grim chuckles from both leaders.

"But you, yourself, have said that we cannot stand against these aliens. We might as well roll over on our backs, show our bellies to be scratched, and piss ourselves. What are we to do?" Madame Gerrot said.

"You have not yet sent one of your own to walk your moon," Kris said.

"We have talked about it. It will be very expensive," President Almar said.

"It will also be very productive. It will require you to advance your science and technology. It will put you into space."

"But we still won't be able to stop these attackers," snapped Almar.

"But you will have started down that path."

"And if we are attacked in the meantime?"

"Empty your cities. Spread out. Be prepared to be attacked with nerve gas. Fight them. Make this victory so expensive that they turn away in disgust," Kris said.

"But you will not sign a defensive pact with us," Madame Gerrot said.

"No," Kris answered.

Madame Gerrot's tail was thrashing now.

"Mort, don't have yourself a coronary," President Almar said to her sister politician. "She's an admiral, for pity's sake. Yes, she may be the whelp of her king, but still, she's just an admiral here. Would you want some admiral, even of your royal bloodline, negotiating a military treaty for you to sign? And negotiating it with no authority and no guidelines?"

"Thank you for understanding the limits of my authority here," Kris said.

"I think there are more limits here than you want to talk about. You are going into battle at three-to-one odds. Something tells me that you don't have the resources to protect us if you did sign that treaty Mort is so hot to get your paw print on."

"You will understand that such issues might be covered by the State Secrecy Act."

"We have one, too," Almar agreed.

"Just how much danger are we in?" Almar asked after a pause. "What do these aliens want? Slaves? Resources? Control of the means of production?"

"They want your heads," Kris said bluntly. "They want to sanitize your planet down to the smallest signs of life."

The big cat visibly gulped at that. Madame Gerrot had been consulting with her aides. Now she turned back to Kris. "Our heads?"

NELLY, PROJECT THE INSIDE OF THAT PYRAMID FOR THEM, Kris thought as she turned to face the opposing wall.

The hologram was very solid. Suddenly, the walls were no longer marble but lightly worked granite. The pillars became figures encased in cubes of glass.

The floor showed piles of heads. Skulls, carapaces, whatever.

"Sweet ancestors," came from somewhere, but otherwise, the room was dead silence.

"These aliens are not like any other aliens my species has encountered," Kris said slowly. "We enjoy encountering different species." *Unless, of course, they go to war with us, but the less said about the Iteeche the better.* "These people hate all life not of their own kind. They search space, hunting for life, and then kill it."

Kris let that sink in.

"Then, once they have plundered a planet down to even its air and water, they take one sample of that life, encase in this plastic cube, and a pile of heads, and take it back to their trophy room. Their room of horrors."

Kris left the hologram up for a bit longer, then had Nelly kill it. She said nothing as she turned back to the two leaders of this planet's most powerful governments.

"It seems we have our work cut out for us," said President Almar, "if we are to keep our heads on our shoulders."

"Yes. It seems we do," Madame Gerrot agreed.

Kris's address to the Associated Assembly after that was a minor affair. She gave the nice, generic speech she had planned, adding in the foolish vs stupid reference to Solzen. It went over big now that she was assumed dead.

Kris made no references to heads or raped planets but left it to her listeners to assume the worst.

No doubt, they would assume far less than what they faced, but hopefully, their fear would be enough to unite them.

She, Jack, and Penny were back aboard the *Wasp* before it was time for lunch.

Kris still hurt quite a bit from those two slugs. Nelly told her that several religious groups on Sasquan were claiming the miracle of her survival for their gods.

That was another opinion Kris was willing to leave open to whatever interpretation people wanted to put on it.

Captain Drago interrupted her lunch. "The aliens are braking as they come around the sun, but they have launched stone, iron, and lead bullets at the planet. These are not slowing. They're headed our way at several hundred thousand kilometers an hour, and it looks like they are aiming for major cities."

Kris tossed her napkin on the table. "Enough of diplomacy. Now we get to fight," she said.

46

The five-hundred-ton bullets were coming in fast. Twelve of them, each made of whatever the aliens had been able to get their hands on. No doubt, they'd make a major hole in whatever they hit.

And what they would hit would very likely be a major city. If not intercepted, every one of them was headed for an impact within one or two kilometers of the center of a major urban area.

The twelve largest cities on the planet.

"Good shooting," Captain Drago was heard to mutter.

"Too bad we'll have to spoil their shoot," Kris said.

She'd ordered the *Endeavor* to cast off and head out immediately. As she did, Nelly and Kris went over several possible shoot scenarios.

They ordered the simplest one.

The *Endeavor* did a deorbital burn, dropped down to graze the planet's atmosphere, then slingshot herself up into an orbit that put her fifty thousand kilometers above the planet, headed for the incoming slugs.

A hundred thousand kilometers below the targets, she hit the first three with a head-on shot, cutting them in half. *Endeavor* then did a flip ship and deceleration maneuver, while using her aft batteries to filet the next three. She repeated that again, and there were twenty-four half-size bullets headed in, but on slightly different courses than they had been a few minutes before.

Kris could only imagine the rejoicing among the Ostriches as their lasers sliced targets exactly as they intended. No doubt, there would be a lot of chest bumping later, but not now.

Now they sliced and diced what was left of the bullets hurtling toward the cat world. Every fifteen seconds or so, the *Endeavor* would lash out at the bullets, dicing them into quarters, eighths, sixteenths, and smaller.

Whatever energy wasn't needed to recharge the lasers went into the engines, braking the *Endeavor* in orbit and heading her back down.

It wouldn't do for the little *Endeavor* to run into the entire enemy fleet all by herself. Captain O'dell reported, however, that the Ostriches were quite willing to do so.

The aliens' first shots did slam into Sasquan, but not as five-hundred-ton streamlined bullets. Instead, they hit the atmosphere as ragged, jagged chunks of thirty tons or less, rolling and out of control. By the time the atmosphere had its go at eroding them, they hit the ground as meteorites of ten tons or less.

That might be hard on the two or three dwellings that got flattened, but they were no longer city killers.

Whatever doubts the cats might have held about Kris's true intent vanished with the demise of the slug strike. The airwaves were unanimous in their praise of Kris as their planet's savior.

"Let's hope they're still saying that after the battle," Kris muttered.

The *Endeavor* made orbit again and rejoined the squadron. The problem was, she was low on reaction mass. She'd used a lot going against the laws of physics.

The *Bulwark* launched its pinnace over to refuel her. The *Bulwark* had come out from the gas giant with more fuel than the other frigates. It was a joke among the skippers that the skipper of the *Bulwark* was always afraid of running out of fuel and always took on extra.

Now, no one kidded him, and Captain O'dell was grateful for the help.

For the upcoming battle, Kris intended to use a similar orbit to the one *Endeavor* had used, only she'd sling herself around the moon to get farther out and be on a better-angled orbit. Like her enemy, Kris would be braking.

But with any luck, Kris would be closer to the cat world as she did so. That would put her in the perfect position to cross the T of the alien line, able to shoot up their vulnerable sterns, hit their engines, and rake their reactors with all her ships while few of them could reply.

At least that was the plan.

And like all battle plans, it didn't survive contact with the enemy.

47

Kris's squadron had reached the apogee of their orbit above the moon and were beginning to fall back toward the cat planet. The aliens were off to her left, still braking.

Kris studied their deployment from her flag plot. On other days, it was her day quarters, but today it was organized to command the developing battle. Screens around her reported the availability of every ship's lasers, armor, reactors, and other critical systems.

Kris had been alone when she fought her last battle from this same space. Today, Jack kept her company. It was nice to have his supporting presence, but she somehow doubted she'd find time to even notice him.

Her eyes roved from screen to screen.

No surprise, the aliens had upped their deceleration for a bit and were farther out than Kris had planned for. The extra deceleration meant they would have to do some reaching to make orbit, but it would allow them more maneuverability when the shooting started. Kris would not always be able to count on having their vulnerable engines and reactors pointed her way.

Trade-offs, trade-offs. This was a surprise Kris had expected.

Then they did the unexpected.

The first seven upped their deceleration, which put the other fifteen rapidly climbing up their rear. However, as the next eight overtook the vanguard, they slewed aside to take station on their far side. Then they also upped their deceleration. The last seven ships slid in smoothly on the side closest to Kris's squadron. That done, they all resumed their previously scheduled fleet deceleration.

Instead of facing a long line whose T Kris could easily cross, she now was confronted by three much shorter lines. One was a few hundred kilometers closer to her, but the other two were in a perfect position to flank Kris if she tried to have her squadron take that line on alone.

"They've formed squadrons," Kris said softly to herself.

"I bet you didn't see that coming," Jack said.

"Actually, I kind of expected something like that," Kris said, still half talking to herself. "I was thinking they'd form a dish like in the last fight, but three lines have advantages as well."

"They aren't dumb," Jack said.

"I never said they were."

"No, I don't believe you have," he agreed. "So, now what?"

"We use our 20-inch lasers for best effect, and boy, do I wish I'd brought along just two of those 22-inch war wagons."

"This will be a slugfest," Jack concluded.

"It's looking that way. They outweigh us. If they manage to come alongside and board, they'll bury us in bodies. However, we have the reach, and, unless I'm mistaken, they don't have any armor."

"Kris, Chief Beni has been doing his best to get a solid-mass determination on those ships," Nelly said.

"And they do have armor," Jack said softly.

"The ships are massing more than they did the last time we met them. Every one of them is different, but there seems to be between forty-five and seventy-five thousand tons more ship there."

"Nelly, how many extra tons were on the ship we shot up at the *Hornet*'s arsenic planet?"

"I estimate there were fifteen to twenty thousand tons of rock, Kris, that we had to punch through before we could hit the soft, chewy center. There is likely double or more armor on these hulls."

"So it's maybe twice as bad as the last time?"

"It looks that way, Kris."

"Pass that word to all the captains with my compliments and suggest that they plan on hitting the same place on their target's hull as hard as they can, as often as they can."

"I've sent it, Kris."

They were at three hundred thousand klicks and closing when Kris ordered the fleet to set Condition Charlie. She saw no reason to let the aliens know any sooner than she had to that their targets could get smaller. The former mutineers pitched in, manning the *Wasp*'s extra reactor. Those who weren't engineers mustered with the Marines to repel boarders.

Sampson stayed sedated in the brig. It was tiny, but it was locked.

Jacques and Amanda joined the twenty alien recruits in a space reserved for them at the center of gravity for the *Wasp*. Hopefully, that would make the jinking around easier on them.

And hopefully, Jacques could find words to explain what was going on.

Kris had so wanted to talk to an alien, ever since the first time they gave her a choice between killing them or dying herself. Now she had her own pet aliens, and she hadn't found a second to talk to them.

The problem, of course, was that these aliens were of a different tribe from the strong, silent types that wanted her dead.

Oh, and the tame aliens didn't have all that big of a vocabulary.

Someday, the world would have to present Kris with a few easy problems.

Someday, hopefully, sooner rather than later.

Physics ruled space warfare. In ancient days, ship battles had depended on the wind. No wind, no battle. Too much wind, and the ships might find themselves struggling to stay afloat more than fight each other.

Space battles were very much like that, only it was gravity that ruled the roost. And while gravity might be more constant than the wind, it was no less a master of the battle.

The alien warships were decelerating, aiming to make orbit around the cat world. What they'd do there was an exercise best left to horror.

Kris was on a course to intercept them.

Gravity ruled both their vectors.

But laser power might very well trump gravity's vectors.

At 160,000 klicks, Kris ordered all her ships to Condition Zed. Thirty seconds later, she ordered them to cut deceleration and face the enemy. Seven of her ships lashed out at the closest seven enemy ships with six 20-inch lasers each.

No surprise, the targets shed rock and droplets of steel. Some shot off steam as ice burned away to gas. The targets got fuzzy but showed no serious damage.

Kris flipped ships, paused for a second or two for the gunk to fall behind, then hit them with the aft batteries.

The targets fizzed as ice and rock armor ablated away under the lasers' probing, but again, no explosions.

Kris brought her squadron back on course and returned to a deceleration burn as her lasers recharged.

Twenty seconds later, she repeated the double volley.

Twenty seconds after that, she did it again.

This time, the closest enemy squadron showed damage from the pounding. One blew up, and two staggered out of line, their engines firing in directions they weren't intended to.

The other four turned bow on to Kris's squadron and charged.

Above and below those surviving four, the other two lines of ships did the same. Their commander was now much less concerned with making orbit than getting in range of Kris's ships and slamming them with their main battery of more lasers than Kris had ever had a chance to count.

Maybe whoever was giving the orders didn't care if they made orbit so long as they destroyed Kris's ships.

Who's your Enlightened One?

Kris ignored the question and ordered her ships to flip. They began jinking and danced away.

Now Kris was between a rock and a hard place. Specifically, the moon she'd been using to swing above now was coming up fast below her. The enemy, desperate to get in range to use their own huge battery of lasers, were coming up nearly as fast behind her.

Kris's ships emptied their now-recharged aft batteries. One more ship blew up, but the surviving close-in three absorbed their hits and kept coming.

The *Hornet* at one end and the *Bulwark* at the other end of

Kris's line took on the new ships coming in range. They fired . . . and got only fuzz to show for their shooting.

Kris flipped ships again. Her middle three ships finished off the first squadron they'd attacked. Two ships blew, and the last lost all acceleration and just drifted in space.

However, the other two squadrons had closed the range as Kris's ships exterminated their fellows. Enemy lasers began to crisscross the space around her ships. In her flag plot, boards began to slip from green to yellow as ships reported their armor taking hits.

Reaction mass and water bled out of the damage into space to disrupt the lasers just as the enemy's rock, ice, and steel armor had splayed out Kris's lasers.

It was the same for both sides, except that while the aliens' gunk quickly fell behind the decelerating ships, Kris's bleed of ice and hydrogen fouled the middle ground between them for a few critical moments more.

Now, fifteen alien ships charged in to narrow the range for their four to five hundred tons of angry, suicidal commitment to Kris's doom.

"Kris, we will miss the moon," Nelly reported, "But if we keep this up, we'll have trouble making a good orbit around the planet."

"We'll worry about that later, Nelly."

Kris studied her boards. Now her ships were slugging it out as best as they could, dancing the crazy jig that never kept them on a straight course for more than two seconds. A dance that dodged the aimed enemy fire.

The enemy's fifteen ships were huge and overweight. They were too heavy on their feet to dance like Kris's, but what they lacked in finesse, they more than made up for with their huge batteries.

Kris's ships fired and reloaded. The aliens fired and fired and fired; never for a moment were they silent. Worse, most of Kris's ships now faced two of them. Only at the head of the line was the *Endeavor* able to fight a single alien, applying her limited battery of six 18-inch lasers as best she could.

The big war wagons, the *Hornet*, *Constellation*, *Royal*, *Wasp*, *Congress*, *Intrepid*, and *Bulwark*, each divided its attention between two ships, firing bow batteries at one, aft batteries at the other. This kept each of the enemy ships shedding bow armor; rock, steel, and steam spread down the hull, dispersing their own lasers and occasionally causing damage.

That was good. The bad news was that her ships weren't hammering through the alien armor to smash reactors inside.

The worst news was Kris's ships were taking hits; damage was accumulating.

Kris could lose this battle if she kept fighting it this way.

"*Wasp. Congress. Intrepid.* Concentrate on one ship opposite you and kill it," she ordered bluntly.

Seconds seemed to take forever, and minutes vanished in a blink. The battle went on with her ships firing, flipping, firing, recharging, then doing it over and over again.

The enemy fire hammered them. The *Constellation* suffered damage to a rocket motor and zigged out of her place in the line. Unfortunately, she also steadied on a course for more than two seconds.

The luckless *Connie* took more hits.

The *Royal* changed fire from the two she faced to slice at the one that had the *Connie*'s number. It worked . . . for a second. The enemy ship's fire faltered and the *Connie* got her engines under control.

But *Royal* paid for saving her shipmate as her own two targets got off scot-free for a few seconds. Now her armor showed bright red on Kris's boards.

Across from the *Wasp*, the enemy ship rocked as a laser slashed through its bow and cut deep inside. It hit a reactor and freed the demons inside. Gouts of plasma shot out its sides, but its huge batteries kept shooting.

Kris watched the readout on her board as the *Wasp*'s armor went from yellow to red.

The *Wasp* flipped, and the bow lasers fired. There must have been nothing left of the aliens' bow. Six lasers cut through it and deep into its guts.

More fire blossomed within the shattered hull. But angry lasers still reached out, cutting through the thin vapor of the space around the ship. Even as the reactors lost containment and the plasma demons gobbled up the ship, it was still spitting death at the *Wasp*.

"Captain Drago, engage one of the ships fighting the *Royal*."

"On it, Admiral." The *Wasp* didn't miss a beat as it flipped ship and began slicing into the ship that *Royal* had been splitting its fire with.

"*Royal*, the *Wasp* has the ship closest to it. You concentrate on the other one," Kris ordered.

"Great, an even fight," *Royal*'s skipper said, and laid into the one target.

The *Intrepid* did not finish off its ship in quite as spectacular fashion as the *Wasp*. Its target ended up rolling in space, a silenced hulk with fires gutting it from stem to stern.

Kris ordered *Intrepid* to turn its attention to the ships attacking the *Bulwark*. She did it none too soon.

The poor *Endeavor* was in trouble. She only had six 18-inch lasers, and her armor had been thin to begin with. She was hurting.

The *Bulwark* switched fire to engage the *Endeavor*'s ship. The forward end of Kris's line was still two ships against four, with the *Endeavor* giving all that it could.

In front of Kris, her boards showed way too much red.

Suddenly, two alien ships blossomed into gas, and there were no ships facing the *Royal* and the *Wasp*.

"*Royal*, help the *Connie*. *Wasp*, help the *Intrepid*."

Now there were four fair fights. The gallant *Hornet* was still being hammered by two, as was the *Bulwark*, but the enemy ships must have been hit just as hard as Kris's.

The end came quickly, but none too soon. Enemy ships began to burn and explode even as the *Connie*, *Hornet*, and *Bulwark* limped out of the fight, reactors dead, overheated, or redlined.

When the enemy saw that the day was lost, all the ships that had fallen by the wayside began exploding, as containment fields were dropped and plasma was intentionally let loose to finish what the fight had begun.

"Not one surrender," Kris groaned.

"They never do," Jack agreed.

48

The battle was won, but the squadron was still in dire straits.

"Kris, did you know that many of the French and Spanish ships the British captured at the great Battle of Trafalgar were lost when a storm came up and blew them all onto the rocky shore?"

"Yes, Nelly, I seem to remember reading that somewhere."

"We're in danger of smashing ourselves onto the planet below."

"Yes, I noticed, Nelly. Now shut up."

Kris motored her high-gee station onto Captain Drago's bridge. "Can the *Wasp* make orbit?"

"Yes. We've got one reactor off-line, but we can make it. I can't say the same thing for the *Hornet*, *Constellation*, and *Bulwark*. They're both down to a single reactor, and none of them are in good shape."

"Could we loan them a pinnace?"

"If I do, I'm none too sure the *Wasp* will make orbit."

"Penny," Kris said, turning to her only staff officer, who had spent the battle on the *Wasp*'s defensive station shuttling Smart Metal™ around to cover for hits on the armor.

"Yes."

"Can you merge the *Hornet* onto the *Wasp*? Say something like a pinnace."

Penny was already shaking her head before Kris finished. "No, Kris. The pinnace is a subsystem of the ship. The programming to generate it is there. Remember, the hull is a special program with all sorts of security overrides. You can't just slide it all away from, say, one beam to let another hull merge with it."

Kris said a most unprincesslike word. But then she was an admiral today, and she'd been told that Sailors cussed.

"We've got ships that aren't going to make orbit if we don't do something. Get me a fix, not back talk."

"Maybe we could adjust the two ship's hulls so they could come alongside and kind of dock together."

"Make it happen, Penny. Find a good chief and do what you have to do. Otherwise, some of our ships are going to burn up on reentry. That's bad for our people but worse for the people on the planet we're supposed to be saving."

"I'm on it," Penny said with a huge sigh her late husband's Irish grandma would have been proud of.

Whether it was Penny, or, more likely, a lot of good chiefs on the *Wasp* and *Hornet*, the two ships did end up docking hard but docking enough that between the *Wasp*'s two good reactors, and the one they could keep running on the *Hornet*, they made orbit.

Once Penny and the chiefs had shown it could be done, the *Constellation* and the *Royal* got cozy, and the *Bulwark* sidled up and not quite rammed her bow into the *Congress*.

Captain O'dell asked permission to try the same with the *Intrepid*. One of the *Endeavor*'s reactors was out, and the other two were none too reliable.

Eight ships had gone out to face the aliens. Four of sorts succeeded in reaching orbit again.

On the ground, you could easily see fireworks and great rejoicing. In Kris's day quarters, there was little to celebrate.

She had the butcher's bill to read.

The frigates were crewed by four hundred men and women; two hundred and fifty boffins and fifty Marines topped them out at seven hundred. The *Wasp* tipped in at some nine hundred, what with extra Marines and scientists.

Her squadron had avoided the catastrophic failure of a reactor that consigned all aboard to a fiery grave. Still, the enemy lasers had cut deep.

Kris read the list: 612 dead, 1,452 wounded with some still likely to die despite all that modern medicine could do. The *Hornet*, *Connie*, and *Bulwark* were hardest hit, although the *Endeavor*'s smaller crew had suffered heavier casualties in proportion.

What had shown up on Kris's boards as bright red for

damaged armor, lasers, and engineering had been real men and women dying as lasers slashed hard into their ships and defensive stations juggled armor around desperately to keep disaster at bay.

Kris leaned back in her chair, stared at the overhead, and found she could fervently pray. "Please, dear God, may I never fight another one like this."

But there was more to do than mourn the dead. The living needed to eat, and they needed to celebrate that they'd once again faced death, looked it in the eye, and walked away from its hungry scythe.

"Kris, do you have a moment?" Captain Drago said after knocking on the doorsill.

"Talk to me," Kris said, putting down the report of blood and loss.

"Cookie tells me that he's got a deal on meat. Cheap. As in free. All we have to do is go down and get it."

"Can we afford the reaction mass?"

"When our longboats go down for chow, they'll be bringing back water as well. That's one way to feed the reactor and feed the crew."

"Free meat. Are you sure we can eat it?"

"The boffins are pretty sure. The meat offer came with a full scientific analysis of what goes into the local's digestion. A certain President Almar wanted you to know that they were providing the full details on their physiology. To make sure, I'll be sending down a doc to make the necessary tests, but I'd rather try it than not."

"If Cookie says he can make it taste good, go for it. And the water. We aren't bone dry on reaction mass, but we'll need to refuel before we leave here."

Captain Drago stepped in and closed the door. "Let me guess. You want to refuel from the gas giant on the other side of the system. The one where the aliens set up a base."

Kris made a sour face. "I'd like to wipe this system clean, but these damage reports," she said, waving her hands at her boards.

"Yeah. It would be nice if we had a repair ship to tie up to, but we have a lot of good ship maintainers, and we can do a lot with this Smart Metal."

"We've done a lot."

"I've got some folks working on figuring out if we can drain the Smart Metal from our two wrecked ships. Maybe move the reactors out of them and into a ship that still has some fight in it. I'll have that report cycled through to you as soon as they're done."

"Do," Kris said.

She ended up studying reports for the rest of the evening. Jack brought her a meal from the wardroom, and Kris ate it at her desk.

It was quite late when Jack finally hauled her off to bed.

When she ignored the wonderful things he was doing to her breasts, he rolled her over like a log and began doing even more wonderful things to her back.

"Am I distracting you, yet?" he asked.

"Well, you are definitely attracting my attention," Kris admitted. She stretched and found it made a lot of her feel very good.

"Good, because I am not stopping, young lady."

"Persistent, huh," she said into her pillow as he did something wonderful to the lower part of her back. And then went lower.

"You fought your fight. You won. I'd like to celebrate that I'm alive if you don't mind."

"And you want to celebrate it with me?"

"Most definitely."

She rolled over and smiled at her persistent husband. "Then I guess I'd better let you celebrate."

So he did. Then she did. Then they both did until they fell asleep in each other's arms.

49

The ship's moaning around them woke Kris in time for breakfast. They quickly showered. Jack kissed her very black-and-blue spots where she'd been shot, then found some cream to put on them.

It seemed he now had a supply of medical ointments and drugs for all the particulars that ailed her.

Husbands were nice.

They made it to the wardroom while the officers were still eating.

"What's with the racket?" Jack asked, as they found a space at Captain Drago's table.

"We're pulling the Smart Metal out of the *Hornet* and re-spinning it into the *Wasp*. The *Hornet*'s hull was barely holding out the vacuum by the time the shooting stopped. Their ward-room and mess, along with most everything else, got smashed up pretty bad, so you may notice some new faces at our tables."

Captain Phil Taussig of the *Hornet* arrived as he spoke. He had a bandage over one eye and an arm in a sling, but he was balancing a plate full of eggs and bacon with great aplomb.

"Welcome aboard," Kris said.

"I can't tell you how glad I am to be aboard. I seem to be making a habit of this. Coming aboard your flag in a roughed-up state. I'll try to avoid it in the future."

"If you need a port, we'll provide the storm," Nelly said.

"That was a joke," Kris said.

"Of course."

Phil took a bite of his bacon and made a face. "I'm not complaining, but this is a bit on the strange side."

"Locally grown," Drago said. "Just arrived last night."

Phil took another bite. "Not bad. Will it mess up my gut anything like the last local rations I had to share?"

"I have it on the best of confidences," Captain Drago said, "that this chow is as good for you as any you got from your mama's breast."

"I was a bottle baby," Phil said, "much to my wife's delight in my adult fixations. So, we have ourselves some locals that are really glad for something our princess did. Isn't that unusual."

"No doubt, and totally," Captain Drago agreed. "But there is no accounting for tastes, and we are enjoying their, no doubt, short-lived appreciation."

"Don't I ever get credit where it's due?" Kris asked the overhead.

"No," "Nope," and "Not likely" seemed to be the table's consensus. At least it was from the general and captains. There were a few lowly lieutenants at the foot of the table who kept their own counsel, and, no doubt, tried not to be shocked by the carrying-on of their seniors.

"How's the reaction mass coming along?" Kris asked.

"Much better than I expected," Captain Drago said. "Thank heavens for Smart Metal, again. We've rerigged several of our longboats into water tenders. They drop down and pick up as much freshwater as their antimatter engines can lift. By late today, we should have enough aboard to allow us to motor quite stately out to that other gas giant you were interested in. By tomorrow morning, I expect to have enough for a safety margin that will warm the cockles of even an old nanny such as myself."

"Gas giant?" Phil said, swallowing his dried eggs and bacon.

"I want to clean out the last of this rat's nest," Kris said.

"They sent twenty-two of their twenty-four ships," Drago said. "That leaves two, plus whoever they have keeping their hands warm around the four large reactors we've spotted over there."

"What do we have left to fight them with?" Phil asked.

"That's what I'm waiting to find out today," Kris said, "and no, Phil, if we don't have enough firepower, we go home. I'll even allow for a fifty-percent safety margin."

"Do we know these dudes well enough to know what fifty percent *is* for our safety margin?" he asked with a grin.

"You've been with me too long," Kris said with a sigh.

"And, I'd like to point out, I've survived all of it. So far." Phil looked around. "Drago, is there any wood to knock on?"

"It's all Smart Metal," the skipper of the *Wasp* reported.

"I have a real wooden desk," Kris said. "You can drop by after breakfast and knock on it. You can also try your hand at figuring out what a fifty-percent safety margin is."

"I think I will."

So it was that Jack and Phil ended up sitting around Kris's conference table studying the schematics of the revised and readjusted ships when Penny and Masao dropped in.

"Is that what the new ships will look like?" Penny asked.

"I have no idea what they will actually look like from the outside," Kris said, "but this is what they will be packing and what will be pushing them through space."

"Each ship is different," Penny said after a quick glance at the boards.

"It all depends on what the BEMs left us after the last fight," Jack said.

"The *Wasp-Hornet* looks to be in the best shape," Kris said. "Between the two of them, we can patch together eight forward 20-inch lasers. We have two of the *Wasp*'s reactors and one from the *Hornet* to go with the one from the *Sisu*. We only have three aft lasers. The bad guys were aiming for the stern, and it was hard on reactors and aft batteries."

"Any chance we can move one of those lasers aft?" Phil asked.

"Not in the time I'm willing to take," Kris said.

"Sorry about the stern," Penny said dryly. "I had armor shuttling back and forth from the bow to the stern depending on which way you had us going. So, what will our armor thickness be?" Penny asked, herself likely to be responsible for the defensive station in the next fight.

"Even at Condition Zed, we'll only have eighty-five percent of the planned defensive depth."

"How much hell will I have to protect us against?" Penny asked no one, then went on, "What about the *Royal-Connie*?"

"Aside from getting the best name in this lash-up," Phil

said, taking over the story, since he was standing in front of that pair of ships' schematics, "it looks like there are only seven lasers surviving from their forward batteries. Aft, we have two lasers and three reactors. Pretty heavy casualties for those two. The armor belt will only have sixty percent of the norm."

"That's kind of thin," Penny said.

"The *Intrepid-Bulwark* has another good name," Jack said. "She also has seven lasers forward. Her reactors are in the same state as the *Wasp*'s, with two of her own good, one of the larger reactors from the *Bulwark*, and the borrowed one from the *Sisu*. Aft, she has three lasers. Her armor has again been thinned down a bit. Sixty percent. Maybe fifty-five, depending on how small we make the ship in Condition Zed."

"The *Congress-Endeavor*," Kris said, taking back the story, "sounds somehow dirty. Or maybe Jack's just having an evil influence on me."

Jack allowed that he might, and Phil congratulated him on that.

Kris went sternly on. "Only two of the *Endeavor*'s six lasers survived—one fore and one aft. The casualties among the Alwans were high. Only one of her reactors is still workable. The *Congress* is in pretty good shape. Four lasers forward and two aft. Two of her reactors are also online. Almost all of the armor they have is from the *Congress*, and it's only going to give fifty-five percent of the depth she had in the last fight."

Penny fixed Kris with a jaundiced eye. "And you want to take this collection of patchwork wrecks into another fight?"

Kris winced. "But there are only two warships over there. For all we know, the reason they stayed behind was that they are not fit for space. We need to wipe this bunch out, once and for all."

"But if they are combat ready and looking for a fight to defend what's left of their wives and kids . . .?" Penny said.

"Then we approach them carefully. Come to a halt well out of range and use the advantage our 20-inch lasers give us."

"Does that sound like a plan to any of the rest of you?" Penny demanded.

"Pretty much," Phil said.

"Have any of you considered that the more time we spend with this crazy woman, the more likely we are to trot along eagerly with her next insane idea?"

"Yep," "Pretty much," and "That's what I see happening." That last came from Masao and was accompanied by a broad smile.

"You men!" Penny said, but her show of exasperation was mellowed by a growing grin as well. "Okay, count me in, too."

Through the day, the schematics of the four compound frigates began to grow on Kris's boards as chiefs and Sailors went about rationalizing and resolving some of the more difficult problems of pulling gear from one ship and mounting it on another. Storerooms, quarters, water mains, and air ducts had to be moved around as reactors were slipped from one hull to the next. Slowly, a single hull began to take shape that men and women could live in, fight in, and, if necessary, die in.

Kris had made the decision to merge her squadron's eight ships into four. With that decision made, she found herself mainly an observer as chiefs and Sailors did the work under the supervision of the division heads. Occasionally, a decision got passed higher up.

Phil left most of the calls to his Executive Officer, but occasionally the XO would call him. He'd listen, then politely excuse himself from Kris's day quarters to consult with Captain Drago on his bridge. They'd talk, resolve the problem, and pass it down.

Kris never had a question passed up to her level. She wasn't sure just how she felt about her new, rarefied rank that left her twiddling her thumbs as all those around her stayed busy.

When she tried to involve herself in Amanda and Jacques's work, she found them pretty much ignoring the aliens on board so they could study the society sprawled across the planet below them.

"It really is amazing," Amanda said. "They have little or no computers, but their economy is complex and global. I know that, historically, we humans did something like this back on Old Earth, but I've never had a chance to closely observe a mash-up like this. It's like I'm in a time machine."

Kris went back to her quarters and watched as more spaces vanished or were moved around in her ships.

As supper approached, Phil ducked out to talk to Captain Drago for a moment, then both of them presented themselves.

"Admiral, you are invited to a dinner in your honor in the Forward Lounge," Captain Drago said.

"Dinner in the Forward Lounge?" Kris said.

"The uniform is dress blues with all your medals and decorations," Phil added.

Kris gave them both the evil eye. "What's going on here?"

"We will see you in an hour," Drago said.

"Don't disappoint us," Phil added, as the two left.

Kris found her day cabins suddenly emptying as Penny and Masao also vanished away.

"Jack, Nelly, what's going on?" Kris demanded of the only two who were still with her.

"Nothing mutinous, my love," Jack said, grinning his most lopsided grin ever.

"So you're in on it. *Et tu*, Nelly?"

"Your Latin pronunciation is atrocious, Kris, but yes, I do know, and no, I won't tell you."

"Honey, you just have time to shower and get dressed," Jack said, bowing and ushering Kris toward their night quarters. "Shall we?" was not a question.

"So, just time to shower and get dressed. Not a second for something else?" Kris said with a sly grin.

"Be a good girl, and we shall see."

"But you always say I'm best when I'm naughty," Kris said. Jack sighed. "Naughty and nice, in one long, tall package." So she was.

50

Captain Drago and Commander Phil Taussig were in dress blues as they appeared to greet Kris and Jack as they came from their night quarters, exactly one hour later and not a second sooner.

"An escort?" Kris said.

"What with all the modifications, I wasn't sure you could find your way to the Forward Lounge," the *Wasp*'s skipper said.

NELLY, YOU'RE NOT PUTTING IN THAT YOU COULD GUIDE ME ANYWHERE. WHAT'S UP?

KRIS, THIS IS A THOROUGHLY HUMAN MOMENT. I'M OBSERVING AND KEEPING MY MOUTH SHUT, THANK YOU VERY MUCH.

This is going to be a very strange evening.

Despite the report to the contrary, they easily found their way to the Forward Lounge.

"Atten'hut. Admiral on deck," greeted them as they entered.

For the first time in her life, Kris didn't immediately shush those offering her this honor. She was too waylaid by what she saw.

The Forward Lounge had been converted into one huge wardroom. As far as she could see, officers stood at their linen-covered tables, china and silverware before them. Every surviving officer, even some who looked pretty banged up, were there. There were even a few Ostriches, doing their best to stand to attention with the humans.

Someone tapped a glass, and they began as one to sing, "For she's a jolly good fellow." The song went on; someone had added stanzas that would never be appropriate for children but seemed right at home among her victorious warriors.

Through it all, Kris just stood there.

Maybe her eyes did mist up a bit, but it must have been a flaw in the life-support system. Some irritant in the air, no doubt.

It must have been. Beside her, Jack was having the same problem.

The song ended with a rousing cheer, and Kris began to make her way to her usual head table. Her progress was slow. Every ship's captain and a lot of their senior division heads were along the main aisle and they wanted to shake her hand. Even Captain O'dell was there with her collection of female officers and four Alwan gun captains who had survived the fight.

Kris got a chest bump from one of them. It was a gentle one. At least gentle enough not to crush ribs.

It took her a long time to get to the head table, but waiting for her there were not only Penny and Masao but also President Almar of Columm Almar and Prime Minister Gerrot of the Bizalt Kingdom.

They greeted Kris with a bow, and Kris returned it from the waist.

Again, Zarra ak Torina stepped forward to translate. Her harness today was red with golden buckles and spangles.

"We are glad that you live to meet us again," President Almar said as the room fell quiet, again in response to someone's tapped glass.

"We all are glad to meet you again," Kris said.

"You have won a most wonderful battle," Prime Minister Gerrot added.

"A lot of people have won that battle. And many of them are not here to celebrate this victory with us."

"Yes. Yes," President Almar said. "Thus it is always. Good young felines die for the homes of their mothers and the graves of their foremothers. We can only offer you our humble thanks that you, who have no homes or graves here, have done us a service we could not do for ourselves."

"We did what our duty to all sentient life required," Kris said.

"Yes, so you have told us," Almar agreed. "But we must offer you tokens of our gratitude, even if they are but minor tokens. They are ours to give, and we give them to you."

The president looked to her right and two cats, tawny gold coats marked off with the same red-and-gold harness as the translator, came forward. One carried a long black pike with silver-and-jewel inlays along the finely worked point, the other a large sword, its two-handed grip wrapped in gold filigree and studded with sparkling jewels.

Almar stepped forward and took the black-handled pike. "A feline is never without her weapons," she said, and where a moment ago had been a softly furred hand, now five long claws sprang forth. "However, we learned quickly enough that a good pike could outreach the sharpest claw. Among our people, the Colnan Halberd with its long reach and its sharp blade has defended us from many an attack. In the last two hundred years, few have been honored with the gift of a Colnan Halberd by proclamation of the Congress of Columm. Today, we hope you will accept this from us."

She handed the ancient weapon to Kris. Kris accepted it with a bow and a "Thank you."

The room cheered. Kris raised the halberd high so all could see it. She twisted it so that its sharp edge flashed in the light. When the applause slowed, she handed it off to Jack. He accepted it with a bow and stood beside her, the Colnan Halberd at attention.

Kris did the handoff to Jack because Prime Minister Gerrot was coming forward and motioning to the sword bearer to approach as well.

The Prime Minister cleared her throat and spoke. "Among our people, the most ancient of honors is to join their king in the charge. We hope you will allow us to bestow on all of your officers the honor of being Members of the King's Charge. We ask also that you allow us to bestow on the captains of your ships the honor of Commanders in the King's Charge."

"I gladly accept these honors in their names," Kris said, wondering where this was going and why there was one sword bearer still standing off.

The Prime Minister's tail twitched, and the sword bearer came to stand beside her. "My king has bidden me to offer you

her highest honor. She wishes to raise you to King's Sword
Bearer and Commander of the King's Charge." The Prime
Minister bowed. "In the thousand years of our recorded his-
tory, we have no higher honor."

The sword bearer presented the sword to Kris, handle first.
She withdrew it from its gold-and-bejeweled scabbard and
flourished it above her head . . . careful not to slice the overhead or dent the blade.

Who knows which is tougher, Smart Metal or this steel?

No doubt it would be the Smart Metal™, but it would be a
shame to find out otherwise.

When the cheering died down, the two leaders of the most
powerful lands on the planet below did not suggest that someone serve the meal. No, two more warrior types appeared with
boxes in their hands. These were made of fine wood, beauti-
fully polished, and just the right size for awards.

Kris recognized the sizes of the boxes. One was as big as
the one that came in the mail from Earth and contained the
Order of the Wounded Lion. The other was about the size of
the box that Admiral Krätz had tossed to Kris and revealed the
Pour la Merit, Imperial Greenfeld's highest honor.

All had come without fanfare.

Apparently, the felines intended to start Kris on a new tra-
dition. When she opened these boxes, they would really *feel*
like awards.

Again, President Almar went first. She opened the smaller
of the two boxes. It showed a silver shield with crossed golden
swords hung from a watermarked red ribbon with golden
edges. "This is the Medal of Highest Valor. For the last two
hundred years, it has been the highest award for valor given by
the people of Calumm. We offer it to you."

So saying, she stepped forward and slipped around Kris to
fasten it around her neck.

President Almar whispered something.

IT'S GETTING CROWDED HERE, Nelly translated.

TELL HER THAT IT IS NO LESS WELCOMED IN THE NAME OF
ALL THOSE WHO FOUGHT, BLED, AND IN TOO MANY CASES
DIED WITH SUCH VALOR, NELLY.

Kris's collarbone spoke softly. The president did not seem
surprised.

Again the Prime Minister came second. She opened the larger box and drew out a long yellow sash with a golden medallion.

"The Order of the Rose and the Thistle is the highest order in our kingdom," she said. "For those who are recognized for their civic contributions, the Rose is first on the medallion. For those who win it on the field of battle, the Thistle takes the place of honor. Your medallion is the first of its kind. The thistle and rose surround an image of our solar system. We suspect there is more to this symbol than we have yet plumbed the depths of." She finished with a wry smile.

Now President Almar came to stand beside the Prime Minister. "All of you will find at your place, a simple wooden box. Please open it now. In it you will find an expression of our gratitude. It is the Defender of the Star award, and it is meant for all of you who fought for us. Unlike what we have been giving here, it is an award that the people of Columm and the King of Bizalt give together. This is the first such joint endeavor. We hope it will be the beginning of a long and fruitful cooperation."

Penny opened hers and showed it to Kris. Like the Medal of Highest Valor, it was in the form of a three-cornered shield. In place of the crossed swords, this one showed a sunburst. Here was an award that looked forward and out, not to the past and what it had meant.

Penny gave Kris a wink.

Yep, we've started something. Now to help them finish it in the best way we can.

Servers began to circulate among the tables, bringing plates full of roasted something, petite red potatoes, or something like it, and a bean that the server suggested that Kris not look too closely at.

Cookie and Mother MacCreedy made it taste wonderful, wherever it came from.

The President and Prime Minister joined Kris at her table. They were served a plate of raw meat, seasoned with flakes of something green and purple.

Kris didn't have to make an effort to not look too closely at that.

"Your general commanding your guard, who I understand

is also your mate, advised us that we should not have a banquet in your honor the day that you came to our Association Assembly," President Almar mentioned as the meal progressed. "Something about it being a fast day for your religion."

Kris glanced at Jack. They both managed to suppress a laugh if not a grin.

"I think that he feared that our culinary preferences might be as hard for you to take as we find your proclivity for burning good meat."

"I think you might be right," Kris said.

"You will forgive us," Penny said. "Our digestion is only able to fully process meat that has been seared. It helps us digest it in ways that our stomachs can no longer do alone. We have been burning our fine meat, as you put it, for half a million years."

"Do you have a wise saying that goes something like 'One woman's meat is another woman's poison'?" the prime minister asked.

"We have one just like that," Kris agreed.

"May I ask what you will do now?" President Almar asked.

Kris put her fork down and turned to face the two leaders. "We intend to clean up the alien holdout base on the other side of your system. We will go there, ask them to surrender and, very likely, have to fight them to their death."

"I noticed that all of the attacking ships were destroyed," Prime Minister Gerrot said.

"Many were disabled in the fight," Kris said. "When they found that the battle was lost, rather than surrender, they chose to do things to their reactors that caused them to blow up their ship."

"We are told that our nuclear reactors cannot explode," the president said, alarm showing at her muzzle.

"I don't believe yours can," Kris said.

THEY CAN'T, Nelly added.

"We use thermonuclear reactors, the next step up from yours," Kris added.

"I keep hearing that thermonuclear power is just twenty years away," the prime minister said. "And it has been for the last forty years."

"It is a difficult jump from fission to fusion. At least it was in our history," Kris admitted.

"If we can make the jump to our moon, might you be willing to share with us that secret?"

"It is possible if the request comes from all of your world's people and a means can be found to share it peacefully," Kris said.

"If that is a deal you are offering, that is a deal we are taking," the Prime Minister said.

"You say that the Order of the Defender of the Star is your first joint effort," Kris said.

"The first of many," both leaders said.

"Then let us give you a system that is all yours," Kris said, and raised her glass of water.

Those around the table raised their own glasses. It seemed the locals did brew a most magnificent collection of beers. The mess was enjoying not only home-grown meat but also home-brewed beer.

Glasses clinked. The deal was done.

Exactly how Kris would keep her side of the deal was something only a Longknife could figure out.

And they always did what they had to do, didn't they?

51

They were still accelerating at a comfortable one gee as they swung around the sun, headed for the gas giant on the other side of the system from the cat folks. Kris was holding her reduced squadron to normal gravity while more repairs and adjustments were made.

Officially, Captain Drago was willing to put on 2.5 gees. So were the others. Unofficially, they all asked Kris to go light on the spurs.

She intended to.

No doubt the coming battle would respect her good intentions.

In a pig's eye.

Clear of the sun, they now got their first good view of the alien base.

"Two ships, six huge reactors each," Chief Beni reported. "The base has five mega reactors, larger than we'd usually build for a major city."

"Are their lasers charged?" Captain Drago asked.

"I can't tell at this range, sir."

"Well, tell me as soon as you can, Chief. That's your main job for the next three days."

"Aye, aye, sir."

Kris tracked the bridge conversation from her own admiral's bridge. Her space was now more formally a bridge. It was a fiction that impressed the visitors, and she had three of them. Two old felines, an admiral and a general, and the young translator Zarra ak Torina.

They sat at Kris's conference table now. Seated on stools, the seniors' tails nervously lashed back and forth.

I DON'T THINK THEY LIKE SPACE, Nelly said.

WOULD YOU WANT TO BE GOING INTO A BATTLE TOTALLY DEPENDENT FOR EVERYTHING, EVEN THE AIR YOU BREATHE, AND COMPLETELY DIFFERENT FROM ANY FIGHT YOU'D EVER BEEN IN?

KRIS, EVERY BATTLE WE GO INTO IS DIFFERENT FROM ANY ONE WE'VE EVER BEEN IN.

Kris almost heard a chuckle at the end of that.

"We're still two days away from any serious fight," Kris told the two. "Nelly, please show our visitors the likely outline of the battle."

"Yes, Kris," Nelly answered primly.

Nelly was no longer a secret though Kris suspected that the general considered her some magic talisman.

Nelly quickly showed the status of the gas giant and its moons ahead of them. The planet had a dozen moons, large and small, as well as a ring system.

"The two surviving alien warships are orbiting this small, planet-size moon. The reactors are also in orbit, so we assume they have built some sort of habitat in orbit rather than a ship. If they should choose to come out to fight us, as we choose to come out to fight them, they'll have to make their decision tomorrow. Their likely course is thus," Nelly said, and several appeared on the screen.

In one, they dived down, grazed the giant, then shot up to intercept Kris's ships faster and farther out. In the second, they swung around the second largest moon and intercepted Kris well before she got to where their habitat orbited. In the third, they rose up from that moon's gravity well and headed straight for Kris as she made her final approach.

"You can forecast your enemy's course of action that accurately?" the admiral asked.

"Gravity defines what can be done," Kris said. "In our ancient days, wind and currents defined what ships could do. Does your history have something like that?"

The admiral nodded. "I knew old admirals who lived by wind and waves. It has been nice to tell a helmswoman to go there, and the ship does. The next generation may look back fondly on the control my generation had."

"But the next generation will have the stars," Kris said.

SHE TRANSLATED THAT AS "STRIDE THE STARS" WITH A HINT OF STALKING FOR THE POUNCE IN IT. KRIS, ARE YOU SURE WE WANT TO GIVE THESE PEOPLE THE STARS?

NELLY, I'M DESCENDED FROM NATIVE AMERICAN WARRIORS WHO LIKED NOTHING BETTER THAN A LITTLE HORSE RAID. MAYBE STEAL A WIFE, TOO, WHILE HE WAS AT IT. YET, TODAY, I HATE WAR AS MUCH AS THE NEXT ONE.

BUT YOU FIGHT THEM SO VERY WELL.

ENOUGH, NELLY.

"Which of these paths will your enemy follow?" the general asked.

"I have no idea. We have a saying. 'You can plan your battle as much as you like, but your enemy gets a vote as to how it will go down.'"

"We have a saying much like that. 'You may hunt the long-toothed one, but she may also be hunting you.' So, you will prepare for all three of these?" the admiral said.

"And a fourth. What if they choose to stay in orbit and not come out?"

"That might be the worst option for you," the admiral said.

"You spotted the problem," Kris answered.

"I watched your battle. You're, ah . . . You call them lasers, right?"

"Yes," Kris said.

"Light. Who would think that light could kill someone?" the general grumbled.

"It seems that we have, but didn't know we had," the admiral admitted. "At least some technical students have created them in their classrooms, but they take up way too much energy and do very little harm."

"And a baby takes a lot of work and shows nothing of the warrior skills she may have someday," Kris pointed out.

"And the first steam boilers were hardly able to cruise around a pond," the admiral said, nodding.

Kris was grateful. These folks shook their head when they meant to shake their head and nodded when they meant to nod. That made it easier for her.

Kris nodded back.

"Knowing how you power and arm your ships will make it easier for us to avoid a lot of wrong turns with nothing to show for them," the admiral said.

Kris chose not to react to that.

"Yes. That may or may not be all it is cracked up to be," the admiral said, and laughed. For the felines, a laugh was something that began deep in the throat and came out more as a loud purr than as a human laugh.

Kris expected that she could get used to it.

Phil Taussig arrived. He was supposed to take the visiting firewomen off Kris's hands for a tour of the ship ending in the Forward Lounge. Mother MacCreedy had laid in a very large supply of beer and a single-malt that aficionados said could easily hold its own against any scotch in human space.

Kris's opinion of scotch was that it shouldn't be forced on anyone, in or out of human space, but she kept her opinion to herself.

Once Phil left, Kris settled herself at her desk and did admiral things. The report from Amanda and Jacques on the culture of the cats was interesting but not complete. Kris doubted it ever would be. Whatever they were at present would not be what they were ten years from now.

The synthesis of the reports on the original aliens and their home world was ongoing as well. Kris put it aside and ducked out to Captain Drago's bridge.

Yes, the repairs and modifications were coming along. Yes, the lasers were online. Yes, the engineering spaces were being reorganized. No, there wasn't a problem bringing in the larger reactor from the *Hornet* to work with the *Wasp*'s two smaller ones.

Not spoken, but bubbling near the surface, was a strong hint that one admiral ought to take herself somewhere else and not bother the working people.

Kris returned to her own spaces.

She used her boards to take a walk through the four ships. It did look like the problem of sorting out two damaged ships and making them into one battleworthy hull was coming along nicely. She had Nelly check the engineering reports and verify that there had been no reactor excursions or burbles in the flow of plasma to the engines during the gentle, one-gee, cruise out.

"Kris, go find something to do," Nelly suggested. "When the fight comes, you'll fight it. They'll fight it. Relax. Go jump Jack's bones or something."

"Computer, behave yourself."

"I'm not a computer. I'm Nelly, and I was never taught by my loving, caring semiowner to behave, so there."

Kris went back and tried to lose herself in the reports on the original aliens.

There was nothing new. No surprises. Her team had about squeezed everything there was from the data. They were refining it, but so far had not found, or stumbled across or fell into anything that changed what Kris knew about them or had made a wild guess at.

Kris decided she should go down and spend some time with the twenty aliens she'd recruited.

Down two ladders, around three passageways, and Kris was totally lost.

"Nelly, where are they keeping the original aliens."

"Take a left at the next cross passageway. Go down the next ladder you come to. Ask me for directions again when you get there."

Kris did.

Or she started to.

Kris had read in the after-action report that half of a Musashi Marine platoon had been hit when an alien laser slashed through the hull. Twelve were dead and more wounded. Somewhere she'd noted that the *Wasp* had opened a memorial chapel to those Marines, but Kris hadn't noticed where it was.

She walked by it.

It was open.

The tori gate had no doors. Anyone, at any time, walking by could not help but see the twelve pairs of boots, twelve rifles, and twelve pictures standing along the far wall.

In front of them was a sand garden. Somehow someone had either lifted sand up from Sasquan or programmed Smart Metal™ to create sand and rocks.

The stonework appeared ancient. Lichen and moss seemed to cover them.

Without thought or reflection, Kris found herself turning into the small memorial garden.

On the walls were simple scrolls. Kris could not translate them for herself and did not ask Nelly to do so.

There was a stone bench.

Kris settled on it. For a long while she stared, eyes hardly seeing, at this memorial to twelve who had given their lives under her command. Twelve who had died defending the feline planet in a space battle they had no real part to fight in.

Something drew Kris's eyes around. She turned on her stone bench.

The wall beside the Tori gate was etched with the names and pictures of all 187 of those who died on the *Wasp* and the *Hornet* in this, their most recent battle under her command.

Now the sobs came.

The grief that she had refused to touch wracked her. Tears flowed as if they would never stop. She wept for those who had died, and those whose lives went on with their flesh and blood and minds slashed and scarred in obedience to her commands.

She almost wished she could think of some error on her part that she could beg their forgiveness for, but she had fought the fight as best she knew how.

The enemy had been good.

She, and those who fought with her, had been better.

Better, but not good enough to fight these bitter killers and come away unscathed.

Somewhere in her grief, Jack appeared at her side. His arms enfolded her. Ever ready, he produced a handkerchief. He held her. Just held her, and said nothing.

"Thank you," Kris said when she found she could finally speak again.

"For what?"

"For being you. For being here. For not lying to me and saying it's all right or some other crap like that."

"I don't lie," Jack said.

"I know."

"Don't I get any credit for getting Jack here?" Nelly asked.

"Jack, is this on the way to the alien quarters from Admiral Country?"

"I don't think so," he said.

"So tell me, Nelly, who gets credit for getting me here?"

"I do, Kris. You had to do something. There's another battle coming, and you had a burr up your ass. You're impossible to live with."

"Nelly, your choice of words is getting way too close to the gutter."

"Blame Granny Rita. She would have told you that."

"She can. Don't you."

"You do feel better, don't you?"

Kris leaned against Jack and found the last of the emotions draining out of her.

"Yes, I feel better. I'm alive. Twenty-two enemy ships' worth of bloodthirsty killers are not. They will *not* wreck that planet full of kitties, bloodthirsty or no."

"How about something to eat?" Jack said. "Lately, you've only been picking at your food."

Kris's stomach picked that moment to rumble. About 6.9 on the tummy-rumbling scale. "You might have a good idea, Jack. I was headed down to pester Jacques about our newly recruited aliens, who seem to be content to eat our meat and rest in the artificial sun outside the cave we've made for them. There's got to be something we can do with them."

"See why I gave her the wrong directions?" Nelly said.

"You're going to have to be careful, Nelly," Jack said. "You keep messing in the affairs of us humans, and we're going to mess back in your affairs."

"Yes," Nelly said, almost sounding contrite, "there is that off button, and if I send you in the wrong direction too many times, you'll hire one of those dumb navigation systems and start using it."

"And you, smart girl, would be out of a job," Kris said, taking the hand Jack offered her to help her up from her stony place. That might not be stone, but the Smart Metal™ seemed to have left her just as stiff and cold as real stone would have.

The wardroom was serving dinner. They ate in good company and retired to their quarters. Kris told Jack they'd just cuddle. That was all she wanted, and he agreed.

Whether Kris changed her mind, or Jack changed it for her, she was glad for what came her way.

She slept well that night, untroubled by ghosts.

She'd have more before she slept again.

Many more.

52

Next morning, after breakfast, Kris connected with Jacques and did make it down to where they now housed the alien natives. Their quarters were more spacious and much more to their liking.

They had what appeared to be three caves coming off a rock overhang. Below was a sandy area and what looked like a stream. When Kris crossed it, she found herself splashing.

Apparently, a certain amount of the *Wasp*'s reaction mass was in use as a creek for them.

They had their own fire and were roasting something that had, no doubt, until recently been alive on Sasquan. They seemed content.

~You chased off the other star walkers,~ the gray-bearded man said, no doubt in his voice.

~They will not walk among the stars again,~ Kris answered.

~Will you take more heads?~ the bald woman asked.

~We will either take their heads or they will take ours,~ Kris said.

The bald woman shook her head. Nelly reminded Kris that this meant agreement among these people.

~Why do you have to take their head? Why do they want to take your head?~ piped up a thin voice.

Kris turned to see the young fellow whose leg injury had started all this. Now he was up and hobbling toward them, a young-girl playmate following him like a shadow.

~They have land,~ the graybeard said. ~If you go in someone's land, you either run away from them or fight them. If you win, it is your land.~

That explanation seemed to satisfy all the adults listening. It didn't satisfy the young fellow. ~But look up in the sky at night. Not this one, but the real sky. There is a lot of land. Every one of those dots of light is a star with land. Why fight?~

~You will know when you are older,~ the bald woman said.

That answer didn't seem any more acceptable to him than it had to Kris when she was his age.

~Can I go with you, Uncle Jacques?~

The anthropologist stepped forward. ~You can go with me if your father's father or your father's mother says you can,~ the anthropologist said. The "if" was in Standard.

~Can we,~ came in two-part harmony from both the boy and girl.

~Go,~ the grandfather said. ~Leave your betters in some quiet. And you be sure to feed them, Jacques. When they walk off with you to pester you with questions, they miss their meat here and come home whining for meat that is already eaten.~

~I will feed them,~ Jacques assured their elders.

The four of them crossed the stream, opened the door painted to blend in with the forest motif, and stepped outside.

~Can I have my "reader"?~ both kids begged.

Jacques produced a pair of readers and gave them to the kids. In a moment, they were lost to a basic primer on letters and numbers, the kind of thing Kris had been given when she was three.

"You're teaching them to read?" Kris asked.

"Their elders can't grasp the concept of symbols meaning anything. They aren't dumb. Drop them in the woods, and they'll track a gnat that we can't even see when it's biting us on the ass, but try to get across to them the idea of three or four? Nope. Not possible. Me, mine. One, two, many. Big many to some, but just many to most."

"But these kids?" Kris said, waving at the two, then grabbing one and pulling them out of the way of a hurrying Sailor.

Kris had almost walked into enough poles, walls, ditches, whatever, as a kid lost in her games to smile as she rescued this girl from a similar fate.

"We caught them just before their brains locked down. They're learning. Their brains are also sprouting synapses like a house afire. Just like one of our kids in their age range."

"They're learning to speak Standard?" Kris said, eyeing what the kids were reading.

"And they're picking it up like a dry sponge does water. They're also learning our vocabulary, a full, modern vocabulary."

"They'll be like the others, only open to talking," Kris said.

"Yep. Doc Meade wants them back in the lab this afternoon. I don't think she'll mind if I bring them in early. She's studying them, matching them against the cadavers we have and the baselines we have from their folks. These kids' brains are so different from those of the elders we've got."

Kris chewed that over.

Jacques kept talking. "So, in answer to the question you're not asking me, yes, it was worthwhile picking them up. But the very act of bringing them into our conversation is making them different. Different from their own tribe. Different from the bloodthirsty killers among the stars. I have no idea where all this is heading, but it's opening up what was pretty locked down beforehand."

"I'm going to judge this as good," Kris said.

"Kris, Captain Drago wants to talk to you."

"Why?" Kris asked.

"There's a problem up ahead. Maybe it's nothing, but he'd like you to know about it sooner rather than later.

Jacques raised an inquiring eyebrow.

Kris shrugged. "You take the kids to the doctor, and I'll see what's worrying the captain."

And she walked off. Quickly. Admirals never run. That might scare the average Sailor and really scare their officers.

But admirals can walk very, very quickly.

53

Kris decided to use her day quarters as a shortcut through to the *Wasp*'s bridge. Captain Drago had told Kris never, ever to even think of doing that, but now looked like a good time to break that rule.

So she was very surprised to find Captain Drago and Chief Beni waiting for her in what they had turned into her flag plot.

"What's the rush?" Kris asked, her stomach already in free fall from the looks on their faces.

"The enemy isn't there anymore," Captain Drago said.

"What?" brought Kris up short.

"Chief, explain this to the admiral."

"Yes, sir," the old retired chief said. He had a black box in his hand and began tapping it. One of Kris's large screens converted to show what Kris had looked at so many times in the last few days: a visual of the gas giant and its moons.

Always, it had shown the enemy base camp orbiting one moon.

Now it showed nothing.

"What happened?" Kris demanded.

"I don't know, ma'am. One minute it was showing the reactors and other electronic hums. The next minute, it's showing nothing. Not. A. Thing."

"Of course, with the speed-of-light lag time, whatever it quit showing," Captain Drago pointed out, "quit happening a while back."

"Yes, yes, I know," Kris said. "But what did they do? Could they be masking their emissions? The Iteeche had a way of throwing off our sensors in the last war," Kris remembered.

"Yes. Somehow the bastards could throw off our radar and laser range finders by a couple hundred klicks, ma'am. We never have figured out how they did it. It's one thing to spoof sensors a bit. It's another thing entirely to hide the emissions coming out of a thermonuclear reactor. That's raw physics, ma'am. You've got to contain the damn plasma. That means a lot of electromagnetic fields. All those I can see. Even a blind man could see them."

"But we're not seeing it anymore?" Kris said.

"I tell you, it's not there."

"So they either blew themselves up or turned everything off," Kris said, naming the only two options she could think of.

"They didn't blow themselves up," Chief Beni said. "We'd have seen that."

"So they turned off their gear," Kris said. "Captain, what's it look like when you dump a reactor?"

"First off, you don't dump a dozen huge ship reactors and five gigantic city-size reactors when you're tied up at the dock. That tends to wreck things you don't want wrecked."

"Things we wouldn't want wrecked," Kris pointed out. "What about them?"

"There's no accounting for them," the captain growled. "Admiral, would you be so kind as to order my chief engineer to report to your quarters and could you scare up that chief boffin? They've got all kinds of sensors. They might be able to add something to our conversation."

"Nelly, make it so."

"Already done, Kris. They're headed here as fast as their legs can carry them. I think the rumor that we've lost the aliens is wandering through the ship at faster-than-light speed. You humans do like to talk."

"And you computers don't," Drago said, dryly.

"We are networked by our very nature, sir."

"We were networked long before you were," the captain retorted.

"Enough, children," Kris said. "Chief, can you take my board back to just before you lost the aliens? Enhance it to maximum resolution and walk it through the loss as slowly as possible."

They were going through that loss for the second time when the chief engineers of both the *Wasp* and *Hornet* reported to Kris, with both Captain Taussig and Professor

Labao only seconds behind them. Not far behind them were the two felines and their translator.

Kris brought all of them up to date on the enemy's status, something that didn't seem to surprise any of them, not even the cats. Then she had Chief Beni run them through what they knew about the sudden change in the aliens' status.

The two engineers were shaking their heads as the reactors disappeared from the screen within a single second.

"I'd never scram a reactor while tied up to the pier," Commander Manuel Ortega of the *Wasp* said. "Even if I had it on minimum power, and what we were getting from our targets wasn't minimum."

Ronnie Thiu of the *Hornet* agreed. "Bad idea, but those shadows on the screen? I think that might have been the plasma dissipating into space, or at least some of it. If we're reading it this far away, it's got to be tearing into something to create that kind of radiation signature."

She turned to the head boffin. "Did any of your people have a better look at this?"

"I have some independent reports of this," the professor began in lecture mode. "However, I must tell you that our most sensitive sensor for this was destroyed during the recent fight, and our best researcher in this area lost her life. Her assistant is doing the best he can with what he has available. Our computers are trying their best to enhance what we did capture."

"My children are all working on this, Kris," Nelly reported. "We should have something for you in the next five minutes."

"Good," Kris said, wondering why she was hearing about this first from Professor Labao rather than Nelly, but this situation was coming at them very fast.

"So," Kris said, thinking on her feet as fast as she could. "We've lost all evidence of reactors. What about laser capacitors? Are the guns charged?"

"We're too far out to read anything like that," Chief Beni said.

"How close will we have to get before we know we've got two huge batteries of lasers loaded and aimed at us?" Kris got in before either captain present could.

"Five hundred thousand kilometers," the chief said. "Plus or minus a hundred thousand."

"We better be really slow on our final approach," Captain Drago said.

"Absolutely," Kris said flatly.

"What about their communications equipment?" Kris asked. "Not that they make a practice of talking to us."

"I'm sorry, Admiral," the chief said. "At this range, they could have comm gear online, but unless they start talking on a wide enough beam, or really jack up the power on their gear, I'm listening to a great big nothing."

"Then please keep listening," Kris said, "and let us know if you hear so much as a twitch."

"You'll be the second to know, right after Captain Drago."

"And you were only about thirty seconds behind me on this," the skipper of the *Wasp* told Kris. "If you'd been home gnawing your liver instead of gallivanting around my ship, you'd have known it then."

"I've had enough liver for this week," Kris said.

She glanced in the general direction of the felines. Zarra was translating like mad.

NELLY, IS SHE GETTING THIS RIGHT?

PRETTY MUCH, KRIS. THERE'S A LOT THAT LOOKS LIKE MAGIC, AND THE GENERAL KEEPS SAYING SO. THE ADMIRAL INSISTS THAT THIS IS ADVANCED TECHNOLOGY . . . AND HE WANTS SOME.

GOOD. CORRECT ANY MAJOR MISTAKES, BUT LET THEM RUN THEIR OWN COURSE.

"Admiral," Nelly announced to all, "we have the analysis of the main antenna's takeaway from the recent event. I'm bringing it up on-screen.

The enemy base again appeared, only this time, each reactor stood out clear from the others. Two pairs of six reactors in the shape of a T, three aft in engineering proper, powering the ships' rocket motors, and three strung out along the keel. The pair of six were docked nose in to a space marked out with five gigantic reactors, roaring away with plasma and the superconducting magnetohydrodynamic racetracks that the aliens used to extract electricity from the superheated plasma in their reactors.

Until only a few years ago, humans had used the same technology. Many starships still did.

Then the lights went out.

On-screen, gossamer shadows showed where the plasma went. There were brief sparkles where the plasma met something and interacted with it. On-screen, it was hard to see. No doubt, in person, it had been horrible to suffer.

"It appears that the reaction from venting the plasma," Nelly reported, "tore the ships away from the station. We can't be sure because the ships vanish from our observation as the plasma dissipates."

"What happened on the station?" Kris asked.

"They stayed put for a bit more than a second after the ships, then they, too, vented. Each reactor vented in several different directions," Nelly reported

On the screen now only the station showed. Shadows went in several directions from each reactor. Here and there were more flashes as structures not meant to face the demons of hot plasma encountered it and became one with it.

"If they were planning on doing this and being in shape to restart and attack us," Nelly said, "I do not believe that it went as smoothly as they wanted."

Kris found herself gnawing her lower lip.

"We'll see what we shall see when we get closer," she said. That didn't have the firm finality that an admiral was supposed to bring to her words, but it was the best Kris could muster in this situation.

"Nelly, send to squadron: 'Continue battle preparation. I don't trust these bastards any farther than I can throw them.' "

"I sent it, Kris."

ALL OF IT?

RIGHT DOWN TO THE "BASTARD" PART.

Kris shrugged. That might not go down with the other deathless words before battle, but it definitely reflected her thoughts. The Longknife legend would, no doubt, edit it appropriately.

54

It is impossible to come to a dead halt in space.

Always, you are orbiting the center of the galaxy at a mind-bending pace.

Usually, you are orbiting a sun at a more reasonable speed, but you are still moving.

Finally, most times a ship is orbiting a planet of some sort. We humans don't go to space for the view, we go for the territory. Maybe we aren't as territorial as the newly discovered felines, but we're looking for living space and resources.

Kris knew all of these laws of physics. Still, from her flag bridge, she ordered Captain Drago to bring her squadron to as near a dead halt as possible when they were five hundred thousand klicks from the moon where the aliens had built their orbital refuge.

Making allowances for the huge gravity well of the gas giant only a few million miles away, the squadron drifted in space. Every mind, every sensor aboard, focused its full attention on the mystery that lay ahead of them.

Every scrap of spare computing power concentrated on analyzing what the sensors revealed.

It pretty much came to one big nothing.

"As far as the electromagnetic spectrum is concerned, there is no there there," Chief Beni reported from his usual place at sensors on the bridge. "Every instrument we've got says there is just nothing happening up ahead."

"Visuals?" Kris snapped from where she sat in flag plot.

"They are still rather vague," Professor Labao reported from her elbow. "We are unsure if that stems from the junk that has been injected into the space around the base, or because whatever we are looking at just doesn't look like what we are looking for."

Kris did not smile although the report was as perfectly noncommittal as she'd expect from a scientist reluctant to admit he had nothing to add to their knowledge base.

No doubt, it was very embarrassing.

"Captain Drago, lead the squadron closer. If there is a creep speed, use it."

That got a heads-up among the feline contingent observing them from the corner of Kris's flag bridge. The admiral actually smiled at Kris.

Of course, a feline smile showed a lot of teeth. Long, pointed ones.

Let's keep these folks as allies, Kris reminded herself. For the millionth time.

At four hundred thousand klicks, the observed results were no better than they had been at five hundred thousand.

By three hundred thousand, they were starting to get a decent picture.

It was ugly.

Two ships rolled and drifted alongside a long cylinder. Occasionally, they bounced off each other.

"There's no guidance there," Captain Drago concluded. "They're totally out of any semblance of control."

"But are they dead?" Kris asked. "I wouldn't put it past them to have their lasers loaded and on automatic. Whoever closes in gets hit with one last, massive broadside."

"They'd need sensors to know there was anyone there," Taussig pointed out from his place at Kris's other elbow.

"There could be something passive," Kris insisted.

"It would have to draw some juice," Captain Drago pointed out on net. "We are not getting anything at all. Not the low hum from capacitors, nor anything in the lower electromagnetic spectrum from something waiting to power up."

Kris eyed Taussig, who sat at her elbow since he was now a passenger on the *Wasp*, riding along with the remnants of his *Hornet*.

"Take us in closer, Captain Drago. Professor Labao, I want that particular sector of space examined like no bit of vacuum has ever been before. I don't trust these folks to give up without a fight."

"There is always a first time," Jack said.

"For a human, maybe. For them, never. It's not 'enlightened,'" Kris spat.

Slowly, as slowly as the laws of physics allowed, they closed in.

"We are getting some electromagnetic activity," the chief reported at two hundred thousand klicks. "It's in the form of low-powered electric servo motors. They're very weak and not much of them. The kind of things we use for minimum life support."

"So someone might be alive?"

"Possibly, on what's left of the space station."

"Give me a picture," Kris ordered.

Kris knew space stations. She'd blown up at least one and fought to save another. A cylinder was the usual design for them. A simple tin can in space.

This one was no exception.

Or at least it had started as no exception.

Now. Not so much.

Unless the aliens had intentionally built a twisted and malformed cylinder, this station had suffered a catastrophic failure. It was easy to see why.

In a dozen or more places, the hull looked singed, burned by the venting of superheated plasma that these spaces on the hull had not been designed to contain. The vent points showed signs of wreckage drifting by them or hanging on by a thread.

No wonder it had been so hard to get a decent picture of the alien base. Its very death had cloaked it in a veil of destruction.

"Where is the activity?" Kris asked.

"In the extreme forward section of the cylinder," Professor Labao said. "The area farthest from a vented reactor."

Nelly highlighted that section. It was well away from the self-destruction of the reactors. While the other end of the station appeared to be completed and done with, this end still showed where construction had been going on.

Had some low-caste workers there chosen life over death? The odds were long against it. But a mother and father had chosen life for themselves and their two babies once in Kris's experience. Only the babies had survived, but still, of the almost hundred billion aliens Kris had slaughtered, at least two had chosen life.

"Captain Drago, I believe the *Wasp* has the best armor left after the last fight."

"Yes, we're at eighty-five percent," Captain Drago reported. "Why?"

"Let's leave the rest of the squadron at this distance. Set the strongest Condition Zed you can on the *Wasp* and nose in there. If I were you, I'd keep my engines away from them for the first pass," Kris said, "but what do I know? I'm just the admiral."

"And the bloody Longknife," Drago muttered under his breath. Almost.

Kris didn't hear him. Very carefully, she didn't hear.

The squadron swung wide of the moon while the *Wasp* crept closer, if a ship traveling at a hundred thousand klicks an hour relative to the huge gas giant looming over them all could be said to creep.

They were fifty thousand klicks out when the aliens made their move.

55

"We've been pinged! Radar!"

Bridge personnel are supposed to be very informative, but circumspect, in their reports. They are never supposed to shout their reports. Sad to say, old Chief Beni failed to follow proper decorum at that moment.

He was definitely shouting.

"There's also communication from the station to the warship wrecks!"

There was no need to order battle stations. Everyone was already there. The *Wasp* even had an admiral at the Weapons station. There was also no need to order a flip of the ship. The frigate was on a nose-forward course, anyway.

NELLY, JINK.

I'M DOING IT, KRIS, BUT WE'VE ONLY GOT THRUSTERS TO PLAY WITH. THERE'S NOT MUCH I CAN DO.

Nevertheless, in her high-gee egg, Kris felt the side movement as Nelly slid to the left, then dropped the ship down.

On her board, Kris held the lasers ready, but she had no target.

Nothing moved.

Captain Drago had arranged his approach so that only one of the warships was over the horizon of the alien station. Kris searched it for a target.

"Enemy lasers are powering up and coming to bear," Nelly reported.

"Kill them," Kris ordered.

Laser 1 on the *Wasp*'s bow shot out a stuttering blast of light. On the hulk, a section of hull exploded.

But there was more movement visible on the dinged, seared, and dented hull. Faster than human thought, Nelly popped one, then another, then four. Finally, she used all seven lasers.

A missile tried to launch from the dead ship. Nelly nailed it before it cleared its launcher. The explosion wrecked several other launchers.

Kris was fighting a zombie. It shambled and shook and tried to kill her with every twitch. The *Wasp* fought back with the clear, intelligent intent of every human and computer aboard her who loved life and intended to keep living.

Almost as suddenly as it had started, it was over. In what seemed like an eternity but couldn't have been more than a blink, the dead ship was truly dead.

The bridge crew took a second to recover their breath.

"What do we do with the other ship?" Captain Drago asked.

"I'd love to send a couple of antimatter missiles its way," Kris said, still working on catching her breath, "but we only have a limited supply of them. Order the *Royal* to scrounge up some rocks and send them at it fast."

"I've sent the order," Nelly reported.

"And what do you want to do with that spark of life we see on the station?" Jack asked from his egg parked beside Kris's.

"Mount up your Marines and see what you find," Kris said. "If there's anyone over there alive, I want a word with them. Clearly, they need to understand what a white flag means."

"Kris, I didn't notice any white flag," Jack said. Kris could almost see the grimace on his face. "They set a trap, and we tripped it. It wasn't a very good trap, and we tripped it with our usual Longknife sledgehammer, but . . ." He left the conclusion to Kris.

"Yeah," she said with a sigh, "I've got to quit expecting these folks to be decent and open to negotiations. Foolish of me to even think so."

"I'll mount up both Marine companies," Jack said. "Captain Drago, can we borrow the *Wasp*'s pinnace?"

"Take all the longboats, too. Better you see what lies over there than me."

It would prove regrettable that anyone had to see it.

56

A longboat went in first. It headed not for any particular hatch but for one of the vents that had been seared in the side of the station by a reactor's hot breath.

They expected a lot of death and destruction; still, what they found was a shock even for battle-hardened Marines.

"Damn, there are bodies all over the place," Gunny Brown reported to them as soon as he and a squad of Marines were inside.

"Was it explosive decompression when the reactors got dumped?" Kris asked.

"The bodies don't look like they died of that, ma'am," Gunny reported. "I got a forensic team right behind me. The sergeant heading it up thinks they were dead before space got to them."

"Any idea what killed them?"

"There's a lot of paper cups floating around here. Droplets of liquid. They captured some of it and they're doing a field analysis. Give us a minute or two, Admiral."

Kris settled back into her chair in flag plot, tightened her belt, and prepared to wait. The *Wasp* had gone to Condition Charlie after tossing a few large chunks of rubble over the horizon of the station at the derelict warship.

It hadn't reacted to any of them.

The *Royal* was headed this way with a couple of good-size rocks and ice hunks from the giant's ring. Next orbit, they'd see if there was any fight left in the wreck.

Show it or smash it.

Kris no longer cared which.

She was starting to develop a very negative attitude toward her enemy.

"We got the results from those droplets and the cups. There was some kind of alcoholic drink in them. Alcohol and cyanide, we think."

Kris turned to where Amanda and Jacques sat at her conference table. Amanda was rapidly going pale. Beside her, Penny's mouth was falling open.

It was Jacques, the anthropologist, who gave voice to what the others were struggling to get their minds around. "They poisoned themselves on their communion wine," he said.

On the huge base ship they'd shot up, they'd discovered a memorial garden where the ashes of the dead were scattered. There they grew a grain and a fruit that seemed readily converted to alcohol. Bread and Wine.

Sacraments, they'd concluded at the time.

Now, with their chances to continue the fight slim and the option of surrender seemingly the only one any rational person would consider, the enemy had taken their own lives with their sacrament.

"Again, the aliens have chosen death before surrender," Kris muttered to herself. Or maybe she spoke aloud.

"But to make mass suicide a religious experience. Dear God," was, no doubt, truly intended as a prayer from Penny.

"My general tells me to tell you that we had a nation very much like that among us not all that long ago," Zarra said from the corner where the feline observers sat.

"What became of them?" Kris asked.

"They learned different. That life is more important than a hollow death," Zarra answered without consulting her officers. Then she had to turn and tell them what she'd said.

"They agree with what I said," she quickly added.

"We have had groups like that also," Jacques said. "They have also learned differently. These aliens we fight are slow learners."

"The general says maybe they are not meant to learn. Only to die."

"I wouldn't mind that so much," Kris said, and was surprised by the words as they came out of her mouth, "but they take a lot of good Sailors and Marines with them."

"My admiral says that is always sad."

"Yes," Kris agreed, dryly.

"What are we going to do?" Penny asked.

"Find out who's still alive in the aft section," Kris said, and tapped her commlink. "Jack, have you been following this?"

"Loud and painfully clear," he reported.

"You about to go in?"

"The pinnace is clamped onto the hull a good hundred meters short of the end. We're about to cut our way into it."

"Jack, be careful," Kris said.

"Wife, I always am."

Kris took a deep breath and gave the order. "Marines, land the landing force."

57

General Juan Montoya did one final check of his lead platoon. All were as ready as they ever would be.

The battle-armored space suits were primed and ready. Their weapons were locked and loaded.

Jack signaled the Sailor, herself in an unarmored space suit, and the hull of the pinnace opened up a hole in it the size of a double door, which sealed to the aliens' hull. A Marine applied a laser torch to the revealed metal. In less than a minute, a huge chunk of plate drifted off where it was pushed.

Another Marine combat engineer put tape on the sharp edges of the cut. The battle suits were tough, but there was no reason to ding them unnecessarily.

Jack motioned, and a sergeant led the first fire team through the hole. As the last trooper of that four shot aboard the station, a second team followed.

Jack had promised Kris that he would not lead from the front. With eight Marines of his battalion aboard the station, he figured he would no longer be in the front, and slipped himself into line as the third fire team of the squad went in.

It was strange how a man trained to be a Secret Service Agent changed his idea of a man's job when he spent all his time with combat Marines.

Well, them and a certain Longknife.

Jack forced his head back into the game and faced what he knew would be waiting for him.

Gunny's warning was hardly enough for what he faced.

Bodies drifted, thick as seaweed on a kelp bed he'd swum in as a kid. There were men and women, elders, kids, and infants.

So many of the bodies were tiny.

Most stared at him with eyes frozen in some hard stare that the poison had brought. A few of the kids almost seemed asleep.

Jack wanted to puke.

Instead, he did his best to ignore what he saw and ordered a follow-up fire team to sling weapons and shove bodies forward.

What they were after was aft.

"Up here, sir. I think I've found what we're looking for."

Jack found a purchase and shoved himself off for the aft-ward bulkhead. It stretched far around, showing clearly that the station's outer wall had been the floor when it spun. The bulkhead went high up for these people, a good fifteen meters.

Possibly they would have put in an extra deck as their population regrew. Apparently, they'd built large, expecting a lot of kids.

From the proportion of the dead, they'd had a population boom in the year since Kris had clobbered them.

Again, Jack had to force his mind to focus on what he had been sent here for.

Ahead of him was a hatch. A hatch with a wheel lock and a window that let you look in.

Jack peered in, shining a light to help him see all there was to see. It wasn't much. Some two meters away was another hatch with a lock and window.

"Kris, I've found an air lock. I think they intended to keep this place airtight. It looks like hurried work."

"Does that sound as much like a trap to you as it does to me?" came in the form of a question, but Jack doubted that Kris as an admiral or as a Longknife intended it to be taken as such. Certainly not Kris as a wife.

"I'm ordering up the air lock we brought along," he said.

Did he hear a whispered "thank you," in response?

Four Sailors came up, their suits equipped with jet packs. Each handled the corner of a large room equipped with air-tight hatches. A combat-engineering type had been taking soundings of the bulkhead. He signaled the Sailors, and they adjusted their drift.

The temporary air lock settled into place, and the Marine with the welder quickly locked it down against the wall. As he did that, the Sailors expanded out the lock, tripling its size.

Two squads began filing into the lock. Jack included himself.

Only when the aft lock was sealed down did one of the sailors open up the Smart Metal™ of the forward bulkhead and turn aside for a Marine to put a long, thin bead of explosives along the station bulkhead. He covered it with armored cloth.

"Get ready to shout folks. I'm using the smallest explosion I think I can use, and the cloth should direct the force inward, but if your ears are precious to you, shout on three."

The count was quick. All had taken themselves off net as Jack had. With the armored space suits, the overpressure was merely annoying, although Jack distinctly felt kicked where he preferred Kris to fondle.

The wall blew in, and the first rank of Marines rolled through the newly created hole.

Jack was in the second rank.

He joined the rest of his Marines, standing there, dumbfounded.

"Are you getting this?" he said, then remembered he'd killed his sound and video feed before the explosion.

"Kris, are you getting this?" he repeated after clicking himself back onto the net.

"My God, Jack," Kris breathed.

The scene was enough to make even a Longknife resort to prayer.

In front of Jack, an old, gray-haired woman stood. She held a knife to her throat as if ready to drive it up into her skull.

Behind her, over a dozen children, ranging in age from maybe twelve to at least three, stood. Each of them held a knife at his or her throat, just like the woman.

Some of the bigger kids helped the smaller kids hold their knives.

There were tears running down the cheeks of the kids.

There were no tears in the old woman's eyes. The face she presented Jack overflowed with rage and vicious hatred.

~Vermin will never touch us,~ she spat in a dialect that was just barely understandable.

Jack struggled to remember what Kris had said. What she'd say in this situation.

He signaled his Marines to hold their ground, chinned his mic to the speaker in the suit and thought. SAL, YOU AND YOUR MOM BETTER HELP ME GET THIS RIGHT.

WE'RE ALL ON IT.

WE ARE NOT VERMIN, Jack began thinking and Sal translated and spoke. WE ARE TALKING TO YOU. WHAT VERMIN CAN USE YOUR OWN WORDS?

The woman actually seemed surprised, but that did not stop her rage. ~Vermin may mouth the enlightened words of the people, but it is still an animal,~ she spat.

YOU HAVE FOUGHT US IN NUMBERS FAR MORE THAN WE EVER HAD, BUT IT IS YOU WHO HIDE HERE, LICKING YOUR WOUNDS.

The woman's eyes grew wider, but the knife never wavered from its place at her throat.

"This is getting us nowhere," Kris whispered softly on net. "Marines, prepare to fire sleepy darts on my word. Keep going, General."

IT IS WE WHO HAVE COME TO SEEK YOU OUT. IS THAT THE PATH THAT VERMIN WALK?

"Fire," Kris ordered.

Jack felt the pressure from the volley of sleepy darts. Maybe some of the soft pop did come up through the soles of his feet.

Now the old woman showed shock. She tried to drive the knife up into her skull, but her arms would not obey her.

Obey her full will.

When the knife tumbled from her grasp, there was blood on the tip.

One or two of the older children tried to follow their elder, but they were less ready to kill themselves, or maybe less enthusiastic at the prospects. All of them collapsed on the floor, with no blood on their knives.

"Kris, we need a doctor here. Doc Meade, how fast can you get in here?"

"I'm on the outside waiting," came the woman's soft voice. "Can I use this hatch?"

"Have a combat engineer check it for booby traps."

A minute later, the doctor was in the room, checking one patient after another. She extracted the sleepy darts from the youngest children. Marines had already policed up the sharp stuff and bound the hands and feet of the older kids and the old woman.

The children were evacuated, youngest to oldest, in survival packs that looked like nothing less than an oversize beach ball, one Marine towing a pack.

Doc Meade came to the elderly woman last. She checked her vitals, then left the darts in her and checked her bindings. "This one is very vexed, even under sedation. Keep an eye on her."

"They will all be on suicide watch," Jack said.

"If we can, try to get some of the youngest kids off to another ship. We don't want them running into any of the older ones. The big kids might kill the little ones."

"You think it's that bad?" Jack said.

"I think she had a lot more she wanted to spit at you," the doc said. "I think you interrupted her grand exit. I suspect she and these kids were intended to send us a message that you interrupted. By the way, I guess our grasp of their language is as good as we thought."

"Thank Nelly and her kids for that," Jack said.

"You're welcome, my mother says," Sal said.

"Well, let's get the kids where they're safe; and then let's get the hell out of here," Doc Meade said. "This place gives me the willies."

58

Kris shivered as she studied the pictures Jack was sending from the station. She'd would never succeed in wiping them from her mind's eye.

What must it be like for Jack? She'd need to hold him tight tonight.

So she was a bit surprised when Jack called and said she needed to come down to the brig. "The old woman's awake. At least as much as we're willing to let her wake up. She's babbling a lot. It's hard to make out, but I think she wants, no demands, to talk to our Enlightened One. Or as she puts it, 'the vermin with pretenses of enlightenment.'"

"I'm on my way," Kris said, and, unbuckling from her desk chair, launched herself at the door.

The *Wasp* was back at Condition Able, big, roomy, and easy to get around in. Assuming you knew the latest configuration.

Nelly directed Kris, and today, she directed her correctly.

The brig, however, was nothing like it had been. Now it consisted of several annexes, with no admittance from one to another.

Kris took the grand tour.

Lieutenant Commander Sampson had her own wing of sorts. It was more like a hospital than a prison. She was still in bed, sedated, and slowly recovering from her brain surgery. Kris might have ordered her to sick bay, but she had no idea what the new normal would be for that woman.

Sampson would stay in the brig until a new baseline for her behavior was established.

Another annex had the youngest children that had been brought aboard. There were five of them. They were likely somewhere around age seven down to three. Now they were bouncing off the walls, literally, in one large room under the close supervision of five young Sailors and Marines and one surprisingly matronlike chief.

The children didn't know it, but the standing orders for their guards was to spoil them rotten. No surprise, the kids were enjoying it and going along solidly with the program. Presently, they were having a pillow fight with the grown-ups and burning all kinds of energy that they had from a lunch mainly of cookies and ice cream.

No doubt, a nap would be next on the schedule.

Jacques and Amanda had been put in charge of designing a program for the seduction of these children from the dark side into the light.

Kris allowed herself a smile. The gray-haired alien woman would gnash her teeth if she knew what was being done to the children she'd intended to have drive knives into their own brains.

The bigger kids, eight to twelve years old, were getting a different approach, one closer to what Jacques was using for the kids from the tribe Kris had rescued, drafted, enlisted, whatever.

The brig for these five kids had been divided into five roomy cells. Each kid shared it with a young Marine or Sailor who came from a large family and had been their age not long ago.

Each room had one young alien, one young human, and two computer games. The human had started off playing the game by him or herself. Inevitably, or at least in four of the five cases, the kids had come to look over the player's shoulder.

Two of the boys were now lost in games involving racing around tracks or over wild country while the animal drivers or passengers tossed fruit at each other. The boys were laughing uproariously.

Two of the girls had joined their guards playing something involved with directing different sparkly things into forming a wall. Then they'd wreck it, if possible, with one swing of the wrecking ball, and do it all over again.

The oldest girl was the one holdout. Instead of coming to

look over her guard's shoulder and get involved in a game, she'd launched herself at the bulkhead, headfirst.

The guard had not been so lost in a game she'd grown out of years ago that she missed the move. She intercepted the girl on the fly. Now the girl was cuffed to her bed.

On the wall directly ahead of her, a coyote chased a roadrunner, with hilarious results. The guard laughed on cue with the video.

As expected, the alien girl opened one eye to see what was so funny. As Kris watched, the girl succumbed to watching as one vermin repeatedly tried and repeatedly failed, to get the other.

"I was betting on the roadrunner to drag her out of herself," Jacques said, drifting up to watch with Kris.

"It she the hard case?"

"Among our kids, yes. I understand from the *Royal* that they have two hard cases. Both older. Doc Meade wanted to spread the kids out among all the ships, but I told her solitary confinement would be the worst thing we could do to the youngsters. As it is now, we and the *Royal* are the only ships with nurseries."

"And most of them are coming around?"

"All the youngsters are moving, at one speed or another. This young woman, hard as she appears to be, is like putty compared to the diamond of the old lady's personality that you're about to meet."

"What are our chances of turning the woman?" Kris asked.

"Somewhere between none and nil," the anthropologist said. "But Jack had us reduce her sedation so you could talk to her. He thinks it's important that you hear what she has to say."

"Is it safe to do that?"

"Jack wants it. We've got a pump in her. We're ready to put her back to sleep at the first sign she's dangerous to herself. Why don't you come see for yourself?"

Kris left the girl. Her guard had just brought a pillow to support her head so she could watch the video more comfortably.

The next room was not much larger than the one Kris had just watched. Here Jack stood, wearing only the sweat-stained liner to his battle armor. On the bed, the gray-haired woman was tied down with padded restraints. Her head lolled gently back and forth in zero gee.

Jacques opened the door but stayed outside when Kris entered. He locked the door behind her.

~Our Enlightened One is here,~ Jack said, as Kris came to float beside him.

The woman opened her eyes, took in the scene with a lazy glance, and laughed. It was a harsh, dry cackle.

~Vermin, your false enlightened one is a *woman*,~ she spat.

~I led the ships that blasted your other ships into tiny pieces,~ Nelly translated for Kris.

The woman turned her face to the wall. ~Yes, yes, yes, the vermin have chewed our toes. You said that before. But you are fools.~

She turned back to face Kris. ~You are a fool. You shot me with your false guns before I could tell you why I chose to live and see the fear in your eyes before I die like my worshipped one, the truly Enlightened One.~

~What will bring fear to my eyes?~ Kris asked.

~They have sent the torch to all the ships. Your luck may have led you to be there when we stumbled, but your luck cannot save you from what is even now moving to obliterate you. We will swim in your blood. We will pile your heads in our Holy of Holies. You will have no children to share the wine of your remembrance.~

She stared hard at Kris. As hard as her drugged state allowed.

~No one will know you ever lived.~

NELLY, SHOW HER THE CRYPT UNDER THE PYRAMID.

WITH PLEASURE, KRIS.

The wall to Kris's right came alive with a holograph of the hall of horrors under the pyramid.

Even drugged, the woman's face took on shock. Horror.

~You cannot have been there.~

~I have walked your horror of horrors,~ Kris said through Nelly. ~I have spat on it. This is the message I left for all of you to read.~

Now the stone Kris had used to block the entrance to the pyramid filled the wall.

~You make war on us,~ Kris said, ~we will bury your pyramid under a pile of your skulls. We will flood your plain of glass with your blood.~

~No. No! NO!~ the woman screamed. ~You are wrong. All the ships will come now that the torch has been sent to them. It is you that will be buried in a flood of ships. We have more ships than you can count. Our women are most fruitful. We will destroy you.~

"Jacques," Kris said aloud, "are you listening in?"

"Yes," came from a small grill in the door.

"Put her to sleep. I think she's said all she came here to say."

"Her vitals are way up. I was about to do it anyway."

"Do it."

The woman's head lolled back on her bunk, and, in a moment, she was snoring.

"They fled here right after the first fight," Kris said to Jack. He nodded agreement.

"I don't see any way that this group could have sent any 'torch' to the other ships."

"It's not likely," he said. "However, there may be some sort of precedence for them rousing the tribes with a torch."

"And she's assuming someone among the others has done that."

"Like the three ships that observed our last fight?" Jack pointed out.

Kris winced. "Yeah."

"Any suggestions what we do next?"

"I wonder if there is a library on the station," Kris muttered to herself. "Someplace that has the history of these people."

"The only way to find out is to search it," Jack said.

"I hate to order your Marines into that place."

"It's ugly," Jack agreed.

"You'll want scientists in the search, too," Jacques said, joining them.

Kris heaved a sigh. "Captain Drago, lay the *Wasp* alongside the station, then please join me on the flag bridge. Have the other skippers come, too."

"Aye aye, Admiral. The Word is already sent to the squadron."

Kris squared her shoulders. It was bad and would, no doubt, get worse.

59

Kris sat in her day quarters, meetings done.

All four of the squadron's ships now lay close to the station. The *Wasp*, *Royal*, and *Intrepid* were able to spawn pinnaces. They were out cloud dancing, gathering in enough reaction mass for the squadron's needs to get them back to Alwa.

Hopefully, it would not take them long to refuel all four ships.

The idea of sending Sailor, Marines, and boffins to root around among all those bodies on the station to see if there was anything helpful left had caused Kris to blanch.

Professor Labao and Nelly had come up with a solution. As Kris sat here, nano scouts were zipping through the station, looking for anything interesting. Nelly and her brood were doing the oversight. Only if they found something really interesting did a human eye get brought in.

Thanks to a merciful God, the A deck with all the bodies seemed to hold little of interest. It was closer to the hub that the scouts found things to refer for human review. There was a file room, huge and full of actual print on paper. There was something that might be a library, but it didn't have all that many books. There was also a series of large halls that might have passed for courtrooms with judicial chambers off them. In them were loads of officious-looking books. The scientists were all interested in these for lack of something better.

"What we haven't found," Professor Labao noted, "is anything like a research facility or labs. Interesting that."

Kris was finding a lot of things interesting.

The ships swung at anchor as close to the station as was safe. Now there were air locks spaced along the station's outer hull where longboats could easily dock. Inside, a small team had spread nets across A deck. If it worked as planned, the nets would hold the drifting bodies well back from the people who actually boarded the station to do the scavenger hunt.

Kris hoped they saw no more than was necessary.

For now, Kris stared at the screens in flag plot.

They were blank at the moment.

That was not what she saw.

Bodies drifted across them. Big bodies. Tiny bodies. Bodies that screamed blood at her.

No, none of the bodies had screamed. It was the live one that screamed defiances at her.

If Kris let them, these people would drive her crazy with their wish for death. Death for all living things except that tiny group that was enlightened just the right way.

Kris shook herself out of her reveries. She had things to do and decisions to make.

Not quite. If she was honest with herself, the things she had to do were pretty much already decided.

She needed to return three felines to their planet and get back where she belonged.

Getting there would be no easy job, what with her having only the wreckage of eight ships flying in four loose formations.

Traveling back to Alwa would have to be careful, and therefore slow.

Once she got back, she would, no doubt, face even more problems.

When hadn't she?

She would also need to get a message back to human space. She'd found out a lot about the aliens. Oh, and she'd found a bunch of talking cats who will need protection, assuming they didn't want to conqueror the whole human race.

If King Ray had been pissed with her the last time she came back from adventuring, he'd likely have kittens over this one.

Speaking of which, should she take the opportunity to deliver the message in person?

She'd offered the chance to Phil and his crew from the *Hornet*. They'd passed up the opportunity to get home, and now more of them had died. Maybe Kris could be the messenger.

Oh, right, Kris was the Viceroy and Commander of the Alwa Defense Sector. For her to go home would be to abandon her post.

She could order others home, but go home herself? Not so much.

Kris stared at the overhead. She was starting to sound crazy. Almost as crazy as that old woman.

The two of them were a matching pair.

Or might be if Kris didn't get a hold on herself.

There was a soft knock at the door of her quarters.

I could use an interruption right about now.

"Enter."

Zarra and her admiral came in.

"Do you have a moment?" Zarra asked, the epitome of politeness.

"Certainly. No one is scheduled to try their hand at killing me today, and I'm not planning on killing anyone myself."

Zarra promptly passed those words along to her admiral.

She growled cheerfully and padded her way quickly to one of the stools around Kris's conference table. She settled there, her tail lazily lashing back and forth behind her.

"Where is your general?" Kris asked for no reason other than it filled the silence.

"She does not take well to space. She is still recovering from, what do you call it? Zero gee," Zarra explained. "I do not think we can get home fast enough to suit her."

"We humans do not care very much for it either, but the early space travelers had to learn to survive it. We should be heading back to drop you off very soon," Kris said.

"That is what my admiral came to talk to you about." Zarra glanced at her admiral, who made a swatting motion with her paw. Zarra swallowed and went on.

"You have challenged us to a race to our moon. My admiral was wondering if there was any way for you to tow or push one of the dead alien ships into an orbit around our moon."

"So if you got to the moon, you would also have a chance to look over all this advanced technology," Kris said.

"Something like that."

"And if one of these ships was orbiting your own moon, would the race to the moon turn into a real race, with all your zones trying to get their first and gain knowledge they could use to dominate the others?"

Zarra did not flinch. "We do not think so. When we left, the decision had already been made that Columm and the Bizalt Kingdom would working together to reach the moon. Since we have been gone, many others have joined in this group effort. Yes, it is the first such effort across zones that we have ever made, unless there was a war driving us to cooperate to bring down a stronger power, but still, it is happening as we talk here."

Kris found herself again staring at the ceiling. Should she refer this to her staff for examination? What would Amanda and Jacques think of this idea?

Kris shook her head.

"Yes, the technology on the alien ships is well ahead of what you have, but no, I will not help you get access to it."

Kris wondered if the admiral intended to roll her body up as if about to pounce, or if it was just ancient body language that no longer presaged attack.

"There are several reasons why I say that, and none of them involve a distrust of you or a desire to keep technology from you," Kris went on quickly.

"First, the technology we have found in the alien ships is obsolete by our standards. Do you really want to begin building ships that you will quickly be tearing up or throwing away?

"Secondly, the technology these aliens use is much different from what we use. If you are to build ships to fight side by side with us, you will need our communications devices, ranging gear, and weapons. No doubt, you will give each of these devices a unique twist to bend them to your needs; however, a certain amount of commonality will be needed.

"Do you follow the logic of my position?" Kris asked.

Zarra turned to her admiral. The officer nodded as the translator spoke.

Zarra turned back to Kris and began to speak for the admiral. "We have found that to be the case with our own allies. And when one smaller power switches sides, it is often necessary for them to scrap their ships, airplanes, and armored fighting vehicles so that they can fit in with their new overlord. She means ally," Zarra moved quickly to correct her words.

Kris wondered if the idea of first among equals was just catching on. Or if it would ever catch on.

"There is one more question my admiral asks," Zarra said.

"Yes."

"Can we join you? She and I. Can we travel back with you?"

Kris would often wonder why she did not reflect more before giving her answer.

"Yes, you may," she said.

"Thank you," Zarra said, and led her admiral from the room.

It would be two days more before Kris could order the squadron to get underway back the way they'd come: first to Sasquan, then to Alwa.

It would be a long voyage.

Kris wondered what she'd find at the end of it.

60

The *Wasp* came through the Beta Jump of the Alwa System with plenty of velocity and began immediately to brake at 1.15 gees.

As soon as Alwa knew Kris was back in system, she was inundated with message traffic addressed to her as Viceroy; Commander, Alwa Defense Sector; and CEO of Nuu Enterprises.

"Must be nice to know you were missed," Jack said with an evil grin, as Kris surveyed the pile of flimsies stacking up on her desk.

"You want half of these?" Kris asked.

"Oh no," Jack said, heading for the door. "There's got to be some nice Marine stuff I can lose myself in. Inspecting the heads. Checking out the storage rooms. Seeing how my deputy did organizing a brigade of Marines and National Guard. Lots of really fun stuff."

Kris made a nasty face at him, then turned back to the first flimsy. It was from Granny Rita, the acting viceroy. It opened with how glad she was to have Kris back.

Considering that Granny Rita had led the survivors of her battlecruiser squadron in scratching out a life for themselves on Alwa eighty years ago, Kris was left to wonder what could make her so happy to lay down her burden.

One quick read, and Kris had Nelly round up Amanda and Jacques. "Tell them to get here pronto."

Two minutes later, they were there. Out of breath, but there.

"We got problems on Alwa," Kris said.

"We knew they were having problems when we flew through here before," Amanda said.

"Well, it's worse," Kris said, passing over the message flimsy to both of them.

"The old-line Alwans want their old ways back," Kris said. "Only now, *we've* got new-line Alwans who like what they can buy with the money they earn working for the humans. Humans will slow down and stop if a Rooster type wanders into the road. Now Alwans are driving the big rigs instead of humans, and they don't stop for nothing. Some old, bald-feathered Alwan wanders into the road in front of them, they don't slow down. And if the old coot doesn't get out of the way, they don't go back to see if they hit him."

"Ouch," Amanda said. "That kind of makes it hard to figure out who did what to whom."

"Exactly," Jacques said. "So the old-liners hold all the new kids responsible for anything bad that happens to them."

"It seems we humans have created a cash-based society that runs on a schedule," Kris said.

"No wonder the old farts want their old world back," Amanda said.

"That old world is not coming back. They have a choice between us and those bloodthirsty alien space raiders," Kris said, and sighed.

"But how do you get them to see it our way?" Jacques said. "We've done just about everything we can to rub their noses in the facts. They just ignore what they don't want to see."

Kris leaned back in her chair and eyed the overhead. "Maybe we have something new for them to look at."

Jacques raised an eyebrow at Kris.

"Nelly, get me Doc Meade."

"Yes, Admiral," came quickly.

"If I were to take the old woman alien down to Alwa, could you keep her sedated for the ride, then cut back on them when I wanted her in full rage?"

"I've got a pretty good idea on just how much to medicate her to keep her out of trouble," the doctor said.

"I may want her to get in trouble," Kris said, vaguely.

"I'm a doctor, Admiral. First, I do no harm. What kind of trouble do you have in mind?"

Kris told her.

"Yep, I think I can keep her meds at the right level for that without hurting her or her hurting anyone else."

"Good. I'll let you know when everything is arranged."

"You think that will do it?" Jacques asked. From the look on his face, he seemed doubtful.

"Nothing beats a try but a failure," Kris said. "Now, about this money-based economy. Amanda, are we doing this right?"

"Kris, you want production, you have to pay people to produce. There aren't enough humans for all the defense you want, so you need to recruit Alwans. They're new to this whole concept, but they like the TVs, computers, and amenities. I understand we've got a computerized egg warmer that is all the rage. I helped develop the advertising for it when it was still in R&D. You're starting to sound like one of the old farts."

"Oh, no, Amanda," Kris said through a grin. "They don't want to have anything to do with our cake. Me, I want it in my grubby little hands, *and* I want to gobble it down whole. We're very different."

"How's the defensive effort going in general?" Amanda asked.

"Admiral Kitano seems happy. They've got the damaged ships back in full commission and spare Smart Metal to boot. I've already sent a warning ahead that the squadron got shot up badly and will need first call on the yards' time. Admiral Benson says he'll be waiting for us, and we can take the ships right into the docks. I've apprised Captain Drago, and he's passed it along to the other ships."

Kris's grin got even bigger. "He doesn't think our shot-up 20-inch lasers are worth fixing. He wants to scrap them and replace them with some of the new 22-inch lasers he's now got coming out of the yard armory."

"That ought to make you Navy types happy," Amanda said. "You may not like businesspeople, but you sure like the toys they make for you."

"No, Amanda, we like staying alive, which the weapons made by the industrial base does for us."

"Same thing," Amanda said.

"Very different," Kris countered.

"Before you two get into a catfight, and may I point out, we now have cat allies to do that for us, may we take our leave?" Jacques said, standing. "Unless there's something else?"

"Only other thing I've got is a rather short and cryptic message from Pipra Strongarm. You may remember her as the woman I left in charge of Nuu Enterprises," Kris said.

"What's her problem?" Amanda asked.

"She didn't say. She did say that she needed to meet me as soon as I got in. Even said she wanted to be ahead of Admiral Benson."

"But not why?" Jacques said, rubbing his chin in thought.

"No explanation."

"You going to give her the honor of first meeting?"

"She's got my curiosity up. I might put someone else last in line just for giving me that 'I got a secret and I won't tell' kind of treatment, but I trusted Pipra."

"If you trust her, you have to go with that trust," Amanda said.

The two left, leaving Kris to wade through production reports from everywhere about everything. The good news was that there was a lot of it.

Kitano reported herself happy that the new squadrons were training up well since the first exercise, a quick trip to the moon and back. Their latest run out to the closest ice giant had been 4.0.

That was good to hear. Assuming every alien ship in the galaxy wasn't standing in line to jump down her throat, she might have a fighting chance.

And if they are?

We'll burn that bridge when we come to it.

61

They made orbit and, as promised, the *Wasp-Hornet* went directly into Benson's yard. The *Royal-Connie* was assigned to the Musashi docks, the *Intrepid-Bulwark* was directed to the Yamato yard, and the *Congress-Endeavor* barely made it into the Portsmouth yard.

They only wanted one ship to a yard until they figured out if it was one ship or two they had.

Kris had signaled that she would move her flag to the *Princess Royal* and was on her way there when Pipra intercepted her.

"We've got to talk."

"You're talking," Kris said. "I'm listening."

"We've found the pot of gold at the end of the rainbow."

"I take it that's a metaphor. What are you really telling me?"

"When we got here, you pointed out, and you were quite right at the time, that there is nothing here that we could ship back to human space and make a dime off of."

"The transportation costs alone would eat up any profit," Kris said.

"Well, we've found something light enough and worth enough that we can make all our fortunes shipping it back there. Assuming that they don't synthesize it or start growing it as soon as they get a good look at our first cargo."

Kris slowly came to a halt. This *could* be a game changer. Assuming she could ever get Pipra to spill what it was.

"Okay, what is in this pot of yours?"

"It's a plant," Pipra said. "We found it on their south continent in a river. Can you believe it, it can uproot itself and move! Really move, like scoot out of the way of some hungry fish."

"A plant," Kris said incredulously, "that can move?"

"And has sensors. At least it can sense a fish moving toward it and run away."

"That sounds like an animal."

"No, it's a plant. It does that photosynthesis thing. Boy does it ever. It can store up energy like nothing we've ever seen before, and when its mitochondria start burning that energy, it can pull its roots up and take off upstream or wherever it wants to go with the kind of speed that leaves most fish behind."

"Does it have a brain?"

"We don't think so. It seems to react more than act," Pipra said, but not confidently. "Any scientists who can get their hands on some of this are in it up to their ears. This is going to be worth megatrillions."

Kris closed her eyes. She kept hearing this was a game changer and worth money, but she wasn't hearing a whole lot of why.

"How does it work?" Kris demanded.

Pipra made a face. "We're working on that. There are flying fish and a batlike thing that can move fast enough to catch this plant and also have the stomach enzymes necessary to use it."

"So it's complex."

"Complex as hell."

"And people are going to want to pay money for this because . . .?" Kris said, waving her arms vaguely.

Pipra looked at Kris like she was a particularly dumb three-year-old. She started to open her mouth, then seemed to think better of it. A moment later, she finally said, "You use nanos, don't you?"

"Lots of them."

"I've never met a Soldier that didn't like their nano scouts," Pipra said.

"It can save your butt."

"But they don't have much endurance. Not enough power."

"Right," Kris agreed.

"And you want to recover them, right?"

"Right."

"But if a wind comes up, they might not have enough power to fly back to you."

"Yes, then you lose them, and commanders and budget

folks get very cranky. Speaking of which, I'm getting very cranky."

"Yes. Okay. Now, assume that your nano has one of these mitochondria powering it."

A light went off inside Kris's head.

Pipra went on. "Marines gobble down candy bars before a fight. It gives them energy. Now, what if we could give them a candy bar with this stuff inside?"

"Would it work?"

Again, Pipra made a face. "If we can figure out what the flying fish and bats have in their bellies that allow them to access the full power of this stuff, yes. Maybe."

"How close are we to making this work?"

Pipra shrugged. "Six months. Six years. Very likely not six weeks or sixteen years."

Kris made a face. "So we're talking raw science with lots of unknowns."

"And we're dealing with people on one end."

"But nanos don't have civil rights," Kris said.

"But there are a lot of people that wouldn't want weeds or spiders running around with this kind of strength. This could be the invasive species from hell," Pipra said. "I suspect that a lot of people won't want this anywhere near them."

"Ouch," Kris said, seeing the downside for the first time.

"Most of our research is taking place on a new lab on the moon."

"Who paid for it?"

"We all did."

"And how much will it take away from the defense effort?" Kris demanded.

"Not a lot," Pipra answered vaguely. "Listen, you said the first day we were here that no one cared if we lived or died, so long as we died hard and the aliens figured we belonged here. Well, some of the scientists have pointed out that our DNA won't pass the smell test if the aliens do any checking."

"That thought has crossed my mind," Kris admitted.

"Now we have something on this planet that humanity needs, really needs. And we *really* don't want the aliens to get their hands on this stuff, assuming they'd look before they raped this planet down to the bare rock."

"Yes," Kris said, feeling like the word hardly carried enough meaning for the job.

"So, I invested your money in this."

Kris nodded, thinking hard and fast. "I think you did good." Then she changed the subject to her own concerns. "By the way, have you hired a lot of Alwans?"

"Lots of them. Kris, our consumer products are catching on like a house afire. They love our microwave ovens. Down south, our solar-powered riverboats are selling just as fast as we can deliver them. That's what they're using to troll up this plant."

"Everything is changing."

"Damn right it is."

"Some Alwans don't like it," Kris reminded Pipra.

"They can disagree with it all they want, but they better get out of the road. We're coming through."

"No doubt," Kris said. "Are we done?"

"Pretty much. I hear your ships got shot up pretty bad. We've got a decent supply of Smart Metal that should be good for repairs. We're also building our own reactors and lasers."

"Twenty-two inchers, I understand."

Pipra grinned. "You bet they are."

The businesswoman left, to get about her business.

Kris turned back to her walk to the *Princess Royal*.

For Pipra, business was business.

For Kris, it was complicated.

She had two cultures she needed to bring together in harmony. No, make that three. She couldn't forget the felines.

She might have a good job for them.

She was lost in thought, and almost to the *P Royal* when an ensign ran up to her.

"Admiral Kitano sends her respects and requests your presence on the flag bridge immediately, ma'am."

"Nelly?" Kris said.

"I'm in the dark about this as much as you."

Kris began walking briskly.

62

Rear Admiral Kitano was waiting for Kris in her own day cabin, which looked very much like a flag bridge at the moment.

The place looked downright homey. It had a wooden desk just like on the *Wasp*, only its carvings looked like angels rather than Greek pillars. It had several sofas and armchairs. These were in a lovely royal blue rather than the *Wasp*'s earth tones.

Kitano wasn't seated at any of them but stood before one of several large screens.

"You didn't rob the chief's mess for the screens, did you?" Kris asked.

"I wouldn't dare. These are all local production. Among hardworking Alwans, sixty-inch screens are catching on. I got half of the first production."

Kris went to stand by her subordinate. The screens showed the Alwa System in the middle and jumps covering a dozen systems out.

Two were flashing red.

"Is there a problem?" Kris asked.

"No and yes. Or maybe yes. Do you want the good news or the bad news first, Admiral?"

"Make it Kris among admirals."

"And I'm Amber," Kitano said.

"And we are faced with?"

"What looks like incoming reinforcements, headed for Alpha Jump. That's nice, but also headed for Alpha is something else."

"Does this something else have some substance?"

"It just jumped into that red system farthest out. Six I

think, but if we're right, if it's going fast enough and puts on some turns, its next jump takes it to our system."

Kris frowned. "You know about what we found when we caught up with Sampson and her mutineers."

"It's a big report, Kris. Did I skim over something I shouldn't have?"

"Some of the alien warships from the mother ship we first blew away put on some speed and revolutions and didn't try to slow down until they were quite a ways from here. I don't know if what they did was common knowledge or just something they stumbled across."

"It looks to be developing into common knowledge, Kris. A week ago we had a ship jump into a system five out from our Beta Jump. It built up speed crossing the system and hit the jump at close to eight hundred thousand klicks an hour."

"What did it do here?"

"It never got here," Amber said. "It must have missed the jump. You know how the normal jumps do wiggles. We figure it zigged out of their way, and they went flying past it."

"I wonder if they had enough fuel to slow down?" Kris said.

"We don't think they did. Not if it was like the fast movers they used against us last time."

Kris mulled that over for a bit. "So they sent a fast mover on what can only be a suicide mission, and it killed itself with nothing to show for it."

"It looks that way. Now we've got another one incoming. I don't think we can expect to be that lucky again."

"Admiral, please get two 22-inch frigates moving toward both of your jump points."

"You think we can shoot it down?"

"We better be able to. Because, if we don't, I suspect it intends to make one hell of a hole in the planet below."

63

Several hours later, Jack had rejoined Kris on the new flag bridge aboard the *Princess Royal*. He'd brought their private gear. Amanda and Jacques, Penny and Masao sat around the conference table with Professor Labao and Admiral Kitano.

Reinforcements were arriving.

The first ship through was the *George Washington*, with Rear Admiral Yi of Earth. It was a 22-inch frigate and led the *Abraham Lincoln*, *Franklin D. Roosevelt*, and the *John F. Kennedy*.

"Our problems have even Old Earth rearming?" Jack observed.

"With frigates, Jack," Kris pointed out. "They're cheaper, and their smaller crews cost less come payday."

"It's still nice," Penny said.

"I'll take any help we can get," Admiral Kitano muttered.

"Next up we have the *Lenin*, *Khrushchev*, *Bismarck*, and *Frederick the Great*," Kitano reported.

"Do they have the *Lenin* and the *George Washington* in the same squadron?" Amanda said. "I thought those groups didn't like each other."

"The bigger reach," Nelly said, "is the *Kennedy* with the *Khrushchev*. The two men almost blew up Old Earth during the first atomic crisis. I am told this class is made up of great war leaders or peacemakers."

"Well, they didn't blow up Earth, and we got to be here," Kris said. "I'll put those two down as peacemakers."

"Kris, Chief Beni is having a problem with these ships."

"What kind of problem?" Kris asked. *Haven't I exhausted my supply of new problems yet for this month?* she managed not to whine aloud.

"The radar image he gets off these ships is nowhere near as large as his mass-density detector says it should be. His laser bounce from them is even less. Our gravity detector says there's a good fifty thousand tons of ship out there. The reactors are what you'd expect, but the radar bounce is more like a fifteen-thousand-ton corvette and the laser reflection is more like a five-thousand-ton schooner."

Kris eyed her staff. She got a lot of blank looks in return.

"I guess Old Earth's dog may have taught itself some new tricks," she said.

Nelly went on. "The next division is led by the *Charles de Gaulle*; there's another *Churchill*, *Clemenceau*, and *King George V.* They're all 22-inchers."

"Nice. Very nice," Jack said.

"Get your history book ready for this one," Admiral Kitano said. "*Admiral Yamamoto*, *Chairman Mao Zedong*, *Admiral Togo*, and *Sun Tzu*. All 22-inchers again."

"No, Nelly, we don't want a history lesson," Kris told her computer as it began a dissertation on who these ships were named for. "Earth can name their ships after anyone they want. Just so long as we get them to fight with us, it's all very fine by me."

"But, Kris, a lot of these people were at each other's throats."

"That was four hundred years ago," Jacques said. "A lot can change in four hundred years."

"Unless you've got an 'Enlightened One' passing down the same old same old," Kris said.

"Yes," came from everyone present.

"Leading off the next division is the *Nelson Mandela*, followed by the *Shaka Zulu*, the *Simon Bolivar*, and the *Jose de San Martin*."

"I guess we know who paid for them," Amanda said.

"Here comes the last division," Kitano reported. "*Julius Caesar*, *Alexander*, *Saladin*, and *Genghis Khan*. Behind them are a dozen merchant ships named *Apple Blossom*, *Cherry Blossom*, *Pear Blossom*, and the like. Lots of flowers. Oh, and what looks like two more stations. At least, that's what I hope *Shang-hi* and *Plymouth* mean when you put the names on huge ships."

Kris stood and walked over to examine the board with her order of battle.

Of the thirty-four that had sailed out to meet the enemy in the last battle, twenty-six were ready to answer bells and get underway. There were seven more in dock. Maybe four could be made battle ready in a few days.

It was anyone's guess when the *Hornet*, *Constellation*, *Royal*, and *Bulwark* might sail again. If they ever did.

Admiral Kitano had trained up another thirty-two. They were drilled and ready. The twenty-four that Earth had just provided would need to adopt to Alwa battle methods and be put through a few shakedown cruises.

With luck, the enemy would give them the time they needed.

Kris really did have a fleet now. Eighty-two, maybe eighty-five frigates.

Almost triple what she'd had the last time the aliens attacked.

Of course, at least three times as many aliens were likely to come at them.

The screams of the old woman echoed in Kris's mind. "All of them are coming for us. Jacques, how many is all of the alien base ships?"

"We're studying the writing on the wall, Kris. As best we can tell, there are at least thirty of them. There are some that seem to have left only one memorial and pile of heads. If they are still out there and come calling, there might be as many as fifty."

Kris shook her head. "We'll worry about them later. Just now, we have this other problem—fast movers. Let's see how we handle them."

64

Kris studied the screens with Kitano. This was a Navy problem.

The civilians stayed at the conference table. Even Penny and Masao.

The felines slipped in and settled down on stools in the corner. Kris didn't object. They'd come to see what the humans could do. She'd give them a show before she took them out to meet the Alwans. The cats might like the Ostriches.

Assuming they didn't try to eat each other.

Admiral Kitano spoke first. "We've sent warnings through Jump Point Alpha telling the reinforcements that they might have something following them through with a high-speed vector on the boat and unable to steer clear of them. Admiral Yi is taking his ships down a bit below the planetary plane and slowing them at 1.25 gees."

"Except for those two," Kris pointed out.

"Yes, the *Saladin* and the *Genghis Khan* are decelerating at 3.5 gees and are rising a bit above the direct exit from the jump. They've got those new 22-inch lasers with a range close to two hundred thousand klicks. If they can anchor some three or four hundred thousand klicks from the jump, they'll be in position to take solid shots at our fast visitors for a long, long time."

"And the ships you sent up from here?"

"I've got four of the 22-inch frigates of the ghost division headed out. *Phantom* and *Voodoo* to Alpha, *Banshee* and *Daemon* to Beta."

"But they've got a ways to go. When do you expect our hostiles?"

"I hate to say it, but your guess is as good as mine. They

don't maintain a constant acceleration. The report on jump activity will likely arrive after they do. Assuming they don't miss the jump point and not show up at all."

"Your best guess?"

"Anytime from five minutes ago to an hour from now. They could be later. Obviously, they weren't earlier."

"Nelly, do you have an opinion?"

"No, Admiral. The admiral's guess is as good as mine."

"Smart computer," Masao was heard to whisper.

"May I get you some coffee?" Jacques asked.

"Do you want some coffee?" Kris asked the anthropologist right back, arching an eyebrow.

"I would, thank you so very much, Admiral. And I do believe Amanda would as well."

"Me too," Penny put in.

"Zarra, would you and your admiral like some?"

"May we have some of that other dark warm liquid?"

"Chocolate?"

"Yes, please."

"Get me some hot water for tea," Kris said. "Please bring a few bags of that relaxing kind."

"Me too," Jack said.

"Masao, would you lend me a hand? I'm going to need a pack mule to haul all this," Jacques said.

"Of course, since you ask me so kindly," the Musashi officer said, smiling.

"Oops," Amanda said. "And he calls himself an anthropologist."

"Maybe I'm just a little bit worried and off my game," Jacques said as he opened the door for his putative pack mule and intelligence lieutenant.

No sooner had he closed the door than the screens lit up.

No doubt, what was now showing up had taken place hours ago. That made it no less nail-biting.

A bright blip shot out of Jump Point Beta.

The *Saladin* and *Genghis Khan* were still braking, their bows with six 22-inch lasers aimed at the jump point. However, the alien raider was moving fast, some six hundred thousand klicks an hour and *accelerating* at close to 3.5 gees.

It was also spawning bullets, lots of bullets.

Were they just iron slugs or atomics? No way to tell from here.

It seemed like forever, but it couldn't have been more than a minute before the two Earth ships opened fire.

Their first shots missed; the alien was accelerating and jinking. They'd learned something from watching Kris's fights.

The ship was a haze on the screen as it went up first, then down. Then right, then right, and finally left.

The Earth ships fired, then fired, then fired again. They must have fired their forward battery empty because it looked like they paused, cut deceleration, then flipped ship and started firing their aft battery.

One of those must have scored a hit because the aliens' vector went off hard and long to the right. And it held its course.

Lasers from both ships transfixed it before it could make corrections and get back into a jinking pattern.

Where a ship had been, was now only a quickly gone cloud of hot gas.

The *Saladin* and *Genghis Khan* took fifteen seconds to finish recharging their forward battery, then flipped ship again. They were braking at 1.15 gees as they took on the bullets.

They were just dumb iron with no engines, no jinking. They were melted to drops of slag quickly under the cuts and slashes of 22-inch lasers.

The battle was over before it had barely begun.

"That was well done," the feline admiral said.

"But how much more of these will we face?" Jack asked.

"There was no way for this one to report on their success or failure. They likely already have more on the way," Kris said.

"Ships hurled at us blind," Penny said softly, "with crews that have no chance to survive."

The war had entered a new phase. It was now a war of attrition where the enemy could hit them anytime, and only had to succeed once to rack up a terrible butcher's bill.

"We'll have to be on guard every hour of every day," Jack was heard to mutter.

65

TWO days later, the Old Earth fleet arrived above Alwa.

With the *Wasp* in dock, Kris had no Forward Lounge to meet with all her skippers. She briefly considered having the *Princess Royal* grow one but quickly dropped that idea. Her adjustments to the fraternizing rule was quite enough. No need to reintroduce alcohol to the fleet as well.

She'd connected Admiral Benson and Mother MacCreedy and in two shakes, Canopus Station now had a very nice Officers' Club.

As Kris crossed the brow to the station, Captains Taussig and O'dell met her. She'd asked for them, and they'd obeyed her gentle order.

"I'm converting four empty supply ships into two fast warships," Kris began without preamble. "They'll have four reactors and twelve rocket motors. Design tells me they'll easily maintain three gees for as long as needed. One will have all eight of the 18-inch lasers we have left. Four forward, four aft. O'dell, she'll be your new *Endeavor.*"

"Yes, ma'am," the merchant skipper answered evenly but with no visible reaction.

"The other will have six of the new 22-inch lasers. Three forward, three aft. Phil, we'll name her *Hornet.*"

"And I take it that she's mine?"

"Yes."

He nodded. "The last two *Hornets* have been good to me and my crew. Though, I must admit, we've been hard on them."

They walked in silence for a moment.

"As many guns fore as aft," Phil finally said. "What do you intend?"

"I'm sending you two back to Wardhaven with a cargo of information and biologicals that is critical to our survival effort. At least one of you must get back."

"Ma'am, do we have to take the ships back?" Captain O'dell asked. "I know that me and my crew don't want to leave you."

Kris eyed the two. "I'll make it a written order if I have to."

"Yes, Your Highness," Phil said. He knew how much Kris hated to be Highnessed.

"Yes, Phil." Kris tried to keep her reasonable voice. "This is coming from My Highness and your admiral and the Viceroy all rolled up into one mean package. Both of you saw what's under that damn pyramid. For the first time, we've got a full physiological study of those bastards. We've got their intent in their own words as well. There's something more. The scientists have found a plant here that all sentient civilization needs and we can't let the aliens destroy it or, worse, let it fall into the aliens' hands."

"Are you going to tell us what this is?"

"Not now. Not until you leave. But you will be carrying boffins and cargo that you cannot let the aliens capture."

"We've already had this discussion," Phil said. "No doubt you've had the same one with her," he said, nodding at Captain O'dell. "If worse comes to worst, they don't get our ship. They get an expanding ball of gas."

"That's why I'm sending you two," Kris said.

"Will we be taking any other people?" O'dell asked.

Kris grimaced. "If we have space, I guess we could allow some. Likely, we wouldn't have space enough for everyone who wanted to go. We could hold a lottery for them."

"Do you really want to send back those who want to go back enough that they'd risk this passage?" Phil asked. "They wouldn't likely be your best friends."

Kris scowled. "I need you two to be my ambassadors of goodwill. To tell folks we need more help, and we're doing good with what they've sent us."

"I think we could be that," O'dell said. "I'm not so sure that the folks who really want out of here would be much help if someone shoved a mic in their face."

"More likely, they'd grab the first mic they could get their hands on and never let go," Phil said.

"I may have to rethink sending you with excess passengers," Kris admitted.

"If we're going to be using the three gees you mentioned, I'd prefer a light ship," Phil said.

"Thanks for giving me your thoughts, folks."

"Always glad to help a Longknife out," Phil said with a huge grin.

Rear Admiral Yi was waiting for Kris outside the new Officers' Club. O'dell saluted him, but Taussig, being in the presence of a vice admiral, acknowledged him with a nod, then saluted Kris and headed into the club.

Kris returned Yi's salute, the OCS cadet she'd been not all that long ago wondering who was saluting who, as Phil and O'dell slipped away.

"I've got good news for you, Admiral," Yi said, handing Kris a package.

She opened it to find the flag and shoulder boards of a full, four-star admiral.

"You're out of uniform," Yi said with a broad grin

"Again," Kris said, and sighed. "I take it this is still a frocking up? Nothing added to my base pay."

" 'She's a Longknife, she doesn't need the money,' was what your king told me."

"That sounds like Grampa Ray," Kris muttered. Admiral Yi was in Earth dress blues. Kris was in dress whites with all her medals and orders; most were human, but now some were feline.

It added quite a bit to her weight.

Jack was nowhere in sight, unfortunately.

"Yi, would you do me the honor of replacing my shoulder boards?"

"Gladly." As he did, he spoke softly for her ears only. "There's a major reinforcement fleet building up to ship out here. It's holding for something. Just exactly what that something is, I don't know, and I was specifically told that I didn't want to know because if I even guessed about it, and guessed too close, I would no longer be deployable."

"So, what is your best guess, now that you are deployed?"

"Honestly, I don't know. What I do know is that there are three humongous ships taking shape in orbit over Wardhaven,

Pitt's Hope, and Savannah. No one can tell you what's in them that makes them need to be so huge, but I can tell you, there are Iteeche crawling all over them right beside the humans."

He paused to grin at Kris. "At least, that is what I hear."

"Iteeche?" Kris said, with a raised eyebrow.

"I swear, the demilitarized zone is more like a transit zone these days. We shipped them the specs for Smart Metal. What they paid for it is likely what's going on around those three monster ships."

"But you don't know what that is."

"Really, Admiral, I haven't a clue. I was told that when it gets here, you'll fall in love with it, but until it's here, they don't want to risk anything's being captured."

"Well, that's nice to hear," Kris said. "Now, want to tell me why our radar and lasers are being so attenuated when they sweep your ships?"

"Oh, that's a surprise of our own. I'm surprised you didn't ask me on the way in."

"If it's a secret surprise, would you want it on the radio?"

"Right, well, quantum computers have been slowing down itty-bitty bits of light for years to speed up their computing. Ever wondered if we could slow down laser beams, spread them around, and maybe send them back the way they came?"

"The thought has crossed my mind," Kris said. "I understand the small quanta of light in computing are a whole lot more manageable than an 18-inch laser beam."

"That's been the thinking for centuries, but back on Earth, we've had some of our best research centers and universities working on the concept. You know, not all the smart people are out on the Rim, no matter what you've heard."

Kris knew that the Rim worlds prided themselves on their lead in most scientific and technological advances for the last hundred years or so. She'd never visited Earth, and never had a taste of its chauvinism. Hopefully, the admiral would not be a problem.

But he was still talking. "We made a major breakthrough last year just as we were designing this class of warships. My command is coated with hundred-millimeter-thick specially doped and grown crystals. Once we go to Defensive Condition 5, our whole hull is covered with that stuff, and you can't get a laser range finder to locate us, and not a lot of radar will bounce off us. And if one of those bastards you've had trouble with out here should hit us with a laser weapon, you better believe they're going to be in for one hell of a surprise."

"Interesting," Kris said, trying to stay noncommittal. "That's wonderful, because I'm about to brief you on just how bad it is out here."

"Worse than us having to save your bacon from a suicide attacks before we even got to Alwa?"

That wasn't exactly how Kris would have put it, but she tried not to let her irritation seep into her words. "That's just the battlefield prep."

The Earth admiral just kept grinning. "Well, we came out here looking for a fight. It looks like we came to the right place."

Kris could agree with that. "You most certainly did."

66

"Atten'hut. Admiral on deck," seemed to place a special emphasis on "Admiral."

This was an Officers' Club, and as such, honors were neither required nor expected. Still, the entire room was on its feet, even the civilians.

Kris didn't stand them at ease, but began the long walk to the front of the room where Penny and Jack waited for her at a table below four large screens.

It might as well have been the Forward Lounge, but the Forward Lounge gussied up to be the king's Officers' Club. The long bar was to Kris's right. Paintings were on the walls, and battle flags hung from the ceiling. It was exactly the way the Forward Lounge had looked to receive the king.

The only thing missing were pictures of King Raymond and his old commands.

Added were two huge mother ships painted above the screens . . . with bright red slashes through them.

Someone was keeping score.

The place was a whole lot larger. Each of the eighty-plus frigates was represented by its captain, XO, engineering officer, skipper of the Marine detachment, and science lead. Though most of the scientists were civilians, the new arrivals from Earth all sported a uniformed lieutenant commander in that slot.

For the fleet auxiliaries and merchant ships, there were a captain, second officer, and chief engineer. Some in Navy uniform, others in merchant marine colors. A few wore rough civilian clothes.

Kris was halfway to the front when the applause began. Kris had no idea where it started or why some of the Navy types concluded they could clap their hands at attention. However it began, the applause filled the room.

Maybe Kris spotted the origin of the clapping. A table close to hers held Granny Rita; Ada, the Chief of Ministries for the Alwa Colonial government; and several more humans and Alwans.

Granny Rita tossed Kris a wink as she kept on clapping.

Kris reached her own table. Jack greeted her with a grin and "Congratulations." Kris threw him a smile and turned to face her new team.

She took them in as some of them got their first solid look at that damn Longknife who now commanded them and would determine if they lived or died.

On her dress whites, they saw not only the shoulder boards of a full admiral, but most of the highest honors their planets could bestow. No doubt they also spotted awards that no human had ever worn before.

"As you were," Kris said in a commanding voice that carried.

The room fell silent, as if a switch had been turned off.

The officers were seated at long tables, by divisions. Still, many of them had been circulating. No doubt the newcomers wanted The Word on how things were out here. No doubt battle-hardened skippers had been passing The Word of what the new arrivals would need to do to get shipshape and up to Alwa Sector battle standards.

Some officers needed time to scurry back to their seats. Kris waited until the last was seated.

"Welcome to Alwa. I'm glad you could come," drew the usual soft chuckle.

"The first drink is on me. No doubt you new arrivals from Earth have had a chance to taste an Alwa Special."

"It's bloody undrinkable," came from somewhere in the back of the room.

"It's what we've all been drinking, and will drink until they start harvesting the new crops next month on Alwa. Alwa needs defenders, but Alwans were on the ragged edge of survival when we got here. We're staying one step ahead of starvation, planting crops, bringing new lands under cultivation, getting reinforcements, and plowing more land."

Kris paused to let that sink in. "It wasn't what anyone expected, but it's what we've got. We are making do."

She addressed that to the tables with the oldest hands. They rumbled their agreement back.

"However, tonight we're lucky. Our new allies, the Sasquans, have provided us with a delicious, or so I'm told, beer. The second drink is on the Sasquans. You may call them felines. You may call them tigers. Don't call them kittens to their face. They have long claws."

The feline admiral, arms spread wide, claws extended, and her interpreter stood up and received their own round of applause. It might have been shorter than Kris's, but it sounded much more enthusiastic.

"I will begin our briefing tonight the way I always do. Old hands may think they can sleep through it. Don't. Halfway through, it gets very new and horribly interesting."

Kris turned to the screens as they came to life, showing the huge mother ship hovering before PatRon 10's tiny corvettes. Then the Hellburners did their work. The view did not end there, but showed the slaughter of the battleships.

The screens quickly switched to up-front and personal shots of the two fights the *Wasp* had been in, first with the three, then the one. As they blinked out, the screens went dark, but quickly showed the green pips on black space as the most recent battle here in Alwa space took place in fast-forward mode. It finished with the gigantic mother ship blowing itself to dust.

"Now we begin the new stuff," Kris said. "Somebody wake up whoever is snoring."

The room enjoyed the joke.

"This is the planet we went out to visit. The one Commander Pasley and the *Endeavor* found. It has been sterilized down to the microbe level," Kris said, as a view of the ravaged planet came up. "We wondered who did it. My computer hijacked a lander and used it to study the central weight on a temporary elevator that was used to spew all this planet's water and air into space. It didn't originate there."

The scene changed. "Here is the planet it came from. Notice the battle damage," Kris said, as rock strikes were highlighted in circles and the glass plain came in view.

"That pyramid was made of stone from the first planet you saw. And yes, it's large enough to stand out from space."

The view switched to walk them down the entrance hall of the pyramid and right into the Horrors.

"We think that was the king of the sterilized planet. The king and his entire family."

There had been some scuffling, a few coughs in the room. Now it was dead silent.

The camera took the viewers for a quick walk down horror lane.

"Here are samples from every planet they sterilized. There are four hundred twelve of them. Including this one." The view settled on the sole figure from the planet Kris had found and surveyed during the daring Voyage of Discovery.

"In the last hundred thousand years, they plundered four hundred twelve planets. In the last two hundred, they've wiped out five. In one hundred thousand years, this vicious plague of space raiders has grown from one ship to at least thirty. Maybe fifty."

Kris paused, eyeing the screen. "So far, we've killed two of them."

Kris turned back to her officers. "In the Sasquan System, we found the survivors of the first mother ship we blew up. They were licking their wounds. Rebuilding themselves, no doubt, before they set out to slaughter the felines. We blew away their attack."

She turned back to the screens as they showed the enemy adjusting their deployment from twenty-two in line ahead to three divisions of seven or eight.

"To those of you who have fought them, they are becoming more tactically flexible. They learn. We must learn faster."

That got a rumble of agreement.

Now came the view of dead bodies floating in the blacked-out space station.

"Rather than surrender, they killed themselves. All except one group."

The view showed the old woman and the children, knives at their throats. From offstage, Kris's voice said, "Fire," and sleepy darts sprouted in several small arms, legs, and in the old woman's chest.

"We stopped them from their final act of defiance. But the woman was not grateful."

Now the view was of the old woman, strapped to a bed. The room listened as she ranted. "All the ships will come now that the torch has been sent to them. It is you that will be buried in a flood of ships. We have more ships that you can count. Our women are most fruitful. We will destroy you."

The room fell silent as the woman was sedated and lolled back on her pillow.

Again, Kris turned back to her officers. "What's the old saying? You do a good job at a tough assignment, your reward is a harder one. We've blown away two of them. It looks like we now get all of them."

Kris let her eyes sweep around the room. Here and there some blanched. One woman took a long pull on her Alwa Special.

Not so bad when you really need a drink, huh.

But what she saw most were eyes going hard. Lips going tight and determined. Warriors putting on their war face. These men and women had volunteered to come all the way across the galaxy to face a tough enemy. That the enemy was mad took nothing away from them, and maybe, for some, added that extra spice that humans had so often longed for.

A fight against terrible odds for all that they loved.

Kris forged her next words from hardened steel. "I swear that not one more head will be added to that horror show. What say you?"

"Yes," was a primal roar, almost enough to bowl her over. Bowl over a damn Longknife.

"Tomorrow, at 1600 hours, the fleet will sail on its first training exercise. Those of you who are new may ask those who have fought my kind of battle what changes you will need to make to your ships between now and then. Vice Admiral Kitano, you will take the fleet out."

Without missing a beat, Rear Admiral Kitano was on her feet. "Aye aye, Admiral. May I ask why you aren't taking the fleet out, ma'am?"

"I've got a battle dirtside with the Alwa Association of Associations," Kris said. "So I'll have to let you have all the fun. By the way, I've got some shoulder boards you may want to borrow."

Kris went on before Kitano could react. "I'm authorized to promote three vice admirals. Vice Admiral Kitano is the first. No doubt the rumor mill will tell you who the next two are well before I cut the orders in three days, after I get back from the fun and games on Alwa."

Kris left them laughing.

67

Getting a meeting with the Association of Associations was never an easy process. Of late, it had gotten nearly impossible for anyone to agree on anything, even to meet.

Kris found she'd have to wait for two days for the Association to assemble.

After one day of going over food-production reports that looked good and incidents reports of Alwa-on-Alwa blood and even Alwa-on-human attacks, Kris decided she knew all she needed to know.

That evening, Jack drove her to Joe's Paradise Cove in time for supper.

Next morning, they sat on the beach, feeling the warm sun on their bare skin, and stared at the ever-the-same, ever-changing ocean.

"So much has changed since we first came here," Kris muttered.

Jack nodded. "We've lost a lot of clothes since that first time," he said with a sort of leer.

"Do you still love me?" Kris asked.

Now Jack got serious. "You mean with you and me going about our jobs all day long and sometimes into the night, have I somehow forgotten how much love I have for you?"

Kris felt vulnerable, almost little girlish as she admitted, "Yes."

Jack leaned over, enveloped her in his arms, and kissed her. Seriously kissed her.

One thing led to another, and a long while later, Kris found herself looking up at Jack and him looking down at her.

"Should I take that as a yes, you still love me?"

"If you have any doubt about it, let me say yes, I really do love you, and nothing is ever going to change that."

Kris looked into his eyes and saw reflected back at her a love that was eternal.

"I promise you, Jack. Someday, we are going to have a job. Me in one office. You in the next one. We'll have lunch together every noon and supper at night. Maybe we'll even have a little one to feed french fries to."

"That would be nice," Jack admitted. "But that is not a promise I will hold you to, Kris Longknife. You and I both know we go where we are sent."

"You will not have to hold me to that promise. I will hold myself to it. No one, not even Grampa, his royal-ass majesty, will keep me from that job."

He kissed her, and they began to make love slowly this time.

There was nothing in the galaxy but the two of them. At least for a little while.

68

The Association of Associations was to meet at noon. Kris was there well ahead of time.

The plaza where the Alwans met was open, as was necessary to accommodate their endless shuffling about. Kris had two tables set up.

At one she held center place with Jack to her right and Granny Rita and Ada seated in comfortable chairs of Smart Metal™ to her left. The other table was shared by the two felines, with four Ostriches from the south. Again, Smart Metal™ adopted itself nicely to allow the two cats stools that let their tails twitch, as they eyed the birds not too obviously as prey. The Ostriches had a kind of nest for each of them.

They sat there as the Roosters strutted in, putting on minor displays and, in general, waiting for the acting *pro tem* leader. It had been years since they'd actually elected someone to call them to order. Now they passed the lead position from one to another according to some plan Granny Rita confessed she could not decipher.

Straight Tongue and his crew from the Alwa's Sharp Eye View network arrived a bit after Kris. Their cameras today were much smaller than the one Kris had first been interviewed with. The mic the producer pinned to Kris's shirt was downright dinky compared to what Kris had talked into a few months before.

Things were changing on Alwa. That was a problem for some and a joy for others.

Whoever the leader was, he finally crowed, and things got as quiet as a meeting of Alwan Roosters ever gets.

Behind her, Straight Tongue talked into his mic. Nelly translated.

"The heavy one, viceroy for her crowing leader, Kris Longknife, crowing leader in her own right, has petitioned to speak before the Association of Associations. We are bringing it to you live."

MY TRANSLATOR IS WORKING FINE, KRIS. YOU TALK TO THE HUMANS. I'LL COVER THE BIRDS.

As Kris stood, two Marines ushered in a cylinder. Doc Meade in medical whites followed right behind them.

"I have shown you the battle that saved your planet," Kris began.

A large white wall behind the speaker showed a hologram of the destruction of the first mother ship.

MY FEED OF THE BATTLE IS GOING OUT LIVE AND IN HIGH DEF THROUGH THE NETWORK, Nelly reported.

"You know that we heavy ones and many of your own fought the next alien mother ship that came to ravage your planet."

Now the picture changed to show Ostriches manning lasers; humans, Ostriches, and Roosters working together to launch a Hellburner; and the second mother ship blowing itself up.

"I have found the aliens' home world. I have found their holiest of holies. I have walked it with my own feet and seen what they crow about."

The picture changed to show the contents of the pyramid.

"Here they bring one sample of the people of every planet they plunder. Here they bring a pile of heads. That is all that remains of the life on four hundred twelve planets."

Around Kris, the Roosters came to a dead halt. Not one moved. Not one made a sound. All looked at the wall and the pictures on it.

They said they didn't really believe what they didn't see with their own eyes. From the looks of what Kris was seeing of them, some Alwans were making the connection.

"If the sight of what they put in their holiest of holies is not enough, I have an alien to crow to you here. Now. Dr. Meade."

The cylinder folded back to show a bed. The gray-haired woman slept on it.

"I remind viewers," was whispered by Straight Tongue, "that the aliens look exactly like the heavy people who have lived among us since our grandfathers' times. However, they are very different. I am told that the two cannot mate and bear an egg."

"Awaken her," Kris ordered.

Doc Meade did something with her instruments, and the woman stirred. The doctor did more, and the woman rolled over and sat up on the edge of the bed.

Her eyes widened as she took in the view.

~Vermin. You are all vermin,~ she shouted.

Nelly translated for everyone present and watching over the net.

"I present you with an alliance of three sentient races," Kris said evenly, as Nelly translated in bug-eyed monster. "They say to one and all that you will not add their heads to your house of horrors beneath that pyramid."

~You are vermin,~ the woman spat.

KRIS, THE NETWORK IS GETTING ALL THIS. AND MY TRANSLATION.

GOOD, NELLY.

~You are all nothing but shit-eating vermin, and you will all die,~ the woman stormed on. ~The Enlightened One has sent the torch to all the ships. Together, we are more numerous than the stars. Our women are fruitful. We bear many warriors and workers. We will drown you in your own blood, and no one will ever remember your name.~

The woman was off her bed now and strutting around the plaza.

Before her, Roosters in her way got out of it. Those not, stood stark still.

KRIS, THERE'S A RISK THESE DAMN ALWANS WILL SURRENDER RIGHT HERE AND NOW TO HER, Granny Rita said on Nelly Net.

Kris stepped out to face the alien woman, almost chest to chest.

The Ostriches will like that.

"I have fought you five times," Kris said curtly as Nelly translated for all. "Five times I have destroyed your people. Rather than face me, your so-called great Enlightened One took poison. You were ready to kill yourself once you had roared your empty threats at me."

Kris turned her back on the woman and faced the Roosters. "You say you will drown us in our blood, but we have blown your ships to gas. It is you who have no one to remember you ever lived."

The woman screamed. Kris whirled to find the alien charging her, arms out, fingers grasping for Kris's throat.

Two pops sounded, and two sleepy darts appeared in the side of the woman facing Jack. He held his service automatic in the proper two-handed stance.

The woman collapsed face-first into the dirt of the plaza. She skidded to a halt with her arms still out, fingers twitching as if they might still clutch Kris's throat.

Kris turned around slowly, addressing her words to the Association. Three cameras were carrying this. Three much smaller ones. "That is your enemy," Kris shouted. "Will you cower before the likes of her, or will you fight with me? You must decide."

Kris paused. "No, I am wrong. You may not cower before her. To her, you are only something to kill. Will you line up to fight with me, or will you line up to be slaughtered like chicks before her and those like her?"

Kris returned to her seat.

One of the Roosters shouted. "The Association has a proposal before it. Yes, it is from a heavy one, but it is a proposal. I call for a vote."

"We must discuss this," the *pro tem* said.

"What is there to discuss? With her we fight. With this monster, we die. I call for a vote."

More voices were raised, calling for the vote.

I'VE NEVER SEEN THIS BEFORE, Granny Rita said on net. THERE'S NO MOVEMENT. THERE IS NO TALKING AMONG THEMSELVES. THEY ARE JUST STANDING THERE ALONE AND CALLING FOR A VOTE.

THE TIMES THEY ARE A-CHANGING, Kris answered.

The vote was taken. It was unanimous. Another first. Even Straight Tongue remarked on that.

69

Kris remembered all too well from her days following Father around on the campaign stump that the meeting was never over when it finished.

There were interviews to give.

Kris promised Straight Tongue that the heavy people would fight for the Alwans like a son hunted with his father, like a younger brother hunted at his older brother's side. She was none too sure the analogy was going in the right direction, but it pleased the Alwans around her.

Zarra introduced her admiral to the Sharp Eye Viewers and, in a way, introduced her to Kris. "Admiral Furzah says we will fight beside you to the last drop of our blood."

So saying, the admiral raised her right fist to the camera and used a claw on her left hand to draw blood.

The Alwans seemed half-impressed, half-startled by the gesture. Kris was in dress whites with long sleeves, so sharing blood was out. None of the Roosters stepped forward to offer their arm.

Finally, one of the Ostriches offer his arm. He pecked it until blood flowed and held it out so the two species could mingle their blood.

"I didn't see that one coming," Granny Rita said, coming up beside Kris.

"You weren't the only one," Kris agreed.

Doc Meade came forward to slap a bandage on both cuts. She had a carefully neutral look on her face, but Kris could almost hear the mother's voice scolding. "Children."

The doc did get close to Kris's ear. "You're going to have to quit sleepy-darting that old woman. Especially after I've just woken her from a sedated nap. Her heart can't take much more of this."

"She gave the performance I expected," Kris said. "We shouldn't need that again."

Which turned out not to be quite so.

With bandaged arm, the Ostrich they had flown up on a transport plane for the show presented himself with his spouse. "We wish to speak for our association of the Slow Flowing River Valley. We all wish to invite you to come to speak to us about this war. We have a range we would like to talk about settling some of your heavy people on to live among us. We can offer you the entire river valley. We can hunt farther away. If you grow crops there, we can help you."

And, no doubt, they'd love to get some of the consumer items that working for the humans brought.

KRIS, THAT VALLEY THEY ARE TALKING ABOUT IS JUST A COUPLE OF RIDGELINES OVER FROM THE VALLEY WITH THE PLANTS, FISH, AND BATS WE'RE NOT SUPPOSED TO TALK A LOT ABOUT, Granny Rita put in on Nelly Net. IT'S JUST A BIT SHORT OF THE ISLANDS FULL OF BIRD GUANO THAT WE'RE SHIPPING UP HERE. IF FOLKS DON'T MIND RIDING DOWN THERE ON THOSE BOATS, WE COULD GET A TRIANGLE TRADE STARTED.

Kris offered to come address their association. She asked if she needed to bring the alien. The Ostriches glanced over at where she slept fitfully and declined. "Everyone saw what we just saw, or will see it on tonight's news," the one with the bandaged arm said.

"Once is enough," the female beside him assured her.

Kris would have loved to escape to the beach with Jack, but the fleet was ready for another sortie. This time, it needed its admiral present.

Kris excused herself and followed the Marines with the sleeping alien back to the longboat.

70

The *Wasp* was in dockyard hands and likely to stay there for some time.

"Couldn't you at least have kept the eight ships separate?" Benson asked as he reported to Kris upon her return from a hard day dirtside.

"I had a fight on my hands," Kris pointed out. "I needed four patched-together warships more than I needed eight wrecks."

"Well, while you may have gotten yourself something you could fight, what you did was totally scramble those eight ships' basic matrices. If you ask me, you'd be better off just sucking this metal into a holding tank to use to patch the other ships with human-space Smart Metal. We could start all over again with eight new ships. Say we use *our* Smart Metal and pour it around new reactors and 22-inch lasers. I'd bet Drago would love that."

"No doubt he would. How long will it take?"

The yard manager shrugged. "Your guess is as good as mine, but, for what it's worth, I've already told Amber to get your flag quarters ready on the *P Royal*."

So it was that Kris found herself again in the comfortable quarters of her flag bridge on the *Princess Royal*.

At the moment, the screens running around her bulkheads showed her new order of battle. With Jack at her side, she studied it. Two divisions of four ships made up a squadron of eight under a commodore. Two squadrons could make a task force under a rear admiral. Two task forces could make up a task fleet of thirty-two war wagons commanded by one of her new vice admirals.

Only who gets what?

"It looks nice and simple, if I go by the numbers," Kris said. "I've got twelve squadrons. They fold into three task fleets under three vice admirals."

"Only which squadrons go into which fleets?" Jack said. He had such a wonderful ability to put into words what was nagging at her gut.

Kris sighed. "I've got four squadrons with combat experience, but their ships are all the old 20-inch frigates. The six squadrons with those nifty new 22-inchers have never been shot at. They have never dodged and weaved the way you have to to survive the way I fight."

"And who will fight best alongside whom?" Jack added.

"Yeah, do I show some respect for local alliances back home, or just dump ships where I think best? I've already done that, merging the Helvetican ships into other squadrons to bring them up to strength."

Jack nodded. "All except Miyoshi's BatRon 3. He's still down one."

Kris nodded, her mind already racing. "I'll need to keep ships grouped by their support ships?"

Jack nodded. "Are you feeling the headache I'm feeling just looking at this?"

"Where'd you hide the painkillers?"

"I'll get you one."

"Please do. I don't usually complain about cramps, but between this pain in my head and that pain in my belly, I could use something."

"Going to bite my head off?"

"Have I ever?"

"Nope, but the last couple of days have been a bit more of a pain in the ass than usual."

In a moment, Jack returned with two capsules and water.

"The first two vice admirals are easy. I already gave Kitano her third star. Miyoshi is easily my second pick."

"He's been good to us," Jack said. "He didn't have to take us aboard the *Mutsu* when you called."

"He's getting his third star because he fought his battle well, not because he saved my head from the chopping block."

"I know. So, who gets the third?"

"Hawkings is from Wardhaven. Bethea is from Savannah. Both are battle experienced, but they're both from the U.S., as is Kitano. Do I go with two U.S. task fleet commanders even though we're only putting up a third of the ships?"

"Who else is there? No one else is battle experienced."

Kris nodded, but something told her it wouldn't be that easy. "Earth just gave us three squadrons," she pointed out. "That's only one squadron shy of a task fleet. And they are all 22-inchers." Kris brought Jack up to date on the new Earth armor.

"Interesting, if it works," Jack said.

Kris started moved squadrons around on her board.

"If I gave Yi the third star and build a task fleet around the Earth contingent, would that make him happy enough to give up one squadron of 22-inch frigates with their fancy armor? I'd swap in the two 20-inch squadrons from Scanda and Savannah. Bethea would be rear admiral commanding that task force . . . ?"

"That might work," Jack said. "The Earth battle fleet would have one battle-tested squadron, and if Yi listened to Bethea, he might save himself some time adapting to our way of fighting."

"Then, if I give Miyoshi both the Musashi squadron of 20-inchers and the Yamato squadron of 22-inchers, we'd have another. Add in the New Eden squadron of 22-inchers and the Esperanto and Hispania squadron of 20-inchers, that would give us another, well-balanced fleet."

"And if Kitano had an Earth squadron and the Pitt's Hope contingent mounting 22-inchers, you'd be pairing them with the battle-experienced 20-inchers of old BatRon 1 and 2, what's left of them," Jack muttered.

Kris nodded. Of course, right now BatRon 1 was pretty much the *Princess Royal* that she was riding in at the moment and the *Resistance*. Until Benson worked a miracle of spinning up new ships for the crews that had followed Kris into that hellish alien world and back, Amber's fleet would be a bit short.

Kris looked it all over and found it good. Still, before

she spoke, she ambled over to her desk and knocked on its wood.

"That looks good. As good as we're going to get. I don't want to sound unusually optimistic, but it doesn't look like anything can go wrong with this."

Later, she wished she'd knocked a whole lot harder.

About the Author

Mike Shepherd grew up Navy. It taught him early about change and the chain of command. He's worked as a bartender and cabdriver, personnel advisor and labor negotiator. Now retired from building databases about the endangered critters of the Pacific Northwest, he's looking forward to some fun reading and writing.

Mike lives in Vancouver, Washington, with his wife, Ellen, and close to his daughter and grandchildren. He enjoys reading, writing, dreaming, watching grandchildren for story ideas, and upgrading his computer—all are never-ending.

He's hard at work on Kris's next story, *Kris Longknife: Relentless*, as well as *Vicky Peterwald: Survivor*. He's also writing some e-novellas that fill in small spaces in Kris's world.

You can learn more about Mike and all his books at his website mikeshepherd.org, e-mail him at Mike_Shepherd@comcast.net, or follow Kris Longknife or Mike Moscoe on Facebook.

VICKY PETERWALD

TARGET

When her brother was killed in battle by Lieutenant Kris Longknife, Vicky Peterwald, daughter of the Emperor, had to change her life from one of pampered privilege to one of military discipline. Though the lessons are hard learned, Vicky masters them—with help from an unexpected source: Kris Longknife.

M1505T0614

FROM NATIONAL BESTSELLING AUTHOR
Mike Shepherd

TO DO
OR DIE
A Jump Universe Novel

Retired Colonel Ray Longknife and Marine Captain Terrence "Trouble" Tordon come to Savannah via different routes, but what they find is the same. One bully strongman is intent on keeping power no matter what the new rules are for peace. He's got the population cowered by thugs and tanks at the ready. He expects to win the coming elections handily. But Ray Longknife, Trouble, and Trouble's wife, Ruth, are standing in the way...and nothing is going to flatten them.

Praise for the Jump Universe novels

"Fast-paced." —*Library Journal*

"Entertaining...Fun." —*Locus*

mikeshepherd.org
facebook.com/AceRocBooks
penguin.com

M1521T0614

From National Bestselling Author
MIKE SHEPHERD

. . .

The Kris Longknife Series

**MUTINEER
DESERTER
DEFIANT
RESOLUTE
AUDACIOUS
INTREPID
UNDAUNTED
REDOUBTABLE
DARING
FURIOUS
DEFENDER**

. . .

Praise for the Kris Longknife novels

"A whopping good read . . . Fast-paced, exciting, nicely detailed, with some innovative touches."

—Elizabeth Moon, *New York Times* bestselling author of
Limits of Power

mikeshepherd.org
penguin.com